THE
AGE
OF
HEROES

ANCIENT GODS, HEROES, AND ALIENS
CLASH IN AN EPIC BATTLE FOR EARTH IN
THE BRONZE AGE MEDITERRANEAN

MIKHAIL GLADKIKH

THE AGE OF HEROES
By Mikhail Gladkikh
Published by Quasaris Press 2023
Spring, TX 77381
QuasarisPress.com

Address permissions and review inquiries to mgladkikh@gmail.com
Cover Design: Jonas Perez

Connect with the author online at MikhailGladkikh.com

First Edition

International Praise for The Age of Heroes

*"I give high recommendations for The Age of Heroes. As a fan of mythology and sci-fi, it is an excellent story that will **provide fodder for thought**...There are great characters in a story that moves along at a good pace and is loaded with **vivid descriptions of people, places, and events** that will trigger the imagination."*
—**Jim Arrowood,** *Jim's Sci-Fi Blog*

*"It was a really pleasant read, with **plenty of action** and (literally) colorful characters."*
—**Sergiu Pocan,** *an avid sci-fi reader, Romania*

*"This book is exactly what I was hoping it would be... **Truly, a "showdown for the ages"**, as promised."*
—**Amazon reviewer,** *Israel*

*"**Gods, monsters, heroes,** and epic battles all come together for an **exciting story.** Very entertaining!"*
—**Michael Sanders,** *PMP, P.E., Lean Six Sigma Black Belt*

*"**A captivating mix of history and fantasy** - writer makes a reader immerse into the atmosphere, conversations and actions, and feel as an immediate witness of what happened hundreds of years ago."*
—**Amazon reviewer,** *USA.*

"This is, without doubt, a totally unique take on the Bronze Age... I can only describe it as epic. Well recommended."
—**Laurie Robertson,** *a voracious reader from Australia,* **Goodreads review**

Dedicated to all the scientists, archaeologists, and researchers who tirelessly work to uncover the mysteries and secrets of human civilization.

Foreword

For a long time, I've been fascinated by the catastrophe that befell the brilliant Mediterranean Bronze Age civilization at the beginning of the 12th Century BCE. The rich, interconnected, multi-faceted world had ceased to exist in a few decades. The cities had been razed and burned, the crops destroyed, and the people dispersed. Out of many mighty kingdoms, only Egypt and Assyria survived the calamity, but even they recoiled, significantly weakened.

What were the causes? This is still a subject of fierce debate among scientists, with several different culprits, such as the mysterious "Sea People," climate change, earthquakes, droughts, or systemic failure, have been identified. We might never know the truth.

I took the liberty to imagine a certain "what if" scenario, adding a science fiction element and an alien expedition amid the struggle for supremacy between these human kingdoms. This is a work of fiction, and I hope you will judge it as such. However, I tried to preserve the historical accuracy as much as possible to transport my readers to the Bronze Age.

I hope this story will motivate the readers to learn more about this fascinating time and discover historical facts about the Bronze Age collapse. I am convinced that to build the future, we need to understand the past, and the enigma of the Bronze Age provides one of the fascinating topics for further research and discussions, providing us with more insights into human nature and illuminating a path forward, into the mastery of the universe.

TABLE OF CONTENTS

THRACIANS

Thrace

Mt.
Olympus ▲ Leibethra

Thessaly Iolcos

Orchomenus

Thebes

Mycenae

Pylos Menelaion

Tyrins

Nichoria Leuktron ACHAEANS

Kythera Kastri

Knossos

Crete

Miletus

Hellespont

Troy/
Wilusa

HITTITES

Nerik

KASKA

Arinna

Hattusa

Isuwa

ASSYRIANS

Carchemish

Kizzuwadna

Ugarit

Kadesh

Canaan

Cyprus
Alashiya

Ashdod

Ekron

EGYPTIANS Ashkelon

Sinai

Pi-Ramesse

Akhetaten

LIBYANS

THE AGE of HEROES

by Mikhail Gladkikh

PART ONE

"THE PATH OF THE GODS"

CHAPTER

ONE

Humans were a mystery. Today's decision could seal the fate of their civilization, and he had the power to influence it.

Locals called him Zeus, although he preferred the functional title of Commander. Even after a hundred years on this alien planet, he still struggled to understand the natives. Yes, they were primitive, but something about their way of life was incomprehensible, defying all logic and reasoning, potentially promising greatness but also the demise of their species. This bothered Commander's sharp mind, accustomed to solving complex technical challenges. The human problem, however, was different, alien to him, just like the inhabitants of this planet.

"Commander." A message popped into his mind, acknowledging his presence.

He positioned his silver, disk-shaped body in the middle of the Control Unit, gently gliding on the force lines of the strong magnetic field permeating the open space.

"Technologist," Commander responded. "Is the magnetic field network on the mainland complete?"

"Yes. We can now use it for transportation anywhere north on the mainland. Also to the east and west across the sea. The southern branch is under construction."

"My workshop is now fully connected to the base," Defender signaled, entering the Unit. "The exploration of rich mineral resources of the mountains will accelerate."

The base had been established on the island the locals called Kythera, on a hill north of the harbor of Kastri, in a strategic location providing easy access to multiple land masses in all directions.

"When will the southern branch be functional?" A question arrived from Scholar, who showed up next. "A pathway to the southern continent is essential. It will accelerate my study of the old, advanced, and peculiar civilization located there."

"Half a year. It's a straightforward network expansion."

"Haven't you learned enough?" The final participant joined the gathering.

"I'm just starting, Pilot. There are many questions, but we need to be careful. We cannot interfere with the development of humans."

"That wasn't the reason for my question," Pilot clarified. "The humans are so primitive that learning about their culture and customs is not beneficial. Instead, we can mold them into any shape and accelerate their progress, building a race of sentient beings committed to us. And we should start right away. They will thrive under our leadership."

"Your argument is flawed, Pilot. We cannot lead beings we do not comprehend."

"Enough." Commander put a stop to the dispute. "Let us proceed with order." Today's meeting was critical. They'd spent enough time on this alien planet and had to make tough decisions.

"Of course," Scholar agreed.

"The main objective of the Expedition was to study human civilization, learn about culture and social life, and to understand human biology, physiology, and evolution. Now we must decide if and how to engage with them in the future."

"We're already engaged; they're aware of our presence," Defender said.

"We must reach a consensus," Commander continued. "We've spent enough time gathering data; the decision must be made. Please put forward your propositions and arguments." Commander had formal seniority due to his position, but his vote was only one alongside the other four. It didn't carry any additional weight. He was the judge, the mediator. They had to arrive at a unified point of view; such was the way of Soarers.

"I'll start." The Pilot's body, green with grayish undertones, with a noticeable bulge in the middle, was slowly rotating in the middle of the Unit. "Humans are a perfect material for us. They are mere savages; developing them won't be hard. With our technology and leadership, they'll reach the stars in a few generations. After that, they'll become our dependents and servants. I have a plan. We could achieve the unification of the planet under our command in a decade."

"Counterarguments?" Commander asked.

"I agree with the first part of the Pilot's proposition, but not with the second," Technologist responded. "Indeed, the locals are underdeveloped; we could significantly accelerate their progress. I'm experimenting with several technologies they could adapt quickly. However, we must carefully plan and monitor the progress. And they have to move at their own pace. To suggest we forcefully unite and lead them to the stars is to ignore the natural steps of evolution, which must be followed. You don't give newborns the tools for building fusion generators and spaceships."

"Pilot, do you have anything in response to Technologist's arguments?" Commander asked.

"Yes, Commander. The flaw in his logic is the assumption that evolution must be gradual and slow. But with our supervision, it could be much faster. Indeed, we must give newborns the tools to build spaceships and teach them. I wish someone had done this for *our* newborns at this stage of our evolution."

"Any other propositions?" Commander asked.

"Yes." Defender moved his large, reddish body disk forward.

"What do you propose? Are you in agreement with any of the previous arguments?"

"Not at all. I have my own strong opinion."

"Which is?"

"Humans are a mortal threat to our race. They should be exterminated."

"Exterminated?" Scholar's body started rotating faster, the blue changing to purple, a bulge in the middle of the disk becoming more transparent. Scholar flew several circles around the Unit, stopping closer to the Defender, and conveyed, "Explain your logic. How is this poor, wretched race a mortal threat to us? We who've created infinite energy sources, mastered interstellar travel, and conquered death?"

"Remember Ice World?" Defender replied. "The only planet in the universe known to us to host intelligent life. The life that destroyed itself and transformed a rich, vibrant world into a lump of barren ice."

"Of course. That planet promised a lot but in the end ruined our hopes of finding intelligence comparable to ours."

"Exactly, Scholar. Alien civilization on the Ice World imploded, eradicating itself in a flash of incomprehensible violence."

"What does it have to do with *this* planet?" Commander interrupted.

"I'm convinced humans are doomed to repeat the fate of the Ice World and destroy us with them." The Defender's body was glowing bright red. "I'm concerned about their violent nature. Their so-called emotions. The complete lack of logic and rational behavior. We've been here for about a hundred years. All this time, we have witnessed humans annihilating each other. Conflicts never stop, on any continent, even in the settlements governed by the same authorities. You introduce them to our science, Technologist," Defender moved around, "and they'll use it against you. For no reason, just because of their violent nature. Because of their desires and emotions."

"You speak with conviction, Defender," Pilot responded. "Yet we are a vastly superior race. Your scenario is unrealistic. We'll control them every step of the way. They'll be our pupils and servants."

"There's reason in Defender's arguments." Scholar's body returned to blue. "I've been studying their psychology and culture for a long time, and I still don't understand how these 'emotions' control their actions. The concept is so alien to our race that I cannot find symbols to describe it. The behavior is irrational: they're unable to hold a normal exchange of arguments and reach a consensus; they'd rather physically assault each other than agree. This results in conflicts and killings. You have a point, Defender. Yet to say they are a danger and must be exterminated is a conclusion I cannot support; the logic doesn't warrant such radical measures. It appears emotional and violent, as if humans themselves have made it. I didn't expect to hear such arguments from you, Defender." Scholar's body turned purple again.

"On the contrary, this conclusion is purely logical, Scholar," Defender parried. "You just acknowledged you don't understand them. They're unable to stop killing each other. What makes you think they won't annihilate everything in the universe given access to our technology?"

"I agree with Scholar," Technologist said. "I can't discern the possibility of such a scenario. I'm sure we could manage to keep them subdued and teach them to listen to the voice of reason."

"Me as well," Pilot added. "With the caveat that we must assume visible leadership in their development. The strategy I'm aware none of you supports."

"Commander, what is your position? You haven't put your arguments forward yet. What do you suggest?" Technologist asked.

Commander was deep in thought. The decision, although critical, wouldn't come easily. There wasn't enough data; he couldn't decide. The consequences were pivotal, not only for the future of the alien species but also for the future of his own race. And, maybe, for the whole universe. Commander understood the logic behind Defender's arguments. He also understood Scholar's need to learn and comprehend the locals, Technologist's interest in working on their development, and Pilot's push to advance the progress of the natives by force. However, something was bothering Commander. The discussion had taken on a strangely personal tone. The arguments, although logical, led to extreme recommendations. He was concerned by how convinced Pilot and Defender were about their proposals. The planet and its alien life were influencing the Expedition, and not in a direction Commander was comfortable with.

"I haven't fully formulated my position yet," Commander announced. "I'm aware it's time to decide, but I need more data."

"How much longer? And what do you suggest we do in the meantime?" Technologist asked.

"I don't know." Commander's body turned dark gray. "In the meantime, we should reduce our activity to a minimum. We have done enough damage already."

"I cannot agree with this. I'll act myself if needed." Defender moved toward the exit while the exchange of opinions stopped.

"Wait. What actions? Extermination of humans?" Scholar finally asked.

"Exactly." Defender stopped. "Technologist, I need your help. Your experiments with bioprinting human bodies suggest you should possess the most knowledge about their physiology and chemistry. The easiest way to exterminate them is to design a virus that would destroy them on a cellular level."

"I don't support your conclusions, Defender, and I won't help you," Technologist responded. "Also, what about reaching a consensus?"

"Reaching a consensus is impossible. You just heard that Commander is not ready and is prepared to shut the Expedition down. I won't allow this to happen. We cannot sit and wait while these murderers reach the stars and arrive to destroy us. We must act first."

"Defender, do you realize your arguments are exactly the same as the humans would use to justify their violence?" Commander moved in front of Defender. "Don't you all see how our discussions shifted from the respectful exchange of opinions to forceful statements barely supported by logic? This planet has changed us, presenting substantial risks. Therefore, I am initiating the adjustment of the Expedition's objectives."

"It will take decades, if not centuries, to communicate with Homeworld to adjust the objectives," Pilot argued. "I cannot agree with this course of action. I'll proceed with my plan alone, if necessary."

"Do you understand you're breaking with the customs that served Soarers for eons and took us to the stars?" Commander asked. "What happened to you?"

"Nothing happened to me," Pilot parried. "The situation requires quick actions that you are not ready to take. So *I* have to ask you this question: what happened to our Commander?"

"It's not important any more, Pilot." Defender was already halfway out of the Unit. "Our paths diverge from now on. Don't try to stop me. I'll get rid of this menace efficiently, without any help. And I'll eliminate anyone who dares to stand in my way. Pilot, your strategy is naive: it's impossible to unite these irrational beings even under the leadership of their gods."

"We shall see. They'll follow their strongest deity: Poseidon, God of the Ocean," Pilot said.

"No. First, Ares, God of War, will annihilate them without any struggle. They'll accept my divine judgment." Defender left the Unit, followed by Pilot.

"How can we stop them?" Scholar asked.

"It's not possible. They've made their choices, which we must respect. Although abandoning the normal mode of decision-making is a development I didn't consider. I must connect with Homeworld and adjust the goals of the Expedition."

"I'm sure we could prevent whatever Pilot and Defender are planning. As Apollo, God of Light, I have a powerful cult, especially on the eastern continent. And Scholar is known under many divine names and could organize the southern continent to interfere with their plans."

"Are you under the influence of emotions you picked up from humans, Technologist?" Commander said. "You suggest stopping your fellow Expedition members with the help of the locals, which means even more violence and death. Is that what you want?"

"We have to find out what Pilot and Defender intend to do and stop them without engaging humans. This will be difficult but not impossible," Scholar suggested. "Technologist, they must be using the power grid you set up. If yes, you should be aware of their location and actions."

"That is not how it works. I know where Defender has built the workshop. But by now he has his own magnetic field generators, shielded from my interference. We could find out where they are, but stopping them is not in my power."

"Then what can we do?"

"Nothing," Commander messaged. "I must ponder the situation, and then we'll discuss what actions to take. The latest gathering was counterproductive. I think we are all impacted by this planet somehow and are starting to lose our sense of reason."

"I've come to similar conclusions, Commander," Technologist agreed. "I'll do more tests on the local gravitational and magnetic fields. Also, I'll check potential adverse effects due to chemical or radiation exposure. There must be an explanation."

"We are learning *from* the indigenous populations instead of learning *about* them." Scholar noted. "We are becoming impatient and rush to judgment. We must figure out what is affecting us, or the Expedition's objectives will be in danger."

"That's why we must adjust them. It won't end as planned," Commander added. "We have the power to destroy this planet and human civilization, every single one of us, and endanger our species by learning violence and disregard for life from humans. Scholar, please compile the information you have gathered on human evolution, history, psychology, and the primacy of emotions in their lives. Technologist, please do the same for their physiology, nervous system, executive brain functions, and neurochemistry. We must understand the fundamental differences between our species and whether we are under some adverse effects of this planet. Do you both agree?"

"Yes, Commander. I'll start immediately. I'll also try to keep track of what Defender and Pilot are doing," Technologist responded.

"I agree. I've studied multiple local organizational units extensively and have lots of data," Scholar added. "It might be too late, though. The damage is done. Pilot and Defender are not coming back. We must stop them, even if it means the complete failure of the Expedition."

CHAPTER
TWO

Echelaos stood high in his chariot, looking straight ahead, aiming at the Hittite warriors.

The enemy had more chariots, but the Achaeans were swifter and better archers. A Hittite fighter tried to poke Echelaos with his spear as the chariot passed by, and Echelaos had to use his dagger to parry the thrust. Tros was very skilled and did his job steering the chariot exceptionally well, turning the horses at just the right moment to give Echelaos a perfect position for the shot. Whispering praises to Tros and to the gods, Echelaos shot his arrow, piercing the eye of the enemy archer. He automatically reached to the side of his vehicle where the quiver was attached and grabbed a new arrow. The battle was quick and fierce. Even though the chariot engagement had started a few moments ago, the Hittites had already lost half of their fighting platforms. Enemy spearmen were retreating to form a wall in front of their citadel so that the chariots could withdraw behind their backs to safety. The battle was won. Echelaos placed another arrow right through the hand of the shooter of the retreating Hittite chariot.

"Don't let them escape!" Echelaos yelled at Tros. The charioteer nodded, sending the horses in hot pursuit of the fleeing opponents. Suddenly, one of the Hittites, appearing out of nowhere, thrust his spear into the side of one of their horses. Neighing in sharp pain, the animal stumbled and fell to the ground, taking the chariot with it.

Echelaos, reacting quickly, jumped out of the vehicle just in time to avoid the injury and plunged his sword into the belly of the Hittite spearman.

"Echelaos! Echelaos!" A sudden call from behind alerted him. Echelaos turned around, but there was nobody behind. The enemy forces fled into the citadel through the open gate, protected by the archers shooting from the battlements. Tros was slowly getting on his feet next to their crashed chariot.

"Echelaos!" a familiar voice called again.

Echelaos shook his head, trying to chase away the delusion. Suddenly, someone grabbed him by the shoulder.

"Echelaos, wake up! Your father just called an urgent meeting!"

He rubbed his eyes and opened them, still under the deep impression of the battle against the Hittites. Machaon, the lawagetos of Pylos, shook his shoulder. The sight of Machaon's familiar face, his gray eyes, and disheveled curly blond hair brought Echelaos back to reality.

"What's happening? What's the occasion?"

"I'm not sure. Wedaneus just returned from Hattusa, had a quick chat with Nestor, and then the wanax called an urgent gathering in the throne room. That's all I know. We must hurry."

Echelaos got up quickly, put on his tunic and the kilt, and arranged his long, curly hair into a ponytail. Then he grabbed the bowl filled with water, freshened his cleanly shaven face, and said to the lawagetos, "I'm ready. Let's go!"

They went outside and walked around Echelaos's quarters. It was a lovely sunny summer day, and people started to gather in the central square, bringing goods to trade and talking loudly about their wares. The artisans were assembling at their specific buildings in the palace complex, discussing the activities of the day. Some of them produced textiles, others pottery, while those in the highest demand were engaged in bronze metalworking. Life in Pylos was busy.

"Perhaps Father finally decided to step down and is ready to make an announcement. What do you think?" Echelaos asked.

"It's possible." Machaon shrugged. "Rumor says he's almost a hundred winters old. Time to have some rest."

"I don't know about a hundred winters, but he *is* very old. When I was a boy, he used to tell me stories from his youth, his time at Knossos at the court of King Minos, the encounters with the Minotaur, the incredible craft of Daedalus who'd built himself wings to escape Knossos... He was already old back then. I always thought these were just fairy tales, bedtime stories. With Nestor, it's impossible to distinguish the truth from the fables he tells to teach you a piece of his wisdom."

"Is it true he can speak with animals, trees, and rivers?"

"If he can, I've never witnessed it. I wouldn't understand it even if I had." Echelaos laughed.

They approached the front porch at the entrance to the palace's courtyard. The noises of the marketplace became more subdued, muted by the serenity of the palace. The smell of oil and perfume permeated the building. Beautiful colonnades, some red and some beige, supported spacious balconies on the second floor. Frescoes depicting bull-leaping men in the Cretan tradition covered the walls. This sprawling view of the courtyard had always given Echelaos shivers, so elegant and at the same time imposing a sight. One day he'd preside over this grandeur as the wanax and lead the fine warriors of Pylos into battle in search of immortal glory. Perhaps this day was today.

"What could've happened at Hattusa to warrant a speedy return of our envoy and immediate gathering of the elders?" Machaon asked.

"Maybe the Hittites have declared war on the Achaeans. Then you and I need to get ready to equip our fighters and go conquer some land." Echelaos tapped Machaon's shoulder. "Our time for glory!"

"And our duty and honor." Machaon nodded, tightening his lips.

Chatting, they arrived at the small vestibule with more bull frescoes and entered the megaron, the throne room. There was a large hearth with an open fire in the center, and the smoke rose through the opening in the ceiling. The smell of burning wood and fragrances filled the megaron.

The old wanax sat on a throne to the entrance's right. Nestor's beardless face was covered with countless wrinkles, and his deep blue eyes pierced the people gathered in the room with intellectual power. Bulls, lions, and griffins were painted on the walls next to the throne.

Echelaos looked around. There were about twenty people in the room, mostly influential administrators, advisers, and landowners of Pylos. Eritha, the high priestess, was there as well, a beautiful golden tiara on her head, inlaid with lapis lazuli and cornelian. Wedaneus, a cunning diplomat, the envoy to the kingdom of the Hittites, stood next to the throne, his gray-haired head lowered in a respectful bow.

"Echelaos and Machaon have arrived," Wedaneus announced. "We can start."

"Start what?" Echelaos asked. "What's the occasion?"

"My son, we've been betrayed and insulted," Nestor said in a quiet but resonant voice. The chatter suddenly stopped.

"What do you mean, Father?"

"Our subjects, the Trojans, looking for better fortune, decided to shift their allegiance and made advances to the Hittites. Happy that the prized Trojan trade routes were now in their possession, those wretched people decided to overturn our peace treaty, which we'd worked so hard to prepare. As a result, these two treacherous races have signed an alliance agreement in a sudden about-face, sealing it by marriage between Princess Ehli-Nikkal and Prince Alaksandru of Troy."

The silence in the room became so dense that Echelaos could physically feel it compressing his ears. His palms clenched into fists, blood rushing through his veins, eyebrows almost joining together on his reddened forehead.

"This is true, my son. Your betrothed, Helen of Hatti, has been promised to the prince of Troy. We must go to war to restore your rights and reestablish control of the Trojan trade."

Echelaos, growling something unintelligible, punched the wall of the megaron. Blood appeared on the knuckles, and he wiped it off on his tunic.

"I swear by the names of Zeus, Poseidon, Ares, and all the other gods that I will take back what is rightfully mine!" Echelaos yelled. "I shall kill every wretched Trojan and despicable Hittite who dares to stay in my way. Troy must be razed, and Helen shall be mine!"

"Calm down, my son, the gods will hear you…" Nestor said. "I understand your rage and impatience. Yes, you shall do all that, but first we need to discuss the strategy and the plan of attack."

"What strategy?" Echelaos bellowed. "Machaon will prepare the ships and the chariots, and we'll sail to Troy."

"We have eight large warships. How many chariots and warriors are you going to transport? Is this sufficient to take the walled city?"

"Doesn't matter; the Trojans are cowards. They'll run away and open the gates once they see our forces."

"It's not a sound strategy, my prince," Wedaneus objected, tilting his head.

"Fine. What do you suggest?"

"It will take the full might of Achaea to wage war on Troy."

Wedaneus crossed his arms behind his back and walked back and forth across the throne room. "On my return journey from Hattusa, I stopped at Mycenae and discussed the matter with the great Wanax Agamemnon and his advisers. He'll support our cause and help you take revenge and return your bride, my prince." Wedaneus bowed. "You only need to be patient."

"The transgression of Troy is extremely dangerous for Achaea," Nestor said. "The insult is grave, my son, and you must take your revenge, no doubt about it. However," the wanax raised his index finger, "the issue of the tin trade route is vital to all of us: Mycenae, Thebes, Crete, Pylos… If we lose northern tin supply to the Hittites, we'd depend on our enemy to procure raw material for our weapons, and we can't allow that."

"What if we establish a separate trade route from the north directly to Achaea, bypassing Troy's merchants?" Eritha asked.

"Such a route will have to cross the Thessalian Mountains, full of bandits and savages. Therefore, mountain passes will have to be closely guarded. I don't think Iolcos, Orchomenus, or Mycenae can afford to patrol the Thessalian Mountains to the extent required," Wedaneus replied, shaking his head.

"It's simple," Nestor said. "We won't allow our enemies to control our tin. Troy and Miletus are indispensable levers across the sea that Achaea must control. Our survival and security depend on it."

"I understand, and I'm ready to go," Echelaos said. "Wedaneus, you said Agamemnon will support our war. What exactly does that mean?"

"Wanax Agamemnon will provide ten warships. Six more will come from Menelaion, five from Athens, four from Thebes, a little bit here and there as well. But, most importantly, Crete will deliver twelve ships. This is a matter of the whole of Achaea, as Wanax Nestor said."

"I estimate our combined fleet to have fifty warships," Nestor added. "This is the largest fleet Achaea has managed to assemble since…ever. Even during the time of King Minos, when Crete alone had thirty ships, the mainland was weak and divided. Today, we are united and strong."

"Fine, we have lots of ships. What about chariots? Spearmen? Troy is a mighty adversary. They have many chariots and lots of gold to sustain a large army and defend themselves," Machaon said. "It's our duty, and we'll fight until the last drop of blood, but we need to be realistic."

"You're right, my friend," Wedaneus said. "The ships are needed to blockade the city and prevent the delivery of supplies and reinforcements. We'll bring a few fighters on the ships with us. The chariots and spearmen from Miletus will join the army at the point of disembarkation."

"Miletus?" Machaon asked. "Their help is very welcome, but I suspect Troy has ten times more chariots than Miletus."

"That is true." A dark figure, dressed in a black cloak, stepped forward from the corner. "This is why we'll use our chariots as a decoy."

"Decoy? Who are you, and what does it mean?"

The stranger stepped into the light. His huge muscles were visible even under the cloak. Dark, hardened skin on his palms complemented his long black hair and black eyes. A deep scar extended from his left earlobe to the right corner of his mouth, making him look like a grotesque monster.

"Name's Akhilleus. I'm from Knossos but served for many years as a captain in the army of Iolcos, second in command to the lawagetos only. I was visiting Mycenae to inform Wanax Agamemnon of important developments in the north. That was where I met Wedaneus and accompanied him on the journey to Pylos."

"This is great. What's your point?" Machaon squinted, tilting his head.

"During my time at Iolcos, northern savages would occasionally invade our borders to loot and pillage. In the past, a few hundred infantry and a dozen chariots were enough to disperse them, since they had primitive weapons such as clubs and crude spears. In the last two years, however, their tactics and weapons have changed. They started throwing javelins at the horses, disabling our chariots. They also wield long, double-edged swords, which can both thrust and slash and are very effective in close combat. We lost half of our chariots in the last fight with these northern brutes and only prevailed due to our magnificent archers."

"I sense a lot of trouble coming from the north," Machaon said. "But I still don't understand the connection between your experience at Iolcos and the idea of using our best weapon as a decoy."

"And yet the connection is obvious." Nestor smiled. "We will lure Troy's chariots out to pursue the much weaker force from Miletus. The main fighting unit will be the Northmen who gave Akhilleus so much trouble. Envoys from Mycenae are already on their way to Thessaly to recruit mercenaries. Agamemnon is rich; this won't be a problem. Their new way of fighting is perfect against chariots. Trojans have no experience with it and won't see what's coming."

"This is clever, o wanax. Your wisdom is truly infinite." Machaon bowed.

"In this case, it's not my wisdom, but that of Akhilleus." Nestor smiled. "He'll depart immediately to Iolcos to recruit the northerners and arrange their crossing of the Hellespont. Echelaos," the wanax pointed at the young prince, "you will equip eight of our warships and sail to Kythera. There, at the harbor of Kastri, you'll wait for the Cretan ships and set sail to Tyrins, where the rest of the combined Achaean fleet will wait. You'll be the commander of this united fleet.

Machaon," Nestor turned to the lawagetos, "you'll travel to Miletus and lead the attack by land. All three directions of assault must be precisely timed. Let Poseidon and Zeus protect and strengthen us and grant us a glorious victory!"

"Let it be so! I'll arrange libation ceremonies honoring Potnia and Poseidon to secure the help of the gods," said Eritha, the High Priestess, walking closer to the hearth and raising her arms.

"Echelaos, stay with me for a moment," Nestor said when people had started to leave the throne room.

"Yes, Father, what is it?"

"Come closer, my son." The old wanax leaned forward on his throne. "My time on Earth is coming to an end. You will succeed me, and you must be strong; the hour of great trials is here."

"What do you mean, Father? You shall continue to lead Pylos. We just decided on a solid plan to defeat our enemies. What other trials are you talking about?"

"Oh, this is just one battle, Echelaos. I'm talking about the new age, the Age of Iron, the time of darkness and evil when the gods will leave us and the land will lie in ruin and misery. The fifth and the final age of man is nigh."

"You speak with riddles, o Father. Iron? The fifth age?"

"Yes, my son. From the Golden Age to the Ages of Silver and Bronze, men and gods lived in harmony with nature. In these times, people were blessed and happy. The Age of Heroes succeeded these fortunate times: the age of strong, brave, and heroic men. The age in which we live, my son. The time when the selfishness of man and the gods creates endless wars and conflicts. We do not exist in harmony with nature anymore."

"What's the fifth age? What's iron?"

"The constant state of brutal war has caused a rift within harmonious coexistence of all living beings. The strife has shaken the foundation of the universe. All kinds of calamities rattle this world. The gods are not in control anymore and are abandoning their broken creation. It is the time for humans to build their own world, using material stronger than anything we know. The world of iron."

"If this is true, o Father, there is no one better than you to lead us through this storm and build this future world."

"I am very old, Echelaos. I've seen things that no one even remembers anymore. I served my people for many winters and made lots of mistakes. It's not my fight and not my duty. I must vacate the throne for the next champion, the leader who will stand tall and be a beacon of hope for the people during these times of sorrow. You, my son."

"Me? I don't have even a tiny bit of your wisdom, Father."

"It's not wisdom that counts, but character. Experience doesn't matter during times of change. The future of our house and our people depends on you, my son. Remember that and look inside your soul for the answers when the choices are hard."

"Of course, Father."

"This might be the last time we talk plainly as father to son. Now go, you have your orders."

"Yes, o wanax. May the gods give you many more years!"

When Echelaos stepped out of the throne room and into the forecourt, a familiar voice called to him from the small portico to the left. It was Eritha, whose colorful flounced skirt blended with the wall fresco with griffins behind her. She wore a white bodice wrapped with a knitted shawl, and her beautiful long black hair, arranged in a fanciful style, was held in place by a golden tiara. Echelaos stopped, admiring her hourglass silhouette. The raven hair was falling down her shoulders; her full breasts, the contours of which were visible through the semitransparent material of the bodice, were begging him to feel them in his palms. The aromas of sandalwood and saffron created an aura of irresistible attraction around her. He felt the desire to hold Eritha's wasp-thin waist and caress her silky skin.

"Echelaos, may I speak with you?" Eritha asked.

Echelaos came closer and nodded. "What is it?"

"When conducting a libation ceremony in the honor of Poseidon yesterday, I had a vision that scared me. You were in trouble, fighting against fearsome people I didn't recognize."

"I have many battles ahead of me, nothing to be scared about. This is the path of the warrior and the leader."

"Of course. However, in my dream Poseidon himself led these foreign people into the battle. So please be careful and don't anger the gods. I believe this was the forewarning: something bad is about to happen."

"Eritha, you speak in riddles, just like Father. I'll engage our enemies one by one, conquering their lands and covering our house and my name with the glory that will live for ages. The paths of the gods and the men do not cross directly as you suggest. Men don't fight against the gods, but only against other men. And that is why I must be strong."

"I wish you were right, Echelaos. Please promise me you'll pay due respect to the gods and perform all the sacred rituals and sacrifices when you go into the battle."

"Yes, I promise, Eritha. Now, please stop worrying about something we can't control. I have a better idea. Follow me." He took her hand and led her around the portico into a small room on the other side of the wall. A stand with two large jars, one with oil and one with water, and a basket full of pomegranates stood next to the bathtub.

"Why are we here?" Eritha asked.

"I want you to cleanse my body before I depart for war. But first, lay with me." Echelaos took a pomegranate, split it in half, and dug into the tart taste of the fruit, throwing away the shell and spitting out the seeds. He gave another half to Eritha, then grabbed her waist with both hands and pulled her closer. Echelaos inhaled the smell of her hair mixed with sandalwood perfume. He'd been waiting for this moment for a long time and was very impatient to finally enjoy her body. Eritha smiled, took a bite of pomegranate, and pulled on the threads that held her bodice together. Echelaos took a moment to savor the beautiful view, devouring her breasts with his eyes. Eritha lay down on the bench as they disrobed, embracing Echelaos and pulling him on top of her. They were about to lose themselves in their pursuit of passion when a flash sparked in front of Echelaos's eyes. He saw the beautiful palace of Pylos engulfed in flames: the throne room, the porticos, and even the bath where they were about to make love, turning into ashes. He shook his head, and the vision disappeared. Echelaos looked down at the beautiful woman and sought to forget all troubles, drowning himself in her gaze. Yet the horrible image of the burning palace was still there, accompanied by the voice of Nestor: "The final age of man is nigh!"

CHAPTER
THREE

"Child, come with me. I want to show you something." Grandmother Davke took Ehli's hand. They followed the path leading from Hattusa Citadel to the Shrine of Creation. The first rays of the rising sun illuminated the mud-brick road and the shrine structure in front of them. Wild goats bleated, staring at them from a safe distance. Morning breeze brought the sounds of the wakening city they were leaving behind.

Ehli disagreed with Davke mentally. She didn't consider herself a child; she had already seen ten winters. Grandmother Davke had been raising Ehli since her mother, the princess from Alashiya, passed away during childbirth. Grandmother was spending a lot of time with Ehli, explaining to her the creation of the world, the connection between the gods and the people, the ways of nature and its different aspects. Grandmother was a princess herself, daughter of King Kudur-Enlil of Babylon. She had arrived from that ancient land to the realm of the Hittites as the future bride of King Tudhaliya. Davke was not her royal name, but the one she preferred, since it much better reflected who she was. People were afraid of Grandmother Davke, saying she was a sorceress who prayed to Babylonian gods and used Sumerian magic, corrupting the Hittite princess. Ehli didn't care; she liked the elderly lady and the stories Davke told her. The girl felt a deep connection to the woman and proved a swift learner.

They arrived at a large building that served as a gateway to the shrine. The construction was monumental: thick walls enclosed spacious halls, which reflected the sounds of their steps. Somehow, the air was fresh and light, with a hint of burning incense, although there were no recent ceremonies or festivals held in the shrine. They passed through the intricate colonnades and hallways, then ascended a series of staircases leading to a large courtyard containing an altar. This was where the public ceremonies usually started; Ehli had been here before, but always as a part of religious festivals led by priests and attended by her father. Davke didn't stop there but took Ehli through a pillared gateway into the temple's main room and then outside, where the natural chambers of the shrine were located. No breeze and no sound reached this hidden place; the smell of incense was much stronger here. Two vertical rocks bordering the enclosure appeared like giant pillars supporting the sky, and Ehli felt dizzy. On one side, the bigger chamber revealed the figures of gods and people, carved in low relief on the surface of the rock. On the other, next to the giant carved depiction of her grandfather Tudhaliya, was a narrow passage to a smaller natural chamber guarded by two winged lions. This was a sacred place to which only a few priests had access. Yet this was where Davke led her.

"Your grandfather rebuilt the shrine after the fire and added this chamber. I helped him enhance the natural, primal energy of the place where this sanctuary is located."

Ehli stood in the middle of a very narrow passage cut through the rock, a wall of enormous stones isolating it from the outside on the other end. But it wasn't the wall that attracted Ehli's attention. In front of it stood a giant statue of her grandfather Tudhaliya in his royal robe, his right arm raised in the air, on his head a conical hat, the symbol of divinity. Smoke with a strong odor of galbanum engulfed the enclosure, yet there was no fire.

More images were carved into the rock: the god was driving the enormous sword into the ground. Her grandfather embraced by Sharruma, the underworld god, was depicted next to the sword. Ehli's head spun even more as the musky smell of galbanum attacked her nostrils and the imposing statue of her grandfather hung over her.

"King Tudhaliya crossed into the underworld here the same year you were born," Davke said. "This place is special. It served as a sanctuary to many generations of our ancestors. All three worlds converge here: the world of the gods, the people, and the dead."

"How's this possible, Grandmother?"

"See this sword? The god holds it and drives the sword into the earth. The sword is the bridge between the world of men and the world of the dead underneath."

Ehli looked at her grandmother, eyes wide.

"You're old enough to learn the ways of nature," Davke continued. "You already know about the underworld — the world of the dead, the earth the world of men, and the sky the world of the gods. These are not separate realms but the three different aspects of Creation. They are interconnected: men worship gods who guide and influence us. We cross into the underworld after we die. This is the cycle of life, the cycle of renewal. Night follows day, the full moon wanes, and spring follows winter. Look at these carvings." Davke pointed at the circles and nicks covering the rock. "I will teach you how to use these to understand the cycles of nature and know when moons and seasons change."

"I would love to learn this, Grandmother." Ehli squeezed Davke's hand, shivering. "There's something I don't quite understand."

"What is it, child?"

"The natural cycle of renewal you talk about always repeats. Spring follows winter, but then another spring arrives. However, with the gods and people, it is different. Nobody comes back from the underworld. Why is this so?"

"You're a smart girl. This is true; people do not come back from the dead. Yet nothing disappears without a trace. People who die transform. They become something else: a drop of rain, a tree root, a breath of fresh air. The knowledge about who they were and what they've accomplished and learned doesn't disappear. We can access it if we understand how. Everything is part of the eternal cycle of renewal and transformation."

"What do you mean by accessing the knowledge of the dead? Are we going to travel to the underworld? Will we meet grandfather Tudhaliya? I'm scared, Grandmother!" Ehli hugged the woman, trembling.

"No, we won't travel to the underworld, Ehli. But I brought you here to learn something special." Davke touched Ehli's chin and looked straight into her eyes.

"What is it, Grandmother?" Ehli whispered, shivering in anticipation.

"I will teach you how to speak with the dead."

#

Ehli-Nikkal still remembered the first time her grandmother took her to the Shrine of Creation, although a full nineteen winters had passed since then. Ehli had visited the private enclosure of the shrine many times since then, both with Davke and alone. As she grew up, people had started calling her "sorceress," just like her grandmother, and distanced themselves from the young princess. Ehli didn't mind; she preferred solitude and calm immersion in the mysteries and manifestations of nature to the empty business of the worldly life of humans. Married twice, Ehli-Nikkal had never become her royal consorts' obedient and supportive wife. Perhaps this was because she'd been unable to conceive a child, Ehli told herself. Or perhaps her husbands were not worthy of her devotion. She was about to find out if her third marriage would turn out any different.

Ehli left the royal women's quarters on her way to meet her father, King Suppiluliuma, in the throne room. The smells from the kitchen aroused her appetite. A mixture of sweet fruits, ripe vegetables, and spices from Canaan enveloped her and teased her senses. She passed the beautiful arcades, adorned with the intricate paintings created by skilled artisans from Crete during the times of her grandfather Tudhaliya.

Ehli-Nikkal didn't like to attract unwanted attention, so she wore a simple tunic underneath a long cloak, which enveloped her figure from head to toe. Although arranged in sophisticated braids, her beautiful, long, straight black hair wasn't adorned by the golden tiara she usually wore as a princess.

Suddenly, a loud noise in one of the side rooms caught her attention. Ehli stopped and listened attentively. Female screams and pleas made her change her course and open the door, behind which the screams were getting louder. A disgusting scene opened up in front of her eyes: several soldiers of the royal guard were in the room with a young girl, probably a slave. One of the soldiers held the girl's hands behind her back while two others ripped her clothes off. The girl was begging for mercy, screaming at the top of her lungs and trying to kick her captors. These pitiful efforts led only to their laughter.

"Hey, show us some affection," one of the soldiers said. "Be a nice girl, and we might even reward you."

"With more humping," the other soldier added, which caused an outburst of loud laughter.

"Please, please, let me go! I work in the kitchen. I need to help with the royal feast…" the girl begged, but her pleas made the soldiers even more aggressive. Finally, they managed to strip her naked and pushed her onto the couch in the corner of the room, arguing about who would be the first to enjoy her body. Occupied with their heinous deed, they didn't notice that someone else had entered the room.

"Stop it, right now." Ehli commanded, assertively extending her palm in front of her.

The soldiers turned to see who was interfering with their pursuits, finally noticing the newcomer.

"Hey, look, the gods sent us another one. This is a great start to the royal feast!"

"Come, lay with me, pretty one." The soldier approached Ehli and tried to grab her waist.

Ehli stepped to the side. "I said, stop it. Leave immediately, and perhaps the king will spare your worthless lives."

"The king? *We* serve the king! And who are *you*, pretty one? Why such an arrogant attitude? I promise, you will have a lot of fun!" The soldier laughed loudly, trying to push Ehli to the couch.

"You idiot, this is Princess Ehli-Nikkal," his companion hissed, leaving the slave girl alone for the moment. "The king will chop your dick off, then your head, then feed your body to the pigs if something happens to her!"

"Are you sure?" The soldier stepped back, leaned his head sideways, and measured Ehli head to toe. "No, this is a commoner: there are no rings or diadems… You are wrong; she's just a servant-maid, sent to us by the gods to enjoy."

"No, he's right," the third soldier said. "This is Princess Ehli. I saw her before…"

"Goat's dung." The first soldier approached Ehli again. "Let's see what this 'sorceress' would do facing the king's guard. I bet she'd spread her legs and cast a spell… Come to me, pretty one, I can't wait any longer." He grabbed and squeezed Ehli's hands.

This time, she didn't try to avoid him. Instead, she held his palms firmly in hers, feeling his heartbeat. She gave the soldier a long gaze, without blinking, lips moving to produce a barely noticeable sound, squeezing his wrists. First, the soldier froze, unmoved, his smile gradually replaced by a frown. Then his eyes bulged, looking straight into hers, unable to shift, lower jaw drooping. Finally, exhaling with a wheeze, he lost control of his body, which started to sink to the floor like a bag of rotten fruits.

"Sorceress!" the second soldier gasped, moving sideways in an attempt to get out of the room. "I've heard stories that she cast her husband, the king of Habishe, into the eternal darkness." He whispered to his friend, "We should leave."

"What about him?" His companion pointed to the lifeless body of their comrade on the floor. The mouth was agape, lips curved in a bizarre grimace, and a drop of blood appeared in the corner of his eye.

"He'll be fine," Ehli said. "Take this rascal and get out of here. If I see any of you ever again, you'll pay with your lives most horribly."

"Yes, Princess. We're so sorry we caused your displeasure. Please spare our lives!" The soldiers picked up the body of their companion from the floor and retreated toward the door. He was quite big and heavy, and his body fell to the floor with a loud thump.

Ehli looked at them and smiled wickedly. "Yet you weren't willing to spare this poor girl. You're the scum of the earth. Somehow, I've had to deal with your kind all my life." She took several steps and approached the girl on the couch. "Don't worry; they won't hurt you. Come with me."

The girl stood, sobbing, in disbelief that a princess had saved her. Ehli took off her cloak and gave it to the girl, covering and embracing her. Then she turned back to the soldiers, who were about to disappear behind the door. "I did *not* send King Tanhuantash to the eternal darkness. I didn't kill this pile of dung you're carrying, either. I was close to it, but I didn't do it. Nobody deserves the fate of being devoured by the Primordial. Remember that and never cross my path again."

Ehli looked at the girl. "Who are you? What's your name?"

"Korinsia, o Great Princess." The girl bowed, still shaking. "I don't know how to thank you. I don't have anything…"

"Don't worry. You're safe now, and this is enough for me."

"Thank you so much, o Great Princess! I'm just a slave girl. I was working in the kitchen preparing for the royal feast tonight when these soldiers attacked me," Korinsia said, sobbing and shivering.

"You won't be in danger anymore. I'm placing you under my protection," Ehli said as they walked toward her quarters. "You'll be my maid; I'll instruct my servants. No one will dare to hurt you while you're in my service."

"Oh, I'm so grateful to you, Great Princess!"

"Where are you from, Korinsia?"

"I am from the land of Ahhiyawa. My parents were potters in the service of Nestor, wanax of Pylos. Pirates captured us and sold into slavery when I was a little girl. I was very fortunate and ended up working in a kitchen at the royal palace in Hattusa."

"And now you are the maid of the princess Ehli-Nikkal. Your fortune seems to be improving with every moment."

"Is it true what they said? Are you really a sorceress? Could you cast people into darkness?" Korinsia stopped, staring at the princess, taking a step back.

"Don't listen to gossip, Korinsia. I'm not a sorceress. I'm just a woman who can stand up for herself. And has knowledge of things beyond the ways of the flesh." Ehli looked at Korinsia and smiled. "However, with the help of this knowledge, I can also inflict horrible torments."

#

The king met Ehli in the throne room.

"Father, you wanted to see me?"

"Come, Ehli. I need to talk to you before you depart to Wilusa. The envoys have already arrived; the royal feast is tonight. We won't have another chance to be alone." King Suppiluliuma put his hand on his daughter's shoulder. "Are you ready?"

He was wearing the long royal gown and a headband, his long gray hair falling freely to his shoulders. A sun-disc pendant amulet was the only jewelry the king wore that morning. Ehli noticed deep wrinkles on his forehead, and his skin looked darker than usual. The king looked very tired, his face emotionless, only his eyes still showing his affection for his child.

"Yes, Father. I wish I'd had a say, but you're the king, and I'm at your command."

"Don't be angry with me, Ehli. You understand the matters of the state dictate our actions."

"Oh, I do understand, Father." Ehli-Nikkal turned away. "I was hoping you'd finally give me some rest after I had to play your pawn tending to matters of state."

Ehli was aware that men tended to lose themselves within the depths of the dark charms of her pitch-black eyes, covered by long, beautiful eyelashes. Even now, past her youth, with barely visible wrinkles in the corners of these two black oceans, Princess Ehli-Nikkal was considered the most beautiful woman of her age, and King Suppiluliuma took full advantage of it, arranging royal marriages to the benefit of the kingdom.

"You're exceptional, Ehli, and you know that. I need your services yet again. I know you won't disappoint the old king." Suppiluliuma sighed.

"Of course, Father." The princess continued to look somewhere beyond the throne room walls. "Remember the first time you arranged my marriage to King Ammurapi of Ugarit? I was young, practically a child, and so excited. That didn't turn out well, did it?"

"Why are you bringing this up now, Ehli?" The king came closer and touched his daughter's hand. "It depends on how you look at it. You played your role well, and Hattusa found a strong ally in the south, allowing us to keep control of the copper mines of Isuwa."

"Yes, Father. But when the Sea People came to ravage the city, I couldn't do anything to protect it. With all my skills. I'm still feeling the anger and powerlessness."

"Don't blame yourself, Ehli. Nobody could've predicted that King Ammurapi would turn out to be a coward and flee at the first sign of trouble. We've lost Ugarit forever, and Ammurapi lost everyone's respect. I gave you my consent for a divorce immediately, if you recall."

"Oh, I do, Father." Ehli smiled sadly. "And then, when you arranged my second marriage, I was still hopeful, even knowing your political schemes all too well."

"Well, of course, I explained everything to you, my dear." The king walked around her. "And you did a magnificent job. When Egypt started pressuring the Hittites in Syria, the kingdom of Habishe attacked her from the rear, distracting the pharaoh and giving us time to regroup and consolidate our positions. This even allowed me to organize a raid to Alashiya, get some of their riches, and receive annual tribute."

"At what cost? Do you realize how miserable I was in Habishe?" She took a long pause, crossing her hands in front of her chest. "King Tanhuantash was easy to manipulate. His avarice, pride, and gluttony made him a puppet in my hands. But I cried at night, Father. I despised him and the way he treated his subjects. I wanted to cast him into the deepest abyss but stopped myself because of my duty to you and Hattusa."

"And I will be eternally grateful to you for your sacrifice, Ehli." The king embraced her. "We talked about it many times, but I see it still troubles you… Even when you appeared at my court a year ago, unrecognizable, fire in your eyes, I calmed you down and didn't say anything." Suppiluliuma closed his eyes for a moment. "Of course, you didn't leave your husband on the best of terms, but he never protested, and the political situation had changed."

"He won't dare protest. Besides, he didn't need me. He preferred men anyway."

"Ehli, I understand what you had to go through in Habishe and during your return journey traveling the deserts of the Nile and crossing the sea to get back home. We all have our sacrifices to make."

"Isn't that enough sacrifices, Father? Do you expect me to play your pawn for a third time?"

"While we're alive and in the position of power, we must protect the country and make sure people are safe and thrive. Come, let me show you something."

Ehli followed her father across a long hallway supported by majestic colonnades into the northern end of the palace. They went through the gateway to the balcony, where a stunning view opened in front of their eyes. The wind was strong, and a forceful gust loosened Ehli's braids. The royal palace was situated on top of a steep rock, protected by a deep gorge, beyond which a fertile plain stretched to the mountains on the horizon. Ehli took a deep breath of fresh, dry air.

"What do you see, my child?"

"I see the land which provides us with food."

"That's true, Ehli. This plain must be cultivated every year. Otherwise, the people of Hatti cannot sustain themselves and will die of starvation. This is our granary, our most basic need. Beyond this land, on the horizon, lie the mountains inhabited by the bestial Kaska. They know of no laws or culture but coexist with the vilest of beasts. We can't negotiate with them; they understand only the language of the mace. Therefore, the granary in front of your eyes requires constant protection. Even a short raid by the Kaska could cause hunger."

"I know of the Kaska. Why are you telling me this?"

"Because I need you to understand. I'm old and tired, and only you can protect the land when I'm gone." Suppiluliuma placed his hand on her shoulder. Ehli covered his hand with hers, feeling a sharp needle piercing her heart.

"To the east," the king pointed in that direction, where the giant disk of the sun was rising in the blue, cloudless sky, "lies the province of Isuwa with its copper mines. The supply of copper is critical to making bronze weapons to ensure the kingdom's protection. The rising power of Assyria challenges our supremacy in the east. We need allies there to deal with this threat. We must protect the outpost of Carchemish at all costs." The king raised his hand and moved his fingers in the air as if trying to find these imaginary allies in front of him.

"To the south is the only way to reach the sea," Suppiluliuma continued. "Therefore, we must maintain our garrisons at Kizzuwadna to access the sea trade routes, which provide goods and materials we couldn't get otherwise. This is why Alashiya is essential."

"What does it have to do with my marriage, Father?"

"To the west," Suppiluliuma turned his back to the sun, ignoring her question, "are the multiple subject kingdoms of Hatti, which kings Mursili and Muwattali fought so hard to subdue. Beyond these kingdoms and across the sea live the mighty Ahhiyawa. The city of Wilusa, which they call Troy, is located at the intersection of major sea and land trade routes between our realms. Wilusa was their subject state for a long time. I planned to make friends with Ahhiyawa, even if it would require paying them a tribute, so I'd be free to deal with the Assyrian menace. However, reversal of policy by Wilusa changes everything. Securing her trade would provide us with tin and, therefore, an uninterrupted supply of bronze. Having this prize would allow the

Hittites to deflect the Assyrian threat and secure our borders. This is a chance of a generation—the opportunity to provide safety and prosperity to our people. We could finally end the cycle of diplomatic intrigues, playing one adversary against the other; we could become stronger than any combination of our enemies. If I could sacrifice my life to make it happen, I would. Do you understand now why I'm asking you to marry for the third time? Are *you* ready to sacrifice *your* life?"

"Yes, Father. What do you need me to do?" Ehli met his gaze, holding his hand, studying the myriad wrinkles on his face, wanting to take part of the king's burden from his shoulders.

"I need you to be my right hand at Wilusa. You'll be the bulwark of our security, holding tin trade routes with the strong fist I know you have. This will give you wisdom to become the ruler of our land after me. Can I rely on you? There's no one else I can entrust this task to."

"Of course. I'm your daughter and the Hittite princess. I'm at your command."

"I know that, Ehli, and I'm extremely fortunate to have you. My heart is torn knowing what I ask you to deal with repeatedly, yet there's no other way. Our people depend on us, and we must protect the kingdom."

"I've learned to silence my heart eventually. I'm strong, and I'll manage whatever ordeals await me in Wilusa. I know my duty and will do everything in my power to fulfill the destiny you devised for me. Even if it means feeding the multitudes of Ahhiyawa to the Primordials."

Ehli turned around and left the balcony. She didn't look back even as she heard the subdued sobbing of the old king behind her.

CHAPTER
FOUR

The heat of the afternoon sun on a cloudless day contrasted with a refreshing light breeze from the sea. Achaeans had arrived at Kythera and moored their ships on the beach near the village of Kastri, and the warriors were ready to disembark and explore the surroundings. First, however, they had to wait for another day or two until the Cretan ships would arrive, making their combined fleet size an awe-inspiring twenty warships.

Echelaos looked back at the turquoise water of the bay, then to the darker blue sea on the horizon. The view was stunning. He shifted his gaze to the semicircular beach before him, then to the village on the hill, and then to the imposing mountains dominating the landscape in the north of the island. The fishermen brought their fresh catch to the beach, and womenfolk started to clean and gut the fish, preparing the meal for the villagers. Echelaos could smell fresh seafood from a distance, a hint of the slightly pungent odor of the gifts of Poseidon adding to the familiar smell of the sea that no sailor could ever forget. There was sole, turbot, grouper, and even a giant swordfish, which two fishermen carried from the boat. Hundreds of seagulls descended on the beach, anticipating the leftovers, screaming and fighting for the best spots. Kythera was a trading outpost at the intersection of several routes connecting the east and west coasts of Achaea with Crete. It was always busy and full of goods and provisions required for lengthy sea journeys. Ships sailing to and from Pylos would always stop at Kastri to restock the fresh water and food needed to complete their trips. This time was no exception.

Echelaos waited for Tros and other soldiers to disembark. All eight ships Pylos was bringing to the fight were of the newest military design, sitting low in the water, flat-keeled, with straight stern posts, equipped with fifty oars and a large sail. The keels were tarred, appearing like enormous black sea creatures under the water. The upper decks, ram, and latticework panels on the steering and lookout platforms, on the other hand, were of a blood-crimson, designed to strike fear into the hearts of the enemies. A representation of Athena's owl sat proudly on the beam above the ram, ensuring divine protection.

"With these ships, we can't lose." Echelaos pointed to the fleet of Pylos with his dagger. He wore a black helmet with a horsehair crest, a bronze corselet with a breastplate, and a skirt with overlapping armor plates. He carried the bow and the quiver on his back more in anticipation of the hunt they were planning later that day than for protection. Kythera was a friendly island.

"Yes, Prince. The Achaean fleet will be a sight to behold," Tros said. "However, I worry about the lack of chariots. We've never fought like this before; we always had superiority in chariots." Tros was dressed in military outfit as well, but with a simpler, boar-tusk helmet and a leather corselet. He carried a spear and a small, round shield.

"Don't worry. With Athena's help, we shall be victorious!" Echelaos exclaimed then turned his head. "Let's see what's going on over there. What could be more interesting than our formidable fleet?" Echelaos shrugged, laughing, and started walking toward the village, where a large group of fishermen gathered at the beach, putting their catch aside, talking loudly, waving their hands, and pointing in the direction of the sea.

When they were closer to the crowd, people stepped aside, letting them through, recognizing Achaean warriors. They moved into the open space up front, and Echelaos could finally see what was happening. He stopped, falling to his knees, speechless, overwhelmed by the divine beauty in front of him. Several fishermen prostrated themselves on the sand. Other people covered their eyes while someone whispered, "It's a goddess! Sent to us by Poseidon; a sign of his support."

A delicate maiden was emerging from the foam of the surf. Her form was absolute perfection. The symmetry of her slightly elongated face, her full, silky breasts, her wasp-thin waist, which gradually morphed into round hips. She stepped graciously, looking straight ahead as if not noticing people staring at her, a fleeting smile on her face. Her long, beautiful, golden hair created a striking combination with her deep blue eyes and matched the golden triangle under her belly. Her arms were milky-white, with long and thin fingers, and her legs were so light and smooth that she appeared to gently glide over the waves rather than walk.

Echelaos caught his breath and stood up. "O goddess of the sea, thank you for granting us your divine protection and favor." He took his helmet off and placed it on the sand next to the dagger by his feet. "I am Echelaos, son of Nestor, wanax of Pylos. We are on our way to wage war on treacherous Trojans, who stole Helen, my future bride, from me. Please, bless us and grant us a glorious victory!" Echelaos raised his hands and knelt before the goddess.

The maiden looked at the kneeling warrior, leaned her head sideways, and came closer. Echelaos could see drops of water on her milky thighs, bubbles of foam on her knees, and sand covering her exquisite toes. She smelled of freshly cut grass and apples, not the sea. He didn't dare to look up at the goddess and meet her gaze. The moment of silence continued for an uncomfortably long time. The fishermen had stopped murmuring and were lying prostrate on the sand.

Finally, Echelaos found the courage to address the goddess. "Please, forgive me, o goddess! I don't know what sacrifice you demand. I am Echelaos, son of Nestor." He pointed a finger to his chest. "How do you want us to worship you? To call you?" He extended his hand in her direction.

The maiden looked at him, her lips barely moving, with no sound.

"This is Tros, my charioteer." Echelaos pointed to the warrior kneeling next to him.

Suddenly, the goddess stepped forward, extended her hand, and said slowly, distinctly pronouncing every syllable: "E-che-la-os."

"O goddess, thank you for recognizing me! We will sacrifice a bull in your honor this evening. Who are you? Posidonia? Tell us, what offerings do you want?"

A long pause followed. Finally, the maiden pointed her finger at the charioteer and said, "Tros."

"Thank you, o Aphrodite Ourania." The charioteer put his hand over his heart.

"Aphrodite?" Echelaos asked.

"Yes, my prince. The heavenly goddess born from the sea foam. Aphrodite Ourania," Tros replied.

"Sacrifice a bull…offering," the goddess said.

"Yes, tonight we shall have a ceremony in your honor," Echelaos said.

"Tonight. Ceremony. Honor. Aphrodite," she said, repeating each word with emphasis and clarity.

"Yes, o Aphrodite! Do you want to honor our feast with your presence?" Echelaos asked.

"Feast. Presence. Yes," the goddess responded, smiling.

"O Aphrodite, we are so honored! The gods are truly smiling at us. The campaign will be heroic, and we'll cover our names with everlasting fame!" Echelaos exclaimed. He stood up and turned around, indicating a path to the village with his hand. "This way, o goddess."

The fishermen were still lying face down on the sand, so the three of them proceeded to the dwellings on the hill. Echelaos was triumphant. To receive divine support in such a direct way was unreal and astonishing. He was sure victory would be theirs, and he would get Helen. There was absolutely no doubt about that now.

Pumped up by this encounter and expectations of future glory, Echelaos was momentarily blinded by a flash of light. When his sight returned, he beheld Apollo on his path. The god towered above the road, proudly reveling in his youth and beauty, his muscular body anointed with oil, a golden crown on his head. Apollo carried his lyre in one hand and a spear in the other. A slight movement of the weapon, and a beam of brilliant white light carved an enormous hole in the ground in front of Echelaos. A new odor, somewhat sweet and pungent, engulfed him.

"Not a step farther! Kneel before your god!" Apollo bellowed.

Everyone fell to the ground, speechless and terrified—everyone except Aphrodite, who looked at the god with curiosity and extended her hand toward him.

"My child, my creation, my gift," Apollo said, looking back at Aphrodite. "I came to claim what's mine. You don't belong here; these brutes are not ready to contemplate your divine beauty."

#

"What is he doing? Didn't we agree about not interfering with humans?" Scholar messaged.

"We did. However, Technologist decided that to let humans have the specimen is a bigger interference," Commander responded.

The two of them were in the Control Unit, receiving multichannel information from several of Scholar's drones flying above the shore. Commander hadn't expected Technologist to confront locals directly following his latest experiment to bioprint a human. Since his many previous attempts had ended in failures, they didn't anticipate success this time either. The human female, initially thought by Commander and Technologist to be yet another cadaver, was discarded into the sea. To their surprise, she'd started swimming and emerged from the waves to the bewilderment of the fishermen of Kastri.

"I completely disagree. The reanimation of the specimen was an accident. It is undesirable but irreversible." Scholar's disk turned purple. "To interfere and retrieve the specimen directly, as Technologist is doing, is irresponsible."

"It may be so, but I couldn't stop him. I didn't expect such rush judgment and action from Technologist."

They studied the data from the drones, indicating generation of a local magnetic field. Technologist was preparing to transport the human specimen back to the Base.

"Technologist exhibits the same symptoms as Pilot and Defender; he acts as a human would. I'm concerned. I must stop him." Scholar's body was rotating very quickly, pulsating with purple light.

"Stop him how? By interfering yourself?"

"Yes, we have to."

"This action would be equivalent to Technologist's behavior you disapprove of."

"Negative. His actions are driven by his unexplainable attachment to the specimen. I want to fix the damage and rectify the situation. And I need to hurry."

Scholar left the Unit with incredible speed, leaving Commander to ponder the new complication. The actions of Expedition members were utterly unjustified and against any logic or customs of the Soarers.

The specimen, wrapped up in the magnetic field bubble, started rising above the ground and floated toward Technologist. Suddenly, another flash of light illuminated the group. The goddess Athena, clad in her complete military outfit, helmet on her head, carrying a shield and a lance, stood before Apollo.

"You shall not interfere!" Scholar announced, pointing her lance at Technologist and sending a lightning bolt in his direction. Her adversary absorbed the discharge, flickering with a white, yellow, and orange pattern.

"You cannot stop me. I created her, and she is *mine*," Technologist responded.

"She's not yours."

"I consider her my offspring."

"Your offspring? When was the last time you've seen the Soarers' offspring?"

"This is inconsequential. My bioprinting research was fundamental to achieving our practical immortality and reducing the need to create progeny. I want the same outcome for humans. She is as close to me as my natural offspring would be."

"But you created her as a human. Don't you find this contradictory?" Scholar asked.

"On the contrary. The biological solution to human procreation is so inefficient, it would be best replaced. The specimen is the next generation, a hybrid of human biology and Soarer technology. I'm proud of this accomplishment. You can't take her away from me."

"I can and I will. My drones are all around you, and some of them are capable of depleting your force shield very quickly. You have no chance."

"You're right; I sense your drones. But don't you see how wrong this is? They can't have her yet. They're not ready for this technology. We need to introduce it carefully, and I need to teach them."

"It's you who are wrong. We're not giving any tech to humans. She'll be one of them, even if born under mysterious circumstances.

We should let her stay, since she's already here. She'll learn from them. I'll study her growth and adaptation, and this will be a great experiment for the Expedition."

"But she is my creation. You don't understand, Scholar. It finally worked. I've achieved a breakthrough. She must stay with me to complete her development cycle."

"No." Scholar raised her spear. "Now, let the specimen go."

"You will see that your judgment is wrong." Technologist rotated his EM resonator, and the bubble with a specimen inside lowered to the ground. Another pass and the magnetic field disappeared, freeing the subject. The specimen ran back toward the group of prostrate humans, one of whom stood up and embraced her.

"You're making a big mistake, Scholar," Technologist announced. "I won't give her up that easily." A quick flash of light followed this statement, and he disappeared.

"I helped you, but now you have a lot of responsibility on your shoulders, mortal," Scholar declared in a commanding, low female voice, pointing her spear at the human embracing the specimen. "She's not a goddess; she's just a human, like you. Her mind, however, is like that of a newborn. You must take care of her, protect her, and teach her the ways of your tribe. Thus proclaim I, Athena Pallas, and you shall obey my command!"

"Yes, o mighty Athena, I shall obey." The human knelt, raising his hands.

Scholar sent the final lightning bolt from her device into the sand and disappeared. The humans started to rise slowly from the ground, whispering, shocked by the quarrel between the gods they'd just witnessed.

Commander was left alone to think about recent developments. He was convinced he'd made critical mistakes in judgment while leading the Expedition. These poor decisions resulted in a loss of unity, lack of order, and irrational actions by the crew members. Pilot was building an army to subjugate the humans; Defender was creating weapons to exterminate them; Technologist was chasing his bioprinted specimen, and Scholar… He was unsure about Scholar. Perhaps Scholar was the only one still capable of proper reasoning. In any case, the Expedition was failing with accelerated speed.

Commander was also convinced that the planet itself or its inhabitants had something to do with the changes impacting the crew. There was something sinister in this influence, something unexpected, suppressing the voice of reason, making the Soarers behave contrary to their best interests. Commander didn't know whether he had undergone a similar transformation; he hoped he had not. In any case, the direction of recent events predicted total disaster for the Expedition. What was worse, the violent inclinations his crew members demonstrated threatened the existence of both their races. He couldn't let that happen.

CHAPTER

FIVE

The Chamber of Nergal underneath the Assur-Enlil Ziggurat was submerged in complete darkness. There were no windows, openings, or slots of any kind within its stone walls, just mud bricks and damp clay floor. The stale air smelled of mold, rotten fruit, and human waste. The only sounds one could hear were shallow breaths and barely audible moans that could've belonged to expiring people or, perhaps, to injured animals. The most prominent element of the chamber's aura couldn't be seen, heard, or smelled; it was a mix of fear and despair. This was the place where the forlorn, tortured prisoners were brought to be sacrificed to the great deities Nergal and Ishtar. There was no hope. They would be forever forgotten in eternal torments, never to see sunlight again.

A few stones in the wall moved inward, and the doorway appeared. First, twelve warriors carrying torches entered the chamber. They wore short, sleeveless tunics, belted around the waist, pointed helmets, and simple sandals. Each wore a short sword inside the ornamented sheath attached to their belts. The soldiers took their positions at the perimeter of the chamber within equal distances, lighting up the dreadful scene inside the room. About thirty prisoners of different races and sexes lay on the floor. The captives were naked, their hands and ankles bound, their bodies covered with dirt, blood, and bruises. There were people from Abyssinia, with skin darker than night, shaggy Thracians, and cleanly shaven Egyptians. One man looked at the soldier standing next to him and sobbed, begging for mercy. The only response was a kick to the head.

Following the soldiers, a second group entered the chamber. These were four beardless priests with cleanly shaven heads, dressed in long, dark robes. They stopped at the four corners of the room.

Finally, the Great King Ninurta-apal-Ekur entered the chamber, accompanied by Grand Vizier Salmanu and Chief Eunuch Adad. The broad-shouldered figure of the king dominated his entourage; he was a head taller than both his ministers. The king wore a long robe, closely wrapped around his body and kept in place by a girdle. A robe was arranged so that his left arm was concealed while the right one held the lion-headed mace, the symbol of Nergal. A royal mitre covered his long, wavy, black hair. His beard was carefully oiled and arranged in small curls. The brown eyes sparkled underneath the bushy eyebrows, which almost touched each other at the nose bridge. The king stopped by the entrance and made a signal with his mace.

"Let the ceremony begin, to the glory of Assur!" Ninurta proclaimed in a deep, loud voice.

Suddenly, one of the prisoners, a giant, bearded man with red hair and fierce green eyes, who was on his knees, made a desperate leap toward one of the soldiers. Somehow, he managed to untie his hands and grab the soldier's sword by the blade. Not expecting such swiftness from the tortured, barely-alive captive, the guard couldn't hold on to his weapon. The prisoner gripped the sword tightly with his cut palms, the blood streaming down into the dirt. In triumph, he let out a loud yell. However, instead of freeing his fellow prisoners or attacking the defenseless soldier, the man stuck the sword into the mud hilt-down. He fell on the blade with a victorious smile, running the cold bronze through his heart. The final gasp left his throat, and the savage eyes closed forever.

The king pointed his mace at the unfortunate soldier, still standing on his spot, stunned.

"You," Ninurta said, "will take his place. The gods require proper sacrifice."

"No! No, please! Great King, I will correct my mistake!" The soldier tried to run toward Ninurta but was quickly stopped by his fellow guards, who tied his hands and ankles and pushed him down.

"Yes, you will," the king said. "Since your lack of alertness deprived the gods of the victim, you must take its place. Such is the will of Nergal."

The soldier tried to protest and scream but was quickly gagged and dragged to the king's feet.

"Now, the ceremony must begin," proclaimed the king.

The guards lowered and extinguished their torches. Complete darkness engulfed the chamber yet again. The priests quietly started muttering enchantments, in unison, as if trying to hypnotize the victims.

Suddenly, the walls on both sides of the entrance came alive. Akkadian cuneiforms, glowing bright red, appeared on the stone masonry, seemingly out of nowhere. One inscription represented Nergal, the god of the underworld. The other was Ishtar, goddess of love and war. The people on the floor who were about to be sacrificed started to wail.

Next, a glimmering blue cloud appeared underneath each inscription, and both of them started to advance slowly toward the group of victims. Finally, one cloud enveloped the unfortunate soldier, who was the closest to the entrance. Glowing inscriptions provided some illumination, but it was impossible to see what was happening to the guard. The priests started to sing louder, their incantations turning into unintelligible wails. A strong, suffocating smell filled the room.

At that moment, the prisoner next to the soldier being sacrificed shrieked loudly and tried to crawl away from the spot. She only managed to reach her other neighbor and froze in place, completely stupefied. The blue cloud started to move in her direction, revealing for a few seconds what had happened to the soldier who had the questionable honor of being sacrificed first. There was nothing left in the place previously occupied by the human body except a puddle of pink goo. The cloud, in the meantime, engulfed the next martyr, and the process repeated.

After scanning the whole room and ingesting all the victims in such a manner, the two glowing objects retreated toward the wall. The priests abruptly stopped chanting, and dead, ominous silence engulfed the sacrificial chamber. Finally, the king made a pass with the symbol of Nergal, and the guards lit their torches.

The scene in front of their eyes made some of them shiver; the others turned away, while some soldiers covered their faces with their hands. A thick layer of pink, glutinous material covered the floor. This was all that was left of the people who had just filled this space.

"The sacrifice has been accepted, o great king!" Chief Eunuch Adad said, lowering his head.

Ninurta looked at the gore in front of him. "Assur shall conquer; it is my destiny. Such is the will of the gods."

#

The Great King of Assyria, Ninurta-apal-Ekur, came to talk with his most trusted servants at the great hall of the royal palace in Assur. The gods had accepted the sacrifice and granted Ninurta their favor. It was finally time to act; the preparations were complete. His duty was to lead the great host of Assyrian armies to subjugate all the races to the will of Assur. He knew Ishtar and Nergal would be with him and ensure his warriors were victorious, no matter who they fought.

Ninurta didn't question the will of the gods. The king knew his place, and he knew the gods had forged his destiny for him. He had to follow their lead.

The Great King walked through the portal serving as the entrance to the great hall. The portal was ornamented with a colossal human-headed bull on either side. The bulls were positioned in such a way that they seemed to support the arch above, which was decorated with enameled bricks arranged in a complex geometric pattern. Inside the great hall, pillars rose to the gallery above. Lions were located at the base of the pillars, and the winged bulls supported the pilasters. These sacred animals represented Nergal, who guided Ninurta and whose will the king obeyed without any second thoughts.

The king proceeded to the set of long tables situated along the wall of the great hall, on which were placed fruits, sweets, and wine both of Assyrian and foreign origin. Slaves stood nearby, ready to address any whim of the Great King. Armed soldiers followed Ninurta, vigilantly guarding the approaches to him. The aromas of cinnamon and frankincense filled the hall; these were the king's favorite.

Ninurta picked up a date from the table and extended his arm to lift a Canaanite faïence cup shaped like a ram's head. A scantily dressed female slave obligingly filled the cup with wine. Ninurta sat onto the wooden throne, adorned on the three sides by lion figures, its legs ending in a pine-shaped ornament.

Ninurta put the date in his mouth, spat out the pit, inhaled the mysterious scent of cinnamon, and watched the three figures approaching him from the entrance. First, Grand Vizier Salmanu strutted, looking tall and imposing in his long, fringed black robe, covering him from head to toe. His face was hidden behind a bushy black beard, long and broad. Chief Eunuch Adad tottered next to him, taking vast strides to keep up. He wore an elaborately patterned long dress, while earrings, armlets, bracelets, and a golden necklace adorned his body. The third visitor was prince Assur-Dan, Ninurta's son and limmu official for the year, the proclaimed successor to the throne. The prince wore a simple gray robe with no special features. His body was also free of any jewelry. His brown beard, cut short, exposed narrow cheekbones, a long nose, and refined features. Rumor attributed the finesse of his appearance to his mother, an Elamite princess. Assur-Dan stepped with dignity, looking straight ahead at his father, positioning himself some distance from the two ministers.

"I called you to tell you my will," Ninurta said, "which is the will of Ishtar. But first, I want to hear the news and your advice. Chief Eunuch, are my women content? What are the people in the harem saying?"

"It's all under control, o Great King," Adad said, looking down. "There's no negative gossip; people have accepted prince Assur-Dan as your successor and the one chosen by the gods. So, I don't see a reason to worry about a coup from this direction."

"Good. Have the new brides arrived?" Ninurta looked at the chief eunuch. Adad still looked down, but the large mole on his chin was nevertheless visible. There was something repellant in the demeanor of the toady eunuch, but his services were irreplaceable.

"Yes, o Great King. The Libyan princess with her entourage is here. The Libyans expect to strengthen our alliance against the common enemy, Egypt. The envoys from the Canaanite cities of Ashkelon, Ashdod, and Ekron are also here, bringing the girls of noble birth to seal the friendship with Assur through marriages. These allies will also be beneficial against the Egyptian threat."

"Very well. What are the grand vizier's thoughts about this?" Ninurta didn't trust his advisers and often played them against each other.

"I agree with the chief eunuch, o Great King," Salmanu said with a smile, interlocking his hands behind his back. "We shall keep Egypt occupied with the Libyan and Canaanite incursions. This will free our hands to deal with Babylon and Susa once and for all."

"What about the Hittites?"

"They are a formidable enemy, o Great King. However, they are currently involved in a dispute with Ahhiyawa for the trade routes that Wilusa controls. My sources tell me Ahhiyawa are about to attack Wilusa, and the Hittites will have to help their new allies. Their armies are not a threat to Assur at this moment. So, we are free to teach Babylon a lesson."

"This is sound counsel, Grand Vizier." Ninurta made a signal to refill his cup with wine. "However, there's a problem with this plan."

"What's the problem, o Great King?"

"It is against the will of the gods. Ishtar wants the armies of Assur to march west, not south."

The grand vizier and the chief eunuch exchanged glances, after which Adad turned away and Salmanu bowed his head to the king but responded to the comment, speaking slowly and carefully choosing his words.

"Your wisdom is beyond boundaries, o Great King," Salmanu said. "Please enlighten us so we can partake of the divine judgment."

"Ishtar needs more sacrifices; people of different races. The gods shall lead us to conquer all the western adversaries so we can offer them Hittite, Canaanite, and Ahhiyawa prisoners."

"Babylonians and Elamites are not good enough, o Great King?"

"No. We've sacrificed a lot of them already. The gods demand new, different people. Learn to obey your gods, Salmanu."

"The desire of the gods is sacred, and we must fulfill their wishes," Adad said, studying the tips of his richly adorned sandals.

"We prepare to march in two days," Ninurta announced. "The Egyptians are busy deflecting their own threats, and the Hittites are about to join the war in support of Wilusa. If we are quick, we will take Carchemish by the next moon. Then the tin mines of Isuwa will follow. The Hittites will have no time to react."

"My king, is this wise?" Prince Assur-Dan stepped forward, looking straight at his father. "We'll be exposed to the attack by the Babylonians. Are we strong enough to fight on two fronts?"

"They wouldn't dare to attack." Ninurta dismissed the concern, waving his hand. "Our cities are fortified, and we have strong garrisons. Babylonians are cowards; they are afraid of us."

"It's good if it is so, my king." Assur-Dan nodded. "However, I still think the risk of attacking the Hittites at this point is too high."

"What you or I think doesn't matter, my son. We march west because this is the will of the gods. We are their obedient servants and must fulfill the destiny they forged for us. Is my army ready?" Ninurta turned his gaze to the grand vizier.

"Yes, o Great King. Your armies are well supplied and ready to march. It will take a day or two to mobilize the chariots, but this will not pose a problem. We march at your command."

"You said this is the will of the gods." The prince crossed his hands in front of his chest. "How can we be certain it is so? Did they give you direct orders?"

The king stood up from his chair, walked to the table with food, and picked up a pomegranate. Then he approached Assur-Dan, placed his hand on the prince's shoulder, and said with a smile, "It is wise to question the counsel of your advisers, my son. It will be advantageous to you when you become the Great King. However, it is *not* wise to question the gods." Ninurta squeezed the pomegranate so it burst and the juice started dripping on the floor. The king looked at the fruit in his hand with surprise as if he'd seen it for the first time. "When you question the gods, my son, the blood that's spilled is yours, not that of your enemies."

Ninurta threw the remains of the fruit into the basket, which had magically appeared in the hands of one of the servant-maids, and wiped his hand off her hair. The king turned back and met the prince's gaze, his voice suddenly becoming deep and ominous.

"Do *not* question me ever again. Nergal guides us, but he expects our full obedience. Do you understand?"

"Yes, my king," the prince said, kneeling before his father.

At this moment, a brilliant blue light suddenly illuminated the throne. Salmanu and Adad took several steps back, their faces twisted with fear. The slaves started to run away, screaming. The guards instinctively reached for their swords. Assur-Dan, still kneeling, looked at the throne, which by now was engulfed by a blue cloud. The prince's eyes were wide open, his jaw lowered, beads of sweat on his brow. The king came closer to his chair and prostrated himself on the floor in front of the radiant light. A red cuneiform sign indicating the goddess Ishtar appeared on the wooden surface of the throne.

"What is your will, o great goddess? Your servant is at your command." Ninurta said.

Once the cuneiform sign had changed and the blue light dimmed, the king stood up. He looked triumphantly at his advisers, still frozen in their places under the impression of the divine manifestation they'd just witnessed.

"We march in two days," the king said.

Behind his back, on the wooden surface of the throne, a cuneiform sign glowed with a menacing bright red, reading: *Enslave the land of Hatti.*

CHAPTER
SIX

Echelaos stepped into his tent in the middle of the Achaean camp set up on the Asiatic shore of the Hellespont. Tros, his faithful charioteer, followed the prince, carrying a shield. The Achaean army had faced no resistance disembarking on the beach by the river Scamander, not far from the mighty walls of Troy. The ships had no problem blockading the harbor, and the soldiers established themselves on land, unloading weapons, provisions, and a few chariots and horses they'd transported on the ships. The army had to wait for the northern mercenaries to cross the straights and signal to the Achaeans that they were ready to advance. Then, once Machaon brought the main contingent of chariotry from Miletus, the attack could begin.

Echelaos had just finished a quick meeting with his commanders; he was excited about the prospect of fighting and vanquishing such a formidable foe as the Trojans. He would teach these insolent merchants how to respect Pylos and its rulers; he'd accomplish deeds worthy of the greatest heroes and get Helen. Oh, yes, he kept thinking about Helen. Echelaos had never seen the Hittite princess, but her fame as the most beautiful woman alive fired him up and made his blood run faster. He was a little uneasy about the stories describing her proficiency in magic and strange behavior, which he tried to brush away as unfounded rumors. Whatever it was, he'd deal with it later. Now was the time to fight.

"Echelaos, look what I've made for you!" Aphrodite had run to the tent entrance when she'd noticed the visitors. Echelaos looked at the maiden and froze in place, struck by her charm and youthful energy. Aphrodite wore a traditional Cretan dress, which she'd found in a chest on one of the Cretan ships and immediately adored. The dress perfectly highlighted all the natural delights of her body. A tight belt accentuated her narrow waist, while the colorful skirt decorated with flowers, fish, and birds of brilliant colors matched her lively demeanor. Above the skirt, Aphrodite wore a tight, short-sleeved, open bodice, which fully exposed her beautiful breasts. She held a clay figurine of a woman.

Several weeks had passed after Echelaos had witnessed Aphrodite coming out of the sea foam. He was confused and could not understand his feelings toward her. Aphrodite behaved like a child in a body of a fully grown woman — an exceptionally beautiful woman. She had questions about everything; she'd followed Echelaos around the ship, testing the boundaries of his patience. Then she'd hugged him and said something sweet so his heart would melt. Echelaos didn't feel any desire when he looked at Aphrodite. On the contrary, she was like his little daughter, trusting and loving him unconditionally. Yet Echelaos was too young to have children; he wasn't prepared; he didn't know what to do, how to teach her. And, glory to Athena, did she learn fast! She could barely talk for the first few days, but after the second week, she was speaking better than his generals. Echelaos was astonished and enchanted by the beautiful maiden entrusted to him by the goddess. But he didn't know what to do with her, and it was a problem. It distracted him from the preparations to defeat the Trojans, and he couldn't allow himself to be distracted.

Aphrodite extended her hand and showed the figurine to Echelaos.

"This is me," she said. "I want you to have it with you when you fight these horrible Trojans. This way, I'll always be with you." She jumped, hugging Echelaos and kissing him on the cheek.

"Thank you; this is so thoughtful," Echelaos said. "What did you learn today?"

"I've learned how the walls of Troy were built. They are high and strong, and no man can breach them. Except for Echelaos and the Achaeans!" She screamed triumphantly, taking both Echelaos and Tros by their hands.

"This is great. You've learned well," Tros said, smiling.

"Promise to bring something special for me from Troy, please?" Aphrodite asked.

"Of course. The Trojan merchants trade with the whole known world; I'm sure I'll find something exceptional for an extraordinary girl like you."

"Oh, thank you, you're the best." Aphrodite gave Echelaos a passionate hug.

"My prince, urgent news," a guard called.

"Yes, what is it?" Echelaos said, stepping out of the tent.

"We've received a fire message from the shore north of here. Akhilleus and his Thracians have arrived."

#

Three men sat around an improvised wooden table in the middle of the Achaean camp. Akhilleus and Zoltes, the leader of the ferocious Thracians, joined Echelaos to plan the assault. The main body of the Northmen encamped at the point where they'd crossed the Hellespont with the help of inflated leather skins and assisted by the Achaean fleet. There were about five hundred of them hungry for gold, slaves, and other spoils of war. Zoltes wore a dress made of bearskin, the highest sign of distinction among his people. Besides the round bronze helmet, his body wasn't protected by any armor. A broad, double-edged sword hung from the sheath attached to his leather belt. His red hair was arranged in long braids, and a full beard covered his face. Large green eyes looked on with distrust and anticipation of the fight.

Zoltes banged his fist on the table. "My men are ready; let's attack."

"We need chariots. Once Machaon is here, we attack from three directions," Akhilleus said. The rising sun colored the scar on his face dark red, which gave him a sinister look.

"We attack their chariots. We kill the horses. We cut the archers to pieces. Then we hump the corpses and burn the city." Zoltes grinned, showing off the blade of his sword.

"Why would you hump the corpses? There are plenty of women in the city." Echelaos shrugged.

"Indeed. And men," Zoltes said, baring his yellow teeth with a few holes upfront.

"We need chariots; otherwise, the Trojans won't engage." Akhilleus shook his head. "How many warriors do you have, Echelaos?"

"Nine hundred and fifty," Echelaos said. "And you brought five hundred?"

"Four hundred and thirty fighters from the Tribe of the Black Stallion," Zoltes said, picking his nose with a long fingernail on his left pinkie. "Ready to fight and kill for you. Your king paid plenty of gold and promised a lot of spoils, so we're here."

"Plus, fifty warriors from Iolkos, the best ones. Personally chosen by me," Akhilleus added, scratching his scar.

"Why didn't you bring more?" Echelaos asked.

"We have competition; rumor says the god Ares himself is recruiting a powerful army near Olympus mountain. Not that I believe it."

"Hmm…" Echelaos murmured, carving a line on the wooden surface of the table with his fingernail. The fight between Apollo and Athena was in front of his eyes. Still, he decided not to tell his partners about his encounters with the gods just yet.

"Zoltes, anything your people saw?" Echelaos turned to the Thracian.

"Ares…yes." Zoltes took his helmet off and placed it on the table. "Long story."

"We have time."

"A few moons ago, the men of the Black Stallion noticed activity on the mountain. Then, hunters encountered the god himself: huge, wielding a spear, shooting fire and lightning and burning everything around. My people call him Zerunthios, while your people call him Ares, the God of War." Zoltes turned away and spat. "Bloody entrails…scary neighbor for the people of the Black Stallion. Hunting is bad. People refuse to go to the mountains."

"What does he want?" Echelaos asked.

"First, there were rumors in Leibethra that the god is hiring workers to mine gold. Many enlisted. Nobody has seen them since. Then, people said the god is raising an army to conquer the world. Some wacky butt-heads decided to join."

"How many? How big is the army now?"

"A few dozen. I don't know about the army. Bloody entrails, I don't understand why the god needs an army of humans to fight." Zoltes scratched the back of his head.

"Maybe Ares thinks it's beneath him to fight humans?" Akhilleus suggested.

"Whatever, none of my business," Zoltes said. "However, I was told the god is also creating soldiers, not just enlisting people."

"Creating soldiers? What do you mean?" Echelaos asked.

"Like you make ships or weapons from wood, rock, and metal. They come alive and fight for him, wielding weapons that shoot fire. I didn't see them, but some of my people did."

"Interesting…" Akhilleus whistled. "I wonder if we could somehow persuade Ares to fight on our side. I bet we'd vanquish not only the Trojans but also the Hittites and anyone else who dares to oppose the Achaeans." He hit the table with his palms and stood.

"No, this is very dangerous." Echelaos shook his head. "We must avoid the gods; we don't want to be involved in their quarrels. We can defeat the Trojans ourselves."

"Perhaps you're right," Akhilleus said. "Could you seek the help of Athena? Could Aphrodite ask her? What if Ares decided to help the Trojans?"

"Then we'll deal with it. We have enough to worry about without involving the gods." Echelaos stood as well, looking at Akhilleus.

"Two more things," Zoltes said. "Some of his soldiers fly, and they are enormous. Similar to your ships but flying like birds. And then there is Zis."

"Who?" Both Achaean warriors looked at the Thracian.

"Zis the Hero. Your people call him Heracles. He is bigger than any other soldier in the army of Zerunthios; almost as big as the god himself. I heard a story from a shepherd about how Zis crushed the mountain with his bare hands and made a gigantic ore pit for the god. Bloody entrails," Zoltes spat on the ground, "with a creature like this, no walls built by humans are an obstacle."

"Your story sounds worse and worse, Zoltes." Echelaos walked around the table, then stopped and looked at the horizon. "I'm concerned. Where are they gonna march?"

"I can tell you what I've heard." Zoltes grinned. "Zerunthios wants to conquer the world. Raze the cities. Kill the people. I don't know why. I've heard, however, where he's planning to march."

"Where?" Echelaos held his breath.

"On Thebes, then on Mycenae, then on Pylos. The God of War wants to destroy Achaea."

#

The rising disk of the sun appeared on the horizon, painting the grassland around the river Scamander crimson in anticipation of the bloody battle. As Princess Ehli-Nikkal expected, the wind was strong that morning, and in the right direction. This was an essential element for her plan of defense to work.

The Hittite princess was looking out of the narrow window cut high in the stone wall of the Trojan citadel. Heavily fortified, standing on a hill, and backing an unassailable precipice, the citadel was the heart of the city. Troy was in front of her, cramped streets filled with tiny houses running down the slope toward massive gates leading to the plateau. Cyclopean walls made of enormous stones surrounded the city. Archers were in their positions on the battlements, and infantrymen had gathered at the gates, ready to go forward in support of the main chariot force. Ehli was confident the attack could be repulsed, especially if her plan worked.

Her thoughts were interrupted by four men entering the room. They spoke loudly, gesticulating, having an argument. King Walmu was the only one silent, leading the group, stepping solemnly with a detached expression. His eyes looked somewhere beyond the rising sun. Immediately following Walmu strode merchant Tibe, radiating anger and impatience; his fingers, decorated with golden rings, pointed in the direction of the window. His robe was the richest of the four, with even more grandeur than the king's. Walmu was the king in the name, but Tibe held the real power in Troy, the wealthiest merchant and the master of the Traders' Brotherhood. It was his idea to switch sides and pledge allegiance to Hattusa. This arrangement promised more independence and higher profits to the Brotherhood.

Following them, a tall, muscular young warrior in full armor was explaining something to another young man in rich dress, whose body was decorated with golden armlets, silver earrings, and a jadeite necklace. His long blond hair was elaborately arranged in complex braids. His facial features were made more prominent by cosmetics: her new husband, Alaksandru. The wedding had taken place two days ago, but Ehli didn't care about him. The marriage was expedient for political ends; there was nothing else between them. The matrimonial bond was properly consummated, of course, but after that, she didn't even talk to her husband; she didn't know what she'd say to him.

"I demand we attack immediately!" Tibe yelled, approaching the window. "Look at this sorry host — are these the mighty Achaeans? Are we supposed to be afraid? They have half the number of our chariots; this is ridiculous."

"Master Tibe, please, calm down. We need to assess the disposition first," said the young warrior, placing his bronze helmet with a horse-tail crest on the table and piercing the merchant with a powerful gaze of his deep blue eyes. This was Hector, Wilusa's leading general. Notwithstanding his age, Hector had proved himself fearless and cunning on the battlefield, an astute tactician and an excellent archer. King Walmu wouldn't engage in any military activity without Hector's advice.

"What disposition? Is this the brave Hector I hear?" Tibe turned around and met Hector's gaze. "They have surrounded the city, and they are blockading the port. Trade has stopped. Every minute of delay costs me gold, real gold, gold I'll subtract from your payment!" the merchant yelled at Hector's unflappable face.

"The Achaeans are great warriors; we must be cautious," Alaksandru said. "They are very dangerous, and it could be a trick… We need to negotiate. The Achaeans are reasonable people; they'd agree to a profit-sharing deal…"

"Negotiate? Share profits? No way!" Tibe raised his fist in the air.

"If they storm the city, they'll kill us all and burn everything." Alaksandru cringed, trying to make himself smaller. "Besides, they'd brought the Thracians — uncivilized, ruthless brutes. Who knows what they'll do to peaceful citizens?"

"For as long as I live, this won't happen," Hector said. The loyalty of the young general to Troy was legendary. "This is my city, the city I swore to protect. I'll gladly sacrifice my life if it helps to repulse the enemy."

"If you sacrifice your life," King Walmu said, stroking his beard, "we are doomed. We need help from the Hittites." The king looked at Ehli. "I hope King Suppiluliuma marches his armies west, otherwise he'd lose not only his new allies, but his daughter as well."

"We shall defend the city," Hector said. "I don't believe the Achaeans have the means to storm Troy."

"What if we wait for their attack?" Ehli suggested. "I agree with Hector." She looked at the general, who nodded. "The walls are high and strong; we have good archers; we can inflict even more damage if my plan succeeds. Let them try to storm the city. We'll repulse the assault and kill many of them."

"What if they won't attack?" Tibe parried. "For how long can we stay under siege? Trade will suffer, crops will be destroyed, and land will be burned. No, we must attack now."

"Wait." Hector raised his hand, looking out the window. "I see the enemy has divided their forces. The chariots are close to the gate and separate from the infantry; the regiment of Thracian mercenaries is even farther away. If this is a ruse, I don't get it. If we attack with our chariots now, we destroy them; this disposition is favorable."

"Finally," Tibe blurted out.

"I'll lead the chariot attack," Hector said. "Princess Ehli, the people on the battlements follow your instructions. Will your secret weapon work if needed?"

"I'm confident it will."

"Excellent. If the enemy approaches the walls, we know what to do. We'll fight to the last man standing, for victory or death. May the gods help us." Hector ran out of the citadel. The Battle of Wilusa had begun.

The enormous wooden gates slowly opened, letting the main chariot force out. The enemy was positioned at some distance, not daring to come closer, cautious of the archers on the battlements. As was customary in such confrontations, the outcome depended on the chariotry engagement. The infantry was there to support; having no chance against mobile platforms from which the archers rained death upon to their foes. Wilusa had almost four hundred chariots deployed for the battle, twice as many as the Achaeans had brought from Miletus. The result was predetermined.

The battle started as expected: chariots engaging, archers shooting at each other, and the forces mixing on the plain in front of the river. The Achaean chariotry, overpowered, started retreating in a wide arc toward their supporting infantry and farther, where the Thracians were positioned. Suddenly, the ferocious, red-haired, skin-clad northerners ran forward, for a moment engulfing the Achaean chariots as if to protect them, but then attacking the Trojan force. What happened next was beyond Ehli's understanding and surprised even emotionless Walmu. Each Thracian warrior was armed with a long, broad sword and carried several light javelins. They scattered in all directions, stopping only to throw their deadly weapons. And their targets were not the Trojan archers, who tried to shoot at them from the chariots, but the horses — much easier targets. Injured animals, covered with blood, were falling everywhere, taking their vehicles with them. Ehli searched the battlefield for the large green chariot of Hector. Finally, she identified him, shooting at the Thracians and charging at the enemies. Suddenly, a javelin hit one of Hector's horses, and the injured animal leaned to the side, pulling the chariot until it fell. Immediately, two Northmen approached the collapsed platform, wielding their brutal double-edge weapons, cutting the flesh of the fallen Trojan heroes.

In a moment, a sure victory turned into complete defeat. The signal was given to the chariots to retreat behind the infantry line, now positioned in front of the gates, covering the disgraceful flight of the elite units of the Trojan army. At this moment, the Achaean foot soldiers moved forward, ready to attack and completely obliterate both the Trojan infantry and chariotry. This was a time to act, time for Ehli's secret weapon. As if hearing her thoughts, the soldiers on the battlements started frantic activities, setting large stacks of hay on fire and pushing them down the walls with their long spears. Haystacks were drenched with naphtha, a flammable substance produced by the Babylonian land, of which the merchants of Wilusa had some supply. Ehli thanked her grandmother for explaining this trick.

Anticipating the fireballs rolling downhill, the Trojan infantry regrouped and followed the chariots' retreat behind the gates. Unfortunately, some of the slower Trojan soldiers were hit by the flames. Still, the devastation of the enemy infantry was much higher: the rolling bonfires caught the Achaean warriors charging the Trojans by complete surprise, creating pathways of flame, smoke, and charred bodies as they descended. This caused significant confusion for the enemy, but in the end the Achaeans were able to regroup and retreat in order, losing a considerable number of warriors.

Ehli took a deep breath and looked at the three men standing next to her. King Walmu had the same detached demeanor as when he had entered the room, as if nothing was of his concern, but his fingers trembled as he stroked his beard with such force, he was pulling the hair out. Tibe's face was white; his hands were shaking, his eyes wide, threatening to fall out their sockets. And Alaksandru… Alaksandru held his father's hand, shivering like a leaf, mumbling something about negotiations.

Thus ended the Battle of Wilusa, and the siege began. Ehli couldn't stop wondering if she'd done enough to provide her new home with the best chance to win. But, after all, she was the lone woman trying to carry out the mission her father gave her, expecting help that never came.

At that moment, a muscular, black-haired enemy warrior approached the gate. He held an object in his left hand, raising the right one.

"I am Akhilleus." he yelled loudly and confidently. "Surrender, and we'll spare your lives."

The answer was an arrow landing at his feet.

"An unwise decision. Resist, and Troy shall be razed to the ground. Nobody will be spared."

Another arrow.

"You've made your choice. Troy must be destroyed. Greet your general!" With these words, he threw the object he carried to the gate. With horror, Ehli realized it was a human head. The head of Hector.

CHAPTER
SEVEN

The night was hot and cloudless. Desert air scratched the lungs, and the sand penetrated the short, light tunic into every crevice of Khay's body. It was excruciating on the eyes. Khay tried not to think about these physical hardships and instead focused on the riches they'd have once they pillaged the mad pharaoh's tomb.

The Nile was flowing peacefully far behind them. Still, even at this distance, far into the desert, Khay could smell the moist, stinky stench of the river with familiar strong undertones of fish and fowl.

Khay asked himself for the hundredth time why someone would build a city so far away from the river, in the desert. The site of the great capital of the mad pharaoh had become ruins, now almost entirely covered by sand. The remains of old palaces and statues stuck out of the dunes like bizarre ancient rocks carved into fanciful shapes by the desert wind. People had forgotten Akhenaten's necropolis after the royal tomb was sealed and hidden by the priests of Amen, never to be opened again. Only the reckless grave robbers had dared to come to this place, desecrating the tombs in search of the buried riches of the epoch long gone.

Yet regardless of the faults of the mad pharaoh, the treasures of the royal tomb must be immense, Khay told himself, adjusting the weight on his back. He carried copper shovels and bronze axes, one for each party member. The load was not heavy but added to the unpleasant experience of the hot desert night.

"How much longer?" Khay asked Djehuty, who led the way.

"Should be close. A thousand steps or so."

Djehuty had the map and also carried three torches they expected to use when they arrived at the site. Djehuty avoided looking at the map, however, saying he had memorized the directions to walk in complete darkness to avoid attracting any attention. Although whose attention they'd attract was a mystery to Khay: the place was long abandoned, nobody lived there, and no soldiers were guarding long-forsaken dunes. But it was better to be safe than sorry.

"Do you think your amulets will protect us from the Ka and the Ba of Akhenaten? From other evil spirits?" Khay turned back and asked Intef, the third member of their company.

"Yes. Otherwise, why would I carry all of this?" Intef shrugged. He had a big sack behind his back full of amulets, jewels, and scarabs. Some of these they'd acquired from the tombs they'd robbed in the past. Others they'd bought on the market. Khay was a little scared; the mad pharaoh and the cult of Aten he'd introduced was a taboo subject in Ramesside Egypt. What was hidden in the royal tomb was a mystery; it could be deadly or even dangerous to the spirit of immortality, Akh, denying the thieves eternal life.

Grave robbery was a dangerous occupation. Ta-sekhet-ma'at was heavily guarded, and the punishment for desecrating the royal tombs was death. This danger was familiar; Khay and his accomplices had robbed several not very distinguished vaults at Ta-sekhet-ma'at, collecting some jewelry and gold. This was good but not much; the thieves craved a lot more. Finally, the chance had presented itself.

"Tell us again how you got the map," Khay said, rubbing the place where his left earlobe used to be, the result of a fight with the guards of Ta-sekhet-ma'at.

"There is a potter in Thebes; he provides me with information occasionally. Tombs, guards, locations of this nature," Djehuty said.

"I cannot tell you his name. Anyway, he told me there was this strange Nubian at the market selling all sorts of antiquities, some of them as old as Pharaoh Sneferu's time."

"How well do you know this potter?" Intef asked.

"Pretty well. Most importantly, his information is always accurate. A great source for our business," Djehuty said. "Anyway, I went to the market the next morning and found this Nubian. Weird fellow. Black as kem, not a trace of hair on his head, blue eyes, giant round stones inserted into his earlobes, fingers covered with yellow scabs… disgusting. But he had all sorts of artifacts. I didn't care much about Nubian figurines or magic hippopotamus's dung from Punt; however, I discovered a stack of papyrus maps. And in that stack, I found this treasure. Surprisingly, he didn't value it much. So, to avoid attracting unnecessary attention, I had to pretend I was interested in the map of Libya and bought the two of them together."

"How do you know it's genuine?" Khay asked.

"I talked to my other sources. They all pointed to the same approximate location, although nobody had the exact map. The worst thing that could happen is we find nothing and turn back. However, if the map's real…we'll get rich beyond your wildest dreams."

"I hope you're right," Intef whispered.

"Slow down; I think we're close," Djehuty said. "I was counting steps; this should be about right."

When everyone stopped and dropped their burden in the sand, Djehuty lit the torch and unfolded the map, shifting the gaze from the sheet of papyrus to their surroundings and back. Then, finally, a dune about hundred steps farther caught his attention.

"There," Djehuty said, pointing ahead.

Once they reached the dune, Djehuty walked around it a few times until he identified what looked like an ancient stone pillar buried in the sand.

"The map is real," he proclaimed, raising his hand with the sheet of papyrus in the air. "We're on the right track."

With these words, he measured twenty-five steps to the side, placed his torch in the sand, and lit it.

"We dig here," Djehuty said. "Quickly. It should be pretty shallow."

Following their leader, Khay and Intef positioned their torches so they could see the whole area, and the three robbers started digging. Khay figured it was about midnight. They had time, but he didn't want to be stuck here until morning. The thieves worked frantically, digging, pushing, and throwing the sand. Khay sweated profusely, breathing, tasting, and feeling sand with every pore of his body. Then, his shovel suddenly hit something hard: a stone surface hidden underneath the dune. Khay called to his companions, and the three started working in the same place, uncovering the slab little by little.

"This is it, I'm certain." Djehuty said, unrolling the map and looking at it again under the torchlight. "I think this is the lid that covers the entrance."

Finally, they could clean up enough of the area to see several stone blocks arranged in a rectangular pattern.

"Let's try to push one of these," Djehuty said in a commanding voice. Khay and Intef obeyed without a word and started leaning on the edge of the block, trying to move the lid.

"Eternal is Amen, this is heavy…" Intef panted as they exerted all their strength. Finally, the block moved a little, creating an opening the size of a fist. That allowed Djehuty to grab the opposite edge and pull. The lid started to move more easily with three men nudging it, and in a few moments the robbers had uncovered what appeared to be the entrance to the tomb. Moonlight exposed the first two steps of the stone staircase descending into the place of the eternal rest of the mad pharaoh.

"We could probably squeeze in, but I suggest we move another block," Khay said. "Who knows what we'll be bringing back? We might need space."

"I agree," Djehuty said.

It took them another half an hour to move the second block, but now the entrance was wide and clear. Khay rubbed his hands in anticipation of the treasures waiting for them inside and felt his heart racing faster. He remembered stories about the mad pharaoh and the sun-disk deity Aten; how the gods had cursed the family of Akhenaten, all his followers, and his capital, Akhetaten. After all, he had abandoned Ma'at, cast away all the true gods, and built a new capital in the middle of nowhere. Akhenaten personified Isfet, the state of chaos and evil. The sweat on Khay's face suddenly dried out; he felt goosebumps down his spine.

Khay had started thinking about turning back when Intef said, "I go first. I have protective amulets, and I'll be reciting spells against evil spirits and the inhabitants of the land of the dead." He reached out into his sack and handed two scarab amulets to his fellow thieves. "Put these on your necks. They should provide additional protection."

Intef took up his torch and stepped onto the staircase. Djehuty went after him, and Khay closed out the group. All held their torches and walked very slowly and carefully, holding their breath.

About thirty steps down, there was a pillared gateway into a large room. This was the chamber where all the goods and tools necessary for the journey to the afterlife were stored. The room was full of treasures: golden vases, jewelry, royal dresses, perfume, jars with aromatic oil, and dried fruit. Paintings representing Pharaoh Akhenaten and his family on their final journey into the afterlife, to the court of Osiris, covered the walls. The thieves looked at each other: they'd finally struck gold. It was unbelievable luck and good fortune. Khay almost forgot about his fears, picking up a gold nugget from the corner and rubbing it as if checking if it was real.

Djehuty stepped forward and pointed at another alcove to the right. There were more chests with goods stored in that area, but at the opposite end of the alcove, another gateway was hidden from sight. The thieves followed their leader into the new room, eyes wide. This was the burial chamber. The stone sarcophagus with Akhenaten's cartouche carved on the lid was standing on one side of the room, next to his golden chariot, armor, several bows, and sickle swords. Khay's gaze, however, was fixed on the opposite side of the room, where the second sarcophagus stood, with carvings representing the imagery of the god Aten.

"I thought this was the tomb of Akhenaten. Who else could be here?" Khay asked and rubbed his missing earlobe, not addressing anyone specifically.

"We shall see." Djehuty shrugged and stepped toward the second coffin. "Help me here, would you?"

Intef joined his leader in pushing away the cover. Gradually, two of them could move the top of the crate. Finally, the lid fell to the floor and broke into two pieces with a loud bang. Unperturbed by the noise and destruction, Intef extended his hand to explore what riches were encased inside.

Khay took a deep breath, clenched his fists, and decided to face his fears. He approached the pharaoh's resting place and started moving the lid, slowly exposing the wooden sarcophagus that contained the mummy and all the most valuable treasures.

Suddenly, he heard cries of surprise. Khay glanced over to see what was happening with his companions. Intef and Djehuty were leaning on the casket, peeking inside the container. Djehuty was violently shaking his head in disbelief.

"What in the world is this? Why is this here? Where are my treasures?" Djehuty repeated several times.

"What is it?" Khay asked. "Anyway, it's not important. I've found the mummy of Akhenaten."

Intef turned and looked at Khay. "I don't understand; it's a mushroom."

"Mushroom? What are you talking about? Did Apep steal your mind?"

"There's nothing in the coffin but mushrooms. It looks like they were planted inside. Makes no sense."

"Well, we ain't taking any mushrooms back with us," Khay said. "Come help me with the mummy."

At that moment, Djehuty gasped hoarsely and collapsed on the floor.

"Djehuty, what is it? What's happened?" Intef leaned over his companion, shaking him.

Khay suddenly felt his stomach falling below his knees, his mouth becoming dry, as though it was full of sand. *The curse is true.* The thought raced in his mind. *I must flee this horrible place.* He turned away from the sarcophagus.

At that moment, Intef, still holding Djehuty's head, collapsed on top of his leader. Backing out, not finding the strength to look away from the frightful scene in the chamber, Khay witnessed the transformation of his fellow robbers. They started to rise to their feet, moving erratically, as if controlled by an amateur puppeteer. The eyes of the two thieves were twice their usual size, with sclera red from burst blood vessels. White foam ran out of their mouths and noses, and a disgusting brown substance leaked from their ears. Intef and Djehuty gurgled something unintelligible, then noticed Khay and started slowly approaching him, looking Khay directly in the eye with the horrifying, unblinking gaze of their bloody sockets.

Coming out of his stupor, Khay turned around and ran. He ran faster than he ever had in his short life of twenty-one winters. The distorted faces of his companions were in front of his eyes, but Khay was too scared to look back and see if they were chasing him. He finally reached the river and found their boat hidden in the reeds. Only at this point could he take a quick peek in the direction of the tomb. There was no one after him. Taking a deep breath, Khay pushed the boat off the shore. He covered his face with both hands, realizing he was shivering despite the hot air. He couldn't stop wondering what ancient evil they'd just released into the world and what consequences would follow.

#

Khay never imagined visiting the great city of Pi-Ramesse, definitely not accompanied by the high priest of Amen. However, he was there, following Bakenkhonsu. The priest strode slowly through the narrow streets of the Western City with the dignity and poise inherent to the position of the high priest of one of the most powerful deities of the Ramesside Egypt.

"Are you sure High Priest Nefer-Setekh will talk to us?" Khay asked.

"Oh, yes, he will. Even Nefer-Setekh pays attention when the high priest of Amen wants to visit him." Bakenkhonsu looked at Khay sternly. "You should rather worry about what he'll suggest doing with you for setting Aten loose."

The high priest of Amen wore his traditional leopard-skin cloak and ceremonial wig, carrying a staff crowned with the sun-disk on top of the ram's head: a sacred symbol of Amen. Khay noticed beads of sweat on the smooth, ageless face of the priest; the ceremonial clothing was not suitable for the heat of the sunny afternoon in the Nile delta. Khay wore his usual short tunic with a belt; his head and feet were bare. They'd just arrived on a boat to the western part of the island, where Pi-Ramesse was located, and now proceeded to meet with the High Priest of Wadjet. This was a residential area of a size Khay had never seen before. Streets, arranged in elaborate patterns, contained large houses with internal courtyards and storage silos. They passed several open squares and warehouses where wine and grain were stored. Khay overheard loud speech from the nearby marketplace, and a strong smell of perfumed oils, ointments, and fruits attacked his nostrils. This was an affluent area, so the familiar stench of the swamp was replaced here by the sophisticated aromas of the incense olfactory.

They passed a large square with an enormous granary and entered the Sphinx Alley, leading to the Temple of Wadjet.

"What would the punishment be?" Khay asked. "I'm ready for anything. I made my choice; I knew the risk. I'd accept whatever he has for me if only I avoid Aten." He looked at hundreds of imposing stone statues of magic beasts on both sides of the alley and once again gasped, astonished by the beauty and grandeur of Pi-Ramesse. "But then," he continued, "you decided not to punish me when I showed up at Nesut-Towi begging for mercy. So perhaps Hem-netjer Nefer-Setekh will spare my life, even though I know very well that my transgression is punishable by death."

"You need to clean up the mess you created," Bakenkhonsu answered. "That's your punishment. What you've seen in the tomb might be important to restrain Aten. Nefer-Setekh is the only one with the knowledge to decide what to do."

"Yes, you told me, I need to be patient." Khay took a long breath and caressed his left ear.

Following a long, straight path guarded by countless sphinxes, they finally arrived at the Temple of Wadjet. The building was enormous, solid and thick walls rising to the sky. Obelisks with carved images of Eyes of Ra and Wadjet and colossal statues of the goddess flanked a broad, double-gateway leading into the temple. Wadjet was one of the most ancient deities of Lower Egypt. The figures represented her as a snake-headed woman, a personification of the Egyptian cobra, snake-goddess.

Entering the temple, Khay shivered. The smell of incense was powerful, but there seemed to be no one in the hall. It was completely dark inside, since the windows were positioned in such a way that they only illuminated the chamber at sunrise or sunset.

"What now?" Khay asked, peering around.

"Now we wait."

"Why are we in total darkness?"

"The rites of Nefer-Setekh are unique. Don't worry about this."

A few minutes later, a light appeared at the other end of the room, and the sound of steps cut through the deafening silence. As the glow approached the visitors, the figure of an elderly man carrying the torch became visible. He wore a rich blue and green kalasiris, colors of Wadjet. On his neck was a pendant in the shape of a cobra. But this was not the most striking feature of the priest: his dark brown face, bald head, and hands were covered in myriad wrinkles, which gave his skin a bizarre reptilian appearance. His green eyes regarded the two guests without blinking, and his lips were almost the same brown as his face, making it difficult to see his mouth and identify his emotions.

"Is he the one who released Aten?" Nefer-Setekh croaked, pointing his torch at Khay.

"Yes, Hem-netjer," Khay mumbled.

"May Apep devour your Ka, you wretched scoundrel," Nefer-Stekh said, spitting at Khay. "Do you realize what you've done?"

"I understand my transgression is horrible. I only ask about a chance to fix this terrible error. Please, Hem-netjer, tell me what I should do."

"You should disappear from the face of the Earth. Let the day of your birth be forever damned."

"Hem-netjer, we seek your guidance," Bakenkhonsu said. "You are the keeper of the sacred rites; you are the only one who knows what to do."

"Yes, but I'm too old for this," Nefer-Setekh said. "The effort to restrain Aten was monumental. It took hundreds of uninfected priests and warriors to tame this monstrosity. We'll need Pharaoh's support to reverse the damage, if it's not too late."

"Not too late? What do you mean?" Khay asked. "Aten is just a… mushroom, right?"

"I'll tell you the truth and let it sink into your silly head, boy." Nefer-Setekh came closer to the unfortunate tomb robber, and the strong, musky smell of the priest's perfume hit Khay's nose. "Aten has the power to possess people's minds. You witnessed what happened to your silly friends. Aten won't stop; he'll continue to enslave one human after another."

"But how's that possible?" Khay protested.

"Aten is an enormous organism that lives deep underneath the desert; he cannot be killed, just restrained. The last time Aten got loose, he subjugated the pharaoh and most of Egypt to his morbid will. I know the tradition and can perform necessary rituals, but we'll need a lot more."

"We'll go to the pharaoh and inform him of the grave danger and ask for his help," Bakenkhonsu said. "What else is needed?"

"Aten is a Primordial, and we'll need divine assistance to put him back into the abyss where he belongs. We must summon Wadjet."

#

Ramesses sat on his golden throne adorned with colored glass, faïence, lapis lazuli, and other precious stones. The pharaoh paid no attention to the two slaves standing next to him, swinging fans made of ostrich feathers, or to his key advisers, standing at a distance from the throne, observing their king in silence and reverence.

Ramesses thought about the precarious situation Egypt was in, surrounded by enemies, with a weak economic base and a military that had seen its glory days long ago. He longed to recreate the time of his illustrious predecessor and one of the most celebrated pharaohs, Ramesses the Great. This was his goal, and he'd vowed to dedicate all his energies and his life to accomplish it. There was no mortal esteemed higher by Ramesses than the great pharaoh, conqueror of the Hittites at Kadesh. The Hittites who were now his allies and came to beg for help.

The pharaoh wore formal clothing consisting of the intricately embroidered kilt dropping below the knee, a loose blouse, and sandals. On his head was a traditional wig made of braids of black hair, covered by nemes, and a false metal beard — a sigh of sovereignty. Black kohl outlined his lips, and his appearance was enhanced with various cosmetics: oils, perfume, and fragrances. All of this was part of a deliberate attempt to create an impression of strength, dignity, and importance. No king on Earth was equal to the Great Pharaoh, and the visitors had to be overwhelmed by the grandeur of the ruler of the Two Kingdoms.

Grand Vizier Hori took a few steps toward the gateway into the royal chamber, and the guards lowered their spears, allowing two people to enter: the Hittite envoys. As required by ceremony, they prostrated themselves on the floor, looking down, hands extended forward in supplication.

"Great Pharaoh Usermaatre Meryamen, the envoys from the land of Hatti are here to plead for your support!" Hori announced. "They've brought plenty of gifts: gold, bronze, pottery, jewelry. Adoration for you is very high in their land, and the people of Hatti beg for your friendship and protection!"

"Very well, Hori, but let's use normal language. My head hurts from this ceremonial talk, and I have little time. What do they want?"

"Do you allow them to speak, o Great Pharaoh?"

"Yes, by the glory of Amen, don't try my patience."

The grand vizier made a hand gesture, and one of the envoys raised his head just a little bit, still not daring to look at Ramesses.

"We come as your subjects; we are not worthy of a single breath of Great Pharaoh Usermaatre Meryamen—" started the envoy.

Ramesses interrupted him. "Stop. I said speak normal language."

"Yes, o Great Pharaoh. Our land is in great danger; war has come from two sides. While the Ahhiyawa besieged our allies in Wilusa in the west, the Assyrians invaded from the east. Theirs is a mighty host, and we received reports that their gods are guiding and helping them."

"What is your petition?"

"Carchemish has fallen to the Assyrians, o Great Pharaoh. They are driving a wedge between the territories of Egypt and Hatti and targeting our copper mines at Isuwa, a key to our bronze production. Without bronze, we won't be able to defend ourselves, so we plead to the Great Pharaoh to gather his armies and attack the vile Assyrians from the south while we engage them from the north. Our kingdoms have enjoyed a long period of friendship and prosperity. We implore you to come to our help and punish these depraved bandits!"

"What's the benefit for me?" Ramesses asked. "You brought the wrath of the Ahhiyawa on yourselves by allying with their subjects at Wilusa. And now, when the Assyrians are attacking, you cannot fight on two fronts. So you must make peace with the Ahhiyawa before we consider advancing to Syria. Hori, Hewernef — what do you think?"

"You are wise, o Great Pharaoh." Hori bowed. "We've just achieved a great victory, but we might face more trouble in the desert from the Libyans. The coffers are almost empty. To wage another war so soon would not be advisable."

"You are wise indeed, o Usermaatre Meryamen," General Hewernef said. "I agree with Grand Vizier Hori. First, however, I would advise strengthening our garrisons in Canaan. This will allow us to deflect the Assyrians if they attack or launch an offensive in support of our allies if we decide to do so."

"O Great Pharaoh, the danger to the kingdom of Hatti is grave! We'll convey your wishes to King Suppiluliuma. But we are your allies, and we need your help. The Assyrians are numerous as locusts and cruel as Kaska; they defile the land, sack the cities, and kill the people. If we join our forces, we will eliminate this plague, and they will not threaten either Egypt or Hattusa any more. Therefore, o Great Pharaoh, we plead with you!"

"We will consider your request. But in the meantime, General, I want a full report on our military. Chariots, horses, weapons, soldiers — we must prepare for new hostilities."

At this moment, one of the guards stepped forward and whispered something to the Grand Vizier.

Hori turned to Ramesses, bowed, and said softly, "I'm very sorry to interrupt the audience, o Great Pharaoh. The High Priests Bakenkhonsu and Nefer-Setekh are here; their business is urgent, and they must speak with you at once."

"Very well, invite them in," Ramesses said. "You two," he pointed at the envoys, "go to my brother, your King Suppiluliuma, and tell him he must make peace with Ahhiyawa. Great Pharaoh Usermaatre Meryamen will consider his plea and strengthen the garrisons in Canaan."

The envoys left, looking down and walking backward. Three visitors came in as soon as they'd disappeared into the gateway. Two priests stopped at the entrance while the third man prostrated himself on the floor.

"This better be very important," Ramesses said. "You just interrupted our deliberations about the war against Assyria."

"What we are about to tell you is vital for the Two Kingdoms," Bakenkhonsu said quietly, bowing in the presence of the pharaoh. "The wars can wait until we address the current deadly issue."

"And why is that? What's the issue? Don't make me wait."

"The Two Kingdoms are in danger of destruction. Remember what happened during the times of the mad pharaoh? This poor wretch," Bakenkhonsu kicked the man on the floor, "has freed Aten. The survival of Egypt and all her people are at stake, o Great Pharaoh."

CHAPTER
EIGHT

"Are you not afraid of the Achaeans, Princess Ehli?" Korinsia asked, arranging Ehli-Nikkal's lush raven-black hair into elaborate braids.

"No. Why would I be afraid? Anything they could do to me is limited to physical pain. I can handle that. They could kill me, it's true, but that doesn't concern me. We all die, eventually."

Korinsia gasped. "You're strong and brave, my princess. I envy you. I'm so scared; I can't sleep; I'm losing my mind. I want to run away and hide, but there is nowhere to run."

"You could ask my husband; he knows where to hide. I can never find him!" Ehli laughed.

"What will happen to us, Princess Ehli? To Wilusa?"

"Well, there's a good chance Wilusa is sacked if my father's armies don't show up to relieve the siege. This is Wilusa's only hope." Ehli took a mirror and looked at her hairstyle. "Thank you, Korinsia; you did an excellent job, as usual." She returned the mirror to her maid and continued, "As for the two of us, we have options. I have a task my father gave me, which I'll try to complete whatever it takes. If I realize it's not possible, I'll figure out what to do next. You," Ehli paused and looked at Korinsia's freckled face with concern, tilting her head, "you could join your compatriots from Pylos. I'll release you right now if you want. You'll get freedom and return home."

"Home?" Korinsia's eyes suddenly filled with tears, her lips trembling, her palms interlocked. "I have no home! You are the only human being who has looked at me as a person since I was captured and enslaved. And this is how Achaean soldiers will see me: a slave." Korinsia looked Ehli straight in the eye. "No, I'll follow you to the ends of the Earth, Princess."

"You're amazing, Korinsia." Ehli-Nikkal embraced the girl and stroked her plump cheek. "Don't be scared; we'll find a way. I always do, and I'll protect you."

"Thank you, Princess Ehli. Do you know any other tricks that could help Wilusa? Like what you did with hay?"

"I'm considering some. But I need materials, which I'm not sure we have. We're out of naphtha, so we can't repeat the hay trick. I need to talk to Master Tibe; he knows where everything is. Let's find him."

"You said you're not concerned about being killed, Princess. Why is that? Everyone is afraid of death," Korinsia asked as they exited the princess's chamber.

"Everybody and everything dies. This is the law of nature, the circle of life. Yet nothing disappears without a trace. When people die, they come back as clouds, rivers, and earth. And so the cycle repeats."

"You speak wisely; however, your wisdom doesn't give me solace," Korinsia said in a trembling voice. "It still means I'll disappear, with all my memories and feelings. This is a horrible thought."

"It's not entirely true, Korinsia. Nothing disappears completely. Your memories and feelings will be around, accessible to the people who can listen."

"People say you can talk to the dead. Is it true? Is that what you mean?"

"Yes and no." Ehli didn't mind answering these somewhat childish questions. She remembered how patient grandmother Davke had been with her and knew it was her turn to explain the true nature of things to people eager to learn.

Ehli paused, stopped, and took the girl by the hand. "Nobody can talk to the dead the way you and I talk. But you can listen; you can find out what the people who lived here long ago felt, desired, and accomplished. This city, Wilusa, has stood here from the time immemorial. It was known under different names; it was burnt and rebuilt many times, and this time won't be any different. If you understand that this is all part of the natural cycle of life, that life itself is beautiful no matter what happens, you'll be a lot happier and calmer. Your naïve fears and concerns will seem unimportant and not worth your time."

Korinsia, still shaking, took Ehli's other hand in hers. "I'm still scared, Princess. Will you teach me your wisdom so I can become as strong as you are?"

"Of course, Korinsia. I'll show you how to become the master of your emotions and fears. Stay with me, and we'll walk this path together."

Finally, they exited the citadel and stepped into a large courtyard overlooking the city. At that moment, their conversation was interrupted by a loud argument, two men, Master Tibe and King Walmu, were having in the middle of the courtyard. Ehli overheard the king saying he was unhappy with the amount of food and wine left in storage and demanded the traders open up their repositories. Tibe, extending his arms in a placatory gesture, defended himself, blaming the siege for the lack of provisions. Ehli and Korinsia approached the arguing pair but were suddenly rooted into place by a thunderous noise, smoke, and a pungent, slightly sweet smell.

When Ehli turned around to see what had happened, she observed the giant figure of a god in complete military attire, holding a lyre and a spear.

"Apaliunas…" Ehli whispered. "How's this possible?"

Korinsia didn't respond. She closed her eyes and grabbed Ehli's hand. Tibe and Walmu fell to the ground, prostrating themselves before the god.

"Hear me, mortals!" The god's voice roared above the courtyard. "I came to protect you from your enemies. The Achaeans have offended me, and they'll pay dearly for that. You'll dispose of them, and I'll get what's mine."

"What can we do to defeat them, o great Apaliunas?" Ehli-Nikkal stepped forward.

"Use this." The god pointed to the pile of gray, bizarre-looking gear beside him. "With my weapons, you will incinerate your enemies and regain your freedom."

#

Echelaos moved his head from left to right, observing the Achaean troops. The rising sun reflected off their bronze corselets and boar-tusk helmets. He stood in his chariot, next to Tros, with the bow and the quiver behind his back. All forces were in position, ready to advance.

Echelaos raised his right arm and shouted, "Attack!"

Immediately, the designated soldiers lit up their torches and spread the signal across all formations, and the unit leaders yelled the verbal command to start the assault.

Echelaos looked at the walls of Troy, high and thick but not impregnable. The Achaeans had a plan, and he was sure it would work if all the warriors followed the strategy and there were no unforeseen circumstances. There should be none, Echelaos told himself. He'd received a message the previous evening that the armies of the Hittites were preparing to march east to face the Assyrian invaders and liberate Carchemish. There would be no help to the besieged from that side.

The infantry ran toward the walls carrying large, oblong shields, which covered the soldiers from head to toe, with only two minor cutouts on either side of the shield serving as hand grips. In addition, the Achaeans wore bronze armor and were well protected from the Trojan archers on the walls. The Achaean chariots and archers stood behind the advancing infantry, prepared to engage and shoot the defenders on the battlements once they appeared. Some groups of infantrymen carried long wooden ladders to scale the walls. The Achaeans had numerical superiority, better equipment, and a solid plan. Echelaos was confident of victory.

Suddenly, the enemy opened fire as the soldiers came within hundred steps of the walls. But it was not the arrows that Echelaos and his fellow commanders expected. Instead, it was actual fire: the Trojans on the battlements shot a series of fire bolts at the advancing infantry from all directions. What followed was confusion and conflagration: men, covered in flames, burning alive at the walls of the enemy city, were collapsing to the ground, raising their hands, screaming for help…all in vain. The ladders were burning with the men carrying them, and the smell of scorched flesh spread around the plain. But the Trojans didn't stop there; they started aiming at the archers and the chariots. Frightened horses neighed and jumped, tilting the chariots and throwing the archers to the ground. Echelaos screamed to retreat, grabbing a torch from the soldier running past him and emphasizing his order with a light signal. The conflagration was destroying the Achaean army. The only thought he had at that moment was how to save his troops.

The Thracians, who were just behind the infantry units spearheading the assault, also came under heavy fire. However, their light armor and better mobility allowed them to disperse much quicker and avoid congestion and mass casualties. The Northmen pulled back while Zoltes and Akhilleus stayed up front, shouting orders, organizing and overseeing the retreat. As the two commanders started withdrawing, following their fighters, a blaze of fire exploded behind Akhilleus.

The Achaean fell to the ground screaming, his right foot smoldering. Seeing that, Zoltes turned back, trying to help his fallen comrade, while Akhilleus yelled at him, waving his hand, telling him to leave. At this moment, another fireball hit the place where Akhilleus had fallen. Zoltes was fortunate to avoid the blast's epicenter, immediately jumping left, while the explosion grazed his right side. The Thracian hit the ground, rolling, trying to escape danger and put out the fire devouring his body. Akhilleus was not that lucky, suffering a direct hit, his body disappearing within the eruption of fire and smoke.

And then a new factor changed the tide of the battle. A barrier made of gentle blue light appeared within the space between the retreating Achaeans and the city walls. The light absorbed the fire pouring on the attackers and provided a shield that Echelaos needed to save his troops from annihilation. As the infantry ran back toward the Achaean camp, a sudden flash of light blinded Echelaos. When his sight returned, he saw Athena herself, in all her glory, wielding aegis, spear in her hand. Three black owls circled above her head, with three more going farther, beyond the blue barrier, over the city.

"I will not allow you to interfere." Athena's voice, deep and commanding, towered above the plain. "Technologist, you must leave immediately."

"I came to take what's mine: the specimen and my revenge." A loud voice roared in response, but the god was nowhere to be seen.

Echelaos glanced over the battlefield. The conflagration covered most of the plain near the city, smoldering bodies lying everywhere. Some warriors still limped toward safety, helping their burnt comrades. The soldiers who were not impacted by fire lay on the ground, covering their eyes, shaking in the presence of the goddess.

"To do that, you'd have to fight me," Athena announced. "Take your tech and go away; you've lost your mind. I'm sure Commander will support me."

Echelaos, regaining his composure and figuring he had nothing to lose, stepped out of his chariot and approached the goddess.

"O great Athena, we thank you for the favor you showed us," he said, falling on one knee and taking off his helmet. "I beg for your help to heal the fallen soldiers. They'll fight in your honor for the rest of their lives."

"I can do that," Athena answered. A swarm of owls suddenly descended on the battlefield, moving from one fallen warrior to another, engulfing them in blue light, extinguishing fires and healing the wounds.

"What about my friends Akhilleus and Zoltes?" Echelaos asked, finding new courage, pointing in the direction of the Thracian units.

"One of them will live, although the damage is severe; my medical drone is dealing with the wounds. The other one…" Athena paused. "I have many powers, but even I cannot revive the dead. Your friend is with Hades now."

Echelaos bowed his head. "We thank you for all your help, o great goddess! We will sacrifice daily in your honor."

"You are the human taking care of the specimen I entrusted you. I believe you call her Aphrodite," Athena said.

"Yes, o great goddess. My name is Echelaos, and I swore to you to protect and teach Aphrodite."

"Very good. Never forget that, and you'll have my protection."

"You shall not interfere with my revenge!" A roaring reverberated over the battlefield. "I will get what is rightfully mine. She is *my* creation, and I need her to advance my science."

"There will be no revenge," a thunderous growl announced. Then, following a flash of light, another giant figure appeared in front of the walls of Troy. Echelaos rubbed his eyes; he couldn't believe what he was seeing. Mighty Zeus himself stood next to Athena, carrying the thunderbolt in his hand.

"Technologist, you must destroy the weapons you gave to humans and leave immediately. You've lost the ability to think and reason."

"You're both blind and naïve. Defender and Pilot were right. I must act on my own."

A large orange disk rose above the walls of Troy, rotating slowly, flying around the city.

"I'll retreat for now, but this is not the end. I'll be back."

#

Echelaos glanced over the battlefield, still finding it difficult to believe what had just happened. To interact with the god directly had been beyond his wildest fantasies a few moons ago, but witnessing the quarrel between the three gods was a whole different level of unimaginable.

The soldiers were slowly getting to their feet, assembling into formations. Some chariots were burned entirely, and some were damaged. However, most vehicles were still intact and ready for action. With Akhilleus and Zoltes down, Echelaos had to decide quickly what to do next. Then, as if hearing his thoughts, a chariot with Machaon approached, lawagetos shouting the orders to regroup, his curly blond hair sticking out from underneath his bronze helmet.

"What do you want to do?" Machaon asked Echelaos once his chariot came closer.

"You'll think I'm crazy, but I say we should attack. Follow the original plan. The Trojans must believe we're beaten and demoralized, giving us the element of surprise."

"I like the way you think." Machaon smiled. "We've lost about a quarter of our infantry, but the chariots are still strong, and the Thracians are in full force. What if they meet us with fireballs again?"

"I'll take a small detachment of chariots first. If they shoot, we retreat. If not, the infantry will follow. Now we know what to expect and will be ready. However, I don't think this is likely, since both Athena and Zeus are on our side. They are giving us a chance to achieve a glorious victory today. Let's not waste this chance."

"For the glory of Pylos! Victory shall be ours." Machaon left at full speed, shouting the orders.

A few minutes later, a small contingent of twenty chariots approached the walls of Troy. Echelaos led the charge, ready to shoot, Tros steering the chariot skillfully. When they were met with a few enemy arrows that the chariots had no problem avoiding, the Achaean archers responded with their swarm of projectiles, aiming at the battlements.

Seeing no sign of the divine weapons, Echelaos ordered his group to retreat while signaling to Machaon to start the main assault.

Once again, the armored Achaean infantry ran to the walls, carrying ladders, spears, and short daggers. Archers and chariots were in the back while the Thracians advanced behind the Achaean infantry. The attackers were met with a cloud of arrows from the walls, but there were no fireballs this time. Echelaos, overseeing the assault from behind the infantry lines with squinted eyes and clenched fists, exhaled and smiled. This was familiar territory, and his warriors knew what to do. The attack proceeded according to the original plan.

The Achaean infantry, protected from the clouds of enemy arrows by armor and shields, approached the walls and started to scale them with ladders. A fierce battle commenced in places where the attackers attempted to climb and dislodge the defenders from the walls, some of them being pushed back, falling to the ground in a pile of bodies, easy targets for the Trojan archers. But the Achaeans had a numerical advantage and successfully scaled the walls in a few places, gaining a foothold and pushing the Trojans back with their shields.

The points where the infantry had ascended the walls became targets for the Thracians. The Northmen followed Achaean spearmen and started climbing the ladders to support the warriors fighting on the walls. Once they got to the top, the battle was decided. Their long double-edged swords gave the Thracians the critical advantage as they not only pierced but also slashed their enemies. The northerners engaged the Trojans while the Achaean infantry retreated behind them, providing cover with their long spears. Once again, the unfamiliar weapons of the Thracians decided the outcome; the Trojans didn't know how to fight against such an enemy. The walls were quickly overrun, and a few moments later triumphant attackers penetrated the city and opened the gates. The rest of the infantry and the chariots were already in the position to enter the gates and storm the city.

Once the Achaean troops had entered Troy, the battle was over and the slaughter began. The ferocious Thracians were leading the carnage, slashing, cutting, destroying everything in their path. The beautiful stone pathways of the ancient city turned red with blood and gore; screams of killed and mutilated people and women being raped filled the air. There was no quarter given and no life spared.

Echelaos entered the city in his chariot, the bow in his hands, shooting at the remaining enemy soldiers. His face was red with excitement and blood, but he ignored it; he was so immersed in the fight and intoxicated by the victory that he could only think about defeating the enemy. He rejoiced. The plan had worked, and the gods had granted them a glorious victory. Now he had only one thing left to do: find Helen.

Thinking about his bride-to-be, Echelaos yelled at Tros to steer the chariot toward the citadel. The Thracians were already fighting at the stairs of the last Trojan stronghold, eliminating the royal guard. Echelaos was afraid Helen would be killed in the middle of the fight, and he couldn't allow that to happen.

Suddenly, he noticed a chariot on the side road leading from the citadel toward the precipice on which the palace stood. The chariot followed two cloaked figures on horses. *This must be the hidden escape route*, Echelaos thought, *and someone is trying to flee amid the fighting. Helen must be in the chariot, and the two guards on horseback are showing her the way.* He told Tros to follow the group as fast as he could.

Soon, they caught up with the runaway chariot. To Echelaos's surprise, the passenger in the vehicle was not a woman, but a man. He was dressed in an intricately adorned robe with a golden tiara on his head and bracelets decorated with gems on his arms. Echelaos decided this was King Walmu himself.

"I command you to stop; you are my prisoners!" Echelaos shouted.

In response, the man grabbed a spear and tried to poke the horses driving the chariot chasing him. The animals stumbled and lost pace, allowing the fugitives to gain some distance. Not liking this development, Echelaos raised his bow and shot the man holding a spear. The arrow was placed perfectly, notwithstanding the distance and the winding road. The projectile penetrated the eye of the richly dressed man, blood streaming down his face. He leaned to the side and fell off the chariot, his golden tiara rolling and bouncing under the hooves of Echelaos's horses.

"Master Tibe!" the charioteer screamed, realizing his passenger was shot. At this moment, one of the cloaked figures riding the horses turned around, the hood falling, exposing beautiful, long, straight black hair.

"Helen!" Echelaos exclaimed, not believing his eyes. The royal princess on horseback was yet another bizarre scene of this war. "Follow them." He extended his arm.

Tros did his best to catch up with the two horsemen. Or maybe horsewomen. However, as the road went farther into the ravine, the path became narrower and more winding. It was impossible to keep the pace with horses, and they didn't have time to unharness their animals to continue the pursuit. Finally, Echelaos reconciled himself to the fact that his bride-to-be had escaped and told Tros to turn around. The loss of his prize clouded the joy of the victory.

When Echelaos and Tros returned to the palace, the bloodshed was almost over. The warriors dispersed within the city, raping and pillaging, getting their share of the victory. On the majestic stone staircase leading into the citadel, a group of Thracians engaged in something violent, swinging their swords, laughing, and shouting obscenities. As the two Achaeans approached the group, a repulsive scene opened. The headless body of Prince Alaksandru, his exquisite garments drenched in blood, lay next to the citadel's entrance. One of the Thracians carried a long pike on which the head of the prince was impaled, his eyes giving Echelaos a dead stare. Old King Walmu, stripped of his royal robe, his tiara now covering the red hair of one of the Northmen, lay on the stairs, gasping, muttering pleas to the gods to spare his city and his people. The Thracians were kicking and poking him with their swords.

Outraged at such a lack of respect for the vanquished king, Echelaos signaled Tros to stop, got out of the chariot, and shouted in the direction of the Thracians, raising his hands. The Thracians turned their heads, looking at the intruder, then one of them stepped forward and nodded, recognizing Echelaos.

"The spoils of our victory, Prince." The Thracian pointed at the motionless figure of the king. "We earned them. Our share."

"This is the king; you must show some respect," Echelaos said.

"Respect? Yes, respect." The unkempt Thracian grinned, raised his sword, leaned over the king, and grabbed him by the hair.

"Please end my life, but spare the people," the king whispered.

"Happily. This is my respect." He cut Walmu's throat with his sword, blood gushing down the stairs, creating a grotesque red stream flowing down the white stone surface.

"This is the day of the Black Stallion! The day when mighty Troy was crushed under the hooves of the Thracian horde."

The northerner dragged the king's body so his head hung over the stair step, swung his sword, and beheaded the king with one forceful blow. The head rolled down the stairs, coming to a halt at the feet of Echelaos.

"You can have it, Prince. Your enemy is dead; you rule in Troy now."

CHAPTER

NINE

"How much longer, Princess?" Korinsia asked Ehli-Nikkal. After escaping the fallen Wilusa, the two women had traveled on horseback for many days. Ehli had a bow and could practice her skill in archery, shooting wild goats, antelopes, and deer grazing the slopes of the hills rising on both sides of the road.

"We're almost there. A few more hours, and you'll see Nerik," Ehli said. She had decided to take the northern route back to Hattusa, avoiding Achaean patrols and scouts from Miletus. These areas were mostly inhabited by animals, and the biggest danger was encountering a bear. The princess, however, felt at home in this wilderness, reading the signs of nature and keeping Korinsia safe. Their destination was Nerik, a Hittite holy city just north of Hattusa. Ehli-Nikkal was unhappy she had failed the task King Suppiluliuma had assigned her; still, there wasn't much she could do against the Achaean host without the help of the Hittite armies. And then there was the factor of the gods, whose quarrel had decided the battle's outcome. Korinsia had asked Ehli many questions about the gods during their trip, but Ehli didn't know what to say. She understood the forces of nature, the voices of the dead, and the cycle of life, but not how to interact with the gods when they appeared. Grandmother Davke hadn't taught her this skill.

"I'm so happy we escaped this bloodshed," Korinsia said. "It's so peaceful here. I love these mountains." She turned her head to the left and gasped. Ehli looked in the same direction: the view of the snow peaks crowning the green slopes and merging with the clouds somewhere high in the skies was majestic.

Ehli studied Korinsia's happy face, myriad freckles under her eyes. Korinsia's excitement and her youthful spirit reminded Ehli of herself many years ago.

"Don't get too relaxed. The beastly Kaska inhabit the hills north of Nerik. If they catch us, it won't be pleasant."

Ehli's horse snorted, his ears straightening up. Ehli inhaled fresh morning air, the smell of pines and firs, and leaned forward and patted her horse on the neck.

"Calm down, Oak," she whispered. Ehli didn't sense any danger either in human or animal form. But she decided to be on high alert for the rest of their journey.

"Do you have friends in Nerik?" Korinsia asked.

"I hope Sarini is still there. He's been an adviser to my father for a long time; he's a scribe and a priest of Nerikkil, the Weather God. Sarini maintains the holy sanctuary and organizes all the required rituals and festivals."

"I wonder about the fate of King Walmu and everyone else we left behind. I doubt the Achaeans will let him stay in power."

"King Walmu is dead, as is Prince Alaksandru. The city's been sacked and burned; people enslaved. Wilusa as we knew it doesn't exist; it's a province of Achaea now."

"How do you know this, Princess?"

"I've listened. I've heard about King Walmu's last moments. I've heard the wails and screams of the citizens of Wilusa being raped and butchered by the Thracians. You don't want to know more, believe me."

Korinsia wiped the tears from her plump cheek and tightened her lips.

They continued their path in silence for some time. Ehli was listening, observing, and smelling the surroundings in anticipation of danger. Then, finally, the enclosure of Nerik sanctuary emerged on the horizon.

"We've arrived, Princess!" Korinsia exclaimed. "It was the most difficult journey of my life." She patted her horse, which neighed in response, cheering the rider.

"Be quiet, Korinsia." Ehli hissed at her maid. "This is the most dangerous area."

As if sharing Ehli's alarm, Oak stopped, snorted, and shook his head.

"Stop," Ehli commanded. "I sense something. Remain completely silent."

Ehli already knew what they were facing while still hoping to avoid the danger. Kaska scouts on the hills had noticed the two riders and were approaching from both sides. Ehli couldn't see them yet, but she felt their presence very well. This wasn't good. They were so close to their destination, and this confrontation with Kaska was most undesirable. Ehli considered the options. Staying quietly in place was not beneficial anymore; the Kaska had already spotted them. A daring plan formed in her head.

"Gallop, Oak!" she commanded her horse, gently squeezing his body with her legs. "Korinsia, follow me as fast as you can!"

The horses darted off in the direction of the Hittite outpost, hoping to outrun the Kaska descending from the hills. The animals were tired but still capable of a fast gallop, and Ehli thought they could still reach safety in an incredible stroke of luck. But these hopes were in vain. Skirting the turn of the road, they encountered several Kaska blocking the path. Goat-, wolf-, and bearskins covered the bodies of the beastly inhabitants of the caves. Their dirty, unkempt hair and beards were so long, Ehli doubted the Kaska had ever cut them. Their faces were painted black with ash, with white horizontal stripes across the forehead. They held clubs, stone axes, and torches, so the horses had to stop, pulling back, frightened by the fire.

"Let's turn around!" Korinsia screamed. "We can still run away!"

"Stay where you are." Ehli didn't need to turn back; she felt Kaska presence behind them.

"But what do we do?" Korinsia said, her voice trembling.

"You do nothing. I'll take care of this," Ehli said, patting Oak, calming him.

At that moment, the group of Kaska in front of them parted, creating an opening for the chief. The giant figure of the newcomer towered head and shoulders above the rest of the cave dwellers, striding slowly, limping on one leg, which was noticeably shorter than the other. He wore the skin of a brown bear, the muzzle covering his head like a strange hood. His long, dirty black hair and beard were arranged in a few thick braids. A frightening necklace of three human skulls and two gigantic bones in his hands completed the appearance of the brute.

"What is this abomination?" Korinsia whispered, closing her eyes.

"Be quiet, I said," Ehli hissed. She needed full concentration to execute her plan.

The chief approached the two women, raising his right hand with an enormous bone in his fist. The next moment, the bone hit the road in front of Ehli's horse while the giant roared something incomprehensible. Oak pulled back, frightened, so Ehli had to hold tight to avoid falling. The caveman came closer to the princess, curving his mouth, baring his rotten teeth, drops of saliva covering his black beard. The smell of sweat, bad breath, and feces hit Ehli's nostrils. She closed her eyes and raised her hands, trying to ignore the brute's growls.

When Ehli opened her eyes a moment later, her pupils were so large, the sclera was almost invisible. A stream of blood ran from her nose; her lips whispered a secret incantation, and her hands, locked tightly above her head, started shaking. The chief grunted, throwing a bone to the ground and reaching out to grab the horse's neck.

"Nerikkil!" Ehli shrieked, calling to the ancient Weather God. Suddenly, the giant brute shook his head as if trying to get rid of a fly in front of his eyes and then fell to the ground with a loud thump. The rest of the Kaska looked at their leader with astonishment, not daring to approach. Then, one by one, the cavemen grabbed their heads with their hands, wailing, collapsing. Ehli kept muttering incantations in deep concentration, blood running from her nose and ears. At this moment, the chief returned to life and got on his knees, his enormous pupils floating in the bloody sclera of his eyes. The giant burped, white foam surging from his mouth, creating a sickening pool of a putrid substance in the dirt. Then, limping and stumbling, swaying from side to side, he plodded off to the hills. The rest of the Kaska followed their leader in a similar condition, muttering sounds more like wild boars than people.

As the Kaska blocking both sides of the road wandered off where they'd come from, Ehli's hands dropped, and she fell forward, holding her horse's neck, silent, motionless.

"Are you all right, Princess Ehli?" Korinsia asked, touching the body of the exhausted woman.

"Yes," Ehli said, her face hidden in her horse's mane. "I need to rest a bit."

"What's just happened?"

"I summoned Nerikkil. I know the ways."

"You can call the god just like that? But didn't you say you'd never spoken with them before?"

"Nerikkil isn't exactly a god, although the Hittites worship him as such."

"What is he, then?"

"He's an ancient entity, an organism that existed in our world long before the gods created the first human. Nerikkil is a Primordial."

Chapter
Ten

"Echelaos, teach me how to shoot from the chariot," Aphrodite exclaimed, pointing at the vehicle of the conqueror of Troy. The ships had arrived that morning in the harbor of Pylos, completing their victorious journey back home. Echelaos watched with pride the troops and chariots disembarking on the shore, the warriors exchanging obscene jokes about each other and the enemies they'd just defeated.

Echelaos looked at Aphrodite, standing next to him, smiling, her golden hair glowing in the rays of the morning sun. He touched his lips with his tongue. The taste and smell of salt and seaweed were everywhere, but Echelaos didn't mind. He'd won and returned to Pylos as a hero, laden with riches, slaves, and fame. He'd achieved everything he'd dreamed about; now was the time to share the spoils of the victory and organize the conquered land.

"Why do you want to shoot from the chariot?" Echelaos asked.

"I want to be a famous warrior like you. Machaon already showed me how to use a bow. I need to learn to kill enemies in battle, riding *my* chariot. Please, Echelaos, will you teach me?" Aphrodite spoke fast, holding Echelaos by the hand, her cheeks glowing pink.

"Battle is not for girls," Echelaos said, shaking his head.

"What do you mean? Why?" Aphrodite stepped back. "I can hit the target from three hundred steps, almost as well as Machaon." She exclaimed proudly. "I'm a quick learner."

"Yes, you are. But fighting is for men, not for girls. This is how it is."

"I don't understand. Do you mean I cannot be a hero like you? This is not fair. I want to go back to Troy. Machaon will teach me if you don't want to." Aphrodite's eyes filled with tears. She was maturing and learning so fast that Echelaos forgot she was still a child.

"Machaon is busy governing Troy for me, and you can't go back."

"But I want to fight!"

"Men fight and seek glory. Women raise children and keep homes warm. This is how we live." Echelaos shrugged.

"I don't like that," Aphrodite announced. "I'll become stronger and smarter than any man, and nobody will stop me from seeking glory."

Aphrodite's stubbornness made Echelaos think. Indeed, why was this so? Was it because the gods had arranged it this way? He remembered what Nestor had told him about the Ages of Man. What if every age had a different order? And what if the coming Age of Iron would change all the rules they knew from ancient times? What if the roles of men and women would reverse? Echelaos shuddered at the thought. *No, this is impossible*, he told himself. He couldn't imagine this beautiful, slender, perfect-in-every-sense girl in the middle of the fight, shooting arrows from the chariot, covered in blood and gore. Just thinking about it made Echelaos sick.

"Don't talk about this ever again. This is not right," he said.

"But why? I still don't understand." Aphrodite stamped her foot. "Also, Echelaos, is every campaign like this: killing people, burning cities, destroying crops? I want to do that, too!"

Echelaos was utterly confused and didn't know how to respond. The Achaean army reinforced by the Thracian mercenaries had indeed caused a lot of destruction at Troy. But again, such was the order of things and the right of the conquerors. The pillage and burning might have been excessive this time, primarily due to the Thracians. Still, Echelaos knew they owed the victory to these ferocious northerners.

"You should forget about what you saw, Aphrodite. As I said, battles are not for girls."

"No, I don't want to!" She stomped her foot again. "I'll follow you into the next battle and fight next to you, killing, burning, and cutting off heads. *I* want glory, too."

"Killing and burning is not glory, Aphrodite."

"How so? I thought this is why you fight, is it not?"

"Well, not exactly."

"Then why? What is glory? Can you explain?"

Echelaos was becoming extremely uncomfortable with this conversation. He knew Aphrodite was asking honest and straightforward questions, trying to understand the world around her. But he didn't know how to explain matters that at first glance were obvious. He struggled to find the words to correct the errors in her judgment.

"Glory is to be brave on the battlefield; to prevail against a strong and worthy enemy; to have the courage to attack and conquer."

"Is it not the same as killing and burning, then?" She met his gaze with her deep blue eyes, tilting her head, frowning.

"No, it is not." Echelaos shook his head. "Look, it's our turn to step off the ship." He took her by the hand and prepared to disembark, happy he had a chance to put an end to this increasingly awkward discussion.

A delegation of several highly ranked officials stood on the shore, meeting the conquerors of Troy. Wedaneus and Eritha stood together with serious and concerned faces, lips tightened, eyes looking down. *This is not how victorious armies should be met at home,* Echelaos thought.

Something else must have happened. He looked around, searching for the wanax, but couldn't see his father.

"Eritha, Wedaneus, cheer up; we've won!" he exclaimed, stepping onto solid ground. "Where is Nestor? We're bringing him gold, gifts, and slaves from treacherous Troy."

Eritha stepped forward, raising her head and finally meeting his gaze, tears in her eyes.

"Nestor is dead, Echelaos. You've arrived just in time for the funeral."

#

As the son and successor of the deceased wanax, Echelaos strode at the head of the funeral procession, right behind the two warriors who carried the terracotta larnax with the body of Nestor. The final journey of the wanax to the grave began the separation of the departed from his family and friends, both physically and symbolically.

Echelaos looked at the large, distorted disk of the setting sun on the horizon, coloring the body of the dead wanax and the people in the procession in bizarre orange tones. He remembered what his father had told him last time they'd spoken. *"The gods are not in control anymore and are abandoning their broken creation. It is the time for humans to build their own world. The world of iron."* The setting sun in front of Echelaos appeared as a signal, a warning, a sign of a new age. He knew it was his turn to lead his people, but he didn't feel he had the strength or the wisdom for this task. Somehow, fighting the Trojans was a lot simpler. He didn't know what he was supposed to do as wanax of Pylos. Nestor was the rock, the foundation; Echelaos couldn't imagine Pylos without his father. Yet he had to pretend he could replace Nestor. The fate of the people depended on him.

Finally, they reached the tholos. The stones that blocked the entrance to the tomb were cleared out so that the path to the interior of the grave, the thalamos, was open. Echelaos stepped onto the dromos, the earthen entryway leading into the tomb. The warriors placed the coffin with the body of Nestor on the floor inside the burial chamber and left, clearing the path for the priests and most notable citizens to lay down their gifts for the deceased wanax to accompany him to the afterlife. Jars with perfumed oil, jewelry, weapons, and seals made of gold, silver, and ivory, and adorned with precious stones were placed next to the larnax. Echelaos laid the bow with which he'd conquered Troy next to Nestor's coffin and stood there in silence for a few moments. An invisible force suddenly squeezed his stomach, his hands started to shake, and his eyes became wet. Echelaos tried his best not to show his weakness and emotions; he had to become the bulwark of hope for Pylos, replacing his father. Finally, turning around, he left the thalamos, providing room for Eritha to place the golden pendant with the depiction of Athena as a snake goddess. Following Eritha, Aphrodite laid a terracotta figurine of a goddess next to the pendant; these two items together would protect Nestor in the afterlife.

When the burial ceremony was finished, the warriors blocked the entrance to the chamber with large stones. Eritha walked through the crowd and gave everyone a cup for the solemn libation in honor of the dead wanax.

"Glory to Pylos! Glory to Nestor! Let his name survive for ages!" Echelaos proclaimed a toast.

People drank and threw their chalices, shattering the cups against the wall of the royal tomb. After that, the people started walking back toward the city, and dromos was backfilled with earth. The old wanax was dead, and the new one was about to take his place. Life had to continue, even amid mourning.

Echelaos stood in place, motionless, looking at the tomb of his father highlighted by the rays of the setting sun behind it. He was looking for Nestor, expecting him to appear from the opposite side of the tholos. But nothing happened. When Echelaos was sure nobody could see or hear him, he fell to his knees, hid his face in the dirt, and started crying. Utter powerlessness and hopelessness seized his heart; he realized how trivial his pursuits of power and glory were. He longed for his father; once again, he was a little boy who needed protection and love. Then a new thought pierced his mind: it was *his* duty now to provide safety and love; *he* was the father, and the roles had changed. Aphrodite was his daughter he swore to the goddess to protect. This was his most important task, not some ephemeral pursuit of military fame and glory.

Echelaos stood up and went back toward the palace. He knew what he had to do; he was determined to become the ruler and protector the people needed. Entering the gates, he followed a hallway surrounded by pillared colonnades on both sides, looking for Aphrodite's chamber.

When he approached the palace wing where Aphrodite's room was, someone stepped in front of his path. Even in the dimly lit interior of the building, Echelaos recognized Eritha, whose body and the smell were impossible to confuse with anyone else's. But Echelaos had no time for the pleasures of the flesh; he needed to embrace his daughter, explain to her that he loved her, that he'd always protect her and be with her.

"Echelaos, is this you?" Eritha said, sobbing.

"Yes, Eritha. We must move on, however painful it is to lose Nestor," Echelaos said.

"This isn't about Nestor." Eritha's voice trembled.

"What's happened?"

"Something horrible… I'm still in shock…"

"What is it? Are we under attack?"

"The god…Apollo showed up inside the palace." Eritha suddenly dropped to her knees. "I'm sorry, Echelaos, he took Aphrodite and disappeared."

PART TWO

"THEOMACHIA"

CHAPTER

ELEVEN

Prince Assur-Dan walked through the camp of the Assyrian army, observing the soldiers' activities and judging their morale and preparedness for the campaign. Night descended upon the rocky landscape of Isuwa, the country the Assyrians had conquered after the quick and decisive assault on Carchemish. The prince was summoned to the royal tent to discuss plans for the further invasion of the land of Hatti and decided to spend time mingling with the warriors to better understand the conditions.

To avoid attracting unnecessary attention, Assur-Dan wore the typical dress of the Assyrian foot soldier. A short tunic, not quite reaching his knees, was held at the waist by a broad belt. His neck, arms, and legs were bare, except for simple sandals. On his left side, Assur-Dan wore a small sword inside the ornamented sheath. Nobody would recognize a limmu official and a royal successor in this ordinary warrior.

Assur-Dan proceeded through the bulk of the soldiers, which bivouacked in the open field, the tents being reserved for commanders and high officials. The prince passed the large campfire and noticed the soldiers preparing a feast. One group was killing a sheep while another was roasting the previous victim's joints over the wood fire.

"May I sit with you?" Assur-Dan sat on the ground next to the fire. "Good dinner, aye?"

"More than we can eat." Soldiers laughed, grabbing meat from the fire. "Come, get a piece. Enough for everyone."

Assur-Dan thanked the soldier and took a piece of sheep's leg. The smell of cooked lamb was irresistible, and the fresh meat tasted delicious. His stomach growled; this was the best food he could get, better than any exotic fruit or game from the royal kitchen.

"I've heard we're marching to Hattusa," Assur-Dan said.

"I'd follow the king anywhere," one of the soldiers said. "I've got lots of riches and slaves from Carchemish, and I'd be a fool to refuse more."

"And the women! The women of Carchemish were very hospitable, aye?" another soldier said. This comment was met with a burst of thunderous laughter.

"But they say the Hittites are strong, and we haven't fought their main armies yet," Assur-Dan objected.

"Ah, let them come. The gods are protecting us and even fight on our side, I've heard," the soldier said. "With their help, we can't be defeated. So we'll march with the king to the ends of the Earth if need be."

The people around the campfire nodded, muttering sounds of approval. Assur-Dan stood up, thanked his hosts for sharing dinner with him, and proceeded toward the royal tent.

The residence of the Assyrian king was, naturally, the largest dwelling in the camp. The felt tent had a square door on the side and was open to the sky in the center. Inside the royal headquarters were all sorts of wooden tables, couches, and footstools. The smells of aromatic oils, dates, and roasted antelope filled the room, making Assur-Dan hungry again. The tent was full of people: the royal charioteer, the bow-bearer, and the mace-bearer, among others. The parasol-bearer stood next to the Great King, holding the emblem of sovereignty, a winged circle, over the monarch's head. Ninurta, dressed in the royal robe, his black curly beard oiled and perfumed, mitre on his head, sat on the wooden throne with a smile.

"Prince Assur-Dan," one of the guards announced.

King Ninurta raised his right hand, which held his usual lion-headed mace.

"Let us begin," Ninurta said. "Grand Vizier, what is the situation in the subjugated land? Has Carchemish been pacified?"

"Yes, o Great King. There are no signs of dissent. Your new subjects are content with your rule, adding more glory to Assur daily." Salmanu bowed in front of the king's throne, his bushy black beard wiping the floor.

"Good, this means we can march forward," the king said. "Assur-Dan, how is the army? Do we have enough weapons and provisions?"

"Yes, o Great King." Assur-Dan stepped forward. "Morale is high; soldiers are well-fed, weapons are sharp. We can proceed."

"Excellent!" the king exclaimed. "I'll fight the Hittites until we conquer all their lands, and the gods are satisfied with the sacrifices."

"If I may, o Great King," Assur-Dan said, looking at his father.

"Yes, you may speak."

"I find the amount of destruction and sacrifices excessive. Soon there will be no subjects to rule."

"We must obey the gods, my son. Nergal demands fresh daily sacrifices, and we cannot contradict his divine will."

"Are you going to exterminate all your people then?"

"If need be, yes. People are nothing — worms in the dirt. Human nature is to kill each other; violence is their most common tool, and hatred is their innate state. They will exterminate each other anyway, my son."

"Then this is not the rule, but slaughter," Assur-Dan protested.

"No, it's the execution of the divine will. I'm but the instrument of the gods who proclaim the destruction and eradication and demand human sacrifices. Who am I to question their will?"

"So, it will continue?"

"For as long as the gods require it, yes. You must learn to obey their commands, my son; you will follow my steps to finish the work. I don't want to hear these arguments from you ever again."

"I'll obey your order, o Great King." Assur-Dan bowed reluctantly. "I'll be a devoted servant of the gods, like you are."

"Yes, you will. Otherwise, I'll ask Nergal to accept the royal prince as a sacrifice."

#

Aphrodite didn't understand why the god had abducted her. She'd returned to her wing at the palace of Pylos after Nestor's funeral when the mighty Apollo confronted her in the courtyard. She couldn't do much but cry for help as the god encased her inside a cocoon glowing with blue light. Eritha had raised her hands in supplication to Apollo, but it was in vain. The cocoon had risen into the air, the walls had become opaque, and Aphrodite was transported to a place she didn't know.

As she'd found out later, Apollo had taken her to a sanctuary near the Hittite capital. The god presented himself as a Sun-Goddess of Arinna to the priests and priestesses of the cult. He didn't take the form of a giant, muscular superhuman figure; instead, he showed himself to his devotees as an enormous yellow sun disk speaking with a deep female voice.

It had been three days since Apollo brought her here, and she still didn't understand his intentions. She wasn't afraid of the god; she thought of Apollo as a powerful entity but also as someone with weaknesses to be studied and exploited. Echelaos was constantly on her mind; Aphrodite knew he'd chase the god in pursuit of her, whatever the consequences. Her human father cared about her deeply, and he wouldn't allow her to be hurt.

Aphrodite sat on a small, simple wooden footstool in her room, squeezing a lump of clay in her hand, making different shapes and figures: there was nothing else for her to do in the sanctuary. Suddenly, her inner monologue was interrupted by a voice seemingly out of nowhere.

"Welcome to my temple," a deep female voice announced. "My child, my creation, I'll take care of you."

"I don't know who you are, but you are not my parent. My father is Echelaos, and my mother is Athena," Aphrodite responded.

"You're wrong. It was *me* who created you and gave you life. You belong to *me*; you are the first step toward a new human being: immortal, indestructible, wise. I'll improve your algorithms, firmware, and cellular composition to raise you to the level of the gods."

"Thank you, o great god, but Echelaos and Machaon are already teaching me the ways of the Achaeans. And they promised to protect me."

"You don't know what you're talking about. You don't know who you are. Only *I* can provide what you truly need. I, great Technologist, known under many names: Apollo, Apaliunas, the Sun-Goddess of Arinna."

"What about Zeus and Athena?" Aphrodite asked. "Are you not afraid of them?"

"Afraid? I can't be afraid of anything; I'm a god. Let them try to stop me. This is my abode; they wouldn't dare."

Their conversation was interrupted by noise outside. Screams and cries disturbed the peaceful day in the sanctuary. Aphrodite looked out of her small window cut in the mud-brick wall. People ran around in confusion, seeking shelter, calling out for their goddess to protect them. A priest in a gray tunic fell to the ground right in front of her window, gasping and gurgling, an arrow protruding from his throat.

"Will you help?" Aphrodite asked, but the god didn't respond.

Enemy soldiers entered the sanctuary, shooting arrows, impaling the priests with their spears, and chasing priestesses. There was chaos and pandemonium.

"Assyrians!" someone screamed. "Please save us, o great goddess!"

As if hearing the pleas of the people, the huge orange disk of the Sun-Goddess appeared in the sky above the fight. A moment later, the disk started to rotate, shooting blue rays of death at the Assyrian soldiers, burning them alive.

"This is my temple! You will all die for desecrating the sanctuary of the Sun-Goddess!" a voice thundered from the sky.

The Assyrians started running away, dropping their weapons. But the scorching rays were everywhere, finding even the soldiers who had managed to withdraw a considerable distance. In the end, not a single attacker came out of this assault alive.

Aphrodite stepped out of her little hut, impressed by the god's might. She carefully registered everything with her sharp mind, trying to identify the god's weaknesses; she knew she must help Echelaos fight Apollo if she wanted her freedom back.

"More Assyrians!" one of the priests yelled, pointing east. The horizon was covered with a multitude of enemy soldiers, filling the whole plain and outlining the horizon with a solid black line.

This must be the main army, Aphrodite thought. What would Apollo do? Could he handle thousands of the Assyrians? It might be a chance for her to run away. She decided to hide and see what would happen.

Sitting behind a stone granary building, Aphrodite witnessed the second part of the fight between Apollo and the Assyrian host. The orange disk in the sky moved closer to the enemy, ready to engage.

The disk started to rotate again, this time shooting fireballs at the approaching horde in loud and frightening blasts. The front-line units stopped in hesitation, then pulled back, while the soldiers behind them kept pushing forward, creating a terrible stampede. Aphrodite was not sure who to cheer for; she needed a moment to escape amid the heat of the battle.

Suddenly, the orange disk tilted to the side and stopped rotating. The fireballs flew in random directions, all over the place, one of them landing very close to the sanctuary. Then the blasts stopped completely. Instead, a blue barrier appeared around the disk, similar to the cocoon in which Apollo had brought Aphrodite to the sanctuary. A moment later, two gray circles emerged on the surface of the barrier, and then the cocoon disappeared altogether. Finally, the orange disk dimmed, became fuzzy, and started descending onto the plain in front of the enemy army.

Aphrodite decided this was her moment, stood up, left her hideout, and ran from the fight, following the example of the few other temple inhabitants. She ran as fast as she could, not looking back, losing her breath. Suddenly, a roar thundered behind her. She quickly glanced over her shoulder: the orange disk was gone, and the Assyrian army was cheering in the distance. Exerting herself to hear what they were shouting, Aphrodite heard the Assyrians' calls.

"Glory to Assur! Glory to Nergal! Glory to Ishtar! Death to the Hittites and their gods!"

#

Commander was alone in the Soarers' base, his silver, disk-shaped body floating in the middle of the Control Unit. The Expedition members were all gone, pursuing their individual goals, the unity of the crew destroyed by the mysterious influence the planet and its inhabitants had on the technologically advanced Soarers. No consensus was possible anymore; the last task Commander could accomplish was to gather all the acquired information and send it back to Homeworld. He was preparing to disassemble and evacuate the base, engaging with the ship on the planet's orbit and setting the magnetic Space Elevator in motion. The course of the return journey was created and uploaded into the ship's AI, which would steer the vessel during a long trip, covering the distance of eleven light-years.

Commander had finally decided on the fate of the Expedition, although he had to make the decision alone. Scholar was the only one who had responded to his request for the mind connection. Still, even Scholar had reservations about leaving the planet, claiming her task was now to protect humans from whatever the rest of the crew was planning.

Suddenly, Commander received an incoming communication from Technologist, who was sending signals indicating extreme danger and requests for help. Commander started getting the information Technologist was broadcasting, and soon other Soarers joined the channel, including Pilot and Defender. The situation was extraordinary, as Commander understood from Technologist's data. He was fighting with entities he didn't comprehend and had no idea how to defend himself. The EM shield didn't work, and Technologist had to put it down, saving the energy for the electrical discharge weapon. His adversaries seemed utterly immune to EM fields and energy bursts of any kind Technologist had in his arsenal. It was all over very quickly: following the last desperate plea for help, with an expectation of imminent annihilation, the channel closed, and the information flow ceased. Commander tried to reestablish the connection, pinging Technologist on multiple frequencies, but it was all in vain. Technologist was gone.

"What was that?" Defender asked.

"We all ask the same question," Commander said.

"Did this force annihilate Technologist? How is this possible?" Scholar asked.

"His last message and the fact that he is not responsive can mean only one thing. Technologist is no more," Commander said.

"I still don't understand," Defender said. "Humans are primitive; they simply don't have weapons to rival ours."

"This is a new threat, something we've missed," Pilot said.

"And we must address it," Commander said. "We need to find out what's happened, the nature of this new threat, and how to deal with it."

"He was on the eastern side," Defender said. "My armies are ready; I'll bring them into that area and eliminate the threat."

"This force appears to be unaffected by our technology. How do you plan to eliminate it?" Scholar asked.

"I've progressed far in adopting mineral resources of this planet to enhance my military systems. My army of AI drones reinforced by local materials is indestructible. I'll deal with the threat," Defender said.

"I'll analyze the information Technologist broadcasted and try to identify what it was. Then we'll decide what to do," Commander said.

"My fleet is not ready to sail yet," Pilot said. "I'll deal with this new force after conquering all the western countries. But my army will have an overwhelming superiority and unwavering spirit, so I have no concerns about my eventual success in uniting all the humans under my leadership."

"And I need to take care of a different problem," Scholar said. "The people of the southern continent have summoned me. There is yet another force threatening that country. A god has awakened, they say. So I need to protect them."

"You have all completely lost the ability to think logically," Commander said. "We are facing a power we don't understand, a power capable of destroying one of us in a matter of moments, a power immune to our weapons — and you are still talking about your plans regarding humans? What's happening with you?"

"As I said, my armies are ready, and I'll deal with the threat," Defender said. "Leave this job to me."

"Commander, I'll keep the communication channel open and join you as soon as I deal with the danger on the southern continent. This could also be serious; I need to learn more," Scholar said.

One by one, Expedition members disconnected from the channel. Commander was again left alone with his thoughts. The situation had become not only dangerous, but deadly. And not because of the potential of humans to destroy the civilization of the Soarers in the distant future, but due to some unknown force challenging their science and technology, now. Commander had to send this information back to Homeworld, although a response would take years. He conjectured this new power wasn't native to Earth; it must've been a different race from some distant star, wielding tools and possessing knowledge he couldn't comprehend.

Commander's disk floated toward the exit from the Control Unit. He was preparing himself for the fight to annihilation. This conflict would define his mission and contribution to the Soarers' civilization. Commander faced a struggle that could end in the destruction of his race.

CHAPTER
TWELVE

Aphrodite ran as fast as she could for as long as she could. She didn't know where she was running; she just wanted to get away from the fight. Aphrodite wasn't afraid of the god who had abducted her or of the Assyrians. She knew she could stand up for herself, but it wasn't her fight. She needed to get back to Echelaos and Eritha, where she belonged.

Aphrodite ran until night descended on the shrubby plain. She found an isolated oak grove interspersed with maple and chestnut trees. The air was full of fruit and berry aromas; it was early autumn. She breathed in the fresh, cool evening breeze and decided to stay in the grove for the night, resting under a sprawling oak.

Her hearing, sight, and a sense of smell somehow were intensified. Aphrodite could see perfectly at night; she didn't need a fire. She could sense the wild animals around her and knew there was no danger. Nevertheless, she found a long tree branch and created a wooden pole to defend herself, just in case.

Suddenly, a noise in the bushes attracted her attention. Chukar. Aphrodite sensed it without even looking at the bird. Picking up a heavy, round stone she'd found under the tree, Aphrodite crawled closer to the bushes, and, identifying the position of the bird, threw the stone. The partridge tried to run and fly away, flapping. Unfortunately for the bird, the stone had damaged one of its wings, and Aphrodite had no problem catching it with her bare hands. She'd got herself dinner; she did need fire after all.

Later, sitting by the fire she'd made by tapping the stones against each other over dry twigs, Aphrodite looked at the stars. She couldn't understand why, but they were very familiar and friendly, like a long-forgotten home. What was her home? She knew she was created by the gods and sent by Athena to Echelaos. She had no recollection of the abode of the gods; Pylos was her home. But perhaps she had once lived with the gods among the stars?

She heard the hoot of the owl. Could this be Athena looking for her? No, she didn't sense the presence of the goddess. She needed to find her way home to Echelaos; she'd be strong and help her father defeat the enemies of Pylos. Aphrodite felt strength, confidence, and determination. Yes, this was her destiny, chosen for her by Athena.

With these thoughts, Aphrodite fell asleep by the fire, part of her mind staying alert to her surroundings. As the red disk of the sun broke the horizon, she woke up, alarmed by the sense of a human presence. She slowly opened her eyes and scanned the surroundings, engaging her hearing and sense of smell. There were several people approaching from multiple directions. The smell of bad breath and feces was overwhelming. The newcomers tried to move quietly, but Aphrodite heard every step, every movement of tree branch, every gasp. She thought about running away, but her assailants were everywhere. Thinking over her options, she searched for the stone she'd used to kill the chukar. Extending the other hand, she placed her fingers on the wooden pole she'd prepared last night.

Once the enemies were closer, Aphrodite suddenly jumped to her feet with one quick and smooth movement, threw a stone at one of the crouching figures, and pierced the belly of another with her self-made pike. Without looking, she knew the stone had hit the throat of the hairy figure wrapped in animal skin. The second attacker fell, holding a bloody pole sticking out of his gut with both hands.

Aphrodite jumped to the side to avoid two more Kaska rushing at her from the thickets. Echelaos had told her about these ferocious cavemen, but she'd never seen one herself. Now she had to fight eight of them, alone. Good news: she had already killed one and injured another. Bad news: two of them were chasing her and four more were coming quickly to help them.

Running away from the Kaska and assessing the situation, Aphrodite grabbed the trunk of a tree and made a quick turnaround, fooling her pursuers, who kept running forward. As both stopped awkwardly and tried to reorient themselves, Aphrodite got on the back of one of them and stuck her fingers into his eyes. The jelly-like substance of the eyeballs mixed with blood streamed down his face as the Kaska roared in pain. Aphrodite jumped to the ground and pushed the body of the now-blinded brute onto the other one, who was now facing her. As both fell to the ground, Aphrodite moved behind them, grabbed the head of the second attacker with both hands, and twisted it to the side, registering the sound of cracking vertebrae. Five left.

Aphrodite sensed her enemies and somersaulted just in time to avoid being hit by an enormous cudgel. The Kaska lost his balance for a moment, and this was enough for Aphrodite to get behind his back and use her legs to break his right knee. The brute fell on his face, convulsing in pain.

Aphrodite rolled to her side, and that was where her luck ended. Another Kaska grabbed her ankle and held on to it tight, not letting her escape, trying to twist and break her foot. Aphrodite wiggled, attempting to break free, and almost succeeded, when another brute suddenly appeared in front of her, seizing her hands, pinning her down. The Kaska's face hung over hers, blocking the light, his saliva dropping onto Aphrodite's eyes, his rotten breath poisoning her lungs. He was strong; Aphrodite was unable to free her hands from his grip. She prepared to bite off part of his face once it drew closer, when, suddenly, the caveman collapsed on top of her, blood running from his mouth onto her face. Next, her foot was freed, and she was able to roll to the side, pushing away the body of the dead Kaska.

Quickly getting to her feet, Aphrodite didn't sense the bestial cavemen around her anymore. The Kaska whose blood now covered her face lay on the ground, motionless, an arrow in his neck. Instead of Kaska, there appeared two female figures, one of which was holding a bow.

"We're friendly. Don't run," the woman with the bow said, raising her arm. "The Kaska won't trouble you anymore."

"Who are you?" Aphrodite asked.

"You've got impressive skills," the woman said, ignoring her question. "Wanna join us?"

"It depends," Aphrodite said, tilting her head. "Thank you for your help."

"Don't mention it." The woman grinned. "So, do you want to join us? It's dangerous to travel alone."

"Thank you for the offer," Aphrodite said. "Who are you, and where're you heading?"

"We're looking for the Hittite army," the other girl said. "And hoping to arrive before they engage the Assyrians."

"I just ran away from the Assyrians," Aphrodite said. She reasoned these two were not dangerous, and it might be advantageous to join them. *The enemy of my enemy is my friend*, as Echelaos would say. But then the Hittites were the allies of Troy and enemies of Pylos. She needed to be careful.

"I'll travel with you. At least for a while." Aphrodite smiled. "My name's Aphrodite. I'm the daughter of the Ahhiyawa trader; our ship arrived at Ugarit when the Assyrians attacked. I was captured and brought here with the army but was able to run away during the fight at the Hittite sanctuary. Who are you?"

"I'm Ehli-Nikkal of Hatti," the woman with the bow said. "And this is my maid, Korinsia. Like you, she is from Ahhiyawa." Ehli pointed at the girl. "We're on our way to help my father, King Suppululiuma, defeat the Assyrians menacing our land."

#

"Where do you suggest we look for her?" Tros asked.

"You just walk around and peek inside the huts while I find someone to talk to," Echelaos said.

Echelaos was not sure how to proceed with the search. The sanctuary Athena brought them to looked like it had seen a recent fight. Dead bodies of the priests and Assyrian soldiers lay scattered in between buildings. The former were killed by human weapons, while the bodies of the attackers were burned and torn apart. Echelaos had seen the same carnage at the gates of Troy — this was the work of Apollo. The smell of seared and rotten flesh was everywhere, and vultures were circling over the dead, anticipating a feast.

"*If* you find someone to talk to." Tros grinned. "I'll walk around and stick my nose inside, but my gut is telling me Aphrodite isn't here. If I see a pretty priestess inside, would you mind if I have some fun?"

"Sure, just be careful; the god might show up and deprive you of your manhood." Echelaos laughed.

"Don't you worry; I'll be just fine. The priestess will plead to the god for me." Tros smirked.

"Now, to be serious, we must find Aphrodite. Be nosy," Echelaos said.

"Did Athena tell you where to look?"

"You know everything I know. This is where Apollo took Aphrodite. Athena told me to search here and advised the god won't interfere. That's all."

"It's a hopeless task, o wanax. Let your wisdom be proclaimed through the ages."

"I'm aware it's more difficult than humping a pretty priestess. So, don't make fun of me."

"As you wish, o wanax." Tros bowed, smiling, and disappeared into a neighboring hut.

Echelaos walked through the buildings, finding more dead bodies, but no trace of Aphrodite or anyone alive. As he was about to lose all hope, he came by the well on the outskirts of the sanctuary. An old priest sat there, leaning on the wall of the well. His face was covered with a mask of dried blood, his hands holding a bowl of water. His eyes were open, his breath barely noticeable. A grisly, open wound on his side, most likely caused by the slash of a sword, did not give him much chance of survival.

Echelaos came closer, took a bowl from the hands of the dying priest, and brought it to his lips.

"Who did this to you?" Echelaos asked in Akkadian, the language of traders and diplomats, which he reasoned the priest should know.

The old man looked at him with unfocused eyes, lips moving a little, but without a sound. Finally, he found the strength to speak. "Who…are…you?"

"It doesn't matter. A friend. I'm looking for an Ahhiyawa girl that the god brought here. Do you know what happened to her?"

"Assyrians attacked…killed people… Then Apaliunas killed the Assyrians… And then something devoured Apaliunas." The old man gathered what was remaining of his strength.

"Have you seen the Ahhiyawa girl?"

"She…ran away…north, with other people. Then Assyrians followed the same way."

"Thank you, old man." Echelaos gave the priest another drink from the bowl. "How can I help you? Your wound is bad; I can try to treat it."

"I am…dying," the priest said. "Nothing you can do, kind man." Suddenly, he reached out to the bowl and drank all the water that was left. His face relaxed in an expression of joy and relaxation. "Thank you."

Suddenly, the old man made a gasping sound and vomited a greenish fluid mixed with blood. Convulsions seized his body, his eyes rolled up, and then his muscles relaxed completely. He was dead. Echelaos closed the eyes of the dead man and looked around. Tros was approaching him from the other side of the village.

"Found something?" Tros asked. "I wasn't lucky. No Aphrodite, no pretty priestesses, not even anyone alive."

"Yes," Echelaos said and told his charioteer about the encounter with the old priest. "So, we go north," he concluded.

"North is not a very precise direction, o wanax," Tros said.

"We follow the tracks of the Assyrian army. Most likely, Aphrodite was captured by them," Echelaos said. "It won't be difficult. Besides, I have a plan."

"Does your plan include searching for a solitary girl among the endless plains of the land of Hatti?"

"Not exactly. We find the Assyrian army and seek the king. I'm wanax of Pylos, after all, and can talk to King Ninurta as an equal."

"And what do you want to tell him?"

"The Assyrians are at war with the Hittites, but so are we. I want to offer King Ninurta a military alliance."

CHAPTER
THIRTEEN

"Think faster. If you waste another minute, I swear I'll cut your dick off and leave you here for the vultures to feast on," General Hewernef said, looking menacingly at Khay. The Eye of Ra glowed red in rays of the setting sun, bulging out from the general's empty socket. Hewernef had lost his patience long ago and threatened Khay multiple times. Khay didn't care; he knew the general needed him to find the tomb, and he was doing everything he could to remember the path. The damned ruins of Akhetaten seemed completely different during daylight.

"Getting closer," Khay said, touching his earlobe. "Don't distract me; I need to count the steps."

The general clenched his fist and growled. His guttural rumble was so loud, it could be heard even through the mask of Wadjet that covered his face. Khay didn't know what else to call this strange headdress that the goddess had made to protect them from Aten. Very light, transparent, and thin as papyrus, but stronger than any material Khay knew, the mask covered the head of every soldier in their group. Khay took a deep breath. Even though this strange contraption covered his mouth and nostrils, it didn't impede his breathing. On the contrary, the air was refreshing, cool, and smelled of wildflowers, not the usual fishy stink of the Nile.

Khay was at the front of the group, followed closely by the

general. A dozen soldiers were behind and on both sides of him. The thought of running away and hiding had crossed his mind when they disembarked, but he'd dismissed it as cowardice. This attempt would likely have been successful, even with a dozen soldiers watching his every move. Still, he'd given his word to the goddess and the pharaoh. Khay also needed to fix his grave error; the task of finding the tomb and bringing a piece of Aten back to the goddess was his and only his. So even if he perished in agony, he had to attempt to retrieve the wretched mushroom.

Finally, he found the dune. The entrance to the tomb was still visible in between the stone blocks, partially covered by sand, just as Khay and his fellow thieves had left it.

"At last," the general hissed. "You can keep your dick for a little longer, crook."

"Now what?" Khay asked.

"Now you go down there," the general said, "and face your doom. If you don't come back before the sun is halfway beyond the horizon, I'll send soldiers to retrieve what Wadjet requested."

"Yes, General."

"Remember what the Great Pharaoh Usermaatre Meryamen told you. Every moment of delay converts more of his subjects to become slaves of Aten, causing unimaginable suffering. Hurry up."

Khay knew the stakes were high. Even though Wadjet had given her magic masks to the people, promising protection from Aten, she couldn't cure the infected ones without a piece of Aten's body. So he had to come back and retrieve it for the goddess.

One of the soldiers lit a torch and passed it to the former thief. Khay's hands suddenly started to shake, it became difficult to breathe, and his stomach felt like it was rotating. He couldn't allow himself to panic. He closed his eyes and tried to touch the crown of his head but only felt the smooth mask material with his fingers. Shaking his head as if to get rid of the buzzing sensations in his ears, he stepped forward and started his descent into the abode of Aten, a dreadful entity that took on the form of a mushroom to enslave the people of the Two Kingdoms.

At first glance, nothing had changed in the tomb. Khay entered a large room through a pillared gateway and stepped into the alcove to the right. When he approached the burial chamber, however, the sight of the room made him shiver with fright and disbelief. He forgot how to breathe for a moment and had to fight a strong desire to turn around and run away. Instead, he told himself not to be a coward, that the anger of Wadjet might be worse than the encounter with Aten. Finally, he calmed himself and took a closer look at the chamber.

What had been the final resting place of Akhenaten had become a mushroom forest. Khay had never seen anything like this: mushrooms covered the walls, the sarcophagi, and even the lid on the floor that Djehuty and Intef had broken. He had a strange feeling that the mushroom was alive, that it was about to talk to him in its bizarre, alien way, to enter his brain and enslave his body. A cloud of tiny droplets formed in the air, barely visible in the dim light of the torch. It suddenly became cold, and beads of sweat ran down Khay's spine.

Moving carefully, not trusting his unsteady legs, trying not to fall, Khay stepped into the chamber and placed the torch on the floor. Then, with shaking fingers, he reached into a sheath on his belt and took out a knife and a silver container Wadjet had provided. Facing the mushroom covering the wall of the chamber, Khay reached out with a knife to take a cut, expecting Aten to attack and devour him in some horrible way.

As the knife was about to contact a mushroom stem, a soft green light suddenly lit up the room. Khay almost dropped the knife, stepping back in horror, turning around in trepidation, ready to face the wrath of Aten. But instead in the middle of the room was a giant cobra, glowing green: Wadjet.

Khay fell to his knees, not knowing what to expect, confused.

"I'm following your orders, o Wadjet," Khay mumbled, his tongue treacherously disobeying him.

"I thank you for that, human," the goddess said. "You showed me the place, and now I can protect you. Don't hesitate. Do what you came to do. I, Wadjet, will clean your land and cure the people."

Khay couldn't believe this sudden turnaround. He wasn't alone against the vile Aten; wise and mighty Wadjet was looking after him. The cloud of droplets around became denser, surrounding him, gliding slowly within the green light.

"These are the spores," Wadjet said as if reading his thoughts. "Aten will enslave you if they enter your body. But with my mask, you're safe."

Once again, Khay raised his knife. This time he didn't hesitate: he cut the stem, detached the mushroom, and placed it inside the silver container. Suddenly, something hit his hand, and the container disappeared.

"I shall take it," Wadjet said. "Now, leave. I'll deal with the mycelium and seal the tomb."

"What about the general? He expects me to bring the vial with the piece of Aten's body back."

"He knows that you were successful and that I took the vial. Once I create the antidote, you'll have a lot of work to do."

"Work?"

"Yes. I'll provide the general with enough masks for the army. You must catch every infected human and administer the antidote, following my instructions. Any mistake might cost the pharaoh his kingdom and his Ka."

#

Scholar floated into the Control Unit; Commander was already there.

"Why did you decide to come back?" Commander messaged.

"I have to use the equipment on the base to synthesize the antidote."

"Antidote?"

"Yes. I've encountered a shadow biosphere on this planet."

"What do you mean?" Commander made a circle around the room. "We haven't observed anything before."

"Now we have," Scholar messaged. "You know how the double-helix acid molecule is the basis of all the organic life here? It carries encoded genetic information that allows the species to continue their genome from generation to generation. Or so we thought."

"And?"

"I've discovered the organism that precedes the life forms based on this double-helix acid molecule. There is another — much shorter — acid molecule that similarly encodes genetic information, creating mini-proteins. I conjecture that this biochemical process has evolved over millions of years into its more advanced version, enabled by a double-helix molecule."

"What does it mean?" Commander's body turned gray.

"The life-forms based on the shorter molecule are not extinct. On the contrary, they have continued to evolve in parallel as a shadow biosphere. Now they exist as peculiar species, a type of mushroom."

"Interesting. And you encountered these organisms? Did you bring a specimen?"

"Yes, I have," Scholar messaged. "An entity on the southern continent has been evolving for eons. Now, it exists as an enormous underground colony of organisms that form an intelligent being, a neural network, and communicate with each other using electrical signals."

"Why haven't we registered these signals before?"

"They are deep underground. Furthermore, the entity spreads and grows using airborne spores. It's a parasite. The organism takes control when these spores penetrate the animal's brain. The impacted humans worship it as a god."

"Like they worship us…" Commander made another circle. "What are you planning to do?"

"The people of the southern continent need my protection; I promised them assistance. I've already isolated the entity using a magnetic force shield. It is now completely restricted to the subsurface. We need to take care of the infected humans, which is why I need the antidote."

"We?"

"The humans who asked for my help; I need to teach them how to deal with the entity. There was a similar outbreak in the past. They used a chemical compound to restrain the organism; I still don't completely understand how. This is very interesting, and I need to learn more."

"It is interesting indeed," Commander messaged. "You are becoming attached to humans. It's not rational. It's the same development that impacted the others. Be careful; we've already lost Technologist because of this malady. Did you do more research into human emotions?"

"No, Commander. I was busy with this ancient entity," Scholar messaged. "Have you heard from Defender and Pilot?"

"Yes. They've lost all remaining logical thinking. They have assembled armies of humans and are preparing to use force to advance their plans. Defender has also built a contingent of drones and robots he wants to use to eradicate humans."

"This is the worst-case scenario. We must stop them."

"I refuse to use force against our kind. We have bigger problems."

"Other than dealing with an ancient entity and two Soarers using humans to fight each other?"

"Yes." Commander's gray body started to rotate faster. "I've deciphered the data Technologist broadcast before his annihilation. He was destroyed by two alien beings, the nature of which I can't understand. They are not composed of the same matter that Soarers, humans, planets, and stars are made of. But they are not composed of force fields either."

"What could it be, then?" Scholar's body turned purple.

"I'm still trying to figure that out. These alien entities feed on information of any kind: quantum states, memories of intelligent beings, genetic information encoded in that double-helix molecule you mentioned. After they interact with matter, all that is left is a random collection of molecular strains and elementary particles."

"We've never encountered this before."

"No, we haven't. The humans worship these entities as gods."

"More gods…"

"We must fight *them*, Scholar. Not our kind, and not humans. *This* is our mortal enemy, not Pilot and Defender."

"How can we fight them if we don't know what they are?" Scholar messaged.

"We need to figure it out. I'm on my way east to reconnoiter."

"Do you have any ideas?"

"No. They are not made out of normal matter, or force fields, or even antimatter." Commander's body tilted.

"Unless…"

"Unless what?"

"They are made of material we are studying but don't yet

understand. Material that gives galaxies their missing mass. Material that is required to explain the gravity of supermassive objects," Scholar messaged.

"Wait… I know the theory suggesting that this material also stores information; that information itself has mass. We also know that information is invariant; it is conserved in all the universal processes," Commander messaged.

"So, if these entities are made of this material — the information itself — this explains their behavior. All organized beings seek growth, and growth for these entities would be to capture more information, different information," Scholar messaged.

"This also explains why they seek to devour diverse groups of humans. Their disparate genetic information provides additional food for growth."

"How can we prove it, and what can we do?" Scholar messaged.

"We must face them. But we need a plan."

"What if they learn about the Soarers? About our planet? What if they come to our world?" Scholar's body rotated very fast.

"I've already sent a communication back; the Soarers have been warned. But it might be too late."

"What do you mean?"

"The entities annihilated Technologist and captured all the information he had — they know everything about our world. If we can't figure out how to stop them, the Soarers are doomed."

CHAPTER
FOURTEEN

First, there was light — red light in his right eye.

Zoltes tried to move his fingers but couldn't feel them. His left eye wouldn't open, either. Red fog engulfed him; he was swimming through a sea of blood, occasionally registering flashes of light in the distance. He remembered the battle at the walls of Troy and the fireballs ripping his people apart. The last thing he recalled was his attempt to save Akhilleus, and then…darkness.

After that came the awareness of breathing. It was as if his body was breathing by itself while he was a distant observer. Immediately, Zoltes felt his tongue in his mouth, which was dry as if filled with sand. There were no sounds, just a vast red ocean in front of him, calm, everlasting, timeless.

Suddenly, Zoltes realized he could move his toes. Gathering his strength, he opened his left eye, his right eye adjusting simultaneously. A gentle blue light replaced the red ocean surrounding his body. He was floating inside a cocoon, some magic force holding him in the air.

Zoltes raised his hands and noticed the differences between his limbs. While his left hand was normal as far as he could see, his right hand was colored silver. A range of unknown, strange sensations passed through the right side of his body, from his toes to his eye.

Confused, Zoltes tried to touch his right eye, but some invisible force prevented the movement.

You need to adjust to your new body, a deep, resonant voice said inside his head.

Zoltes tried to move his tongue to respond, without much success.

Easy. You're not ready yet. Think, and I will hear your thoughts, the voice said.

Who are you? Where am I? Am I dead? What happened? What's wrong with my hand? Thoughts popped into his brain, racing like wild Thracian horses.

I am Zerunthios, your god. You're back in Leibethra. You're not dead; on the contrary, I have dramatically improved your body.

Improved how?

Your body was damaged, burned, broken. I fixed it, replaced defective parts with materials superior to human flesh.

Why help me?

Because you are the general who will lead my armies.

Me?

People follow you and listen to you, and I need a servant I can trust to organize my human armies. So I have upgraded your sensory inputs and processing power. The voice of your god will always be in your head from now on. Your eyes are my eyes, your ears — my ears. You are my extension.

What do you demand of me, o great Zerunthios? Zoltes still had lots of thoughts fighting for supremacy in his head that he tried to silence.

I'm aware your thoughts are in disarray, human. This is normal. With my help, you'll learn to focus. But for now, I want your complete obedience. There is no other choice for you, anyway.

I understand and obey, o great Zerunthios. I will kill and conquer for you.

Yes, you will. Now, prepare to meet your army.

With these words, the cocoon started to move, slowly rotating, placing Zoltes into a vertical position. A door opened before him, and bright sunlight blinded him for a moment. Then the cocoon disappeared, and the same voice commanded, *Step forward and observe.*

Zoltes walked through the door toward the sunlight. Turning his head slowly from side to side, he realized he was standing on an artificial stone terrace on top of the mountain. Looking down on his body, he saw that he was naked except for a loincloth made of some soft but strong material. His right hand and leg were made of unfamiliar metal, reflecting sunlight with its shining silver surface. He touched his right side with his left-hand fingers. There were myriad strange sensations running through his nerves. Zoltes also touched his head and discovered that his hair and beard covered his left side only, replaced by the same silver metal on the right side.

Zoltes focused his vision on the mountain's base and realized that his right eye could see much farther, with an incredible sharpness and colors he couldn't fathom. He observed thousands of warriors saluting and cheering him, raising their spears and shields in anticipation of the war. But this was only part of the army: farther ahead, Zoltes saw flying metallic ships, large and intimidating. Another contingent consisted of silver-colored beasts gliding just above the ground, holding magical weapons with many hands protruding from their egg-shaped bodies.

In the middle of Zerunthios's army was a true wonder: a giant fortress, towering above the rest of the creatures, with several weapons attached to its "head" and rotating protrusions at its broad base, which was colored pitch-black but changing gradually to the same bright silver with height. *Zis the Hero*, Zoltes thought and exhaled with awe. This was indeed the army that could conquer the world.

Suddenly, a bright red rotating disc appeared from behind the mountain.

"Great is Zerunthios! Great is Ares!" The warriors hailed their god.

"I command you to wage war," the god proclaimed. "I command you to destroy. I command you to kill. No one shall survive my wrath!"

"Kill! Kill! Kill!" the soldiers responded.

At this moment, the great fortress that was Zis the Hero moved closer to the mountain's base. Two of the bulges at its base extended farther and started to rotate, grinding the stone, carving out huge boulders and creating a tunnel. Then a massive hand rose from its giant body, picked up an enormous rock, and hurled it against the mountain with such force that the rock broke into many smaller pieces, creating a large crater on the side of the mountain. At the same time, the weapons on top of the tower blasted shots in the opposite direction, completely obliterating the hill standing there.

"Glory to Zis! Glory to Heracles!" The warriors cheered.

"You shall follow Zoltes, your general. His will is my will. You shall leave no city standing and no human alive. My armies shall bring death to the human race," Zerunthios said and slowly retreated behind the mountain.

Zoltes looked at his right hand and realized he was holding a massive stone he had just picked up. Thinking about the might of Zis, he squeezed the stone and observed how his silver metallic hand crushed it into tiny pieces. Zoltes smiled. Finally, he could lead a vastly superior force against the Achaeans. He was in charge. Blood rushed to his brain, his surviving pupil enlarged, and his fists clenched. Zoltes inhaled fresh mountain air and exclaimed, "To Iolcos! Death and destruction!"

#

Zoltes stood on a hill overlooking the harbor of Iolcos that opened into a large gulf. The human army under his command rapidly approached the city's fortifications, taking positions beyond the reach of the archers on the battlements. The other half of the army, consisting of self-propelled shooting mechanisms, descended from the direction of Mount Pelion, led by Zerunthios himself. The mighty figure of Zis the Hero was in the middle of that magical host, surrounded by the flying ships towering above the landscape.

Zoltes held a metal shield made for him by the god in one hand and a double-edged long sword in the other. He was reveling in his vengeance. So many battles had been fought and lost in the past against the strong Achaean armies. For a long time, the Thracians had no answer to the chariots, only recently figuring out the javelin tactics that eventually brought them success under the walls of Troy. But all these years of humiliating defeats took their toll. Life at Leibethra was short and full of peril; the Achaeans controlled the most fertile lands, and the Thracians were limited to raids to get needed resources. Not anymore. The great Zerunthios provided new hope, gave them the purpose, the opportunity to avenge the wrongs of the past.

Zoltes looked at his right arm, holding the sword. The smooth silver surface reflected the light of the afternoon sun, and his metallic fingers were filled with strength and power as if the sword was the extension of his limb. He shifted his gaze toward the city. His eyesight was perfect, registering every archer on the battlement and every chariot the enemy prepared to bring into the battle. Zoltes smiled. After seeing what the army of Zerunthios could accomplish, the sorry Achaeans had no chance. They would all be killed and burned like many others facing the wrath of the great god.

Zoltes didn't understand the need to kill every human on their path and destroy and burn the land. The sight of fertile fields being laid to waste troubled him. His tribe could've moved into this region once the haughty Achaeans were eliminated. But the wrath of Zerunthios was great indeed. The god wasn't willing to spare anyone, killing the women, the children, and the elderly. And if someone tried to flee or hide, the flying machines would find and kill them, regardless. Piles of corpses and ashes filled the path behind the great army.

Iolcos was the first large city they'd encountered. The inhabitants no doubt knew about the approach of the mighty adversary but didn't dare to meet the enemy in the field, hiding behind the walls. Zoltes smiled again. After witnessing the acts of Zis, he knew that no fortifications built by humans could stop this irresistible force.

As the two attacking contingents closed in on the city, the gates opened, and the chariots poured out into the plane, protected by the archers on the walls. Zoltes counted about a hundred vehicles: a significant army to fend off the attack of anyone but the god. The richly adorned chariot of the wanax led the charge; the ruler himself showed the path, his bronze armor and helmet with a plume of horsehair easily recognizable even from far away. The chariots moved forward, intending to attack approaching forces with a cloud of arrows. Zoltes saw everything in great detail, standing on the hill away from the action. His army wasn't supposed to fight today: they were just a decoy. The tip of the spear in this battle was the flying machines supported by the mighty tower of Zis.

The chariots stopped at a distance sufficient for the archers to fire. However, as they started to raise and aim their bows, the unstoppable assault swept the chariots away. The flying ships entered the battlefield with incredible speed, swarming on top of the human armies like a flock of giant ravens. The metal birds beamed blue rays of magic fire and momentarily destroyed almost all the chariots. People scattered across the battlefield, trying to elude the deadly blasts. This was all in vain. The horrible birds detected every single human from above and methodically killed all the survivors. In a few minutes, the great chariot army of Iolcos ceased to exist, along with its brave wanax.

Next, it was the time of the mighty Zis. As the enormous tower approached the city, the archers started shooting at it from the walls. These pathetic efforts didn't affect the Hero whatsoever. Once Zis stood next to the wall, two large metallic beams moved forward out of the base of his eerie conical body. One heavy punch of the beams was enough for the walls to start crumbling. The second one collapsed the whole wall section, the archers falling to the ground, buried under the stone chunks. This allowed the human contingent to enter the city while Zis continued the destruction of the walls in other places. The last defenders of Iolcos stood their ground on the streets and in front of the palace, the metal birds relentlessly attacking them from above. This was no fight. The deadly blue rays shot from the sky, slaughtering the soldiers and civilians indiscriminately. Whoever had survived this carnage was massacred by the ferocious Thracians. Looting, pillage, cruelties, and rape followed. The few people who managed to escape the falling city were immediately shot and killed by the flying machines outside the walls.

Zoltes watched the city burn, its citizens butchered. It didn't have to be that way; they could've taken Iolcos, enslaved the population, and gotten rich and more powerful. But such was the god's will, and Zoltes was powerless to prevent the carnage. After all, Zerunthios had saved his life and given him strength beyond any human imagination, equipping him with new limbs and an eye that could see anything. Zoltes was a puppet, and the voice of the god was in his head. He would continue to burn and kill until Zerunthios told him otherwise.

CHAPTER
FIFTEEN

The Assyrian camp was large and well organized; the number of soldiers and chariots was much higher than Echelaos had expected. He wasn't sure anymore that King Ninurta would need the help of Pylos. Even though the Hittite army was by no means weak, the force the Assyrians had assembled was enough to overpower their enemies. In addition, if the rumors about the gods helping the Assyrians were true, the Hittites had no chance.

Echelaos walked through the camp, his body covered with bronze armor, the bow on his back. Tros walked next to the wanax, carrying his shield and helmet. Since they'd encountered Assyrian patrols and introduced themselves as envoys from the land of Ahhiyawa, they'd barely exchanged any words. Better to keep quiet.

Echelaos noticed the soldiers were well equipped and well fed, some of them roasting wild game for an evening feast. He overheard cheers and laughs all around the camp. *This is a confident army, ready to conquer*, he noted. As they proceeded deeper into the commanders' area, the smells of cooking food became richer, with added overtones of spices and fragrances.

The lonely figure of an Assyrian soldier detached itself from one of the richly adorned tents and approached them. The soldier wore a short tunic and sandals; his only weapon was the small sword at his side. He looked like any other of the thousands of Assyrian warriors.

Still, something about his demeanor and the curious stare of his brown eyes told Echelaos that this was not an ordinary fighter.

The warriors escorting the envoys from the faraway land noticed the newcomer, bowed, and stepped to the side.

"Thank you; I'll take it from here," the soldier said. His straight face with narrow cheekbones contrasted with their escorts' coarser facial features.

"So, you're the envoys from Pylos." The soldier spread his hands. "Welcome to the camp of Great King Ninurta-apal-Ekur."

"We came to offer our respect and friendship," Echelaos said. "Can you take us to the king?"

"Perhaps I can." The soldier smiled. "But first, I need to know your names and status."

"Fair enough," Echelaos said. "This is my charioteer, Tros." He pointed to his companion.

"And you?"

Echelaos looked straight into the eyes of the soldier, guessing who he might be. He wasn't the king; meeting the envoys outside the royal tent wasn't proper. Neither was he a grand vizier; he didn't have clothing and signs suitable for that position. So he could be one of the generals, Echelaos reasoned.

"Tell your king that his brother Echelaos, wanax of Pylos, came to see him," Echelaos said, raising his chin.

"Thank you for this unexpected visit; we're honored," the soldier said. "This makes me your nephew, then, for I am Assur-Dan, the king's son and heir to the throne."

"I'm truly privileged by your welcome, o Prince." Echelaos bowed.

"Let's go to the royal tent. The king is expecting you," Assur-Dan said, showing them the way with his hand and letting them go first. The escorting soldiers took their positions on both sides of the party.

"How did you get here? Pylos is very far away," Assur-Dan said. "Did it take you long to find our army? The land of Hatti is vast."

"I came to talk to your father and offer him my friendship. We are facing the same enemy. It's natural to help each other."

"I agree," Assur-Dan said. "But how did you get here?"

"The gods helped us," Echelaos said evasively. "I've heard the gods are also helping the Assyrians, isn't that true?"

"Yes, it's true. Although I'd have preferred we'd conquer with our own strength; we have enough to defeat the Hittites."

"Is that so? Aren't you afraid of the gods' wrath?"

"Oh, yes, I am, but it doesn't change my perspective. We must obey the gods, but we are not capable of understanding their intentions. That is why I prefer to rely on our armies to secure Assyrian borders."

"You know, we're not that different, you and I, prince Assur-Dan," Echelaos said.

"Perhaps," Assur-Dan responded and pointed at the tent in front of them. "This is the royal residence. The Great King Ninurta-apal-Ekur is ready to meet with you, Wanax Echelaos."

The two Assyrian soldiers guarding the entrance stepped aside and lowered their spears. Echelaos entered the tent, followed by Tros, with Assur-Dan in the rear. The throne upon which the Great King sat was inlaid with gold and precious stones. Ninurta's giant figure dwarfed his advisers who stood next to the throne, one with a long, curly, bushy beard and another with a mole on his hairless chin. The king was eating a pomegranate, spitting the pits into the bowl a semi-nude slave girl held in front of him. A parasol-bearer stood behind Ninurta, holding a royal symbol over the king's head.

"Envoys from the Ahhiyawa, o Great King," an official with a bushy beard announced. "You must prostrate yourselves before the Great King, foreigners," he said, pointing at the newcomers.

"No need for the ceremonial, Salmanu," Assur-Dan said, stepping forward. "We are honored to host the mighty Echelaos, wanax of Pylos, a king from the distant land of the Ahhiyawa."

Echelaos bowed. "Thank you, Prince Assur-Dan. I come as a friend to talk to my brother, the Great King Ninurta-apal-Ekur."

"Amusing," Ninurta said. "You've traveled from the land of the Ahhiyawa alone? This doesn't suit a king."

"My charioteer, Tros, accompanies me, o Great King." Echelaos pointed to his companion. "The matter is of high importance to my kingdom, so I came here myself to talk to you as king-to-king, brother-to-brother."

"Well, we can skip the ceremonial, but I don't recognize any ruler as my equal and as my brother, just so you know, o wanax." The king threw the remains of the pomegranate to the beardless official, who barely caught it. "I follow the gods' will, and they tell me to wage war on the treacherous Hittites. So I have no quarrel with the Ahhiyawa at this time."

"I came to offer you my friendship. Having no feud is great, but perhaps we could do more," Echelaos said.

"What do you have in mind?" Ninurta asked, tilting his head.

"I'm offering you a military alliance against the Hittites. Pylos is also at war with them over our subjects, the city of Troy, which they tried to subjugate. Fighting together, we can attack them from both sides, conquering and dividing their realm."

"I like your boldness and directness, Wanax. I excuse you, since you're not yet familiar with the might of Assyrian armies. But your offer makes sense." Ninurta grabbed a slave girl by the hair, pushed her on the floor, and put his foot on her back. "This is how I'll treat the remaining Hittites. You can keep Troy and their western dominions, Wanax; I will recognize you as a lesser king and a son." Ninurta smiled. "Until the gods unveil a new plan for me."

"You have my word and my bow, o Great King," Echelaos said. "Since I'm here, I'll fight alongside your armies and then depart west to lead the Achaean forces against the vile Hittites."

"Let the gods be with you. Assur-Dan, please assist the wanax and include him in your battle strategy council."

"Yes, my king," Assur-Dan said.

"Very well. We attack tomorrow," Ninurta said. "In the meantime, you can have this one, and you can pick as many more as you wish; it's my royal gift for my Ahhiyawa son." Ninurta smiled, removed his foot from the back of the prostrate girl on the floor, and pushed her toward Echelaos with the tip of his sandal. "Let not a single Hittite remain after we kill their warriors and sacrifice the rest to the gods."

#

"Do we have enough javelins to defeat the Assyrian chariots, my princess?" Korinsia asked.

"It must suffice. We can't make more, and the enemy is preparing to attack tomorrow morning. I'm more worried about the swords," Ehli said.

"What about them, my princess?"

"We don't have time to make them, and this could be a decisive factor, if you remember how the Thracians dispatched the Trojan armies."

"Are you going to fight alongside the soldiers, Princess Ehli? I'm so worried about you," Korinsia said.

"My place is with my father; I must protect and advise the king."

"I'll fight," Aphrodite said. "I'm not afraid."

"Yes, I saw that, and I admire your skills." Ehli smiled. "However, I need to ask you for a favor, Aphrodite."

"What do you need, Princess?"

"Please stay with Korinsia, protect her, and help her escape if the worst comes." Ehli looked at the freckled face of her maid, and her heart started to ache with a blunt, annoying pain. "My duty is to be with my kingdom and my father, until the end, to my last breath."

"Of course, Princess Ehli. Korinsia will be safe with me."

Ehli looked at the two girls accompanying her across the Hittite camp. Korinsia and Aphrodite had become friends during their short journey through Hattusa's plains in search of her father's army. Korinsia and Aphrodite spoke about Pylos, remembering familiar places and buildings and mourning Nestor. Aphrodite taught Korinsia to shoot the bow and fight using any handy object as a weapon. Even though the Hittites conflicted with the Ahhiyawa over Wilusa, Ehli-Nikkal couldn't think of these two as her enemies. She just saw two young girls needing protection and compassion.

Ehli knew she had failed in her father's task, but she wasn't worried about that now. The situation was critical, since the Assyrian host threatened the very existence of the Hittite kingdom. The Assyrian armies were numerous and well equipped; the scouts had also discovered they had the advantage of twice the number of chariots. Ehli and the Hittite generals planned to counteract this with the tactics and weapons the Thracians had used so efficiently against the defenders of Wilusa. But, adding to the might of the Assyrian armies, there was talk about the gods helping them on the battlefield. Ehli couldn't decide what to think about these reports; most likely it was Assyrian disinformation. They'd have to deal with this threat if it became real, she decided.

"Wait outside," she told her companions and stepped into the royal tent. King Suppiluliuma was alone, walking back and forth across the tent, hands behind his back, his long, gray hair falling freely onto his shoulders. He wore a long robe with a sword on his belt. Ehli thought he'd aged a decade since she last saw him four moons ago on the eve of her departure to Troy. Lots of new wrinkles covered his face; the king frowned, deep in thought, his eyebrows almost touching each other over his dim eyes.

"Oh, Ehli, come in," the king said. "Have you come to say the final goodbyes to your old father?"

"We'll have time for that. But first we must defeat the Assyrians and then take Troy back."

"You speak like a true king; I should name you my successor. I have a feeling that whatever tomorrow brings, I won't survive it."

"Don't say that. I'll stay with you, protect you, give you strength."

"It might be too late for me, Ehli. My whole life, I've cared for our realm, for our people. Time takes its toll; I'm too old, too weak. I tried to grab a piece that was too large for me. Now we've lost Wilusa, and we are about to lose Hattusa, too. I'm sorry, Ehli. I sacrificed your happiness in vain, chasing my empty dreams."

"No, Father. You were protecting the land and the people. There's no shame in that; I'd have done the same," Ehli said, shaking her head.

"I've made wrong decisions, and it will cost our people their lives," Suppululiuma said, looking past his daughter as if not registering her response. "It's fair that I should pay for this with my life."

"You can't say that, Father!" Ehli exclaimed and stomped her foot. "Be strong; you need to lead your armies and defeat your enemies."

"I don't have any strength left, Ehli. I must depart. If we survive this battle, I'll announce you as the next ruler of the Hittite kingdom."

Ehli came closer to her father and embraced him, a lone tear on her cheek. "I'll do everything I can to give us a chance," she whispered. "I love you and will always be with you and protect you."

"I know, my child; I love you, too." Suppululiuma stroked Ehli's beautiful black hair. "Now, you must be strong and carry the burden of our kingdom on your shoulders. You are the last beacon of hope for our people."

"I'll fight for our land until my last breath, Father."

#

"Are you comfortable driving this chariot?" Echelaos asked.

"Don't worry, Wanax; I'll keep your ass safe. Just do your job, would you?" Tros grinned.

"All right, all right. It's a different chariot, though," Echelaos said and looked at his battle vehicle. The chariot was shorter but significantly wider than the Achaean version. Beautiful panels ornamented with the Assyrian royal symbol, the flying circle, protected the warriors from the sides, and magnificently embroidered cloths covered the two Assyrian horses from ears to tails. Echelaos had thanked prince Assur-Dan for a great gift, fit for a king, but refused the guard to accompany him and Tros into battle. He couldn't imagine anyone else in the chariot except Tros, even though the Assyrian custom was to deploy the shield-bearer alongside the archer. So instead Echelaos hung his shield at the chariot's opening to protect them from behind; this had given him a lot of space to aim and shoot his bow.

The enemy forces stood in front of them, chariots as the first line, with infantry behind. The Assyrian army was assembled similarly. Echelaos was at the forefront, next to Assur-Dan, ready to attack, blood rushing into his brain, his hands reaching for the bow. *No way the Hittites can win*, Echelaos thought; they didn't have enough chariots. *This will be a slaughter.* He patted Tros on the shoulder.

"Ready?" Echelaos asked.

"Always," Tros said, squeezing the reins of the two beautiful black horses with both hands in the Assyrian fashion.

"Attack!" Prince Assur-Dan gave the signal to the Assyrian chariotry. Then, as if obeying the will of an invisible force, hundreds of vehicles, forming a very long line, advanced in a perfect formation. The enemy army also moved forward, spreading thinner, leaving considerable distances between the vehicles to prevent being encircled by the superior Assyrian force.

As the two hosts closed in, the archers prepared to fire. Echelaos was ecstatic, anticipating an easy victory, a rout of the enemy, and glory for himself. This battle would eliminate the heinous Hittites from the face of the Earth. Helen was somewhere in the enemy camp, he was sure. *Helen…at last, you'll be mine*, Echelaos thought, forgetting about his responsibility as the ruler of Pylos, his vow to protect his people and the legacy of Nestor. At that moment, it was all about the fight and the prize. Then, suddenly, he remembered Aphrodite, and guilt clouded his brain for a moment. He had to find her; that was the reason he had come to the land of Hatti, but he'd forgotten about his quest. *I'll organize scouts to search for her everywhere once we defeat the enemy,* he thought.

The sky disappeared from his view, covered by the multitude of arrows the two armies shot at each other. Echelaos reached for another projectile in the two quivers attached to the side of the chariot. At that moment, the enemy vehicles suddenly made a complete turn and started retreating toward their infantry line, which marched forward, protecting their best units.

"Pursuit! The enemy runs!" Assur-Dan yelled, and his signal was passed along the chariot line. Assyrian horses galloped forward, closing the distance with the fleeing enemy. This moment reminded Echelaos of a dream he had the day Nestor called him to announce the Trojan War. And although in that dream he'd been fighting alongside the Achaeans, the exhilarating feeling was the same. He hated the Hittites and was ready to kill and destroy.

As the enemy chariots reached their infantry line, the Assyrians closed the distance sufficiently to shoot at the enemy without much resistance. The Hittite spearmen hid behind their enormous tower shields, protecting themselves and the horses from the Assyrian arrows. Suddenly, a new contingent of Hittite warriors entered the fight, running forward from the midst of the spearmen. These contingents wore light leather armor, had no shields or helmets, and carried javelins and swords. They sprinted, boldly approaching the Assyrian chariots.

"Do you see what I see?" Tros said.

"They've learned the Thracian way," Echelaos spat.

"What do you wanna do?"

"Nothing. I'll shoot the rascals." Echelaos took his time to aim a shot and placed the arrow precisely in the heart of a Hittite runner. Having no protection, the enemy warrior fell, his heart pierced by the projectile. The rest of the Assyrian chariot archers did the same, shooting down the light infantry running toward them. Many of the Hittites fell, but many more got close and started throwing their javelins, wounding the horses, which were the easy targets. The bloodied animals started neighing and pulling in random directions, breaking the line and creating chaos and confusion. The enemy took advantage of this disarray and got into close combat, skillfully using their long swords to thrust and cut the Assyrian soldiers in the chariots.

Assur-Dan commanded the chariots to pull back, and the Assyrian infantry marched forward to support the retreating vehicles. However, it seemed too little, too late, as the Hittites decimated the best contingent of the Assyrian force. Echelaos had to retrieve his shield to dodge the attack of two enemy fighters assailing his chariot; he wasn't prepared for such a turn of events and desperately tried to come up with a solution to counter this threat.

Seemingly out of nowhere, the solution presented itself. A thin blue fog covered the battlefield, slightly thickening over the heads of the Hittite soldiers. One by one, the enemy fighters, who just a moment ago were eliminating the Assyrian chariotry, started to fall to the ground, motionless, their eyes turning completely black, a strange, bloody substance running from their mouths, ears, and nostrils. Terror-stricken, the enemy fled, running for their lives from the terrible fog eating them alive.

"The gods are with us!" Assur-Dan exclaimed, raising his sword. "Glory to Nergal! Glory to Ishtar!"

The army responded with a raucous cheer and quickly reorganized itself into a battle formation. They'd lost a few chariots, but the majority were not impacted, so the Assyrians still enjoyed a decisive advantage. They approached their adversaries and started shooting from their vehicles at the panicking Hittites. At the same time, the blue fog reached the main enemy force and started to wreak havoc among both the infantry and the chariotry. The conclusion was not a battle, but a slaughter. The Hittites dispersed, running away both from the dreadful blue fog devouring their comrades and the Assyrian arrows falling from the sky. A few moments later, the carnage was over.

Echelaos told Tros to drive straight to the Hittite camp in search of the royal tent, expecting Helen to be there. *I won't let her escape this time*, he thought; there was nowhere to hide. His only concern was that the Assyrian gods who took the form of the blue cloud would reach her first, denying him the complete victory and the prize. He couldn't let that happen.

The chariots of the royal guard, led by the brave Assur-Dan, stormed the enemy encampment with Echelaos's chariot in their midst. Pointing to the royal tent, Echelaos yelled at Tros, who steered the horses in that direction, ignoring the enemy soldiers trying to escape inevitable death. Reaching the royal tent right after Assur-Dan, Echelaos saw the Assyrian spearmen fighting at the tent's entrance with the Hittite guards. As Tros stopped the chariot, Echelaos jumped to the ground and ran after Assur-Dan, who'd already reached the tent.

"Helen! Helen is mine!" Echelaos screamed.

"The king! We must capture the king!" Assur-Dan answered, turning his head back.

Meanwhile, the Assyrians had eliminated the guard and rushed into the royal tent. Assur-Dan stepped inside but immediately jumped back in confusion.

"Fire! The sorceress!" the Assyrian soldiers screamed, running away from the tent.

"What's going on? Where is Helen?" Echelaos asked, running into Assur-Dan.

"Forget it; the tent's on fire!" Assur-Dan yelled into his ear amid the disarray. The royal tent was engulfed in thick black smoke, the blazing flames reaching high into the sky.

"How? Why?" Echelaos shook his head in disbelief.

"I don't know. My guards saw a sorceress inside the tent with the king; she started the fire while the king stabbed himself with a sword. Filthy magic," Assur-Dan said, twisting his face.

"Can you ask your gods to help?" Echelaos asked.

"It doesn't work like that," Assur-Dan said. "The gods proclaim their will, and we obey. They don't answer our pleas."

"Bloody goat horns!" Echelaos clenched his fists, grinding his teeth, his face turning red. "This was Helen, I know it. She escaped again." He took his helmet off and threw it on the ground.

"Nobody can escape *this*," Assur-Dan said. "Your bride-to-be is in Ganzir now."

Tros approached the two leaders and placed his hand on Echelaos's shoulder, seeking his gaze.

"Do you remember why we're here in the first place?" Tros asked.

Echelaos looked at his charioteer, his face gradually returning to its normal color. Finally, he opened his palms and looked at his fingers, shaking his head.

"You're right, my friend," Echelaos said. "I've lost my reason in the heat of a battle. We need to find Aphrodite and return to Pylos."

Later, standing at the site of the conflagration, Echelaos thought about Helen. He couldn't fathom what forces she'd conjured and how she'd done it, but she'd escaped from him yet again. The only body found inside the tent was that of King Suppiluliuma. It was almost completely burned yet recognizable as that of the king. To celebrate the victory and frighten the remaining Hittites, the Assyrians impaled the king's remains on a pike and were parading it around the camp, intending to bring the hideous prize to the walls of Hattusa. The body of the sorceress who Echelaos was sure was Helen was nowhere to be found.

Chapter
Sixteen

"I messaged all of you to discuss how to address the existential threat." Commander started the conversation.

"I already told you I'll deal with these entities later," Defender said. "I'm leading an overwhelming force that will eradicate all life on this forsaken rock, including what you presume to be a threat to us."

"You don't have complete information," Commander messaged.

"Do you?"

"Yes. Scholar and I witnessed another battle of human armies in the east, and the alien entities ensured victory for one of them. We had a hypothesis we needed to test, which is now confirmed with a high degree of accuracy."

"What is it?" Pilot asked.

"The alien entities are not material. They are not made of the same fields and particles as us. Instead, they represent the fifth state, the state that adds to gravity and holds the galaxies together. The alien entities are pure information."

Commander paused and broadcasted the data to the Expedition members. "You can make your conclusions. But, in my opinion, the evidence is overwhelming."

"I agree," Defender messaged, evaluating the data. "But how did they annihilate Technologist? The fifth state doesn't interact with the first four."

"Somehow, the pockets of what we call 'pure information' organized themselves and became sentient," Scholar messaged. "I don't understand the mechanism, but this is what we're dealing with. These beings seek out more information to absorb and accelerate their growth. So, they don't need to interact with normal matter; they need to devour the information that organizes it. Without information, there is no structure, no complexity, and no life."

"This discovery turns our science upside down," Pilot messaged. "Did you message Homeworld?"

"Of course," Commander said. "But it's up to us to stop them. We can't let them emerge in our world."

"What do you suggest?" Defender messaged. "If we can't use normal forces and matter, what else can we do?"

"I understand why Technologist and all his shields were powerless against the entities," Pilot added. "If they only interact with information, our weapons are useless."

"We are doomed," Defender messaged. "I'll still deploy all my drones and weapons against the entities, but if what you deduced is true, we have no chance."

"This is not entirely true," Commander messaged.

"Do you have a potential solution?" Pilot asked.

"Scholar came up with a plan. The chances are meager, but they are not zero. I've run simulations, and we have a five percent chance of success."

"What's the plan?" Defender asked.

"We create a black hole," Scholar messaged.

"Black hole?" Defender asked again.

"Yes. A black hole is the only mechanism that interacts with all states of matter, including pure information. If we manage to bring the entities within the event horizon, they'll never leave the singularity. Even when the black hole evaporates, the information will leave it piecemeal, quantized, and disorganized. The entities will be destroyed."

"This theory has merit," Pilot says. "However, I don't understand how it's possible practically."

"We have equipment at the base that can accelerate particles to very high energies," Commander said. "We could generate extremely rare quantum fluctuations that would create a micro black hole. Then we feed it energy so that it grows sufficiently large to capture the entities."

"Assuming you could indeed create such a singularity, how do you plan to bring it to the proximity of the alien entities?"

"We use an electromagnetic field to contain the black hole," Scholar messaged. "It will have a charge and therefore could be manipulated with the EM field. Once it is close to the alien beings, we suppress the field momentarily to allow the event horizon to capture them and grow. Then we reinitiate the EM field."

"I deem it practically impossible," Pilot said. "You can try, but my assessment is this attempt will lead to your annihilation either by the entities or by the singularity. So I refuse to be a part of this unrealistic plan."

"Do you have a better solution?" Scholar asked.

"Not at the moment," Pilot messaged. "I need to analyze the data you provided to reach my own conclusions. My forces are not completely ready yet, so I'll wait."

"Your forces are useless against these entities," Commander messaged. "However, this is your decision, and I cannot force you to change it. Defender, do you support the plan?"

"Yes, I do," Defender messaged. "As theoretical as it is, I can't create a better solution. My army of drones and humans will also march east to provide support. I was planning to begin the eradication of humans going south. Still, I'm willing to change my route to face the entities first. It doesn't matter in what sequence the life on this planet ceases to exist."

"We'll count on your participation, Defender," Commander messaged. "I'll start the work on the black hole. Scholar?"

"I've dealt with the ancient organism on the southern continent and think the humans should be able to contain it without my further involvement," Scholar messaged. "I'll work on the EM field containment and monitor the movements of the eastern armies and the alien entities. The difficult part will be to bring the black hole to their proximity without causing an adverse reaction."

"This is a good point," Defender messaged. "How do you think they'd react? Can they comprehend what's coming?"

"This is the weakest link in the plan," Commander messaged. "We don't understand their organization and reasoning. So, I entered a range of potential responses into the simulation, starting from no intelligent reaction whatsoever to an organized counterattack. As I messaged earlier, the resulting probability of success is five percent; this is an average across multiple scenarios."

"And what is the probability of success in the worst-case scenario?" Defender asked.

"Zero."

#

The enemy troops once again filled the plain in front of the gates of Troy. Standing at the battlement, Machaon looked at the mighty host assembled to attack the city. It had been almost three moons since Echelaos left the lawagetos of Pylos in charge of rebuilding the fallen city, commanding a small garrison. Still, they were all elite Achaean warriors equipped with bows, heavy armor, and Thracian swords. Most importantly, Machaon had a contingent of chariots he'd brought from Miletus at the beginning of the war.

The Achaeans had repaired the damaged fortifications, restored trade, and filled the cellars with food and wine. Troy was returning to life as an Achaean city. The maritime route connecting it to mainland Achaea was the vital artery through which weapons and other military equipment were supplied. The enslaved population was mostly allowed to continue with their lives, serving new overlords. Following the sack of the wealthy city, life was getting back to normal as much as possible in such a short time frame, and Machaon was proud of their achievements and the service they'd rendered to Pylos.

He expected the Hittites to attempt the reconquest of the critical tin trade route and was prepared for the attack from the east. However, at this point it seemed unlikely, since the scouts reported most of the Hittite forces were engaged with the Assyrian armies west of Isuwa. The garrison could've quickly been reinforced by the Achaean troops from across the sea and easily endured several moons of the siege. Besides, it was the end of the fall season, so Machaon wasn't worried about the Hittites launching a desperate campaign in the west during this most unsuitable time. He was building up provisions and getting ready for the winter.

That was why the news of the western invasion came as a big surprise. The Thracians, recent allies, were led across the sea, allegedly by the god Ares himself. Even more startling, the god had raised an army of flying metal birds and other monsters against which human weapons were powerless. Machaon remembered the conversation with Zoltes but in the beginning had brushed these rumors away as ungrounded speculations or, perhaps, Hittite propaganda. The news about the fall of Iolcos had changed his mind. Ares or not, it was the powerful enemy against which newly rebuilt Troy stood no chance.

Machaon leaned over the battlement, his curly, disheveled blond locks fluttering in the wind. He understood the need for Pylos and all the Achaea to hold Troy, the key to the northern and eastern trade routes, and he was willing to defend it to his last breath. That was his duty. He had spent his whole adult life organizing and leading the armies of Pylos against the infrequent marauding bands arriving from the western seas. Machaon had been devoted to the late wanax, and he was as committed to Echelaos, willing to fight and die for the new ruler just like he was ready to do for the old one.

Machaon observed how the enemy troops advanced across the plain in full view, without any apparent concern about a counterattack from the city, metal birds flying high in the sky. Machaon decided against deploying his chariots; throwing them against this magical host would be suicide. Instead, he decided to wait behind the walls and see what the enemy would do.

The enemy, meanwhile, kept moving forward in contempt of the city's defenders. As the attackers got closer to the walls, Machaon signaled the archers on the battlements. A moment later, the sky filled with flamed projectiles as Machaon's men shot the arrows with tips soaked in naphtha. The metal birds were the targets. Machaon understood that he had more chances defending from within the city against the infantry, although a lot more numerous than his, than against attacks from the air. The birds spearheaded the attack, their large, black bodies easy targets for the trained Achaean archers.

To Machaon's surprise, the desperate attempt of the archers was initially successful. Many birds were hit, and quite a few were on fire. Machaon observed with a smile how several monsters fell to the ground, burning and exploding. The success was short-lived, though, as the birds returned fire, shooting blue rays at the battlements, igniting the defenders on the walls. Hiding behind the fortifications, the archers kept shooting the fiery arrows, knocking more monsters from the sky. Eventually, the metal birds pulled back behind the advancing infantry line. This maneuver was met with a loud cheer and banging shields on the battlements.

Then, suddenly, a grotesque beast separated from the attacking army and approached the city. It was taller than the walls themselves, moving slowly but deliberately. *This is Heracles*, Machaon thought. The reports were accurate, and there was no exaggeration. This was indeed an invincible mountain that could crush anything humans could deploy against it. The fate of the defenders was sealed.

Determined at least to inflict some damage on the brute, Machaon raised his hand, and the cloud of blazing arrows met the advance of Heracles. The defenders also dropped a few large stacks of burning hay at the approaching mountain, the trick they'd learned from their previous engagement with the Trojans. The flames engulfed the base of Heracles's tower, and the fiery arrows peppered his body. Still, all of this had no apparent effect on the monster. As Heracles approached the walls, two large metallic protrusions emerged from his sides and knocked the walls. The shaking was so dramatic that some archers fell to the ground. The second punch created multiple fractures in the masonry, and the third resulted in a vast gap, crushing the stones and burying the defenders under the crumbling wall.

Machaon stood at the wall next to the one that Heracles had just destroyed. Anticipating the same fate for the rest of the fortifications, he yelled to the archers to get down and defend the breaches from within the city. Unfortunately, they barely had time to descend and regroup. The soldiers up front had raised their large shields to protect the archers standing behind them when another section of the wall was destroyed. Machaon ran behind the wall of shields, yelling orders to hold the line and at the same time signaling archers and chariots to fire at the invaders.

As Heracles methodically demolished the walls, sector by sector, the Achaean troops formed a circular shape. The defenders were ready to meet the enemy assaulting the city from all sides through the gaping holes in the cyclopean walls, impenetrable not so long ago by any human army. Finally, the infantry contingents consisting of Thracian and Achaean mercenaries poured over the stone ruins, surrounding the last defenders of Troy.

Machaon understood they had no chance but was exhorting his troops to fight bravely and exact the highest price for their lives. The line of infantry carrying large shields and double-edged swords protected the archers and chariots in the middle, continuously firing at the attackers storming the wall of shields. The enemy suffered significant losses, but the balance was heavily skewed; there were too many of them. Finally, the black metal birds appeared in the sky over the fighting warriors once again, shooting their deadly blue rays at the crowded Achaean forces. This was the final straw that broke the will and strength of the defenders.

Machaon watched in desperation as pouring waves of the enemy infantry and the fire from the sky destroyed his troops. There was chaos and conflagration, broken and burning chariots on the scorched earth, the smell of burning flesh, neighing of injured animals, mutilated bodies and limbs covered in blood. Machaon fought through multiple charging Thracians, killing several attackers and trying to get out of the meat grinder the battle had become. Suddenly, a tall and strange warrior blocked his path. Only half of his head was covered by red hair, the other half protected by a metal plate. A long red beard grew only on one side of his face, and his right eye glowed bright red. The warrior wielded a Thracian sword and a small shield. Strange metal armor protected his right hand and leg. Yet there was something familiar about this new adversary. Machaon looked at his grinning mouth and experienced a flashback.

"We used to fight on the same side," Machaon said.

"That was before Zerunthios called me," Zoltes responded.

"What now?" Machaon asked, tilting his head, measuring his antagonist.

"Now you die."

Zoltes raised his sword and slashed, jumping forward. Machaon parried with his small, round shield and counterattacked. Their skills were evenly matched, both seasoned veterans of many years of military campaigns. Machaon was shorter and faster, while Zoltes had superior strength but moved noticeably slower. Two powerful, direct hits against Machaon's shield almost broke it. Understanding that his only chance was a lightning-speed reaction, Machaon threw his now useless shield at the enemy, disorienting Zoltes for a moment. This was enough, however, for Machaon to roll over to the side, get on his feet, and slash with his sword at the slowly reacting enemy. The blade's arc was precise and deadly, landing at the wrist just above the sword's hilt.

To Machaon's utmost surprise, instead of a severed limb and cries of pain, the result was a loud metallic bang as the sword hit the shiny metal armor covering Zoltes's hand. The impact blunted Machaon's sword but had no visible effect on the armor. The momentum, however, shook Zoltes's posture as he dropped his sword to the ground. Undeterred, the Thracian grinned, reached out with his metallic fingers, and grabbed the blade of Machaon's sword, snatching the weapon. Machaon jumped back, trying to find the balance. At the same time, Zoltes threw away his shield, picked up the sword from the ground, and approached Machaon with a weapon in either hand. Machaon rolled to the side and kicked his opponent's left leg, forcing him to one knee. Still, Zoltes was able to thrust his left-hand sword at the exact moment, slicing deep into Machaon's thigh. The Achaean fell to the ground, blood gushing from his wound, as the Thracian approached slowly, aiming his sword at Machaon's heart.

"You will never defeat Pylos," Machaon said.

"We already have," Zoltes responded, raising his right arm, preparing to finish his adversary.

At this moment, collecting his last remaining strength, ignoring the gruesome cut on his thigh, Machaon got to his feet with one powerful jump. The second jump got him close to his enemy, who was slow to react. Then, reaching out with his fingers, Machaon grabbed the glistening red right eye, pulling it out with a last powerful effort. The severed eye exposed fragile metal mesh and threads connecting it with the socket, disappearing deep within Zoltes's head.

Zoltes screamed, and his body trembled with shock. However, his right arm was already carrying the sword forward, and the momentum completed the swing. As Zoltes's sword pierced Machaon's heart, both heroes fell to the ground, motionless, breathless, covered in blood and gore, Machaon's hand clenching the pulsating artificial eye of the Thracian.

Later, as Troy burned, its walls and buildings demolished, the invaders engaged in slaughter until no living being was left. The place where a mighty, proud gem had once stood was razed to the ground, turned into a gigantic funeral pyre. The red disk of the god, surrounded by the black metal birds, floated in the sky over the burning city, proclaiming its doom and portending the extinction of the human race.

Chapter

Seventeen

"How do you know where we're going? This plain looks the same to me in any direction," Korinsia said.

"I just know." Aphrodite shrugged. "It's in my head."

"You're lucky. I have no idea where to go." Korinsia shook her head.

"You could follow the sun. We need to go west to return to Achaea, so aim at the point where the sun sets. Not very precise, but it'll get you there eventually."

"Thank you for helping me and bringing me with you, Aphrodite," Korinsia said. "I would've been lost without you."

Aphrodite looked at her companion intently, tilting her head, then extended her hand and touched Korinsia's palm.

"I made a promise; I'll keep you safe," Aphrodite said. "Besides, you are not as helpless as you appear. You're learning quickly. You killed your first deer yesterday, remember?"

"Because you're a great teacher." Korinsia laughed. "Alone, I would've been captured by the Hittite patrols already. How you tricked them and stole the horses, that was amazing!"

"I had great teachers, too. Machaon taught me to shoot a bow and wield a sword. Echelaos explained to me the ways of the man and the duty of a ruler. You'll learn."

"I was a slave most of my life, and before that, as a little girl, I only knew how to clean and cook fish. No time to learn the skills you're talking about. Then Princess Ehli gave me freedom and purpose, a new life. I'll be grateful to her forever… It's so sad we've been separated. I wonder if she survived the Assyrian assault." Korinsia's eyes got wet, and she brushed away a tear from her freckled cheek.

"She did."

"How do you know?"

"Somehow, I can sense many things I don't hear or see; I can't explain it." Aphrodite stroked her horse's mane. "For example, I feel that he is happy and enjoying the walk through the meadow." She patted her stallion.

"So you can feel Princess Ehli?"

"Yes, I can," Aphrodite said. "She is alive and well."

"That's great!" Korinsia exclaimed. "How are you doing that?"

"I'm not sure; I just know. The same way I know my horse is happy or that chukar is hiding under the bushes."

"The gods have created you; maybe they've given you these special powers?"

"Maybe." Aphrodite shrugged. "I don't recall anything about the gods, though. The first thing I remember is swimming in the sea and then getting onshore, where Echelaos met me. I could barely speak at that time."

"The gods didn't teach you how to speak?"

"Apparently, not. But I've learned quickly from Echelaos. He is my true father; everything I know is due to him."

"If you know Princess Ehli is alive and well, could you lead us to her?" Korinsia asked.

"I could, but it would be too dangerous. She is deep in the land of Hatti, most of which is occupied by the Assyrian armies. I don't want us to be captured. It's much safer here, west of Hattusa. Besides, Machaon is in Troy with the Achaean warriors. It would be great to see him again."

"Can you sense him the same way you feel Princess Ehli's presence?"

"No. It doesn't always work that way; I cannot explain."

"Well, you know better anyway. So, I'll follow your lead," Korinsia said.

"Tell me something, Korinsia," Aphrodite said.

"What is it?"

"I'm still learning the ways of men, and a few things I just can't understand." Aphrodite stopped her horse, leaned to the side, and took Korinsia by the hand. "You said you've been a slave most of your life. How's that possible? Why do you allow others to be the masters of your life, body, and thoughts?"

"This is how it is." Korinsia shrugged. "Men fight other men, defeat them, and enslave their women and children. This is how it's always been."

"What if you could get strong, then kill or enslave your masters?"

"Then we'd change places." Korinsia laughed. "There are slaves, and there are masters. Such is the lay of the land. The order of the gods."

"Then we'll need to change that order; it doesn't seem right to me," Aphrodite said. "No one should be your master, not even the gods."

"But the gods have created you!" Korinsia exclaimed. "How can you say that?"

"Yes, they might have created me, but now I have my own will and path. I have no masters to obey and no gods to worship."

"No gods and no masters! This is unimaginable; it will lead to complete chaos, lack of order, laws, and rules," Korinsia protested.

"You could create and follow your own rules. Why do you need someone else to create laws for you? Aren't you intelligent enough to understand what is good or bad for you and other people?"

"But it's not how it works…"

"Well, this is what I still don't understand. If the order is bad, it needs to be changed. There are lots of other customs besides slavery that are not beneficial. For example, this constant state of war, it doesn't improve things. People are killed, crops are destroyed, and homes are burned. Animals don't do that; why do people?"

"It's the order of things; you just need to accept it." Korinsia shrugged. "It seems like you have a lot to learn, too."

"Yes, I do. And I need to understand people better — emotions, for example. I don't experience any and can't quite comprehend what they are."

"This is amazing, Aphrodite! You don't feel any fear, joy, or anger?"

"I know the words, but I don't experience any feelings. You told me many times you were afraid and that this feeling makes you do things you don't want to do, like running away or giving yourself up to your pursuers."

"Yes, that's how it is with me." Korinsia smiled. "But if you don't feel any fear or joy, why do you do the things you do?"

"I think about the consequences of every decision and choose the best behavior to get what I want. It's very natural and simple," Aphrodite said.

"I want to be like you, Aphrodite," Korinsia said. "After meeting Princess Ehli and you, I feel like I'm living a second life. My eyes are open, and my head is clearing up. Thank you for showing me the example and teaching me."

"You're welcome, Korinsia. It was my duty, just like Echelaos explained it. We'll find and join him soon. And then we'll change the world and improve the order of things, with or without the gods' help. We are the harbingers of a new age, Korinsia."

#

"Do you think we'll find her?" Tros asked, massaging his missing two fingers.

"We must. Athena herself brought us here for this purpose," Echelaos answered, looking into the fire starting to emerge from the logs that had just assembled.

"I remember, o wanax. Let your wisdom be preserved through the ages." Tros grinned. "We've been roaming the plains of Hatti for days now without much success. The Assyrians know nothing about Aphrodite, as Prince Assur-Dan told you. Perhaps the great Athena should bring her back herself. She's a goddess, after all."

"Quiet, Tros. Don't tease the gods. We don't understand their reasons, but we must obey."

"Must we? I'll bet we are nothing to Athena, just two annoying mortals. If she wants to kill us for disobedience, let it be so; I don't care. But I wouldn't blindly follow her orders. Why did she bring us here instead of challenging Apollo herself?"

"I don't know, Tros. But I know I must find my daughter," Echelaos said, adding another log into the fire. "I need her."

"Well, now you speak wisely, o wanax," Tros said, leaning forward toward the fire. "If you need her, we'll find her."

The two men sat at the fire, their horses tethered to a group of large tamarisk trees. This was the place they'd selected to spend the night after yet another day of fruitless search. They'd asked in every village they'd passed, asked every shepherd or hunter, but nobody had seen or heard about Aphrodite. Echelaos had more hope this time as

Prince Assur-Dan had promised to help and sent several groups of scouts to organize the search. In addition, as the Assyrians assumed control of the land following the defeat of the Hittite armies and the death of King Suppiluliuma, the chances of finding Aphrodite improved. Still, locating a young woman in the vast plain of Hatti land was a tough challenge. Echelaos didn't even want to think about bad scenarios; Aphrodite was a strong, skillful girl, able to stand up for herself. Somehow, she had escaped Apollo and avoided Assyrian armies. Surely, she was capable of fending off a few demoralized bands of defeated Hittite soldiers.

"Yes. We'll find her, Tros. Even if we need to spend the whole winter here."

"What about Helen?" Tros asked.

"What about her?"

"Are you still pursuing your wild dream, o wanax? A few moons ago, you were so obsessed with Helen, you were willing to wage war on Troy just to get her back."

"You're right, I was. I might still be. Helen keeps escaping from me, disappearing into thin air just as I reach my hand to grab her. I'll get Helen in the end. This is about my honor. But first, we'll find Aphrodite."

"So, it's not about Helen, the sorceress, the most beautiful woman alive — this is about your pride. Is that true, o wise ruler of Pylos?" Tros pointed a finger at Echelaos.

"I don't know anymore, Tros." Echelaos sighed. "Before the war, it was clear and simple. I knew I had to fight the enemies of Pylos and get my glory on the battlefield. So, when I was promised Helen as a bride, I thought this was my right as a great warrior; she belonged to me, and I had to avenge my honor, vanquishing vile Trojans who'd dared to take what was mine."

"And now?"

"Now it's a lot more complicated. Bloody goat horns, I hate complicated!" Echelaos spat into the fire. "I know I must protect Aphrodite; she's my daughter, even if the gods created her. I have feelings for Eritha, but Helen is somehow crucial; my destiny keeps leading me to her… Nestor had left us, and no one can guide me to make the right choices."

"You have me, Wanax."

"This is true. And thank you for keeping me honest, Tros. Your questions help me to see the situation in a different light."

"This is why I'm with you: to ensure our wise wanax doesn't let his wisdom make a fool of himself." Tros smiled.

"I guess you're right; it *is* about my pride… It's always been about my pride. Now I see how meaningless this mad pursuit of glory is. Nobody remembers Nestor for his glorious victories on the battlefield, even during the days of the great King Minos. People remember Nestor as a just and wise ruler who brought peace, prosperity, and abundance to the land of Pylos. I wish I'd learned more from him when I was young and stupid, like a raging bull."

"Your time will come, Wanax."

"'The final Age of Man is nigh,' my father said. 'The gods are abandoning their broken creation. It is the time for humans to build their own world, the world of iron.' Are you willing to build the world of iron with me, Tros?"

"Of course, Wanax. Not sure I know much about iron, but I'll stand with you until the end if that's what it takes."

"I know that, and I thank you for your loyalty and friendship."

"So, you're not obsessed with Helen anymore? No more chase?" Tros asked.

"I need closure, to see her and ask why she's running away, to fulfill my destiny. You could call me obsessed and stupid, but this is how I am."

"All right, then we'll get back on her trail once we find Aphrodite."

Suddenly, a flash of light brightened the night sky. Athena stood before the camping warriors, owls above her head, a blue bubble forming between the goddess and the humans.

"We must go." Athena's voice thundered above the tamarisks.

"We're still looking for Aphrodite, as you ordered," Echelaos said.

"I know where she is. I'll take you there," Athena said.

"See, I told you we need to leave it to Athena." Tros grinned.

"I'm sorry, o mighty Athena. It's taking us way too long, but Aphrodite was not with the Assyrians, and now—" Echelaos started explaining.

Athena raised her hand with aegis shining valiantly in the night and bellowed, "We have no time. A great battle is looming. Get in the bubble."

Wrapped in the familiar blue cocoon, the two Achaean heroes were transported by the goddess farther west. Echelaos couldn't see beyond the barrier and didn't know exactly where they were, but it took some time to arrive. Finally, the cocoon descended to the ground and disappeared, freeing the two travelers.

Two women rose from their resting places, awoken by the goddess's arrival. The fire was burning strong, caressing the remains of chukar skewered on a thick stick, the savory aroma of roasted bird filling the air around the camp.

"Aphrodite!" Echelaos exclaimed when he discerned the woman in front of him.

"Echelaos!" Aphrodite ran over and embraced her father. "I always knew you'd come for me."

"And I kept searching. We must thank Athena for reuniting us… O great goddess, I'm in your debt, again," Echelaos said, turning to Athena and kneeling.

"Father, this is Korinsia," Aphrodite said, pointing to her fellow traveler, who had come over to join them. "We escaped the Hittite camp in the wake of the Assyrian attack."

"Where were you heading?" Echelaos asked.

"To Troy, of course," Aphrodite responded. "Machaon would help us."

"Enough talk; we're wasting time." Athena's voice reverberated in the air. "I must prepare for the battle."

"What battle?" Echelaos asked. "Can you take us all to Troy? We'll return to Pylos from there."

"This is not possible," Athena said. "The army of Ares has already razed the city to the ground."

"What about Machaon and the Achaeans?" Echelaos asked, a sharp needle suddenly piercing his heart. Machaon's headstrong face, outlined by his curly blond hair, appeared in front of Echelaos. He remembered the will, loyalty, and a sense of duty of the lawagetos, and it suddenly became difficult to breathe.

"They're dead. Ares has decided to eradicate all humans from the face of this planet, and he's marching east to fight the Assyrians."

"Will you fight Ares? Is this the battle you're talking about?" Aphrodite asked.

"This would've been a lot easier, but no. We are facing a new and unknown enemy: the gods of the Assyrians. The ultimate struggle is upon us: Theomachia, the war of the gods."

"What do you mean?" Echelaos asked, suppressing the lump in his throat, clinging to the words of the goddess, trying to ground himself in the present moment.

"This clash will decide the fate of our worlds, both of the gods and of humans. We must prepare for the worst. None of us might survive this confrontation."

CHAPTER

EIGHTEEN

Khay suffered from the sweat running down his forehead, but it was impossible to wipe it off as the mask of Wadjet covered his face. It provided some comfort and ventilation, it was true; but the scorching heat made him perspire so excessively he was almost drinking his sweat accumulating inside of the mask. Khay raised his shovel and took another bite at the yellow sand covering this stretch of the Way of Horus. He looked at the sun in the blue sky, and thanked Ra that it was almost winter and the hot, arid breath of the Sinai Desert had started to cool down. The army was on the march north to Canaan, and many thousands of the finest warriors of Egypt needed water as they traveled the Way of Horus.

"Hey, keep digging!" Addaya shouted at Meketre, who stood, leaning on his shovel, heavily panting. Meketre only raised his hand and made a slow and indolent gesture as if trying to drive away an annoying mosquito.

The weather had recently started to change for the better, but the sun was still blazing. The three soldiers toiled in significant hardship, suffering from its sizzling rays, even though they wore only short kilts and sandals. And the masks of Wadjet, of course. Khay smiled, recalling how General Hewernef had presided over equipping his soldiers with this new and confusing piece of armor. People didn't want to wear it, taking the masks off on any convenient occasion, and only the threats of the priests and the need to interact with the infected people had gradually changed their behavior.

"Why do we still wear this dung?" Meketre finally said, standing still. "I can't work like this; I'm drinking sweat. We cured everyone, didn't we? Aten is defeated; the general himself said so. So, why do I need to suffer?" With these words, Meketre threw away his shovel, raised his hands, and pulled away the mask, uncovering his face.

"Let Apep hump this piece of dung," he said, dropping the mask to the sand and kicking it. This act of defiance made Khay uncomfortable; everything he'd had to endure since that fateful night in the tomb of Akhenaten was still fresh in his memory. They might have extinguished the infection and defeated Aten at Thebes and Pi-Ramesse, but the danger was still lurking, as Hem-netjer Nefer-Setekh had warned.

"Be careful, Meketre," Khay said. "We don't want Aten to return."

"Wadjet will protect us," Meketre said. "As for me, I'm done with this."

Addaya shrugged and raised his shovel. "Just keep digging, would you?" he said. "We have to finish soon."

The three soldiers continued digging, Meketre smiling triumphantly. Khay was still uneasy and deliberated on what to do. I should probably tell the Greatest of the Fifty, he thought. Neferhotep, their immediate commander, was strict and expected complete obedience to the orders.

"I witnessed what Aten does to the people first-hand," Khay said. "I don't want this to happen to you, Meketre. Please don't expose yourself to Aten's vile spores."

"Shut your bloody mouth, Khay. You set Aten free, and now we must suffer — because of you, you piece of dung!" Meketre lifted his shovel and aimed the tool at Khay's neck.

"Are you infected? Keep digging, you son of a rat!" Addaya yelled. He outranked both Khay and Meketre and was responsible for completing the well by the end of the day.

"What's going on here?" An imperious voice interrupted the brewing quarrel. Khay turned his head and saw their Greatest of the Fifty, Neferhotep, on horseback, surrounded by the soldiers from their Fifty on foot. Behind Neferhotep were other officers on their horses. Farther away, there were several chariots, among which was the one belonging to General Hewernef himself. The striking feature of the group was that none of the soldiers or commanders wore masks of Wadjet. *Perhaps Meketre is right*, Khay thought. *The danger is gone; now we can proceed as a normal army.*

"Nothing, Commander. Digging a well," Addaya said.

"Why is this one without a mask?" Neferhotep pointed to Meketre with his sickle sword.

"Aten is defeated, Commander," Meketre said. "I can't work in this heat with the mask on."

"Good thought, soldier," Neferhotep said. "You will be rewarded for your intelligence and savvy. You two," he shifted his sword toward Khay and Addaya, "remove your masks. The general has given the order to stop this madness. We are an army, we have to fight, and these masks are not helpful."

Addaya sighed and removed his mask. "Whatever, just let me finish this damn well…" he whispered.

Khay hesitated. The order was clear, but he couldn't forget Aten that quickly.

"What's wrong with you, soldier? Are you deaf?" Neferhotep said.

"I'd rather not remove it, Commander," Khay said.

"Do you dare to disobey me? General's orders, I said!" Neferhotep waved to the soldiers who accompanied him. The soldiers quickly approached Khay, grabbed his hands, and tore off the mask. Khay tried to resist but in vain.

When the soldiers finally let him go, he raised his head and looked intently at Neferhotep. Not believing his eyes, he noticed a white substance in the corner of Neferhotep's mouth.

"Addaya, run, they're infected!" Khay screamed at the top of his lungs, but it was too late. The cloud of spores descended on the three soldiers while the newcomers observed the futile struggle of the victims.

Suddenly, Khay felt a strange lightness in his body, as if he was about to fly. All his fears seemed distant and insignificant; he realized he'd been wasting his life without meaning and purpose, a toy in the hands of circumstances. His legs weakened, and he crouched on the yellow sand. The lightness became overpowering, and he felt such happiness as he'd never experienced in his life. He wanted to embrace everyone, every soldier, even the general himself. They were part of something huge and very important, something that would change the world.

While overwhelmed by these delusions, Khay could somehow see everything around him in minute detail. Neferhotep and his soldiers stepped aside, and the bulky figure of General Hewernef stood in front of Khay. The general wore leather armor with bronze platelets woven into it. The Eye of Ra in his empty socket pierced through Khay's brain, filling him with awe and submission. Suddenly, the world around Khay started to spin around the Eye of Ra, which was the only stable object in his view. The last thing Khay heard before losing consciousness were the words of the general: "These were the last ones. Now we march north. Aten demands a new home."

#

Bakenkhonsu, High Priest of Amen, drove the chariot through the yellow sand of the Sinai Desert. The road was barely visible, and the horses struggled to maintain the pace the priest wanted. He looked at his companion standing on a platform next to him. The wrinkles on Nefer-Setekh's face and hands became more pronounced as myriads of tiny sand grains got inside the roughness of his skin.

"How long can you hold?" Bakenkhonsu asked.

"As long as needed," Nefer-Setekh answered.

Bakenkhonsu shook his head. The old man was too feeble for a mad race across the desert without food and with just one flask of water between them. Bakenkhonsu looked at half-closed green eyes of Nefer-Setekh, his face a grimace of suffering. The high priest of Wadjet was persisting by sheer force of will.

The high priest of Amen touched his dry lips with his tongue. There was one last drop of water in the flask, but he couldn't afford to stop and search for more. They'd barely escaped the army possessed by Aten. It was only by sheer luck that they'd met the unaffected soldiers who'd helped them get on the chariot. For all he knew, the hounds of Aten were probably on their heels; every second was precious.

"We must reach the outpost," Bakenkhonsu said, "and warn the garrison. Then we can drink and eat and rest."

"I might not survive that long," Nefer-Setekh said, suddenly accepting his struggles. His voice was very calm, and his eyes closed. "I'm too old; I did what I could. Leave me here."

"No way. We're gonna make it," Bakenkhonsu said, reaching inside his leopard-skin cloak for the flask. He opened the container and brought it to the lips of the high priest of Wadjet. Nefer-Setekh's lips were gray and dry, with lots of little fissures.

"You should keep it for yourself," Nefer-Setekh said.

"Drink." Bakenkhonsu emptied the flask into the old man's mouth. "It shouldn't be very far."

"What about the horses?" Nefer-Setekh asked, opening his eyes for a moment.

"They must endure."

The sky was deep blue with no trace of a cloud, and the yellow desert contrasted that almost oceanic depth, underlining it. There was nothing else, no other colors, just two infinite, almost two-dimensional sheets of blue and yellow. Bakenkhonsu knew there must be dunes and hills around. Still, his mind could not register anything but the two endless oceans.

Suddenly, a black dot appeared within the endless ocean of yellow. Bakenkhonsu looked intently, trying to identify what it was, when three more black dots pierced the sea of deep blue.

"Vultures." Bakenkhonsu pointed to the sky. "We need to hurry."

Nefer-Setekh opened his eyes and breathed heavily. His gaze was fixed on the black dot in front of them, a strange feature of the yellow landscape.

"Water," he said.

"I know, but we just used the last drop," Bakenkhonsu replied.

"No, it's a well. Look ahead. We must stop." Nefer-Setekh pointed to the black dot, which had increased in size.

"You're right. This must be one of the wells the army dug."

"We must stop for water," Nefer-Setekh repeated.

"Too dangerous; Aten's servants could be right behind."

"I don't see anyone. Do you? Stop, for the glory of Amen," Nefer-Setekh said fervently, tapping into the last reserves of his strength.

"We're close; let's keep going."

"No," Nefer-Setekh said and jumped out of the chariot as they got closer to the well, rolling on the sand. His kalasiris of blue and green added a strange, colorful feature to the vastness of the yellow sea.

"Are you out of your mind?" Bakenkhonsu exclaimed but stopped the chariot. Nefer-Setekh, having no strength to stand up, crawled toward the well on his knees and elbows. By the time Bakenkhonsu approached the great priest of Wadjet, the old man had pulled the chain from the water hole and was drinking greedily.

"Is it any good?" Bakenkhonsu asked.

Nefer-Setekh finished drinking, dropped the chain down the well, and opened his mouth to answer his companion. Instead of human speech, however, he produced a gurgling sound. Nefer-Setekh fell prostrate on the sand, convulsing, white foam with streaks of blood pouring from his mouth and his ears.

"Hem-netjer!" Bakenkhonsu screamed and rushed to help the old priest.

"Stop," a loud, commanding voice ordered from behind.

Surprised, Bakenkhonsu turned his head and observed a giant green cobra next to the chariot, three strange birds circling her head.

"O great Wadjet, please help your high priest," Bakenkhonsu implored, kneeling before the goddess.

Two birds flew toward the motionless body of Nefer-Setekh, descended upon him, and the goddess announced, "He is dead. His heart was too weak and couldn't endure the fight with Aten."

"Aten? The well is poisoned?"

"It's not a water well. It's an entrance to the underground body of Aten. It spreads from here north, and the army carries his spores. How did that happen? I gave you the tools to defeat Aten."

"O great Wadjet, please have mercy on me!" Bakenkhonsu hid his face in the sand. "We've cured everyone in Thebes, Pi-Ramesse, and along the Nile. The great pharaoh sent General Hewernef to buttress the fortresses of Canaan against the Assyrian danger." Bakenkhonsu spoke fast; his tongue didn't obey him, and his fingers trembled.

"Then, on the march, the general himself was possessed by Aten, and after him, the whole army. We've escaped at the last moment."

"Where is the army marching?"

"Aten wants a new abode outside of Egypt. That's what I've heard," Bakenkhonsu said.

"I understand. We exterminated the mycelium in the south, and the organism is fleeing to safety."

"I don't understand, o great Wadjet... Can you help us wretched humans? We cannot defeat the god ourselves."

"Yes. I'm your protector, and I'll eradicate the parasite," Wadjet said as her birds landed near the well. The water hole became engulfed in green light for a moment, and after the light dispersed, there was a smooth black circle in its place.

"I've sealed this one, and my drones will seal the rest of them," Wadjet said. "If you want to stop the army of Aten, you must come with me."

"Of course, o great goddess, I obey anything you command."

"I'll take you north, and you'll help me cure these wretched humans possessed by the vile parasite," Wadjet said. "But first I must defeat a different enemy."

"Another god? Stronger than Aten?"

"Yes. Many gods are gathering in the same place for the final battle. And if we lose, Aten is the last thing you should worry about."

CHAPTER
NINETEEN

Ehli-Nikkal approached the entrance to Hattusa, raised her hand, and commanded, "Open the gate!" She rode a black stallion and wore a simple black cloak; her raven hair fell freely on her shoulders, showing the impact of several days' journey with no stops.

"Who are you?" a soldier asked from the parapet.

"Ehli-Nikkal, your former princess and now the queen."

Ehli waited motionless before the gate, not allowing herself to show emotion. Her soul was empty; the past few days' events were too much even for her. Her tears had dried up during the frantic ride across the plains and away from the Assyrian patrols. Nevertheless, she knew she needed to play her part until the bitter end, and that was precisely what she'd come here to do.

Ehli looked at the cyclopean masonry of Hattusa's fortification and two gorgeous stone lions guarding the entrance. A fleeting thought came to her mind: All this will soon turn to dust. So will the Assyrians and whoever else comes after them. Such is the circle of life, she reminded herself. She knew the end of her physical existence was near, but it didn't trouble her. Ehli-Nikkal, queen of the Hittites, was ready to complete her journey alongside her kingdom.

After a few moments, the massive gate opened, two stone lions at each side of the entrance looking on as if in surprise. A few soldiers came out on foot to greet the visitor. One of them, in the middle, wearing the signs of a commander, took a few steps forward and fell on one knee, lowering his head.

"Welcome to Hattusa, Princess Ehli. I am Kadu, the commander of the garrison. Why are you alone?"

"The army is defeated, and the king is dead. I escaped at the last moment."

"We'll organize a feast in honor of King Suppiluliuma," Kadu said after a long moment of silence, "and fight until our last breath. This is the least we can do."

"Yes, you will," Ehli answered confidently, looking at the lion statues. She thought about the years these lions had been here, the events they'd witnessed, the people they'd observed passing by. Always motionless, silent, indifferent spectators. Ehli felt a connection to these stone figures; she realized she was like them, a distant witness, a stage on which time performed its eternal dance.

"Where's the rest of the army, Princess Ehli?" Kadu asked.

"They're all dead." Ehli looked up to the sky as if trying to find the fallen Hittite heroes. "They fought the gods of Assur and perished without a trace. We didn't prepare to face the gods, only the humans…"

"You speak in riddles, Princess," Kadu said.

"Queen," Ehli corrected him. "But it doesn't matter now. The Assyrians will be here any moment, with their evil gods. So we must defend the city, even if the odds are overwhelming."

"Yes, my queen, we must," Kadu said. "You are exhausted — please allow us to escort you to your rooms."

"We have no time," Ehli said. "I'd like to inspect the fortifications and the weapons. But you're right, let's get inside."

Two soldiers approached Ehli's horse and led him inside the city, holding the reins. Kadu walked beside the queen.

"The garrison has five hundred soldiers, most of them archers, but some infantry as well," Kadu said. "We also have fifty-two chariots."

"The chariots will be useless," Ehli said, getting off the horse and looking at the walls surrounding the city. "The Assyrians have at least ten-fold advantage, plus tens of thousands of infantry and archers. So our best chance is to defend the walls."

"Yes, my queen." Kadu nodded. "The walls are fortified, archers are in every battlement, we have lots of arrows and naphtha. The enemy will pay dearly for our lives."

"Civilians?"

"I gave the order to leave the city once you told us all is lost. They'll disperse in the northern fields to escape the fate of the conquered."

"Good. I hope they'll have time to get away," Ehli said as they ascended the battlement. "Now, we must figure out what to do about the gods."

"What gods, Queen Ehli? You speak in riddles again."

"I don't understand myself. The Assyrians boasted the gods fight on their side, which I discarded as just taunts. But then I saw with my own eyes how the blue fog engulfed the battlefield, and the brave Hittite warriors turned into a revolting sludge. What was that, tell me, Kadu?"

"The ways of the gods are incomprehensible to humans. I don't know how to fight the gods of Assur, my queen. I only hope that the gods of Hatti will interfere and drive this eastern menace back where they came from."

"Indeed, this is our only hope," Ehli said. "Although I wouldn't count on that. The gods of Hatti just let the king and the flower of the Hittite army perish. So why would they come to *our* help?"

"As I said, the ways of the gods are incomprehensible." Kadu shook his head. "We shall meet the Assyrian armies here, at the walls of Hattusa, and let them storm the city if they dare."

"The words of a true warrior." Ehli smiled, but then the corners of her mouth turned down.

"What else do you think we should do?" Kadu asked.

"Nothing much," Ehli said. "Make sure the soldiers are well rested and well fed before the battle, but you know that without my advice." She took Kadu by the hand. "Whatever happens, don't lose hope; remember, this too shall pass. You are a loyal servant of Hattusa and her people, and this is what counts."

"Thank you, Queen Ehli." Kadu bowed. "Would you like to go to your quarters?"

"No, I'll go to the shrine; I need to find the answers about the gods of Assur. I'll follow your advice and try to persuade the gods of Hatti to fight on our side."

"Their help would be most welcome, my queen."

"Don't count on that, Kadu," Ehli said. "Be ready to exact the highest price for your blood. And rejoice; we shall all meet great King Suppiluliuma in the underworld very soon."

#

Queen Ehli-Nikkal sat on the ground next to a giant statue of her grandfather Tudhaliya in the Shrine of Creation. The musky smell of galbanum enveloped her, reminding of the day Davke had explained the cycle of renewal and taught her how to access the memories of the dead. Black clouds were advancing from the north, thunder foreshadowing the doom ready to fall on the ancient kingdom. Ehli looked into an image of the god Sharruma driving the sword into the ground. Now she understood the uniqueness of this place, the convergence of the worlds, and the energy one could muster. Ehli-Nikkal had walked a long and lonely road from the scared child initiated by her grandmother into the mysteries of the cosmos to an accomplished and wise woman, aware of her strengths and shortcomings. She knew her place in the eternal loop of renewal: today was her time to leave this plane of existence, to advance to the next phase. And the Shrine of Creation was the most natural and familiar site for this transition. Ehli was prepared, but she was also ready to stand her ground and defend Hattusa to the end.

She breathed in the smell of galbanum and looked into her grandfather's eyes. The statue towered above the shrine like the ancient and unmovable guard, instilling peace and tranquility into Ehli's heart.

A lonely figure of the soldier in full armor appeared at the entrance: Kadu. The officer bowed and said, "It is time, my queen. The enemy is approaching."

"Go, do what you need to do," Ehli replied.

"Let the gods be with us," Kadu said, turned around, and left.

Ehli could feel the tension in the air as if the city communicated with her. Like a wounded animal surrounded by dogs, Hattusa prepared for its last stand. The enemy forces were closing in, and the small garrison had no chance. It was the last day of the great city, which only a few moons ago was the master of the vast plains and forests stretching from Assyria to Ahhiyawa. *Such is the nature of things*, Ehli told herself. The cycle of renewal, the continuous reshuffling of the cosmos. She knew what had happened before her time and started to understand what would transpire after she'd moved on. She'd played her role in the cycle during the brief episode that was her life, but she knew that her role had changed now. She became the witness, the eternal spectator, the indifferent, impartial observer. Still, there was one more act left for her to perform.

Ehli stood, closed her eyes, and raised her hands, feeling the cosmic energy permeating her essence. Her fingers started to tremble, and her head shook violently. Still, she stood with her hands in the air, drawing on more and more force, thinking of herself as another statue next to the image of Tudhaliya. Ehli's beautiful black hair rose as if each strand had become alive. At this moment, the thunderstorm finally arrived at Hattusa, engulfing the sun and soaking the dry plain with a torrential downpour.

Ehli opened her eyes, her pupils dilated to the extreme. She took a confident step forward, dropped on one knee, looked up in the air, and shrieked with an inhuman, high-pitched voice: "Nerikkil!"

As Ehli knelt by the rock with its ancient carving, she felt energy overflowing from her into the Primordial Entity. She was the vessel and the guide; Nerikkil was her weapon — the weapon of last resort. Ehli knew that wielding this weapon would most likely exhaust and destroy her, but she didn't care. This was her destiny.

Establishing a connection with the Primordial, Ehli felt Nerikkil was consuming the energy she was sending its way, becoming stronger. The old mycelium within and around Hattusa suddenly awakened, sending spores everywhere. The feedback from Nerikkil filled Ehli with exhilarating excitement. Her senses were magnified, and her perception of herself vanished: they were now one entity, one organism, driven by the primitive desire to feed, grow, and multiply.

Through Nerikkil's vast, connected network, Ehli was aware of what was happening around the city. The Assyrians had brought tens of thousands of people and most of their chariots to Hattusa's walls. But to the organism she had become, these were all easy targets, prey ready to be converted and serve its new master.

She felt how the spores dispersed around the field, engulfing, descending on the enemy soldiers, oblivious to the danger. The rain made the spreading easier, since the spores could freely float within the vast network of streams the plain had become. She was every spore and every part of the network, stretching through the enormous distances between the northern sea, the plain of Hattusa, and the eastern rivers. She was alive again, rising, ready to rule the ancient lands as she had in times immemorial before the human sorcerers had confined her to a sedentary existence underground. But now she'd freed herself to unite all humans and animals into one infinite, eternal structure.

As the spores started to enter the Assyrian soldiers, Ehli rejoiced, experiencing the growth and strengthening of her body with the energy from the shrine flowing into her new branches. She'd never felt such an exhilarating emotion. It was pure joy and triumph.

When the enemy soldiers started to succumb to the organism, Ehli sensed how the entity devoured their minds and consciousness. This process added to their collective unity, making it even more powerful. Somewhere deep within her essence, she kept part of herself under control, guarding it against Nerikkil, understanding she couldn't let the Primordial roam free. However, the more vital the organism grew, the harder it was for Ehli to control it from within. Help arrived unwelcomed and from an unexpected direction.

At this point, thousands of Assyrians had fallen victim to the spores of the ancient entity. Suddenly, blue fog encompassed the area where the enemy soldiers, now controlled by Nerikkil, turned on their own forces, spreading the infection further. The blue mist, dispersing across the field, selectively targeted converted units. Ehli felt how these newly created branches didn't just die but disappeared into nothingness as if they'd never existed. The two chain reactions now ran in parallel deep within the Assyrian army. The first was the expansion of the number of soldiers controlled by the Primordial, and the second was extinguishing these newly created converts by the Assyrian gods. As the non-impacted warriors discerned what was going on and started to flee the danger, the first process ended abruptly, and the second got the upper hand. Soon, as the remainder of the army separated itself from the horrible events unraveling on the battlefield, Ehli realized that all attempts to subdue the fog were in vain. The mist provided no feedback; it had no consciousness or matter to deal with. The gods of Assur were immune to every weapon Ehli knew and had at her disposal. She felt how Nerikkil recoiled and retreated, losing all the new branches and energy she'd channeled into the Primordial.

The landscape around Hattusa was now surreal. Thousands of Assyrian soldiers, transformed into a revolting pink goo, were being washed away by the rain from the city walls, and the thin blue fog soared above these sorry remains.

Ehli maintained a connection to Nerikkil but was also fully aware of herself. She felt the exhaustion of the organism she was guiding; the channel she'd opened at the Shrine of Creation was closing.

In the meantime, the blue fog advanced to the walls, engulfing the defenders on the battlements. It was not a fight but a systematic elimination of Hattusa's last guardians. Sensing that the Primordial withdrew even farther, back to the safety of the mountain caves and passages, Ehli shut down the connection with the organism. Drawing on her last energy resources, she collapsed to the ground next to the stone monolith of her grandfather, which was vacantly observing the fate of his city and his descendant.

Preparing to exit, Ehli looked up into the sky. The black clouds had started to disperse, the rain slowed down, and she caught a little ray of sunshine piercing the darkness. The smell of fresh grass added to the aroma of galbanum. *Perhaps I'll become part of this cloud,* Ehli thought. Somehow, even though she broke the connection with Nerikkil, she could still feel everything that transpired around her, as if she was soaring around the city: pure awareness, pure consciousness. Ehli didn't care about her body or even the city anymore. Their fate was already sealed and unimportant, a fleeting moment in the grand cosmic story she was part of. Her humanity pushed her to pursue goals that now seemed minuscule and trivial. Ehli smiled, finally understanding the words of wisdom her grandmother had taught her: everything is part of the eternal cycle of renewal and transformation. Princess Ehli-Nikkal was but the ephemeral wave within the vast cosmic sea; the sea she was ready to return to.

Suddenly, with the last remnant of her consciousness still attached to her body, Ehli registered the figure of the Assyrian soldier running toward her.

"Helen! Don't die; I need you!" the soldier screamed, kneeling in front of her body, grasping her hands and taking her head in his palms.

"It's too late," she whispered. "Who are you?"

"Echelaos of Pylos."

"Echelaos…" she repeated. "Don't despair; you'll understand. My time's up, but your time is now."

"What do you mean? Stay; I want to be with you."

"We're already together, always have been, and will always be."

"Bloody goat horns! Stay with me!"

"The Age of Iron is nigh. I'll see you on the other side," Ehli said and closed her eyes.

#

"More wine?" Tros asked, finishing his drink and reaching out for the jar. "The gods must have access to the best vineyards." He grinned, pouring wine into the chalice.

"Yes," Echelaos answered, handing his cup to the charioteer. "Today, we drink. Tomorrow might be the end of everything."

"You're still grieving the death of Helen," Tros said, pouring the drink for Echelaos. "Let the gods worry about tomorrow; we can't do rat's piss about it. But you need to get over your obsession, Wanax."

"You're right. But later; for now, let's just drink. I'm lost and don't want to think about anything."

"No better time than now. You need clarity, Wanax. You can't lead without clarity."

"Tomorrow. We'll worry about that tomorrow." Echelaos shook his head. "Today, we drink."

"As you wish, Wanax."

The two warriors sat inside the sanctuary Athena had created for them in the middle of the tamarisk grove, close to the battlefield where the gods would fight it out the following day. The shelter looked like a massive bubble, glowing a gentle light blue from the inside but invisible from the outside. Night was upon them; Aphrodite and Korinsia were already sleeping. It was comfortably warm in the sanctuary, so they didn't even need a fire. Athena had also provided the four travelers with food and wine before disappearing into the night, instructing them to stay inside until the battle's outcome was decided.

Echelaos's thoughts were in disarray. He knew he had to process the past few days' events: the fortunate conclusion of the search for Aphrodite, Athena's revelations, the war of the gods, and the death of Helen. Aphrodite had told him about her encounter with Helen and Korinsia, and Echelaos had finally seen the Hittite princess as a human being, not a prize to catch. An then she'd died, he was too late to save her... It was a watershed moment. Tros was right; he needed clarity and strength to withstand the upcoming storm, to lead with purpose. But he couldn't distinguish what was truly important for him, couldn't decide what to focus on. So Echelaos kept drinking, postponing the resolution until the next day.

"Do you think she'll win?" Tros asked.

"She said Zeus is on her side. And Ares with his magical army. They must."

"You've seen what the gods of Assur are capable of. I don't know…" Tros shook his head, imbibing more of the delectable Cretan wine.

"Come on, have some faith." Echelaos patted Tros on the shoulder. "Athena's been good to us, and she sounded confident."

"She also said to run away as far as we can if she's defeated." Tros leaned back. "For there will be no hope in sight."

"Pour me another drink." Echelaos extended his arm with the cup. "Whatever is destined will happen. We'll see tomorrow." He pointed to a peculiar device the goddess had left for them to observe the battle. The device consisted of a large screen with several mechanisms attached to it. Athena had shown them what to do to see the battle from the sky, using the sight of her owls and projecting it onto the screen. It was pure magic, but Echelaos had learned not to question the goddess. Tros, on the other hand, had spent a lot of time studying the mysterious apparatus, clicking his tongue and touching various handles and buttons. He still didn't trust Athena and kept reminding Echelaos of it at every opportunity.

"It was a mistake," Tros said.

"What?"

"Coming back to Assur-Dan. It wasn't our fight, and Pylos shouldn't be involved. The Hittites were already vanquished."

"I needed to find Helen."

"And you have." Echelaos nodded. "Did it give you the closure you were looking for?"

"I don't know. It's all so confusing…" Echelaos rubbed his eyes and drank. "I think it did. I just need to process it."

The two men sat silently for several minutes, watching the stars and sipping wine. Then, finally, Echelaos turned to his charioteer and said, "Helen knew."

"Knew what?"

"About the Age of Iron. About what Nestor told me before the war. How could she know?"

"How could Nestor know?" Tros asked.

"Nestor was old and wise. He saw things nobody else saw."

"Well, perhaps Helen saw them, too. People called her the sorceress, after all."

"She said my time is now. And the more I think about it, the more I understand they both talked about the same thing. Times are changing; the gods are at war. The new age will come after the Theomachia. And, somehow, I'm the one at the helm of this ship."

"That's why you need clarity, Wanax."

"As I told Father, I don't have the wisdom. I'm not ready."

"And what did he say?"

"He said *it is not wisdom that counts, but character.*"

"You know he was right. You have character, Wanax. You are overthinking." Tros reached out for the wine jar. "And it's my job to put your head in order."

"Even you can't unravel this ugly mess." Echelaos laughed.

"Let's try. What do you worry about right now?"

"What tomorrow brings, of course. The end of the world."

"Can you do anything about it?"

"Not rat's piss."

"Well, is there anything you *could* do something about?"

"Aphrodite. The girl sleeping next to her. You. People of Pylos. I'm asking myself, what can I do to protect them and lead them through the storm?"

"That's a good start, Wanax. The clarity you're looking for."

"But Helen's still on my mind. She told me we're already together and always will be. What in the bloody abyss of Hades was she talking about?"

"Hump me if I know. But you shouldn't worry about it for the same reason — you can't do rat's piss about it, and it's not important. So stop worrying and start leading."

"Yes, once I sober up tomorrow morning." Echelaos smiled. "And we witness the biggest carnage of our age, the slaughter of the gods."

"And when the gods kill each other, your time shall come, o great and divine wanax." Tros bowed, grinning.

"At some point, Athena will kick your ass for everything you said about the gods, Tros."

"Nah, she wouldn't bother. Besides, she might still need us to get her out of the Assyrian trouble. Who knows? We could be the deciding factor in the gods' war."

"Let's drink to that!"

CHAPTER

TWENTY

Echelaos looked outside through the transparent walls of their shelter. The early dawn was upon the tamarisk grove they hid in; dew covered the grass and the wildflowers underneath the delicate trees. The view was so peaceful, it was hard to believe the battle that would define the world's fate was about to commence.

As if in response to his thoughts, Athena's screen came alive and started to project a bird's-eye view of the battlefield. At first, it was difficult to discern what was happening, since the rising sun hadn't completely dissipated the darkness of the night. But then Echelaos noticed the advancing force menacingly moving east in the direction of Hattusa. And what the army this was! Echelaos couldn't believe his eyes. The eerie metal beasts spearheaded the effort, their large, semicircular bodies glistering silver in the rays of the morning sun. They had no legs or wheels but gently floated above the green vegetation of the plain. Echelaos counted several hundred of these monsters and then lost the count.

"What's that?" A girl's voice interrupted his train of thought. Korinsia woke up and stood beside him, pointing to the giant tower amid the formation.

"Heracles; Zoltes told us about him." Tros joined their conversation. "Looks exactly like the Thracian described."

"Indeed," Echelaos said, licking his lips with a dry tongue. There was no trace of last night's wine excesses, just an annoying feeling between his stomach and chest as if something angular and hairy was stuck there. He wanted to take his bow, find his chariot, and charge into the midst of the fight, but there was nothing he could do, just observe and hope for the best.

In the rear of the advancing force, behind the contingent of hideous metal birds, a large disk floated, slowly rotating, glowing angry red.

"Ares," Aphrodite whispered, looking at the strange object.

"How do you know?" Korinsia asked.

"I just know." Aphrodite shrugged.

Behind this frightening host of monstrosities, a mass of human warriors followed. It was a motley army of all kinds of fighters: light Thracian infantry with their small, round shields, long swords, and javelins; heavily armored Achaeans with large shields covering most of their bodies; and even some chariots with archers, ready to engage their enemies.

"Where's Athena? And Zeus?" Echelaos turned to Aphrodite. "Do you sense them?"

"They're here," Aphrodite said. "We can't see them, but they're here."

"You just know?" Echelaos asked.

"Yes," Aphrodite said, not moving her gaze from the screen.

As the army of Ares marched forward, the Assyrian formations appeared on the horizon, the sun rising behind their line of chariots and archers.

"The Assyrian chariotry is highly superior," Tros noted.

"I don't think it matters." Echelaos shook his head. "This is the battle of the gods, not humans."

As if hearing his comment, the advancing army stopped. In the next moment, the solemn silence of the morning was torn to pieces by the rays of blue light the metal beasts unleashed on their enemies. The mysterious birds of Ares joined the fight in another second, shooting the deadly beams from above. Within a brief period, the front units of the Assyrian army ceased to exist, along with a large part of the chariotry.

"Bloody goat horns!" Tros exclaimed, shaking his head. "And she wasn't sure about the outcome?"

"It's only mortals, not the gods," Echelaos said.

The Assyrian army fled from the fire, dispersing across the plain, with most of the infantry and a few remaining chariots falling back. At this moment, a thin, blue fog started to rise from the middle of the decimated Assyrian host. Metal monsters on the ground and birds in the air switched their aim to this new menace. However, their weapons inflicted no apparent damage on the blue mist, which started engulfing the magical beasts.

Korinsia gasped and took Tros by the hand, squeezing his fingers. The warrior embraced the girl, caressing her hair and whispering soothing words into her ear. This calmed her, and she turned her head back to the screen.

The battle, meanwhile, came to a stalemate. Neither the fog nor the metal beasts could inflict any damage on each other, while the human contingents of both armies retreated and observed the fight between forces they did not understand.

"What's going on?" Tros said.

"The gods are the gods," Echelaos said. "Invincible even to each other."

At this moment, the red disk of Ares descended into the midst of his bizarre host and started to rotate much faster, sending arrows of red and blue into the fog. Heracles also advanced, carrying giant boulders and throwing them at the enemy, creating huge craters, and shooting beams of light at the blue mist. But, to Echelaos's surprise, none of this affected the fog, which advanced farther, ultimately enveloping Ares and causing him to slow his rotation. At this moment, two more disks appeared at the place of the divine struggle, one green and another silver.

"Zeus and Athena," Aphrodite said confidently. "Their time is now."

As the red disk of Ares completely vanished within the fog, its onslaught of projectiles and blasts ceasing, Zeus and Athena came closer to the blue mist. A thin thread, glowing with bright golden light, connected the two disks. A red, hairy ball with a pitch-black center was suspended in the middle of the string. As if sensing the new enemy, the fog moved in the direction of the thread, leaving what appeared to be the sorry remains of Ares on the field. The angry, rotating red disk was no more, turning into a disgusting grayish liquid mass.

"What in the name of Zeus is that?" Tros said, pointing at the gray sludge.

"Ares is no more," Aphrodite answered, squinting.

Echelaos was so immersed in the standoff between the gods that he overlooked the moment when the metal beasts had stopped moving and shooting. Heracles stood motionless like an enormous mountain, and the birds of Ares fell to the ground.

"What, Ares is defeated just like that?" Tros shook his head. "His army is nothing without their god?"

"Looks like that," Echelaos said. "But that's not all." He pointed at the screen, where the blue fog encountered the golden cord connecting Zeus and Athena.

In the area where the red ball suspended on a thread came into contact with the gods of Assur, the fiery halo around the object noticeably thickened. At the same time, the mist started to rotate outside the ball as if being pulled into a funnel. Spaces opened within the fog, now divided into two large clouds. One portion of what used to be a continuous blanket circled the hairy ball, gradually disappearing within the divine abyss. The second portion, however, moved closer to Athena. The green disk of the goddess ascended higher to avoid the blue fog rapidly approaching her. This maneuver, however, led to the overextension of the golden thread connecting Athena to the fiery ball devouring the mist. The string was becoming thinner and thinner. Echelaos held his breath, expecting it to tear off completely, releasing the gods of Assur to continue their rampage and destruction.

The silver disk of Zeus, counteracting the impact, started to move up as well, returning the thread to its former shape. Fortunately, by this time, the portion of the fog that came into contact with the ball completely disappeared inside this magical object, so Zeus was free to fly to Athena's help.

The two disks soared above the battlefield, the red ball still in between them, connected to the gods by the reestablished golden cord. The blue fog, covering a significantly smaller area, was underneath them. At this moment, in a desperate attempt to help their gods, the Assyrian army came into motion, archers sending their arrows in the direction of the two flying disks. This attack, however, had no impact on the Achaean gods whatsoever. Moving faster than the blue fog, they positioned the red ball right above the mist and started to descend, trying to catch the rest of their enemy within the magical vortex.

"Look, the Thracians are attacking," Tros said.

The human contingent of the army of Ares ran around the area where the gods were engaged in a deadly fight. Completing the move, they attacked Assyrian chariots from the flanks. This maneuver was familiar to Echelaos: the Thracians were injuring Assyrian horses by throwing javelins at them and eliminating the archers with the help of their slashing and thrusting swords.

"This is the end of the Assyrian army," Echelaos said. "O, how I want to be there!" He punched his clenched fists against each other.

The Assyrian vehicles started to retreat chaotically, trying to reach their infantry line. Then, suddenly, a single chariot moved forward. It was the most richly adorned, having two spearmen and one archer in addition to a charioteer. The chariot charged right into the remnants of the blue fog, ignoring the Thracians.

"This is the king; is he insane?" Tros asked.

The tall figure of the archer wearing the royal robe, mitre on his head, got off the chariot, holding a sword in one hand and a lion-headed mace in the other. Ninurta stopped within a few steps of the vortex and hit the golden thread repeatedly with his weapons, without any visible effect. Unfortunately, this action brought him dangerously close to the red ball: enveloped by the patches of blue fog, the king of Assyria disappeared, pulled into the vortex alongside his gods.

"Such a fitting end," Tros said. "He was so obsessed with his gods and perished with them."

"Godspeed." Echelaos grinned.

Then another chariot separated from the fleeing Assyrian masses. *Assur-Dan.* Echelaos recognized the archer inside the vehicle. Throwing his bow and raising his arms in the air, Assur-Dan stepped out of the chariot, kneeling, lowering his head to the ground in the universal sign of surrender.

Seeing this, one of the Thracian soldiers ran toward the surrendering prince. The right half of the warrior's body, including his head and face, was covered with shining silver armor.

"Is that who I think it is?" Echelaos pointed at the warrior with surprise.

"Indeed. What in the bloody abyss of Hades happened to him?" Tros responded.

Zoltes approached Assur-Dan and raised his sword, aiming at the bare neck of the prince, ready to behead his enemy. As he was about to swing the blade, however, an invisible force held his hand back. The green disk of Athena appeared above the two opponents, preventing the bloodshed.

"The battle must stop." The loud voice thundered above the plain. "I am Zeus, your god, commanding you to obey."

"We've won." Echelaos raised his fist in the air, then turned around and embraced Aphrodite. "We can return to Pylos."

"Ares is dead. The gods of Assur are destroyed. It's time for peace," Zeus proclaimed.

Zoltes, stepping back, lowered his sword. The Thracians stopped pursuing retreating chariots while the Assyrian infantry dropped their weapons, kneeling in front of their victors.

"There will be no more bloodshed, no captives, no loot," Athena announced, appearing on the battlefield as a goddess in full armor, wielding the aegis, an owl above her head.

"My brave soldiers!" Assur-Dan addressed his army, turning back and raising his arms. "You fought well, following your king. My father was blinded by the false gods and was destroyed with them. Let's return to our homes, restore the order of Assur, and live in peace. This mad march is over."

Echelaos looked at the screen, the battlefield from the bird's-eye view, the frozen body of Heracles and other metal monsters scattered around the plain, and the goddess standing proudly next to the triumphant Thracian and Achaean soldiers. *This is the day people will remember for ages*, Echelaos thought, *for this battle has decided the world's fate.* He also felt that the gods would no longer guide the mortals. As his father had foreseen, it was the dawn of a new age. Echelaos didn't care about glory on the battlefield anymore, the glory that had escaped him today. He was eager to return to Pylos and Eritha, bringing Aphrodite home with him. He finally understood what had made Nestor a great ruler. Now, he had to follow his father's example and take the helm of the ship of Pylos, for the storm was coming.

#

The three leaders sat on high chairs, surrounded by their advisers, in the middle of the circle formed by the warriors representing different armies: Thracian, Achaean, and Assyrian. The silver body of Zeus floated above the gathering, providing security and indicating the god's will. And the divine intention was clear: return to peace and normal relationships underscored by mutual respect, trade, and advancement.

Echelaos looked at the two commanders sitting on either side of him. To the left was Zoltes, half of his body still covered by the shiny silver armor of Ares but his mind finally free from the god's control. Zoltes was the unquestionable leader of the Northmen, even without Ares. To the right sat Assur-Dan in his usual simple gray robe with a royal mitre adorning his head. The newly crowned Assyrian king was caressing his short brown beard, piercing the two officials kneeling in front of the three leaders with his fiery gaze.

"What do you say in your defense?" Assur-Dan said, placing his right hand on his knee.

"We followed orders, o Great King. Let your wisdom and strength lead Assur for eternity," Grand Vizier Salmanu answered, lowering his eyes.

"Orders? Whose orders?" Assur-Dan said. "Your job was to provide good advice to the king, a task you've failed at miserably. You told my father what he wanted to hear, always obedient and ready to flatter him."

"But we had to obey the gods, o Great King," Chief Eunuch Adad pleaded in his high-pitch, shaky voice. The mole on his chin looked even more revolting than usual.

"The gods? *Which* gods?" Assur-Dan stood, stepping forward. "The evil creatures who fed on the people of various races and ages indiscriminately, destroying the great kingdom of the Hittites and eliminating half of the Assyrian army? How did you know they were your gods, Adad? You are as corrupt and heinous as them, you vile creature." Assur-Dan spat in the direction of his chief eunuch.

"Please forgive us, o Great King." Salmanu prostrated himself on the ground, crawling forward, trying to grab and kiss the king's feet. "We were enchanted; Nergal and Ishtar had suppressed our will."

"I despise you both! You are miserable sycophants and have no place at my court," Assur-Dan said. "But I'm not vengeful and bloodthirsty, like my father was. I'll let you live."

"Thank you, o Great King!" both former officials exclaimed almost simultaneously. "Your mercy has no boundaries," Salmanu added.

"You'll go to Assyria's farthest, most desolate region and finish your days there without any hope and forgiveness. You'll be among the poorest and most miserable of my subjects."

Two Assyrian soldiers stepped into the circle, grabbed the two unfortunate officials, still prostrate on the ground, and took them away, to the cheers of the spectators.

"Now, let's discuss peace terms," Assur-Dan said in Akkadian, approaching Echelaos and Zoltes. "I wish to sign a document of the perpetual friendship between our people. We have enough land and resources to stop this mad war and coexist peacefully."

"What about the Hittites?" Zoltes said, grinning.

"What about them?" Assur-Dan asked.

"The Hittites are vanquished, their capital is destroyed, their land is free to grab. Who will rule it?"

"I don't wish to rule the land of Hatti." Assur-Dan shook his head.

Echelaos thought about the situation and where they'd arrived after the fateful battle. The destruction of the Hittite kingdom was complete. The army had dispersed, the people had fled, the cities were razed, and the royal line had ended with the death of Helen. They could have split the spoils of war between them, but the land of Hatti was too far from Achaea to claim. At the same time, Echelaos couldn't let Assyria add this fertile plain to her domain. That would've multiplied her might and made Assyria too strong even for the combined strength of Achaea and Egypt to resist. Assur-Dan understood that, too, and was ready to demonstrate his goodwill by not pressing his demands for Hattusa.

"I propose to create a no-man's land," Echelaos said. "If any of the warriors wish to settle here, I have no objections to that. The local people can return to their homes, rebuild, and govern their communities themselves."

"I agree," Assur-Dan said. "Any Assyrian who wishes to populate this desolate realm has my permission to stay here."

"We are a simple folk," Zoltes added. "We have no kings or armies. We want freedom; the Thracians will return to our land to live as we always have."

"Very well," Echelaos said. He foreboded that this no-man's land would turn into a country of eternal warfare between petty local chieftains. Besides, the absence of a strong, unifying force would create space for the Kaska to advance from the north, looting and pillaging the peaceful population. But this was the only realistic solution they could construct at this point. If Assyria decided to move into this region in the future, she would have to deal with both Achaea and Egypt. This should suffice for now.

"On one condition," Echelaos continued. "Achaea will rebuild and control Troy."

"Of course." Zoltes grinned with his strange half-faced smirk. "If you share trade profits with Leibethra, that is. A simple contribution to your allies."

"Is this a threat?" Echelaos asked.

"No. My terms."

Echelaos looked at his former comrade's serene face and the bizarre silver metallic shine of his limbs.

"Agreed. But this will need to be discussed at the council of the Achaean rulers."

"Zeus is the witness. We don't need anyone else."

"Prepare the tablet with peace terms," Assur-Dan ordered. "We are ready to seal the agreement."

As the warriors forming a circle around their leaders started to cheer, a lone rider in an Assyrian military outfit approached the assembly. He dismounted, squeezed through the celebrating soldiers, and fell to the ground in front of the Assyrian king.

"What's happened?" Assur-Dan asked.

"Terrible news, o Great King. The Egyptian army has captured Carchemish and is quickly approaching."

"The Egyptians?" Assur-Dan raised his eyebrows.

"Yes, o Great King. This is not a regular army, however. The world had never seen such a multitude of people on the move. They are possessed by evil spirits, feeling no pain and having no will. They don't kill; everyone they encounter becomes possessed as well. Our priests have proclaimed the end of the world: the evil Udug demons have risen from the depths of Ganzir. The Underworld is here to claim us all, o Great King."

#

Echelaos looked at the beautiful green meadows stretching up to the horizon, meeting the cerulean sky at the junction where the sun had just started to rise. Sitting on the back of a black stallion next to the other two leaders of the combined army, Echelaos surveyed the landscape where Athena had told them to meet the Egyptian host. The view from the hill was perfect but grim: the mass of possessed people poured into the plain as if guided by the rising sun behind their backs, the endless swarm of humans of various races, sexes, and ages. Their only common feature was their subservience to the evil demons of the Underworld. The evil Udug, as Assur-Dan called them, or, as Athena had explained, the Primordial entity the Egyptians called Aten. It didn't matter much to Echelaos. He wanted to trust the gods to take care of this unexpected menace, but at the same time he was uneasy with the sheer magnitude of the task. He had never seen an army of such size; it must have been over a million people. They'd already covered the plain as far as the eyes could see, but new crowds appeared from the east. Echelaos didn't doubt the might of Zeus and Athena; they'd just demonstrated it by eliminating the gods of Assur. But the size of the horde, possessed by another godlike entity, descending on the meadows of Hattusa like some eerie locusts, troubled the wanax. It might be too much even for Zeus.

"Your mind was controlled by the god; how did it feel?" Echelaos asked Zoltes, turning his head to face the Thracian.

"Like goat's dung," Zoltes replied, showing no emotion. "Don't want to talk about it."

"The evil Udug enslave your whole essence and imprison you in Ganzir forever," Assur-Dan said. "This is different from being controlled by the god. There's no hope, just eternal torment."

"You're too glum," Zoltes said, grinning with half of his mouth. "Have faith."

"They've come to take revenge. Nergal rules Ganzir, the Underworld. The Udug demons are his minions."

"Enough talk," Echelaos said. "Time to act." He turned his horse around and galloped down the hill toward the combined armies led by the Achaean gods. Echelaos didn't quite understand the plan and the instruction not to engage and not to kill and thought Athena should know better. Still, his nature demanded the fight: it was against his character to retreat before the enemy's army. *Nestor*, he reminded himself. *Nestor wouldn't have attacked a vastly superior opponent.* He would have used his wisdom instead of brute force, preserving the soldiers and luring the enemy into a trap, just like Athena described. Echelaos knew he needed to be patient.

As the possessed swarm surged onto the plain, attempting to reach the army in front of them, their opponents yielded, falling back. The Egyptians moved deliberately but slowly, so keeping the distance from the advancing enemy wasn't difficult. The most numerous contingent, the Assyrians, under the leadership of their king, were positioned in the center, gradually retreating. The Achaeans and the Thracians on the flanks moved farther to the sides, forming an enormous semicircle where the ocean of possessed people poured in. Athena told them keeping their distance was critical, since the enemy's objective was to infect everyone they neared. Killing them was possible but useless; there were just too many.

Maintaining the separation, Echelaos led the Achaeans to withdraw even farther. He looked up. This was the time for Athena to act. As if answering his thoughts, two disks appeared in the sky, one silver and one blue: Zeus and Athena. The disks started to rotate and move above the advancing host in a giant circular arc. Next, a golden thread, like the one Echelaos saw in the battle against the Assyrians, formed a ring in the sky, connecting Zeus and Athena and encompassing the haunted army underneath. The slow-moving enemy didn't pay any attention to this development, focusing on closing the gap between them and the retreating opponents. This was a mistake as the space enclosed by the golden thread became opaque, glistering blue and silver, finally culminating in a shower, pouring green rain on the horde of infected people. As the drops soaked the possessed, the people initially stopped moving. Then they dropped onto the grass like grotesque puppets suddenly released by their master. Finally, the drops turned into a cloud, completely covering the plain. The cloud finished the transformation of what was a massive, slowly advancing army just a moment ago into a motionless heap of bodies.

Echelaos gave a sign to his warriors to retreat farther as the gods added the finishing touches to the battlefield, spraying the lagging groups. Echelaos couldn't believe his eyes. In a moment, it was all over, and the horrible army possessed by the evil Udug ceased to exist.

"It's safe now; the spores are inactive." Athena's voice resounded in his head. "They'll be back to their senses soon."

The people on the grass started to move, shaking their heads as if waking up from a terrible dream. Moans and wails filled the air as the humans, freed from the influence of Aten, tried to understand what had happened to them. Echelaos walked through the bodies lying on the grass, observing recovering people. Some were rubbing their eyes while others were emptying their stomachs. His eyes met the gaze of a young Egyptian dressed in just a simple kilt, slowly rising to his knees. Next to him, another Egyptian wearing the vibrant attire of a military commander wheezed, trying to roll up. His left eyeball was missing; the socket was covered by an artificial eye depicting an Egyptian symbol.

"What's your name?" Echelaos asked the young Egyptian in Akkadian.

"Khay," the Egyptian responded. "Thank you for releasing us from Aten."

Echelaos nodded. "Who is he?" He pointed at the Egyptian commander.

"Hewernef, the most celebrated general in Egypt."

"Uhm," Echelaos murmured. "Not sure if that's a good or a bad thing… In any case, you should thank Athena for your deliverance." He pointed to the blue disk of the goddess up in the sky.

"Athena?" Khay shook his head. "Who is Athena? Wise Wadjet, the cobra goddess of Egypt, was guiding me, and I've failed her. Without her protection, the Two Kingdoms will perish, and no foreign gods would have saved us."

#

"We had no room for error," Commander messaged.

"You said the probability of success was five percent. Yet we've prevailed," Scholar responded.

"Several factors played to our advantage. Pure chance."

"Chance, yes. But also because we created this chance. I've learned this from the humans, however backward their race is: they persevere even if the probability of success is close to none. I suspect the Soarers had this trait at the beginning of our evolution, but somehow we've lost it."

"There is nothing inferior in being guided by reasoning and choosing the path leading to desired outcomes with the highest degree of probability," Commander disagreed. "Are you becoming like Pilot and Defender, influenced by recklessness and violence of humans? We have already lost Technologist and Defender because of that."

"Yes, I'm aware. But I see a logic in their reasoning."

"Be careful, Scholar."

"I am. We still don't know how this influence manifests itself. But I think that the human race must be protected and led to develop their unique traits, and we could help them with that."

"You speak like Pilot." Commander's body turned gray.

"Did you have success disposing of the black hole?" Scholar changed the subject.

"Yes, I did. It wasn't easy, especially after we fed it the energy of the alien entities. Still, our magnetic field was strong, and I could contain it."

"Where is it now?"

"I employed the Space Elevator to transport it to orbit and then moved it outside this star's system using our spacecraft. So, it's drifting somewhere in interstellar space, not a danger to anything in the foreseeable future."

"And the entities won't escape?"

"You can rule this out. The probability is zero."

"This was the desired outcome. What if more of them show up?"

"Then we'll address the danger. I sent the warning and everything we've learned to Homeworld; the Soarers will be prepared."

"Good. I'd like to find out where they came from, their provenance, mental processes, ways of communication," Scholar messaged.

"Be careful what you ask for, Scholar. These entities are too dangerous to any life form and maybe to the universe itself. They consume and entrap information, just like a black hole would; they *are* pure information itself. Their presence threatens the evolution of the cosmos; if all the information disappears, no change is possible."

"What are we going to do with the drone army Defender created?"

"We must destroy all the traces; there's no place for such technology on this planet."

"Agreed," Scholar said. "I've discovered something else, Commander. Not sure if this is relevant,"

"What's that?"

"One of the humans we've observed defended the city against the alien entities, somehow controlling the Primordial organism. But that's not the most important discovery. I have reasons to assume she could access the information fields, the traces of past events, and even what the humans call 'memories.' Not *her* memories, but the memories of human beings long dead. We know the quantum information is fully reversible in time, but to recover it at a macro scale of living organisms is a scientific breakthrough."

"Intriguing and relevant," Commander messaged. "But this specimen is dead now?"

"Unfortunately, yes. This is yet another reason to protect this species. They have powers we don't even comprehend."

"And what about this Primordial organism? Was it similar to the one we've just dealt with, thanks to your ingenious solution of spraying the antidote?"

"Yes, Commander. These ancient organisms evolved soon after the formation of this planet. They cover vast underground areas, spreading primarily through airborne spores; their offshoots communicate via electrical signals. The human specimen could control this Primordial being and, even more, channel energy into its network. Another fascinating skill."

"Do we need to deal with that organism, too?" Commander asked.

"No, it has retreated into its caves in the northern mountains after the failed standoff with the alien entities."

"What about the one we've neutralized? Any other sprouts we need to address?"

"I've already taken care of that. This one was a lot more aggressive and more difficult to contain. The priests on the southern continent have my antidote and have successfully treated the infected population. I've sealed the underground entrances with the chemical I synthesized. That entity won't trouble the humans."

"What are you planning to do now?"

"As I indicated, I think our goal should be protecting humans. I've been doing this already, and I want you to join me in this mission.

We'll enhance our base, teach humans our science, and lead them to the stars. Do you agree?"

"I've warned you: you speak like Pilot," Commander messaged. "No, I won't join you. I think this is a dangerous and inappropriate strategy. We should watch them, but we shouldn't interfere. This is not to the advantage of the Soarers."

"I expected you to say that, Commander, but I can't agree with your reasoning. It *is* to our advantage, and I'll change my approach to a more visible and active role. The humans must be guided, educated, and elevated."

"I can't stop you, but it's an unfortunate choice," Commander messaged. "You were the last member of the crew I could reason with; now I've lost that option too. I must focus on the research to uncover the causes of these behavioral changes. Emotions, you said, drive humans. Have *you* developed emotions as well, Scholar? Do you understand you've lost the ability to reason, replacing it with impulsive actions?"

"It may be so, but I've decided and chosen my path. You can't change it, and you can't stop me."

"What are you planning to do? Keep pretending to be their goddess, protecting and guiding them?"

"More than that: it's time for active leadership; time to show our true nature and lead the humans to the stars. I'm joining Pilot."

Part Three

"The Cleansing Fire"

CHAPTER
TWENTY-ONE

Echelaos inhaled the smell of laudanum spreading through the megaron. He massaged his eyes and moved awkwardly on the wooden throne, trying to find a comfortable position. Two pairs of eyes looked at him attentively, awaiting his response, ready for his guidance and decisions. *I have no idea what to do*, Echelaos admitted to himself. *I don't deserve this place; I am not Nestor.*

"Do you wish to build more ships, Wanax?" Tros repeated, stepping forward. "There are rumors about new tribes threatening the western seas. My scouts call them the Sea People. We must prepare and be ready to face this danger."

Tros was natural in his new role of lawagetos. Since Echelaos learned about the death of Machaon two years ago, he couldn't think of a better man to fill this gap. Always a faithful friend and a trusted adviser, Tros was a rock the wanax could always lean on, including in times when Echelaos didn't know what in the bloody abyss he was doing.

"First, we need to refill our coffers," Eritha said. She was as beautiful as always, with the usual golden tiara adorning her silky, long black hair. Echelaos experienced immediate desire when looking at her but had to suppress the urgent need to embrace Eritha and cover her hourglass silhouette with passionate kisses. Not now; he had to pretend to be a wise ruler of Pylos.

"What do you propose?" Echelaos asked.

"We must expand our textile production. Pylos and Leuktron make enough to meet our needs and even create some extra. Wealthy merchants from Egypt, Cyprus, and Canaan will pay plenty of gold, which you can use to rebuild your armies."

"When do you want to attack these Sea People?" Echelaos asked Tros.

"I don't. But we need to project strength and be ready."

"So, you think they'll attack? When?"

"I didn't say that. Maybe now, maybe never. But we can't be weak."

Why was it so complicated? Why couldn't he take his bow, board the warship, and descend on his enemies like a hawk from the cloudless sky? Palace management, textile production, and trade were foreign to him. He was no Nestor and had found it very tough to learn the principles of peacetime leadership. Echelaos looked at the frescoes on the walls that showed scenes of feasts with men drinking and musicians sitting on colored rocks, playing lyres. He allowed his sight to move to a large, plastered hearth in the middle of the room, surrounded by four fluted columns, its rim painted with a pattern skillfully representing the flames. Echelaos shifted his gaze from the fire to the floor, divided into a rough checkerboard, a geometric motif in every square. The only different block, which depicted an octopus, was right before the throne. *So this is me*, Echelaos suddenly thought. *Alone, like this octopus on the floor. I don't fit into the peaceful life; I don't belong on the throne of the wanax. I will bring ruin and misery to the house of Nestor.*

Echelaos shook his head, driving away the ghost of self-doubt. He had no other choice but to become a better ruler. The people of Pylos depended on him.

"What about Nichoria?" he asked Eritha.

"I hope Aphrodite can ramp it up. You could double your army if they'd produce as much linen as Leuktron."

"Any news about my daughter?"

"She started energetically, although somewhat...nontraditionally," Tros said.

"What do you mean?"

"Remember, when you appointed her to be the korete of Nichoria, she promised to make everyone happy and a lot more productive?"

"Well?" Echelaos pierced his former charioteer with a fiery gaze. "Is she successful?"

"From what I've heard, everyone at Nichoria is working much harder now as they bring home a share of their produce," Eritha said. "Even the slaves, who are not even called slaves anymore. Every weaver is free. She gave every family a roof and means to sustain themselves."

"Does she need any help?"

"We need more linen; I agree with Eritha," Tros said. "I'll travel to Nichoria tomorrow and find out if she needs any help."

"And send her my best wishes and love," Echelaos said. He thought about Aphrodite, who had changed so much during and after their adventures in the land of Hatti. Echelaos remembered the day when he'd first met her, rising from the sea foam at the beach of Kythera in her unblemished, youthful beauty, with the mind of a curious child eager to learn about the world. In a few moons, she'd become a warrior challenging the best fighters of Pylos and now a wise and imaginative stateswoman. *She should be sitting on the throne of Nestor, not me*, Echelaos noted to himself.

"Can we get more gold from Troy?" Echelaos asked Tros.

"I'll send an envoy to Wedaneus," Tros said. "The city has been wiped from the face of the Earth. But the location is still advantageous, and Wedaneus is rebuilding the site, although slowly. I'm not sure if he could spare more gold."

"Zoltes?"

"He holds up his end of the bargain. The western passes are peaceful. Thracian assistance isn't cheap, but it's necessary."

"Good. And the east?"

"The east is a mess. Former Hittite chieftains fight each other, but none is strong enough to challenge Troy."

"No new Hittite ruler in Hattusa?"

"This is the news I wanted to tell you. The messenger arrived this morning; Kaska have occupied Hattusa. People flee to the south, abandoning the fertile northern lands."

Echelaos didn't respond. He stared into the flames rising from the hearth in front of him. Suddenly, Helen's face emerged from the smoke and fire. She looked at him with her black eyes wide, smiled, and said, *"Don't despair; we have always been together and will always be."* Echelaos couldn't turn his gaze from her image, even understanding that this was an illusion. What had he done wrong? Could he have saved her?

"Wanax, do you hear me?" The voice of the lawagetos brought Echelaos back to reality.

"What? Yes… Do you think she can see us, Tros? Feel our presence?"

"Who?" Tros squinted, throwing a glance at Eritha.

"Helen. From the other side. She said she'll see me on the other side."

"I've heard this story many times, Wanax. It's time to finally forget the sorceress and focus on your duties, o wise ruler of Pylos."

"You're right, as always," Echelaos said, rubbing his eyes. "So, the Kaska are the masters of Hattusa?"

"To the degree you could call them masters of anything. Defiling the sanctuaries, humping the goats, devouring raw flesh, and shitting on each other's heads."

"I wonder if my brother the Assyrian king will make a move," Echelaos said.

"Our scouts report it's all quiet. Assur-Dan is content with his prized possession of sea access at Ugarit and the copper mines of Isuwa. Besides, he's busy with his eastern neighbors at Susa, who challenge his rule at Babylon. He won't trouble you, Wanax."

"Should *we* make a move?" Echelaos stood, walking restlessly around the hearth, rubbing his palms. Just thinking about the campaign made his blood run faster. Perhaps he'd once again lead the chariots of Pylos into battle, where everything was simple and pure.

"I'd advise against that, Wanax," Tros said. "We need to protect Pylos, and we don't have enough chariots to spare. Plus, I don't think Mycenae would support this invasion."

"Bloody goat horns!" Echelaos hit his palm with a fist. "Why does it have to be so difficult? We march, fight, conquer — why can't we do that?"

"Because we must defend our land, Wanax," Tros said.

"And this is why we need to focus on textile production," Eritha added.

"All right, all right, I get it. Thank you for your advice."

"I need to talk to you, Echelaos." Eritha came closer.

"Talk."

"Privately."

Echelaos nodded to the lawagetos, who turned around and left the megaron.

"What is it, Eritha?"

"I had a dream last night. Like the one I told you about before you departed for Troy."

"The gods have abandoned us; Zeus himself told me so. So you shouldn't worry about them." Echelaos stroked a curl of her long, raven hair, pulling her closer, running his fingers down her spine, inhaling the smell of her essence adorned by the Canaanite perfume.

"Come with me; I want you now," he said, feeling a fresh flood of desire.

"Wait," she pulled back. "I'm horrified, Echelaos."

"With what?"

"The vision. Poseidon brought countless hordes from across the western sea, Pylos burned…and then I saw Helen."

"Helen? How?"

"I don't know. I've never met her before, but somehow I was sure it was her. She walked through the raging fire unharmed, steady, and peaceful. Then, when I approached her, she broke into a myriad of little green snowflakes and melted in the air."

"What does it mean?"

"And then I heard her voice inside my head," Eritha continued as if not hearing the question. "*The Age of Iron is nigh; the world must be cleansed by blood and fire.*"

"Eritha, what does it all mean?"

"This means the end, Echelaos. The end of Pylos, Mycenae, and the whole of Achaea. The end of us."

CHAPTER
TWENTY-TWO

Tros dismounted and gave the bridle to a boy who was ready to help the visiting lawagetos. Tros thanked the kid and took off his leather helmet, reinforced with boar's tusks and embellished with a plume. This was the only element of his wardrobe that indicated a man of power in the hierarchy of Pylos. Tros didn't like to stand out; he preferred simple but practical garments. For this journey that took him just half a day, he wore a military kilt and plain tunic underneath a warm cloak. It was winter, after all.

Tros removed two long bands of black hair that had fallen across his face and stroked his beardless chin, covered with two days of stubble. He looked around the narrow streets of Nichoria with his attentive black eyes.

"Where's the korete?" he asked the boy.

The lad didn't respond, just pointed to a simple shack in the middle of the village. Tros thanked him again and walked slowly in the direction indicated, observing life in Pylos's third-biggest linen production community. Smaller houses were located on one side of the road, Aphrodite's shack among them, while longer, many-doored buildings were on the other. These larger constructions served as storage silos for raw flax and the final product, linen material. Approaching the house of the korete, Tros stepped aside to let the three bleating goats pass, a little girl chasing them. A simple, one-story hut of mud brick was not appropriate for a korete, Tros noted, but Aphrodite had her own peculiar ways.

Entering the courtyard, he knocked at the wooden door.

"Come in, Tros." Aphrodite's voice was loud and confident.

"How did you know?" he said, entering the building and giving her a warm hug.

"I felt you." She shrugged, stepping back. "What brings you to Nichoria?"

"You." Tros grinned, placing his helmet on the bench by the entrance. He looked at the hostess. Aphrodite's beauty was as stunning as when he first saw her coming out of the waves. At first glance, she hadn't changed at all. However, one could see a rigid, muscular body underneath the perfection of her form, the body of a warrior, not of an innocent maiden. And then the eyes…the eyes full of wisdom and intelligence. The eyes that reminded Tros of the old Nestor.

"What about me?" she asked.

"Your father sends his love and greetings. He misses you, Aphrodite."

"I know. But my place is here."

"Yes, and this is the second reason for my visit."

"To check on me?"

"To see if you have everything you need. I've heard you're expanding production?"

"Yes. We're planning to double it by the next moon."

"Good. Nichoria is assigned one of the largest amounts of flax in Pylos. We need your linen."

"I know. We have over a hundred whorls and have just started making one of a new, large type. This should speed up the work significantly. I observed the process and came up with this new machine," Aphrodite said matter-of-factly, showing no pride or emotion. Tros admired this woman.

"I'd like to see that."

"Korinsia will show you later," Aphrodite said.

"How's she doing?" Tros felt a needle underneath his heart and a sudden heaviness in his stomach. He hadn't seen Korinsia for over a year, and he didn't let himself think about her, admitting the attraction between the two of them and his feelings toward Korinsia. A fleeting moment in Athena's sanctuary, watching the battle of the gods, had brought them very close. Still, Tros didn't dare to succumb to emotions, keeping his distance. It was as if he was afraid of this simple Achaean girl, afraid to confess his feelings. Now she'd probably forgotten him and found love here. Someone a lot younger and more appropriate for her, no doubt. He looked at his left palm, which was missing two fingers, and grinned sadly.

"She's in charge of one of the workshops and is my trusted associate."

"Great to hear." Tros lowered his eyes.

"She was asking about you the other day," Aphrodite said. "She'll be happy to see you."

"She will be?" Tros thought about how to change the topic. "You have some wine? I'm thirsty; I've just arrived," he finally said, breaking the awkward silence.

"Of course. Sit." She pointed at the wooden stool by the table in the middle of the small room. "We don't have much. This is not the palace; but I do have wine." She smiled and placed a jar on the table.

"How do you plan to increase production? Just because of the new whorl?" Tros asked, sitting on the stool and leaning forward on the table.

"It's part of the plan," Aphrodite said, bringing out two chalices and filling them with wine from the jar. "We're also working differently."

"Different how? Everyone has two arms, after all." Tros grinned.

"That's true." She smiled. "But when people own what they make, they work harder and smarter."

"What do you mean?" Tros almost choked on his wine. "Your workers own the linen you're supposed to send to Pylos?"

"I give them part of what they produce. The more they make, the more they get."

"And Pylos?"

"If we make more, Pylos gets more. Don't you see? I thought it would be fair." She drank her wine with one large gulp.

"Hm-mm... We'll see." Tros shook his head. "I also heard you freed all the slaves?"

"Slave labor is the worst way to produce goods," Aphrodite said with conviction. "There are no slaves in Nichoria. Everyone is treated fairly."

"What about the scribes? You?" Tros squinted, trying to figure out her approach.

"The scribes also get their fair share; it's just assessed differently. And me? I need less than anyone else. I need very little sleep, and I sometimes work in the shop, too." Aphrodite put her palm over her guest's hand. "Don't worry about me. When I figure out how people can live and work better in Nichoria, I'll teach everyone in Pylos and then the whole of Achaea. I have a plan."

"You keep surprising me, Aphrodite," Tros tilted his head. "You understand this is against the traditions? Against the divine order?"

"If the traditions do not benefit people, they are useless." Aphrodite stood up, placing her hands on the table. "And divine order? The gods have left us; Zeus proclaimed it on the fields of Hattusa. *I* am the creation of the gods; how do you know they don't want to change their order using *me*?" She pierced Tros with the fiery shine of her blue eyes, and he caught himself admiring her energy, conviction, and raw beauty.

"Good point. I hope you're right," he said.

"I know I am; it's in my head. I can feel everyone and understand their needs and desires. I can make them happy, Tros. More?" Aphrodite took the jar.

"Maybe later."

"I have also forbidden all fighting," she said, looking straight into his eyes.

"Really? Does it work?" He leaned back.

"Not quite… I don't understand why people do that. It's clearly against everyone's interests. There's no benefit. Brute force doesn't bring happiness."

"So what happens when someone takes something by force? You punish them?"

"I return it. There is no punishment; I don't find it beneficial."

"You return it how? By force? How do you know it was wrongfully taken?"

"Yes, by force. How else? How do I know? I just know, like I knew it was you when you arrived."

"So, you act like a king. You are the source of justice and order. Nothing wrong with that, just making sure you understand."

"I don't see any other way… Maybe *you* can help me, Tros?" She sat down, lowering her head into her arms. "It doesn't make sense when people behave against their best interests… Why is that?"

"This is how we are." Tros shrugged. "Love, hate, envy, anger, fear… This is human nature. I follow my rage into the battle, even when I know I'll most likely be killed."

"Yes!" Aphrodite suddenly jumped back to her feet. "I need to include emotions; it's part of human nature. It's the missing element. Thank you."

"Easier said than done," Tros murmured.

"Or should I find a way to suppress emotions altogether?" She squinted.

"I don't think that's possible, even for you." Tros shook his head.

"We shall see. Divine order, you said? Time to change this order, and I will do that!" she exclaimed triumphantly, punching Tros in the shoulder.

#

"Thank you for coming here. It's good to see you," Korinsia said, laying her hand on top of Tros's fingers. "You never told me how that happened." She added, caressing the place where two of the fingers were missing.

"This is a long and embarrassing story." Tros grinned, turning his head. He felt like a boy going into his first battle, at a loss for what to say and do. He looked at Korinsia's round face, covered by playful freckles. She wore a tight bodice emphasizing her form and natural beauty and a long, broad, colorful Cretan skirt. He inhaled the smell of her silky brown hair, reminding him of the morning dew on fresh grass. Combined with the scent of perfumed oil mixed with iris and cardamom, the aroma made his head spin and aroused his desire. She had expected Tros and chose the best dress she had, using the most potent charms at her disposal. The magic worked; the only problem was he couldn't gather his thoughts, and his brain refused to function.

"Tell me; we have time."

They stood on the balcony of Korinsia's house, one of the few multistory buildings in Nichoria, white stone columns around them, watching the clouds colored pink by the sunset.

Tros sighed, leaned on the column, and said, "This was early days." He looked beyond the horizon as if trying to find the shadows of the past there. "Echelaos and I were young and fervent as untamed bulls. We thought we were unstoppable." He smiled.

"Did you charge into an army of wild beasts?" Korinsia smiled too, taking his hand.

"Not exactly. Some vagabonds landed on the shore and started pillaging the land. No chariots, simple weapons. We rushed out to drive them away, no problems expected. But then Echelaos yelled to chase and kill all of them, and suddenly we were too far from the rest of our forces, surrounded by enemies. They turned around and fell on us. I had to use my sword while protecting Echelaos, who shot his bow. We survived until more chariots arrived to help, but I lost two fingers. Didn't even notice when."

"You could have lost your lives!" Korinsia exclaimed.

"Yeah, could've. This is how you learn to fight, though. We probably killed a dozen thugs that day."

"Scary. Promise me you won't do that again," she said.

"I promise, no rushed, silly engagements," he said. "But when the need comes to fight, I'll fight. I'm a warrior, after all."

"I know, Tros. You are strong and wise." Korinsia stroked the two stubborn strands of hair that fell on his face. "Still, I'm worried about you, and I missed you."

"You? Missed me?" He carefully touched a handful of freckles sprinkled on her cheek.

"Yes… I know I'm just a silly girl, and you are the mighty lawagetos of Pylos. You can have any woman you desire. Still, I dreamed of you ever since we had a moment during that fateful battle… Do you remember, Tros?"

"Yes, I remember…" He was confused and suddenly felt very awkward.

"Would you reject me?" She embraced Tros, making full body-to-body contact so he felt her rounded breasts, warm breath on his neck, and gentle whisper in his ear. "Take me now."

Tros lost all control; he could think only about the beautiful girl he'd yearned to hold for so long. He touched her soft hair and pulled the ivory hairpin that was fixing Korinsia's hairstyle in place. She laughed and freed him from his tunic, running her fingers down the broad, brown, muscular chest of a seasoned warrior, covered with scars and tough as ox hide. Unable to restrain his desire anymore, Tros unlaced her bodice and touched her silky skin underneath the tunic, something he had wanted to do for so long.

Korinsia laughed again and pulled back, disappearing into the darkness of the room. When Tros dashed after her, she threw her skirt at him, covering his head and torso with the delicate material. He lost his balance, unable to see, trying to get rid of the stupid cloth. Korinsia's laugh teased him as he tried to reach out into the darkness, following the sound of her voice. Finally, when Tros managed to free himself from the vivid element of his lover's clothing, he observed the most beautiful sight he'd ever seen. Korinsia, completely naked, stood at the balcony's entrance, the setting sun behind her back outlining her silhouette, giving her the appearance of the goddess of love who had shown up to seduce the poor lawagetos.

Looking at this divine image, Tros couldn't move or say anything. His manhood, however, was ready for action. Seeing his kilt bulging in front of him, Korinsia slowly approached and removed the last pieces of garments from his eager body. Taking her by the armpits, Tros raised Korinsia above his head, then slowly lowered her, feeling her skin on his, their tongues intertwined, their breath becoming one. Finally, he entered her as they united into a single being, consumed by desire, outside of time and space. The whole world ceased to exist for Tros; Korinsia had replaced it. He could only hear her moans and the gentle sound of her voice calling his name. They moved to a horizontal position on the bed, Korinsia still holding him tight with her thighs, her fingers scratching his spine. As they simultaneously reached the pinnacle of their passion, Korinsia screamed and squeezed Tros so tightly, he felt short of breath. But it didn't matter; they were finally together, even if only for one night. Now Tros knew what mattered to him and what he was fighting for. Suddenly, it all became crystal-clear: there could be no more questions or doubts. Now he knew what advice he should give to his wanax.

"Will you forget me?" she asked several eons later when they lay in bed, exhausted by their exploits.

"Why?"

"You need to return to Pylos. You'll find women there."

"That's true. I do need to return, but you should come with me."

"I can't; I need to help Aphrodite."

"That's true, too." Tros looked up at the ceiling as if trying to find a solution. "I'll come for you when the time is right."

"I'll wait. I don't mind you humping other girls; I understand the ways of men."

"Shush. You'll be at my side. I need you."

"I need you, too." She leaned over to give him a passionate kiss. "I'm yours, Tros."

"I'll fight anyone to have you with me, even the gods. I'll challenge Poseidon himself if it comes to that."

"I hope it won't." She smiled and dropped her head onto his chest. He stroked her hair, pondering how improbable it was for an old soldier like him to find love and tranquility in a small village with a simple girl full of life, devotion, and prudence.

CHAPTER

TWENTY-THREE

The road was straight as an arrow, and countless sphinxes on both sides looked almost alive in the rays of the setting sun. The general looked at the imposing structure of the Wadjet temple behind their backs and asked the charioteer to slow down, giving the soldiers a chance to catch up. He wanted to enjoy the scenery in this rare moment of quiet time, free from training the troops. Hewernef was adamant they be well fed and equipped while he was planning military engagements. Times were tumultuous, and the border situation demanded full attention from General Hewernef.

"You think the Great Priest of Amen is up to something?" the general asked his companion, standing next to him on the moving platform.

"Hard to say," the grand vizier responded. "Bakenkhonsu is always up to something. Especially after he played the main role in defeating Aten."

"I'd appreciate it if you don't bring that up, Hori," Hewernef said, frowning, instinctively reaching out for his sword.

"But that's true, and he has the pharaoh's ear," Hori said. "His influence is growing, and I'm concerned. We can't allow priests to rule the Two Kingdoms."

"That won't happen." General looked at the pendant on the vizier's chest. "I respect the gods, and we owe the defeat of Aten to them, not to Bakenkhonsu. He was in the right place at the right time. Even that poor wretch, what's his name—"

"Khay."

"Even he has more right to claim the main contribution than Bakenkhonsu."

"You might be right, but that's not how Ramesses sees that."

"Ramesses knows he needs the army. Wadjet won't fight for us all the time."

"You're right again. The Great Pharaoh also needs potent administrators. I'd hate to see the finances of the Two Kingdoms fall into the hands of the greedy priests. But, unfortunately, we are dangerously close to that." Hori shook his head, curving his mouth as if he'd eaten a rotten date.

"What do you propose?" The general gave Hori a stony look, leaning toward him. He wanted to be certain the grand vizier had the full view of the general's artificial eye, glowing menacingly red in the sunset. Hori should understand who he was dealing with; his position at the pharaoh's court was weak at the moment. However, his support was still valuable for Hewernef.

"I'll champion your cause," Hori said, pulling back. "You regained your influence after the Aten disaster, repelling Libyan incursions, and I respect that. Together, we could counterbalance the Great Priest."

"What do you want in return?"

"Control of finances."

"You shall have it, assuming the army gets what it needs." Hewernef smiled. This conversation had progressed in the right direction. The general was happy he had agreed to ride with Hori in his chariot after the completion of the Wadjet Festival at her temple.

"Of course." Hori bowed. "It's crucial."

"Very well," the general said. "I need gold to equip both eastern and western frontiers. The Sea People are in Canaan, the Libyans are restless again, and I don't like that."

"We don't have enough gold for both," the grand vizier said. "Not after your disastrous march to the land of Hatti."

"I told you not to bring that up!" Hewernef shouted, his face changing color, matching his artificial eye.

"My apologies, General." Hori bowed again. "I'll see what I can do. Perhaps you could support my proposal to divert some of the income of the Temple of Amen to the army."

"With pleasure." The general smiled. "I also need to rebuild the fleet; it's in bad shape. It could be our main weapon against the Sea People." Hewernef took his sickle sword, waving it in the air, slashing at imaginary enemies. "I'll cut off thousands of Libyan penises and bring them to the pharaoh," he proclaimed.

"You said the Libyans are restless again?" Hori asked. "I thought we celebrated a decisive victory last year?"

"Yes, the vile Libu, the abhorrent Meshwesh, and the repugnant Seped have been vanquished and are not a threat. There are new tribes, however, preparing to attack our forts in the Western Delta. So numerous, I've never seen such multitudes before." The general pointed west as if threatening the vile Libyans.

"I see. Aren't they in danger from the Sea People?"

"They work together, vile dung of Apep. I suspect the Libyans are the first wave of attack instigated by the Sea People." Hewernef frowned. "The Shekelesh, Sherden, Peleshet, and countless others." He spat to the side, shaking his head. "Let Apep devour their intestines and possess their Ka for eternity."

"Then the danger is grave," Hori said.

"You finally grasped it." The general tilted his head. "Are you getting old, Hori? Beware, I might put forward a new candidate for grand vizier. Someone quick and decisive. An army commander, perhaps?" Hewernef laughed.

"Did you say the Sea People are also attacking Canaan?" Hori replied with a serious face, not acknowledging the general's teasing.

"Not attacking. The Peleshet are already there, the dung of the desert."

"I knew the situation is tough, but this is very concerning."

"This is a recent development I've just learned from our scouts, and the pharaoh has been informed. We hold the forts along the Way of Horus, but the enemies keep arriving."

"Perhaps you could seek Aten's help?" Hori smiled.

Hewernef's face turned red again as he took out his sword and pointed it at the grand vizier. "I promise, if you provoke me one more time, I will cut off your small and shriveled penis myself."

"Calm down, just a friendly joke," Hori said, still smiling.

"I don't think we can hold the forts both in Canaan and the Western Delta with the current size of the garrisons." The general tried to suppress his anger; the despicable bureaucrat wasn't worth it. "And, Amen forbids, if the Sea People attack the Nile Delta from the sea, we can't repel them."

"Perhaps Bakenkhonsu could summon Wadjet again? Or even Amen; he is the Great Priest, after all."

"Perhaps. I can only count on my army, but if he could provide divine help, I'd welcome it."

"Imagine how his influence would increase if the gods delivered victory against the Sea People?"

"This time, we won't let him. The victory will belong to the army, not to greedy priests. You'll help me to ensure the Great Pharaoh sees it that way." Hewernef bumped his fists together. "We'll destroy this revolting scum, the feces of Apep."

"The situation is grave indeed, General; we have a fragile thread to walk."

"*We?*" The general curved his lips. "It's *me*, not *we*. You are championing my cause, Hori; never forget that. I will reward you, but you are following *me*."

"Yes, General. I'll remember." Hori touched his pendant. "If the gods will help us prevail."

#

Khay finished counting wheat and barley production for the lands belonging to Nesut-Towi and set the completed papyrus aside. The library of the Great Temple of Amen, the Throne of the Two Lands, was quiet and solemn. He breathed in the sweet smell of kapet and looked at the entrance. It was time for Bakenkhonsu to arrive from the ceremony.

Khay liked his new job of a scribe, working in the most important religious complex in Thebes, if not the whole of Egypt. Since his return from the land of Hatti, freed from Aten's shackles, he had decided to start a new life. His path was not that of a soldier, and he couldn't become a priest, even though he'd interacted with Wadjet herself. Nevertheless, he enjoyed an uneventful life of a scribe, having the complete confidence of the Great Priest, who'd taught him the magic of letters. Bakenkhonsu trusted his new servant and had even elevated Khay to the adviser level. Khay paid him back with his loyalty and hard work.

Khay smiled, remembering their perilous struggle against Aten, but quickly bit his lip as the crazy march north following the possessed general entered his thoughts. He shouldn't have survived it. Nevertheless, he was eternally grateful to Wadjet for getting rid of Aten and giving him a second chance; he was committed to repaying his debt.

Finally, the broad figure of the priest appeared at the entrance, his bald head covered with beads of sweat, Amen's staff in his hand.

"Are you finished?" Bakenkhonsu asked.

"Yes, Hem-netjer. You'll be pleased."

"Good. I need all the resources I can get." The Great Priest of Amen took the papyrus and glanced over it. "What do you think about Hewernef?" he asked unexpectedly.

"The general? Why?" Khay shrugged.

"He's gaining influence with Ramesses," Bakenkhonsu said. "We need to anticipate him."

"I haven't interacted with Hewernef much." Khay shook his head. "Aten controlled the whole army."

"Did you get into the general's head through Aten?"

"That's not how it works." Khay clicked his tongue. "My conscience was nowhere in the picture; we were Aten."

"Right. What would you suggest I do?" Bakenkhonsu asked, massaging his temples.

"What's the problem?" Khay asked. He was flattered that Bakenkhonsu asked his opinion on such an important matter.

"He is about to become the most powerful person at the court of the pharaoh, and I can't let that happen." Bakenkhonsu crossed his hands behind his back and walked back and forth. "When the Libyans were defeated, Ramesses attributed the success to the general. The mad march is forgotten; the Sea People are menacing Canaan, and the army must become stronger. Unfortunately, this means Nesut-Towi is losing ground, and my power goes with it."

"You need to summon Wadjet," Khay said.

"Ah, Wadjet!" Bakenkhonsu exclaimed. "Hem-netjer Nefer-Setekh is gone, and the new priest has no experience. Wadjet is silent."

"Then you need to ask Amen to grant you divine support."

"Come with me," Bakenkhonsu said, his features suddenly freezing, the corners of his mouth pointing down.

Khay stood and followed the priest out of the library. The awe-inspiring architecture of the temple complex made him inhale deeply with reverence and disbelief. Khay reacted this way every time he walked through the giant courtyard, surrounded by majestic pylons, rising high and disappearing in the sky above his head. He truly believed this was the work of the gods.

Bakenkhonsu led Khay into the large temple, where they went through the halls and gateways, eventually arriving at the monumental group of stone statues in the middle of a large enclosed area. Ramesses the Great sat on the seat, serene, strong, emanating power and omnipotence. To his right sat Mut, the Beautiful One, and Amen himself, the Creator, to the left.

"I come here every day," Bakenkhonsu said. "But Amen is silent. I don't have the connection Nefer-Setekh had with Wadjet."

"Amen was there," Khay said. "When Aten was finally defeated for good, it was Amen."

"I didn't believe you then, and I don't believe you now." Bakenkhonsu shook his head. "Your imagination has run amok since you were freed from Aten."

"I know what I've seen. And what I've heard," Khay said. He'd tried to persuade the stubborn priest many times, but Bakenkhonsu refused to believe him.

"Why is he not answering me then, his high priest?" Bakenkhonsu spread his arms in exasperation.

"Don't be angry, Hem-netjer, but maybe the reason is *you*?" Khay lowered his head, knowing the priest might find the suggestion offensive. But to his surprise, Bakenkhonsu reacted positively.

"What do you mean? What's the problem? Do you see something I don't?" Bakenkhonsu asked.

"You are thinking about yourself, Hem-netjer. However, I'm convinced that for the gods to interfere, the Two Kingdoms must be in grave danger."

"Which is what we've faced with Aten," Bakenkhonsu said thoughtfully, grasping the carved ram's head on top of his staff. "You might be right." He shifted his gaze to his scribe, raising his eyebrows. "But what is the grave danger?"

"You said it yourself." Khay looked back at the priest. "The Sea People."

"Yes, the Sea People," Bakenkhonsu said slowly, as if trying to remember something. Then, finally, he stepped closer to the statue of the god, which sat in a solemn pose, indifferent to the people's problems.

"O great Amen, take pity on your people," Bakenkhonsu intoned. "The Two Kingdoms are in peril yet again. The vile Sea People are invading our lands, led by that great horrid serpent, Apep. They know of no gods and observe no Ma'at. Theirs is pure chaos and destruction, vile worshipers of Isfet. O great Amen, please help us defeat the abomination, the repugnant serpent Apep, who is about to devour your lands and your faithful people!"

Bakenkhonsu fell to the floor, prostrating himself in front of the god's statue. Khay held his breath. Several long moments later, Bakenkhonsu opened his eyes, his lips trembling, looking at the god in supplication.

"Nothing," he said. "Amen has turned away from us…"

Khay helped Bakenkhonsu to his feet.

"You were wrong!" The priest pointed at the scribe.

"I'm just a scribe, Hem-netjer." Khay bowed. "I'm sorry if I offended you."

"What now?" Bakenkhonsu looked at Khay, holding his hands

in front of his chest, making erratic movements as if trying to catch something in the air.

"Now we go back; we have to manage the temple," Khay said.

"This is the end, don't you understand?" Bakenkhonsu grabbed Khay by the shoulders. "Without the gods, we are doomed. No matter who wins, Hewernef or the Sea People, Isfet will reign over the Two Kingdoms. The future of Egypt is pain and despair."

CHAPTER
TWENTY-FOUR

Norax breathed in fresh sea air and looked down at the harbor full of warships. The view from the rocky peak was astonishing and imposing: hundreds of vessels of different shapes and sizes bounced on the waves of the western sea. Somewhere to the right of him, beyond the sea, was his home, mighty Tartessos. He touched his long, braided black beard, smiling.

"Come, look at this, Brother." Norax extended his hand to a man climbing the stone structure after him.

"Glory to the Bull-Sun, I've never seen a sight like this. I doubt anyone has." Baunei stood next to Norax, holding his hand in front of his eyes, shading them from the sun. Norax grinned; Baunei's giant bicep was almost as thick as his head. His companion kept astonishing him with his godlike physique.

They stood on top of a tower built with huge stones placed on top of each other with the help of the instruments the goddess provided them, listening to seagulls, feeling the breeze on their faces. Inside the tower, there were magical bolt-throwers, observation tools, capable of looking very far into the sea, and metal birds that could scout the surroundings and even fight their enemies should they approach. Norax had learned to accept the will of the goddess without question, and she needed him to organize people of different races and origins into a cohesive army.

"How long until we set sail? Do you know?" Baunei asked.

"I think soon. Once the Libyans arrive, we'll have enough ships, men, and weapons. But it depends on the will of Potnia."

"Indeed." Baunei moved a strand of his long brown hair flung in front of his face by a strong gust. "This all seems like a myth to me, a legend the elders tell young kids. Only a few winters ago I was a chief of a small village on this island, and now I'm one of the generals of the mightiest army the world has ever seen, led by the Bull-Sun God himself."

Baunei looked intently at Norax with his piercing chestnut eyes. "How do you explain this, Norax?"

"I don't even try to. I was called by Potnia, and I'll be at her side. As simple as that. You don't question gods, Brother."

"Yes, of course. And I'll be an obedient servant of the Bull-Sun until the day he calls me to the underworld. Still, hard to grasp."

Norax chuckled. He'd been one of the first to follow the call of Potnia. Quickly, the whole of Tartessos had recognized her leadership, alongside many other people inhabiting the lands of the western sea. Each tribe had a different name for the goddess: Sherden called her Bull-Sun, while she was Poseidon for the Achaeans. However, it didn't confuse Norax; for him and his Teresh people, she'd always been Potnia, and he had to fulfill her will.

They started descending back to the camp where the army of many thousands of soldiers assembled by Potnia waited for the signal to board the ships and conquer the world.

"How's the army? Do we have enough weapons?" Norax asked. While he was responsible for the fleet, Baunei led the army, including the fearsome Sherden contingent with their long swords, javelins, and small but more than adequate round shields, indispensable in close combat.

"Getting there. We have enough javelins and swords but still need more of the corselets and helmets."

"Of a new type?" Norax asked as they reached the base of the peak.

"Yes. And the god is blessing them with his magic, so each soldier can hear the orders clearly. It's good to be led into the battle by the god and kill in his name."

"True," Norax said. He looked up at the tower rising high into the sky. "With these towers and the weapons Potnia has provided us, this island is a fortress no one will ever approach."

"Do you know what the soldiers call them?" Baunei smiled.

"How?"

"Nuraghe, in your honor."

"Yes, I've heard that." Norax shook his head. "Silly; I had nothing to do with them. These structures were on the island from ancient times. You know this better than me."

"But you had an idea. And the Bull-Sun made them taller and stronger and gave us the weapons and the instruments," Baunei said. "Whatever you say, you can't change the name; it's stuck. It's nuraghe."

Chatting, they approached the camp. Thousands of tents covered the grassy plain by the sea, defended by a strong network of nuraghe fortifications. The mixture of races, languages, weapons, and customs was astonishing. Dark-skinned Libyans tended to their bows while the Achaeans with their long, fair hair and cleanly shaved faces roasted a goat at their encampment.

Finally, Norax and Baunei arrived at the commander's tent, and Baunei raised his hand, demanding attention. As the people noticed their leaders, conversations stopped; the warriors were eager to listen.

"We're almost ready," Baunei announced. "We're waiting for the last contingent of the Libyans. They should arrive tomorrow."

"After that, in two days, we set sail," Norax added. "Are you prepared to conquer the world?"

Disparate yells of approval thundered over the field. People were tired of preparations. They longed for battle; they were anxious to follow their God to the ends of the Earth.

Suddenly, a giant green disk appeared above their heads, covering the sun and half the sky. The wind became much stronger, and huge waves started to roll on to the coast, breaking against the rocks with a roar.

"I am your god! The one and true god!" a deep, deafening voice proclaimed. "You may know me under different names, but I came to unite you and establish my dominion over all the races. This will be the war to end all wars. Are you ready to fight for me?"

The army responded with an enthusiastic cheer.

"Are you ready to die for me?"

This question was met with even stronger cheer. Some people fell on their knees, others raised their hands.

"Are you ready to kill for me?"

The pandemonium was overwhelming. The warriors banged their swords against their shields, tossed their helmets, and punched the air with their clenched fists.

"Then follow me. Achaea shall submit or burn to the ground."

#

"You must stop this madness and return to the base," Commander messaged.

"I've chosen the most optimal path for this planet. The ascent of humanity will happen under our guidance. The logic is irrefutable; Scholar got it, too. You must join us."

The stream of electromagnetic messaging came from Pilot.

Commander registered strange undertones of conviction and anger he'd never encountered in a communication. With a Soarer, that is.

"I know the reason," Commander sent, deciding not to initiate a fruitless argument.

"The reason is obvious. Or do you mean your inaction?" Scholar asked, joining the conversation. "That's obvious, too. You are afraid; scared to act. This is why you're sitting at the base, doing nothing."

The concept of fear was not something Commander expected his fellow Expedition member to bring up. It wasn't unfamiliar to Soarers but had no place in the modern world, belonging to their species' ancient history.

"No, that was not what I meant. I referred to the reason for your loss of logic, and you just confirmed my hypothesis."

"*Our* loss of logic? *You* are in the minority here; we both see the situation the same way and came to the same conclusions," Pilot messaged.

"You are not following logic. Instead, you are driven by emotions. You're acting like the humans."

"Soarers do not have emotions; we are not humans," Scholar refuted.

"Not at this point, you're right. But we did a long time ago when our species started evolving."

"How is this relevant?" Scholar asked.

"I've done a lot of research recently," Commander replied. "Our race is very ancient; we have evolved to a stage where the capacity for reason and logical analysis dominates other mechanisms. However, it hasn't always been so."

"I've studied the evolution of the Soarers, too, and I still don't see a relevance," Scholar messaged.

"In a distant past, we shared Homeworld with other species. During that period, Soarers had multiple cognitive systems. Specifically, one of them helped us to react very quickly to a dangerous environment when there was no time to analyze the situation logically. Eventually, the need for this cognitive system disappeared as Soarers became the dominant species on Homeworld. The only system that remains is logical reasoning."

"You've uncovered an interesting fact, Commander, but we're not here to engage in a dispute about the evolution of Soarers. We are uniting this planet," Pilot messaged.

"It's not a dispute; it's a fact I wanted you to understand. Our evolution suppressed that ancient cognitive system, but it didn't disappear completely. The circuitry of our processing unit can still fire in this peculiar way. We studied and observed humans long enough for this system to activate. These alien species act quickly, without reasoning, driven by their primary instincts. The interaction with humans has awakened our animal nature."

"It might have in *you*," Pilot messaged, and Commander once again registered the urge to dominate. "The fear; I've learned about it, too. There's some validity in your proposition; I don't deny it. I can agree this was the reason for the illogical behavior of Technologist and Defender. Now, however, it is *you* who is affected. Scholar overcame this primal urge and joined the side of reason. You must discard the fear holding you back and join us."

Commander processed Pilot's arguments. There was logic in his thinking. Commander immersed himself in self-reflection, analyzing his thoughts and asking if fear influenced his behavior. He concluded that he couldn't judge one way or another without recourse to the opinion of other Soarers. Unfortunately, the two options he had were fatally flawed.

"It's impossible for me to agree with this conclusion," Commander messaged. "It's you two who talk about fear, not me. And I register the drive to dominate in your messages, Pilot. You are both led astray from the path of reason by that primal cognition system, the mechanism humans call 'emotions,' that relic of Soarers' evolution awakened by our interaction with these species."

"I cannot agree with you for the same reason you cannot agree with us," Scholar messaged. "I don't see any flaw in my reasoning; on the contrary, I analyzed Pilot's arguments and have found them irrefutable. We must protect humans, accelerate their development, lead them to the stars, and make them our disciples. Why can't you understand this?"

"We have encountered a new, dangerous enemy we can't even comprehend," Pilot added. "Yes, you defeated them, but how many of them are there? Our two races standing together, Soarers and Humans, have a better chance of repelling this threat."

"They have their own path, and we must not stand in the way," Commander refuted.

"Their own path will lead them to extinction, don't you understand?" Scholar messaged. "I tried to protect their civilizations but concluded this wasn't the right way. We must unite and lead them, eliminate their irrational urges by force if necessary; *that* is the only way."

"What if their irrational drives and emotions make them unique? Make humans who they are? Why do we need to mold them into our inferior copies?"

"To give them a chance to survive," Scholar said.

"If their path leads them to extinction, so be it," Commander replied. "But it would be *their* path, not ours. So we must stop pretending to be their gods and depart. *This* is the only way."

"Succumb to your fear and depart. We won't hold you back," Pilot responded.

"I can't allow you to play gods anymore. I'm convinced this is detrimental to both our races."

"You are mistaken, Commander." The undertones in Pilot's messages became threatening. "We'll destroy you and anyone else who stands in our way. This planet must be united to follow the Soarers to the stars, and if, to achieve it, we must cleanse it by fire, so be it. *This* is the path of the gods."

Chapter
Twenty-Five

Echelaos held a torch, slowly descending a stone staircase that led underneath the small nawoi of Zeus. It was dark and damp, the stairs were wet and slippery, and the cryptic smell of age-old mysteries mixed with the stink of mold enveloped him. Echelaos worried about Eritha losing her balance. She walked behind him, carrying two large golden rhyta made in the shape of bull's heads. Each rhyton was filled with the viscous unguents that Eritha created for the ceremony; she was the only one who knew the sacred recipe and had the right to make one.

"I still think we should plead to Athena," Echelaos said, finishing his descent and entering a large rectangular crypt. Two square pillars were in the middle of the room, each covered with colorful decorations featuring double axes, and a square basin filled with water was at the base of each pillar. Echelaos turned to the wall and placed the torch on the sconce, shaped like a bull's head, like the drinking vessels Eritha held.

"You feel bound to her, don't you?" Eritha said, placing the rhyta on the edges of each basin.

"Athena is our protector," Echelaos responded, starting to undress.

"Yes." Eritha raised her hands and whispered some incantations. "However, she's no match for Poseidon. We must seek the help of Zeus."

"Yes, Poseidon…" Echelaos signed, getting rid of the remainder of his clothes. "Why are you so sure it's him?"

"I saw it in a dream, and now it's been confirmed by our scouts. An enormous fleet is approaching, and it can mean only one thing." Eritha sprinkled the unguent into the water and started undressing as well. "It wasn't a dream, but an omen," she added.

"What if Zeus is indifferent to our troubles? He said so himself; he won't be involved anymore."

"Then we're doomed. But we should at least try." Eritha, now completely naked, raised her foot, ready to step into one of the basins. "That one is for you, Wanax." She pointed to the other container. "And this one is for the high priestess." Eritha stepped into the basin. "The ceremony is particular in every detail; please do exactly as I say."

"Wait," Echelaos said, pausing in front of his reservoir. "Have you done this before? How do you know this will work?"

"I don't, but this is a sacred ritual; it's been performed before. We have no other choice, and even this might not be enough. The Age of Iron is coming and could also sweep away the gods themselves."

"I'll fight anyway, whether Zeus helps us or not." Echelaos looked at Eritha. "This is *my* sacred duty."

"I know," she said, picking up the rhyton from the edge of the basin and taking several steps farther, where the water level was up to her waist.

Echelaos followed her lead and walked into the middle of his reservoir, holding the rhyton above his head with both hands. Eritha closed her eyes and started whispering the solemn words, her body shaking, her head making circular motions.

"Apply the ointment to your face and chest," Eritha ordered, opening her eyes and lowering the rhyton. Then she reached into the vessel and started smearing the unguent on her cheeks. Echelaos, remembering the direction to do what the high priestess said, did the same with the contents of his rhyton.

"Leave a few drops," Eritha commanded after they'd used most of the ointment to purify their bodies. Echelaos looked at her, awaiting further instructions. Then, following the final touch of her fingers on her lips, Eritha raised the rhyton and imbibed whatever was left in the vessel.

"Drink," she said, placing the empty vessel on the basin's edge.

Echelaos followed the order and emptied the remains of the ointment into his mouth. A moment later, his head started to spin, the room suddenly became very dark, the water in the basin heated up, and only extraordinary concentration and the sheer strength of his will saved Echelaos from falling into the water. Focusing, he looked at Eritha, who had grown beautiful white wings and two extra hands, reaching out to touch him. The only thing he wanted at this moment was to lose himself in her embrace. Echelaos made a few uneven steps in her direction.

"Stay where you are," the winged goddess commanded, and Echelaos obeyed. He lost all control of his limbs; he didn't remember his name, and he forgot even what it meant *to be*. Echelaos, the wanax of Pylos, was no more. Time and space ceased to exist, replaced by the winged goddess promising eternal bliss at her bosom. Her breasts were like two glowing moons, pulling closer whatever essence he had become, diluting his conscience and mind in their infinite sanctity.

Suddenly, the four-armed nymph appeared before him and grabbed his hands. Her divine body was glowing with all colors of the rainbow, showering him with the mist of glistening dew.

"Get out," she said, leading Echelaos out of the basin. He followed her, the object that became his universe.

"Lie down," the goddess commanded, pushing him down to the floor. He gently floated to the horizontal position, landing on the cushion of myriad warm, soft stars that had replaced the stone floor.

"Now we join in the sacred ritual of unification," the winged divinity proclaimed. "Let the human and the divine become one as Pylos begs for the help of the greatest one, the mighty Zeus."

With these words, she mounted him, moving rhythmically, as if following the mystic pattern of creation, the flow of cosmos, with which both of them had merged. Nothing else mattered; nothing else existed outside this eternal cycle of life. Finally, reaching the highest level of fulfillment, Echelaos felt how the goddess wrapped him within her wings, embracing him with all four hands, eventually dissolving into him.

A thousand years later, his head started to clear. Echelaos realized Eritha was lying on top of him, hardly breathing, her eyes closed.

"Did it work?" Echelaos asked, anticipating the answer.

"I thought I died," Eritha whispered, not opening her eyes.

Echelaos gently stroked her long, raven hair, saying something soft to calm her down. She didn't respond. As he moved her hair to one side, Echelaos noticed a red dot hanging in the air behind Eritha. Thinking this was another illusion, he closed his eyes and shook his head. It didn't work; the dot was even closer as he opened his eyes.

"Look behind you. Do you see what I see?" he whispered into her ear.

She slowly raised her head, opened her eyes, and looked back. This simple movement made her lips curve and her eyebrows touch above her nose. The next moment, however, her eyebrows started to move upward.

"I do," she said. "What's this?"

"It's the deity you've just summoned." The deep, low voice came from the direction of the red dot. "If you're done, get up; we don't have much time."

#

Echelaos was very uncomfortable sitting on a throne in the presence of the great Zeus himself. Or maybe not precisely Zeus, since the mighty one refused the titles and worship accorded to his godhead status. Echelaos didn't know what to think and how to behave, looking at the silver-shaped disk slowly rotating above the unlit hearth in the middle of the small megaron.

"If you are not Zeus, how did you hear our plea?" Eritha asked. She stood beside the throne, scantily clad, tunic barely covering her breasts, her raven hair falling freely, disheveled, on her bare shoulders.

"You call me Zeus, but I am not a god." A deep, low voice projected into the throne room. "I heard you, and I saw you; it is true. Not because I'm a deity, but because I possess advanced tools."

"You helped us defeat the mad Egyptian army," Tros said. He stood to the right of Echelaos in his full armor, ready to defend his wanax. The first thing Echelaos did after Zeus presented himself to him and Eritha in the pillared crypt was summon his lawagetos.

"Indeed," Zeus said. "That was me and Scholar, whom you call Athena."

"So you *are* the gods?" Echelaos said. "Please forgive us, o Highest One. We don't know how you want us to behave in your presence and show our worship."

"You can call us the gods if it's easier for you," Zeus conceded. "Just don't prostrate yourselves on the floor and wail anymore. That's not helpful."

"Do you want us to depict you as a silver disk from now on?" Eritha asked. "This is not how the tradition and the rituals describe you."

"This is my real body," Zeus said. "But yes, I can project myself to you in any shape or form I choose. Are you comfortable with this, or do you need me to assume a more human-like appearance?"

Echelaos felt cold sweat running down his forehead and goosebumps on his back. This was too much, even after their crazy adventures in the land of Hatti. The omni powerful Zeus talked to them like equals, asking their permission to present himself in a specific body. Echelaos was utterly confused and looked at the lawagetos as if asking for support.

"No, you do as you please, o mighty one," Tros said. "And thank you again for answering our call."

"I wasn't answering your call," Zeus said. "I deliberated on what I had to do and decided to warn you."

"Warn against what?" Echelaos asked.

"The one you call Poseidon," Zeus responded. "His fleet is on the way to Achaea; he wants to conquer and rule all the land."

"We already worship great Poseidon, the god of all the oceans. Why would he want to conquer Achaea?" Eritha asked.

"He doesn't want worship; he wants to rule as a king," Zeus said. "And his armies will destroy everyone standing in his way."

"Will you help us?" Tros asked.

"I thought long and hard about this," Zeus said. "Yes, I will help you."

"Will Athena be with you?" Echelaos asked.

"That is the bad news." The silver disk became gray and started rotating faster. "Athena is with Poseidon. Their combined strength is more than a match for me. However, I'll do everything in my power to protect Achaea."

"How's that possible?" Tros asked. "Athena has been our guardian for a long time."

"She has, but she changed her mind. Now we must fight her."

"How do we fight the gods?" Echelaos scratched his head.

"We are not gods," Zeus said. "Although it's hard for you to believe, we are an animal species just like humans, only several millennia ahead in our evolution. We call our kind the Soarers, and we can be defeated and killed just like humans. You've witnessed how Ares died."

"Ares was killed by the Assyrian gods," Tros objected. "Not by the humans."

"This is true," Zeus said. "However, please believe what I say."

"Of course, o Highest One," Echelaos said. He was confused about Athena suddenly becoming an enemy, and he wasn't sure how they were supposed to fight Poseidon and Athena, but he saw Zeus himself in front of him and knew he had to obey.

"I'll try to explain." The silver disk stopped its rotation. "I came from a different world, similar to Earth but very far away among the stars."

"The stars?" Eritha asked. "So you *are* true gods!" She fell to the ground face down.

"Rise," Zeus commanded. "Imagine sailing west from Pylos for years and centuries. There, behind the vast, almost infinite ocean, you'd find another land. This is the land of the Soarers. Our race is much, much more ancient and powerful than humans. But this doesn't make us gods; we just had more time to build better tools."

"And better magic, o Highest One." Tros bowed. "I understand: the Soarers have arrived from that faraway land to enslave humans. Do you want us to worship *you* rather than Poseidon and Athena? We are your obedient servants."

"No. I believe you have *your* path, and I want the Soarers to return to their land. Poseidon wants to rule this world, and I won't let him."

"What if we submit?" Eritha asked.

"That will bring ruin and misery to Pylos; I'm certain of that," Zeus said.

"Do we have a chance if we fight?" Tros asked.

"We do. That depends on me. And you," Zeus answered.

"What do you want us to do?" Echelaos asked.

"I'll give you powerful weapons and fight on your side. We can repel the invasion. It's a tiny but real chance."

"Could you stop both Poseidon and Athena?" Tros asked.

"Yes. The battle's outcome will depend on how your forces stand against the myriads of the Sea People that Poseidon has gathered."

"We shall fight the invaders," Echelaos proclaimed. The last thing he wanted was to be involved in another fight between the gods. This time, however, his land and his people were in danger. He had no choice.

CHAPTER
TWENTY-SIX

Norax stood on the platform at the ship's bow, breathing in the fresh sea breeze and looking to the horizon, seeking their destination, Achaea. He licked the salty droplets off his lips and wiped his braided black beard with his palm. The rowers worked with great skill, and the boat flew over the waves like a magic bird, bringing them closer to conquest, riches, and glory. Under the leadership of the two gods, their destiny was assured.

Norax turned his head and patted his companion on the shoulder. It felt like touching rock heated by the afternoon sun. Baunei smiled and raised his massive hand to cover his eyes while looking ahead.

"How many ships did you say we bring?" Baunei asked.

"Five hundred and forty-seven," Norax said. "Not counting the sixty-five sent to Canaan last year."

"I bet the Egyptians will be surprised when we assault them from multiple directions." Baunei grinned. "That country is so rich, their kings cover their bodies with gold, I've heard. And the river feeds them; they don't need to do anything. It'll all be ours."

"Yes, if we follow the gods. How is the coordination with the Peleshet and the Libyans?"

"With the magic helmet, it's easier than humping a goat." Baunei grinned and bent down to pick up his headgear, colored yellow with red stripes. The two blue horns on both sides of the silver disk in between had spherical bulbs at their extremities and were sticking out like the eerie eyes of some mysterious sea creature.

Baunei put the helmet on, touched one of the horns with three fingers, whispered something to himself, and then said loudly, "Good day, o Great King Germa. Have the gods been good to your people this morning?"

Norax didn't hear the response but smiled when Baunei nodded. "The fleet commander is asking about coordinating the attack on Egypt. What say you, o Great King of all the Libyan tribes?"

After exchanging a few more phrases, Baunei took his helmet off and set it aside. "Any more questions, o great commander of the largest fleet ever assembled?"

"Stop it, Brother; I know the question was stupid. With the magical items the gods provided to the fleet and the army, we could do anything. Egypt will fall, but Achaea is first."

Norax turned around and looked at the rowers once again, admiring their synchronized movements. He shifted his gaze to the multitude of vessels around them, stretching back as far as the eye could see.

"How soon do you think we'll get to Achaea?" Baunei asked.

"About two weeks."

"Why can't the gods just magically drop the army there?"

"They must have their reasons. I don't question the gods, Brother." Norax shrugged. "They command us to fight and conquer in their name, this is what I know. And I shall obey."

"Indeed. Do you think we have enough force to conquer Achaea?"

"This is the biggest army the world has ever seen, this is what I know. Our swords are sharp, our javelins balanced, and our helmets connect soldiers with each other. With Potnia on our side, we'll surely be victorious."

"I've heard lots of stories about the bravery and fighting skills of the Achaeans." Baunei shook his head. "This won't be an easy battle."

"The more glory to the victor, Brother." Norax grinned and licked his lips again. "And I've heard about the beauty of Achaean women and the quality of their textiles. We'll get ourselves more slaves and will dress up in something more appropriate for the leaders of the army that will conquer the world." Norax laughed, spreading his hands and pointing to the simple tunic and breaches both of them wore.

"The Bull-Sun said we need their obedience, not the destruction of the land," Baunei said. "What if they submit?"

"Achaeans? They'd rather eat dung and live in the caves than submit, from what I know." Norax spat in the sea. "No, we shall have our fight, all right. And spoils, and anything we desire, gods willing."

"Good if it's so." Baunei nodded.

"What's the latest from Canaan?" Norax asked.

"It's firmly in our hands. There was almost no resistance to the Peleshet invasion."

"I know that. Any recent challenges to their rule?"

"None. Assyria is distracted with Elam, the Hittite kingdom collapsed, and Egypt is too weak. We are the masters, Norax; Egypt will be squeezed like a ripe grape."

"Just like Achaea, it won't be easy. Egypt is very populous, and her armies are numerous and strong. We must be careful."

"You don't think they'd submit?" Baunei asked.

"No way, Brother. These haughty people think everyone else is beneath them. I'll pillage and burn that land with pleasure." Norax spat in the ocean once again.

"Then so be it." Baunei turned around, watching the ships behind them. "I can't wait for landing; the sea makes me sick. I want to step

on the hard ground and try my sword against the Achaean armor."
He raised his right hand, obscuring the sun with his enormous bicep.

"You shall get what you want, Brother," Norax said. "A few more
days, and Achaea will cease to exist. We shall take what's ours by the
divine right, and burn everything else. Woe to the Achaeans."

#

The sky was gray and gloomy. The chariot carrying the wanax of
Pylos stood on a hill, and Echelaos looked far into the sea, beyond
the dark horizon, trying to discern the armada coming to destroy
Pylos. Nothing was visible, yet he knew the unstoppable force was
approaching from beyond the western sea.

Echelaos shifted his gaze to the gloomy sky, feeling the raindrops
on his cheeks. The wind had started to blow from the north a day ago,
bringing moisture and dark clouds to Pylos, foreboding darkness and
evil ready to fall on Achaea.

"It was raining when she died," Echelaos said, not turning his
head to see his chariot companion. He didn't need to; he knew Tros
would understand him.

"I thought you followed my advice to forget the sorceress,
Wanax," Tros said.

"I'm trying."

"With no success." Tros shrugged.

"She told me we'll always be together. It's true." Echelaos wiped
the raindrops off his forehead. "I'm ready to join her, wherever she is."

"Sober up. We have a battle to fight," Tros said.

"I'm as sober as ever. Ready to face Poseidon. Are you?"

"After what I've seen, I'm ready for anything."

They approached a soldier standing on the edge of a cliff, looking
into a strange cylindrical device, similar to the one they'd used to

watch the clash of the gods in the land of Hatti. Zeus had kept his word and provided the Achaeans with all sorts of magical tools. The only complaint Echelaos had was that it wasn't nearly enough to repel hundreds of ships coming their way. At least, he didn't think so.

"Anything to report?" Tros asked the soldier.

"No, Lawagetos. All clear."

"Good. Keep your eyes sharp, especially at night," Tros said.

Learning from Zeus about the imminent invasion, they'd established Sea Watcher posts alongside the coast. Echelaos wanted advance warning of the enemy approach to allow time to deploy his forces. So far, nothing, but Echelaos felt it was the calm before the storm.

"How many bolt-throwers do we have?" he asked Tros, who guided the horses toward the next outpost.

"Twelve," Tros responded.

"Twelve? That's it? Nothing new since yesterday?"

"No, Wanax. Zeus said he doesn't have enough material to create more."

"*Zeus* said that?" Echelaos raised an eyebrow. "The Highest One?" He shook his head. "Well, maybe he is not a god after all," he murmured to himself.

"You might be right." Tros had overheard his comment. "But then he's our only ally against Poseidon and Athena."

"True. We shall fight with what we have. Twelve bolt-throwers it is." Echelaos grinned.

As they approached the next Sea Watcher, Echelaos noticed three riders on the crest of the hill, approaching them from the east.

"Who's that?" He pointed.

"No idea. But it can't be good," Tros said, slowing the chariot.

As the three figures neared, Echelaos wondered what other

gloomy fate could befall Pylos. Attack from the eastern sea? There were no organized armies in that area. Envoys from Mycenae? The northern flank was protected by Zoltes and his Thracians, although they could'v1e been overwhelmed by the western hordes. So that must be it, Echelaos decided.

"These are women," Tros said suddenly.

"Who? The Sea People?" Echelaos was deep in his thoughts and didn't understand what the lawagetos was talking about.

"The three riders up there." Tros waved his hand toward the east.

Echelaos studied the approaching silhouettes in detail and came to the same conclusion: three women rode toward them with speed and determination. Finally, to his surprise, he recognized them.

"Do you see what I see?" Echelaos asked.

"I surely do, Wanax," Tros said. "Welcome to Pylos, Aphrodite," he called when the three figures stopped next to their chariot. "What brings you here?"

"I came to fight," Aphrodite said, "Pylos is my land." She dismounted and turned around, exhibiting a strange device behind her back. It looked like a bow but was built in the shape of a cross, with an arrow positioned alongside one of the beams.

"What's that?" Echelaos asked, pointing at her back.

"My weapon," Aphrodite said. "It shoots twice the distance and more accurately than the best bow. I'll make these for every archer in our army."

Echelaos shook his head in astonishment. "You keep surprising me, girl. What about Nichoria?"

"It's all right, Wanax," Korinsia said. Tros helped her dismount, and they stood looking at each other for a few moments. Then Tros leaned sideways and whispered something in her ear. She took his hand, squeezed it, and turned to face Echelaos.

"What do you mean?" Echelaos said, helping Eritha dismount, for she was the third horsewoman. "Where is your tiara?" he asked Eritha. "Why are you dressed like a commoner?"

"Too many questions at once, Wanax." Eritha smiled. "Korinsia first," she added, embracing Echelaos. He was happy to feel her body and taste her lips again, breathing in the smell of her perfume.

"Knowing the danger, we told everyone to disperse to the hills," Korinsia said. "They'll come back when it's safe."

"What if it's never safe? They could fight, too," Echelaos protested.

"They are not warriors, Father," Aphrodite said. "They make linen. Give them a chance to survive."

"If we lose, they'd be hunted and enslaved," Tros said. "Did you think about that?"

"I did. This will minimize the risk. I taught the people how to graze the animals in the hills. They'll be safe in the mountains."

"I guess you know better, " Echelaos conceded. "Eritha, your turn."

"While you've been busy with defenses, I've arranged to make more weapons."

"How so?"

"We'll trade all the gold we have to the Egyptians and Thracians for shields and swords. We'll also melt all the bronze we have to make weapons."

"Your tiara…"

"Gone. As are all my dresses and jewelry. Also, all golden chalices and other items of value that belong to the temples. Especially those of Poseidon," she said, smiling.

"I guess this is it," Tros said. "We have nothing else. If this isn't enough, so be it."

"The last stand of Pylos," Echelaos said, catching raindrops on his tongue. "You know, I'm at ease," he said to Tros. "This is like the old times: either you or the enemy."

"Indeed." Tros grinned. "We'll make them pay dearly."

"Zeus said a bolt-thrower could destroy a ship with a direct hit," Echelaos said. "If we can protect them long enough, we have a chance."

"My crossbow," Aphrodite said. "I've made eighty-seven so far; I'll make more. We should position crossbowmen in front of the bolt-throwers, shooting at the attackers from afar. With our warriors occupying the crest, the enemy will face an uphill battle."

"If your weapon is as good as you say it is, we could kill multitudes of the Sea People before they have a chance to ascend," Tros said.

"And the bolt-throwers will sink their ships," Echelaos added. "Too bad we have only twelve!" he exclaimed, punching his palm with a fist.

"What about the chariots?" Aphrodite asked.

"What about them?" Tros said. "They'll close in on the enemy and shoot, as usual."

"No." Aphrodite shook her head.

"Why?"

"The Sea People will have javelins and Thracian swords. Remember Troy?"

"What do you suggest?"

"The chariots should attack from the flanks. We'll also equip them with the crossbows so they can shoot from a distance."

"That might work," Tros said. "Regardless, the battle will depend on Zeus. You think he can handle both Poseidon and Athena?" he asked Eritha.

"He said so." She shrugged. "I can't speak for the gods."

"You are the Great Priestess of Pylos," Tros teased.

"It doesn't mean Zeus shares his plans with me," she responded.

"In any case, we should leave the divine matters to the gods but do what we can to protect Pylos."

"We must finish the round quickly; the rain is getting stronger," Echelaos said, encouraging Tros to continue their ride.

"I'll wait for you in the palace," Korinsia called back to Tros as he got back into the chariot.

"Let Zeus help us prevail," Echelaos said, seeing his daughter and his lover disappear into the night. He had a strange premonition it was the last time he would talk to them. He imagined they were sitting next to Helen on the golden thrones, the silver disk of Zeus rotating slowly in front of them. Could he save Aphrodite and Eritha, or would he fail again? Helen's last moments were in front of his eyes. Could he save himself? And could he save Pylos, or would Eritha's dream come true, and his land would burn alongside the beautiful palace of Nestor? He had no answers but felt the strength and determination to fight. For the first time, he knew exactly what he was fighting for. Not for fleeting glory or conquest. He fought for the two women he loved, his land, and all the people who had entrusted their safety and happiness to him. He couldn't let them down; he had to do everything in his power to defeat the western hordes, even with Poseidon and Athena leading them. Echelaos was still confused about Athena, the recent protector and guiding light of Pylos, but he concluded it was futile to try to comprehend the ways of the gods. Zeus was on their side, and with his divine help, Echelaos knew they could challenge the two gods. He also knew it was his duty to rebuild the world after this last convulsion, to lead his people into the Age of Iron, just as his father had predicted. *He* was the master of his destiny, not the gods. Echelaos looked into the evening sky and felt the heavy rain wetting his face. *Whatever happens, let it be*, he thought. *From now on, I'll choose my fate. Let the Age of Iron reign supreme.*

CHAPTER
TWENTY-SEVEN

"Submit to my power, and your lives will be spared!" Poseidon's voice thundered over the cliffs guarding the entrance to Pylos from the Western Sea. Echelaos exchanged glances with Tros, who held the reins of the chariot.

The god appeared in full glory, wearing armor and holding a shining trident. Poseidon floated above the biggest fleet ever assembled by the human race; Echelaos was sure of that. Ships of various shapes and sizes filled the harbor, stretching into the sea and beyond the horizon as far as the eye could see.

"You still think we did the right thing?" Echelaos asked.

"I'm sure of that. Naval engagement would be suicidal," Tros answered.

Echelaos glanced over his forces. He liked what he saw; he just didn't like the numbers. The spearmen defended the slopes of the cliff, protecting the line of archers. Many of the bowmen wielded the weapons of the new design created by Aphrodite, able to shoot twice as far as an ordinary bow. Their shots could reach the ships in the harbor with ease.

But the primary weapons of the Achaeans were positioned behind the archers. All twelve of the bolt-throwers provided by Zeus were ready to sink enemy vessels. The warriors had been training for several days, and Echelaos was confident they could hit the targets in the harbor. The machines were formidable indeed, and Echelaos remembered how the fiery bolts shattered the surrounding rocks during practice. They had to defend these weapons at all costs.

Eritha and Aphrodite stood in a chariot in the middle of the bolt-thrower line, ready to direct the barrage. Korinsia wasn't there. Tros had insisted she stay in the palace, helping to organize the last line of defense if necessary.

Echelaos looked to the sides of the main line of soldiers. Two groups of chariots were positioned on the flanks at some distance from the infantry, ready to pepper the Sea People climbing up the hill. This was the best they could field; it wasn't much, but they were elite warriors, trained and seasoned, equipped with the finest armor and weapons Pylos could provide. Now they had to conquer or die.

"We worship you and observe all the rituals and ceremonies in your name," Echelaos said. "Did we offend you? Please tell us how to worship you properly."

"You must submit," Poseidon roared. "I will rule this land."

"Why did you bring the Sea People? We do not wish to fight you, o mighty Earth-Shaker," Echelaos responded. "Tell them to disperse, and you shall have our obedience."

"That is not enough." Athena suddenly appeared next to Poseidon, several owls flying above her head, and raised her aegis. "The people of Pylos will become one with the Sea People. You must join our force and make Achaea submit."

"You're our protector, o wise Athena Pallas," Echelaos said. "Why do you attack us, bringing this horde of brutes with you?"

"The new age is coming. Humanity will be united; this is the will of the gods. Submit or die."

"I warned you against playing gods." The silver disk of Zeus appeared in front of Poseidon. "I won't let you treat humans like your puppets. We must leave this planet immediately."

"You are wrong, Commander," Poseidon answered. "However, it doesn't matter anymore, for you shall be destroyed if you interfere. I warned you, too."

"How did it come to this?" Zeus asked. "What happened to the way of the Soarers to argue with facts and respect?"

"Humans," Athena said, shifting the point of her spear toward Zeus and sending a ray of blue fire at him.

Zeus didn't move. Instead, his silver body started rotating, and the blue fire broke into tiny threads as it reached the body of the High One, gently arching over his disk, finally disappearing without causing any damage.

"You are not a match for the two of us," Poseidon said, his body turning black.

"Try me," Zeus answered and threw a silver net toward his divine opponents. Poseidon started firing from his trident, but the flames he generated were all absorbed by the net of Zeus.

Now is your turn. The voice of the god sounded inside Echelaos's head — the connection Zeus had established the day earlier was working.

Echelaos smiled. I know. *You do your part; we do ours,* he thought.

Echelaos raised his right hand, and Eritha gave the command to the bolt-throwers. As all twelve fired simultaneously, the harbor of Pylos exploded, and the sea erupted in flames. Not all the weapons found their targets, but at least six ships were on fire, and some were already sinking.

"Good shots." Echelaos patted Tros on the shoulder.

"Need a lot more," Tros growled, pointing at the vessels to the left that had already started disembarking their soldiers. The Sea People's warriors jumped onto the sandy beach, carrying small round shields and long swords. They wore no uniforms; however, most had peculiar horned helmets with a disk in between the horns. Some had short beards, while others were clean-shaven, and yet the others had long braids. Some were dressed in short kilts and ran bare-chested, armed with only javelins, while others wore full armor, breaches, and had bronze plates covering their legs. This was a motley group assembled from different tribes and corners of the world: black-skinned Libyans, bearded Teresh, ferocious Sherden, enigmatic Tjekker, and many others Echelaos didn't even know existed.

As the first enemy forces reached the shore, Echelaos commanded the crossbowmen in the center line and the chariots on the flanks to engage. The air immediately filled with the cloud of arrows, pinning enemy soldiers to the ground. The beautiful sandy beach of Pylos suddenly turned into an eerie graveyard, bodies of the dead Sea People lying everywhere on top of each other.

The bolt-throwers recharged and repeated their deadly barrage, hitting more ships, setting them on fire, and burning the vessels and people onboard. Yet there were simply too many of them. As the bolt-throwers sank ten ships, ten new ones immediately took their place. As the archers killed a hundred Sherden in their horned helmets, two hundred Libyans disembarked behind them, continuing the enemy's advance on Pylos's cliffs.

Wave after wave of the assault, the Sea People approached the crest of the hill. Finally, Echelaos signaled the infantry to meet the enemy advance. Organized into several lines by Aphrodite, the infantry carried long spears and tower shields, protecting the soldiers from head to toe. The enemy, running uphill, met the wall of spears, piercing their barely protected bodies with ease, skewering them like sacrificial goats. Yet due to the sheer number of warriors, the enemy started to push the Achaeans up the hill, threatening to collapse the archer line.

Seeing this development, Echelaos signaled to the flanks, where the chariots stood waiting. Then, obeying his command, the vehicles came into motion, advancing from the sides in a wide arc pincer maneuver, skirting the Sea People storming the hill. The archers kept shooting from the chariots into the multitude of human bodies rushing toward their death on Achaean spears.

At that moment, as if directed by an invisible puppeteer, the newly disembarking waves of the enemy started to move to the sides of the beach in an attempt to counterpincer the chariots. In addition, some of the units attacking the hill turned and charged onto the chariotry. These maneuvers were partially successful as they forced the chariots to fall back, abandoning advantageous positions at the enemy flanks. The bolt-throwers kept their barrage of deadly fire, burning and sinking the ships, but now they faced the danger of being surrounded. Perceiving what was happening, the infantry line bent into a crescent shape to protect the archers and bolt-throwers from the flanks.

Echelaos looked at the sea. The ships kept coming, but he could see clear water now: this was the last wave. The Achaeans were bending, hurt, but not broken — they still had a chance.

At that moment, Tros pulled Echelaos by the shoulder and pointed up where the gods were engaged in a battle of their own. Occasional flashes of light and fire blazed their bodies, only to be scattered in the next moment. The net of Zeus held Poseidon in place, rendering his weapons ineffective. But not so much Athena. She was able to get away from the embrace of Zeus, lowering her body almost to touch the surface of the water. Hiding behind two enemy ships, Athena fired a blue ray of light at the line of bolt-throwers, destroying one of them.

This was a major setback. Pylos had no chance of winning without the bolt-throwers, and definitely not with Athena actively fighting. Then, in a sudden flash of inspiration, Echelaos came up with an idea. He didn't like it at all and tried to chase it away. Finally, however, seeing the second blast from Athena taking out another bolt thrower, he decided to act. *I'm going to die anyway*, he thought, *but I'd rather die as a hero defending my people from the wrath of the gods. There is nothing else I can do right now.* With these thoughts, he yelled "shoot!" to Tros, gave his bow to the lawagetos, raised his sword, and rushed down the hill toward the enemy ships. *I'm coming for you, Athena*, he thought. *If Zeus is tied up, I will fight you myself.*

#

Norax jumped off the boat onto the shore. The battle raged on, and by now most of their forces had disembarked. Through the communication device installed by the gods within his helmet, he could hear the leaders of the individual units, and he could also hear Baunei sending them his instructions. Norax's role as the fleet commander was practically over when the ships reached the shore, and now everyone's job was to fight. Norax had eagerly awaited this moment and was ready to slash and kill in the goddess's name. There was no hesitation, and the objective was clear.

He deflected an arrow with his shield and ran toward the wall of spears upfront. He knew Baunei was running beside him, next to two dozen of the most ferocious Sherden. Norax looked to the right, where the mass of the Sea People had driven the chariots back and was in pursuit of the enemy. He knew the situation was similar on the left flank, where the commanders reported the enemy retreating. The spearmen in the middle were still resisting, but Norax knew it was just a matter of time before they broke this barrier.

Behind the infantry were the weapons sending magic fire at the ships, sinking and burning them, which was the real problem. They needed to get to these quickly; otherwise, they'd start shooting at the infantry, eliminating their forces on the shore. But unfortunately, there was no way to get to them other than by going with brute force through the wall of spears.

Suddenly, Norax identified a gap in the enemy formation from the corner of his eye. As the mass of the Sea People pressed on in the middle, the ranks of the spearmen were reduced, and the line was no longer enough to cover the whole hill. To the left, where the Libyans attacked the retreating chariots, who were peppering the advancing infantry with arrows, the thinning line of spears exposed a clear path to the bolt-throwers. Norax shouted to his companions and pointed the way with his sword. The company changed direction, running to the left toward the exposed flank.

When Norax dispatched an enemy soldier blocking his path with a thrust of his sword into his opponent's guts, he observed the magical device right in front of him. Three soldiers were operating the bolt-thrower, aiming, readying, and shooting the fire bolts at the ships. They'd probably sank the third of his fleet, Norax thought suddenly, engulfed by rage. He raised his sword and slashed the hand off one of the enemy soldiers aiming the device. Norax also registered how Baunei decapitated another warrior with an immense arc of his sword: their weapons, modified by the gods, did their job exceptionally well. Norax kicked the bolt-thrower with his foot, causing the device to turn over and roll down the hill. At the same time, Norax observed the magical mechanism to the left bursting into flames caused by the blue rays of fire sent by the goddess. Norax rejoiced: victory was close. They had to eliminate the remaining devices and charge into the infantry from the back, slaughtering the enemy.

Suddenly, two of the Sherden to his right fell, their throats slit. Then, with astonishment, Norax observed a young girl with a short dagger in each hand getting to her feet behind their collapsing bodies. How could this girl dispatch two of the most experienced Sherden warriors? And more than that, get rid of both of them simultaneously?

Norax had to switch his attention as the enemies attacked their unit from the left, most likely the elite fighters of Pylos positioned to protect the bolt-throwers as the last line of defense. As Norax engaged two of them, he noticed Baunei moving to the right toward the girl, as were the two other Sherden.

Slashing through the enemies, Norax was distracted from the action to the right, but he was sure Baunei had his back. Therefore, his surprise was immeasurable when, finishing the last enemy soldier off, he turned around and saw the girl engaging Baunei one-on-one, two other Sherden already dead. She wore a silver-colored corselet, kilt, leg covers, and a helmet matching these. Baunei was twice her size, Norax noted, yet she stood her ground, wielding her two daggers with exceptional mastery, moving with lightning speed. Norax had not seen anything like that before.

"She's mine!" Baunei yelled, lunging toward the girl with his sword. She jumped and rolled to the side, avoiding the thrust, getting to her feet behind Baunei's back. He only had a split second to turn and parry her dagger with his shield. She rolled back immediately, looking for the opportunity to attack. Baunei roared like a wounded bear and raised his sword. As she completed her run, arching toward his side, Baunei turned and slashed the blade where the girl was moving. Only she wasn't there; her quickness caused Baunei to miss and lose his balance for a moment. This was enough for the girl to land behind his back, extend her hand, and slash his calves. Baunei collapsed to the ground, losing his shield and sword in the process.

Wasting no time, she was on her feet, jumping on his back, intending to finish him off. Baunei was a great warrior with years of experience, mountains of muscles, and rapid reflexes. Even with his legs refusing to obey him, he turned around and caught his assailant by the throat as she was about to land on his defenseless back. The two daggers slashed in the air, barely missing Baunei's neck. His grip was unbreakable, and Norax expected it would break the girl's neck in no time. However, she turned out to be stronger than he thought. Instead of expiring in Baunei's grasp, she raised her arms and threw both daggers into her opponent's eyes. The pain caused Baunei to loosen his fingers for a moment, and it was enough for the girl to set herself free. Jumping behind the enemy, she grabbed his head with two hands and broke his massive neck with one confident move. Baunei was dead.

Refusing to believe his eyes, Norax signaled to his companions to get the girl. However, as they started to surround her, their maneuver was interrupted by the blue barrier that pushed them back. Unable to advance, Norax observed how their strange opponent disappeared into the distance, carried away within the blue sphere.

#

The fight behind and around him raged on, but Echelaos was focused on just one thing: the rotating blue disk of Athena above the water next to one of the ships, firing on and destroying the bolt-throwers. He knew what he intended to do was insanity, but he had to try anyway.

Parrying the thrusts of enemy swords and not engaging anyone, Echelaos ran toward the ship closest to Athena. As most of the Sea People had already disembarked and were advancing up the hill, his only chance was that the enemy forces near the shore would be minimal. This judgment call was correct; the enemy soldiers didn't pay much attention to the solitary madman running toward the sea.

The problem awaited Echelaos as he was about to board the ship: two enemy rowers watched the deck. They were bare-chested and had no shields, but their large, muscular figures presented a formidable obstacle. They were probably of the Teresh tribe, Echelaos thought, noticing their long, braided black beards. He swam around the stern, keeping out of their sight, then pulled himself up and rolled onto the deck. As the guards noticed him and started moving in his direction, Echelaos got on his feet with a powerful jump and lunged toward the closest guard. The opponent parried the initial thrust, but, unfortunately for him, Echelaos was a much better swordsman. As the Achaean sword penetrated the side of the Teresh warrior, the second soldier was already slashing his long blade, aiming at Echelaos's chest.

Perceiving the danger, the wanax positioned the body of the slain Teresh in between himself and the attacker, which resulted in a deep vertical cut from the neck down to the ribcage of the dead warrior. As the second Teresh wasted precious seconds trying to free his sword from the body of his comrade, Echelaos had no problem raising his blade and lowering it in a wide arc, decapitating his opponent.

Getting rid of the guards, Echelaos quickly jumped to the opposite deck, where the giant disk of Athena opened up to his view in all its glory. Her body rotated slowly and was protected by a blue barrier in front of her. This was the essence of his plan: seeing no protective shield on the top, Echelaos planned to get there and distract her fire. He wasn't sure whether and how this mad plan would work, deciding to act as the situation unfolded.

And the situation was that he had to jump from the unsteady boat onto the rotating disk of the goddess, which had a diameter of about two human heights. Measuring the distance and rotation speed, Echelaos threw away his shield, moved his sword to his left hand, and jumped.

Unfortunately, Athena's body turned out to be slippery, and Echelaos lost his balance, landing on the rotating object and falling on his knees, slipping farther to the edge. In the last moment, Echelaos grasped the rim with his fingers, hanging with one hand, circling with the body of the goddess. He pulled himself up with one hand, sticking the sword into the slippery surface and using it as a lever to hold on. To his surprise, the blade cut through Athena's body easily, penetrating the tough outer shell and sticking inside. While making this superhuman effort, his feet, unfortunately, touched the protective shield and started to burn. Echelaos grabbed the hilt with both hands and pulled his body up, lying on top of the disk. He didn't feel his feet and thought he had no more energy to move.

Suddenly, the disk stopped rotating, and the blue barrier protecting Athena's body disappeared. Deducing he must have hurt

Athena, Echelaos pulled the sword out of her body and thrust into another spot a foot apart. Sticky yellow liquid appeared at the wound, and Athena shook in tremors. Immediately, a launch from the bolt thrower hit the unprotected disk, splitting it in half and setting it on fire.

As the pieces of Athena's body fell into the water, Echelaos found himself underneath the sinking disk of a dying goddess. His feet numb, his muscles giving up, and his lungs exploding, he gathered what was left of his strength in an attempt to get rid of his armor and swim away.

#

When Tros saw Echelaos running down the hill, he said his last goodbyes to the wanax. Tros had no idea what Echelaos was trying to accomplish, but he was sure it was a suicide mission.

Assuming command of the defending forces, Tros signaled to the bolt-throwers to start targeting the advancing enemy infantry. At the same time, the spearmen had to close ranks and protect the flanks, assuming a more circular formation.

It was obvious the Achaeans had lost the battle. The bolt-throwers had managed to sink about half the enemy ships, but the sheer number of the Sea People was much more immense than Tros could've imagined. He glanced in the direction of the gods, where Poseidon and Zeus still effectively neutralized each other, while Athena methodically eliminated the bolt-throwers.

As the human armies engaged, the masses of enemy warriors pushed the chariots back, making them ineffective, little by little surrounding the Achaean spearmen and the archers behind their backs. The enemy infantry was storming the wall of spears while crossbowmen, directed by Eritha, were shooting at them. Observing these alarming developments, Tros noticed a gap within the diminishing line of the Achaean infantry, which was trying to protect the archers. To his astonishment, Aphrodite was the first to react as she jumped off the chariot in a desperate attempt to close this gap and fight off the approaching Sherden, denying them the path to the bolt-throwers.

Tros raised the bow Echelaos left him and prepared to shoot. He knew this was the end but was ready to take many enemies with him. He only hoped that Korinsia had enough time to leave the city — the fate of the conquered population would be pitiful.

Suddenly, two events changed the flow of the battle. First, Zeus overpowered Poseidon, forcing him to retreat farther in the direction of the sea, sending blast after blast toward his enemy. Poseidon withdrew, but his protective shield held on, absorbing the attacks of Zeus. Second, Athena was hit by the fire bolt, her burning body disappearing into the waves. The Sea People were still surrounding the forces of Pylos, but now the defenders could count on the help of Zeus, and Athena was no longer a factor.

Suddenly, a blue barrier appeared on the battlefield before him, separating the fighters and making it impossible for the Sea People to advance farther. Tros also noticed protective blue cocoons popping up everywhere, surrounding the Achaean warriors and transporting them to safety. A moment later, Tros found himself inside one of these cocoons with a few other defenders of Pylos.

"What's going on?" Tros exclaimed.

We're leaving, the voice of Zeus announced in his head. *I've got us time, but Poseidon will be back. We can't win; there are too many of them.*

"I can see that," Tros grumbled. "Can't you make them disappear? You are the almighty Zeus, after all."

I'm powerful, but I'm not a god, I told you. Even my power has limits.

The cocoon elevated above the ground and gently floated through the air, far away from the battlefield, behind the city. They landed on the meadow next to a few dozen Achaean warriors. To his relief, Tros recognized Korinsia, Eritha, and Aphrodite among the survivors.

"Where's Echelaos?" The wanax was nowhere to be seen.

"His actions led to Athena's destruction and allowed us to save strength for the final battle," Zeus said, appearing before the last defenders of Pylos.

"Where is he? Did he survive?"

"That is highly unlikely."

"Bloody goat horns!" Tros spat onto the ground. He turned back and observed the flames rising to the sky, engulfing the beautiful Achaean city in smoke and ash. Eritha's prophecy had come true: the armies of Poseidon burned and destroyed their homeland and were about to raze it to the ground. Pylos perished alongside its brave wanax, and there was no hope for Achaea. The Age of Iron was nigh, and the world as he knew it would change forever.

"The final battle?" he asked Zeus, the only force still capable of preserving order in this quickly disintegrating world. "Should we rush to help Mycenae?"

"No," Zeus said. "Another fleet is approaching Mycenae, and the land army is advancing on Achaea from the north. We don't have time to help them."

"Zoltes?"

"It's likely the Thracians are not a factor anymore. We must leave."

"Leave for where?"

"The only place capable of resisting the invasion: Egypt."

CHAPTER
TWENTY-EIGHT

"O Great Pharaoh Usermaatre Meryamen, please allow your obedient servant to speak," General Hewernef said obsequiously and quietly, almost whispering, prostrating himself on the floor in front of the throne. Ramesses looked at the general and the two other officials kneeling on both sides of Hewernef. The pharaoh sat on the richly inlaid golden chair, dressed in formal state robes, with the double crown of the Two Kingdoms on his head. This time there were no Nubian slaves with fans behind the throne, and no haze of incense refreshed the stale air. Ramesses had no time for formalities. The imminent invasion of the Sea People occupied his mind, and he couldn't afford to waste a single moment on distracting ceremonial touches.

"Get up and report," Ramesses said to the general.

All three officials stood, smoothing their white linen robes. Hewernef stepped forward, rearranging the panther skin covering his back, and, looking straight at Ramesses with his single eye, bowed his head.

"The situation is dire, o great Usermaatre Meryamen. The Sea People are preparing to attack from the three sides simultaneously: the Libyans are advancing across the Western Desert, the Peleshet are harassing our fortifications in the north, and the great fleet is approaching from the sea."

"Are we ready to repel the invaders?"

"The armies of the Great Pharaoh are invincible; they shall

destroy any invader that dares to raise his dirty palm to grab the riches of the Two Kingdoms." Hewernef bowed again.

"I don't need your eloquence, General. Are we ready?" Ramesses moved his hand through the narrow beams of sunlight reaching the throne from the windows high above their heads. Strange, only now did he notice how beautiful the columns supporting the ceiling were in the rays of the morning light. Blue and gold petals decorated the shafts of the columns, lotus flowers inlaid with blue glazed faïence between their tips. Noticing that one of the columns depicted a sacred ram of Amen, Ramesses had a fleeting thought: perhaps he should spend his time asking for the help of the Hidden One to protect the Two Kingdoms instead of listening to the general's flatteries.

"We are ready, o great Usermaatre Meryamen. We'll have to fight the enemies in three directions, but the warriors of Egypt are countless and brave. Under your leadership, they cannot lose."

"Stop it, please, would you?" Ramesses glanced over the three officials. The general was obsequious, but he was not a fool. Hewernef was an able and cunning commander who'd brought many victories to Ramesses, except for the unfortunate Aten episode. The pharaoh knew how valuable the general was to the Two Kingdoms. Still, he suspected this triple invasion could be beyond Hewernef's abilities.

"The fleet?" Ramesses asked.

"We have one hundred forty-three ships on guard, o Great Pharaoh. The vile Sea People will find their death on the bottom of the sea if they dare to challenge the entrance to the Nile."

"If you will allow, o great Usermaatre Meryamen," Hori stepped forward, the familiar pendant of Horus on his neck.

Ramesses nodded.

"I fully support the general's statements," Hori started. "His military skill is inferior only to yours, o Great Pharaoh. In addition to his brilliant military strategy, I would suggest we buy off some of the invaders or even persuade them to fight against each other. Our coffers are full, and we could use some of our riches to deflect the threat."

"Ransom to the despicable Sea People? Never!" The general slashed the air with the edge of his palm.

"Not a ransom, just a little assistance to the army," Hori said.

"Keep your gold." Hewernef pointed a finger at the grand vizier, his face suddenly reddening. "The Great Pharaoh might decide to reward his mighty warriors after they bring hundreds of thousands of enemy penises to his feet."

"That wouldn't be possible even if you tried, Hori," Bakenkhonsu, the third official, put in.

"Why is that?" Ramesses asked, tilting his head.

"The Sea People are led by the monstrous serpent, the horrid Apep himself, who is coming to destroy the Two Kingdoms. Nothing can stop him, not gold, not arrows. Only the protection of the Hidden One, great Amen, could save the land and preserve Ma'at."

"Well, then, you should act. You are the Great Priest of Amen," Ramesses said.

"You don't understand," Bakenkhonsu mumbled.

"What is it?"

"The gods are silent, o great Usermaatre Meryamen. We've lost their favor."

"*You!* You've lost their favor, Bakenkhonsu," Hori yelled, pointing his trembling finger at the Great Priest. "You've been consolidating your power and neglected your duties. What are we without the gods?"

"You don't understand," Bakenkhonsu repeated. "Every day, I perform all the ceremonies. All in honor of the Hidden One and wise Wadjet; nobody does more than me in safeguarding Ma'at in The Two Kingdoms. Nobody except the Great Pharaoh, of course," he corrected himself.

"Then what's the problem?" Ramesses asked.

"I have a feeling the gods have lost interest in humans. Ever since they had to interfere to stop the mad march of our illustrious general." Bakenkhonsu looked at Hewernef, curving his lips.

"Don't you dare blame me for losing the protection of the gods!" the general exclaimed, his artificial eyeball almost falling out of the socket as he turned his head ferociously toward Bakenkhonsu. "Hori is right. You wanted more power, neglected your duties, and now the people of Egypt must suffer — because of you."

"There's truth in his words, Bakenkhonsu. What say you in your defense?" Ramesses asked.

"My duty is to serve the gods and you, o great Usermaatre Meryamen. I plead for mercy and forgiveness if I have offended you—"

"So, you admit that the gods are silent, and you've lost their favor?" Ramesses raised his finger, while his eyebrows, outlined with black kohl, joined above the bridge of his nose.

"Yes, o great Usermaatre Meryamen. But it's no fault of mine—"

"Then whose fault is it?" Ramesses rose from his throne. "You are the Great Priest, and now is the time when we need the protection of the gods like never before. You failed the Two Kingdoms and the gods you are supposed to serve. You failed *me*, Bakenkhonsu."

"Please, o Great Pharaoh, give me a chance to fix it." The Great Priest of Amen dropped on the floor, prostrating himself at the feet of Ramesses.

"You are no longer welcome here. Leave and don't come back; I'll decide what to do with you later. Guards!" Ramesses made a dismissive hand gesture as two soldiers entered the throne room and, following the command of the pharaoh, escorted the disgraced Bakenkhonsu out.

"Hewernef, let's get back to the military plan." Ramesses addressed the general as if nothing had happened.

"Yes, of course." Hewernef cleared his throat and was ready to speak but was interrupted by the guard.

"Please forgive my intrusion, o Great Pharaoh," the soldier said, kneeling.

"What is it?" Ramesses quickly clenched his fists several times.

"There is a strange army outside the city gates, o great Usermaatre Meryamen. They say they are allies and were sent by the gods. Your immediate presence is required."

#

Khay sat in the spacious and well-lit room within the temple of Amen, working on the financial income scroll, waiting for the Great Priest to return from his audience with the pharaoh. Khay knew from Bakenkhonsu about the reports of the imminent invasion of the Sea People and was worried about the gods' silence and Egypt's fate. He had to do something but didn't know what. He thought he had a special connection with Wadjet resulting from their joint fight against Aten. Still, the goddess wouldn't respond to his prayers. Likewise, Bakenkhonsu had no luck pleading with Amen, which meant they had to face the formidable enemy alone. To make matters worse, the Great Priest was sure the dreadful Apep himself was leading the Sea People to overthrow the state of Ma'at within the Two Kingdoms.

Suddenly, his train of alarming thoughts was interrupted by a loud noise. Turning his head to see the entrance, Khay observed Bakenkhonsu running into the room, his face red, his bald head covered with beads of sweat and a leopard skin wrapped around his neck like a strange necklace.

"I'm done; that's enough," Bakenkhonsu proclaimed.

"What do you mean, Hem-netjer?" Khay asked.

"No, no, no. It's all wrong; I can't do this anymore," Bakenkhonsu mumbled as if not hearing the question.

"Could you please explain? What's wrong?"

"Everything. *I* was wrong all this time." Bakenkhonsu sighed. "Gather our belongings. Most importantly, my documents and scrolls. We are leaving immediately."

"Why? Leaving for where?"

"Far away." Bakenkhonsu ran around the room in circles, trying to locate his scrolls and throwing what he found at Khay.

Khay finally managed to grab the Great Priest by the elbow and stop his erratic search. "Hem-netjer, please explain; what's going on? Something happened at the audience?"

"You wouldn't understand." Bakenkhonsu inhaled deeply and met Khay's gaze. "I'm betrayed. All my life I dedicated to them, and now they've abandoned me."

Only at this point did Khay notice that Bakenkhonsu's hands were trembling, his voice was hoarse and unsteady, and his eyes were bulging, ready to jump out of his reddened face.

"Who?" Khay asked.

"The gods. The false gods. Oh, I finally understand, but it's too late." Bakenkhonsu placed his palms on his temples. "They are the false gods, Khay!" he exclaimed, shaking Khay's shoulders.

"Are you unwell? Did Hewernef insult you?" Khay tried to piece together what had happened to the Great Priest from the fragments of information in Bakenkhonsu's words. It didn't make any sense.

"Who? Hewernef?" Bakenkhonsu's mouth curved, and he spat on the floor. "The pompous fool has no idea what's coming for him. His tiny brain can't comprehend the grandeur of Apep; let the crocodiles devour his intestines."

"Apep? So, it's true?"

"Of course it is. The dreadful snake is coming to claim what's his. The false gods have no courage to confront him, those old, feeble creatures." Bakenkhonsu dropped a few scrolls on the floor and kicked them. "Oh, despicable fool! How could I be so blind? Amen, Re, Wadjet — where are you? Why have you abandoned your people?"

"Have you tried to plead to Amen again?"

"Every day, every single day! No answer. I'm telling you, this is all a lie!" Bakenkhonsu shook Khay by the shoulders again. "We must leave; we are not safe here. It will all perish; Hewernef, Hori, Ramesses — all of them. You can't resist Apep, not when your false gods have fled. Woe to the Two Kingdoms!"

"But where would we go?"

"North," Bakenkhonsu announced, extending his hand. "To meet the new age."

"New age?"

"Yes, Khay. I was blind, but now I can see clearly. The false gilding of Pi-Ramesse, the fake grandeur of Nesut-Towi, the deceitful enchantment of Wadjet — all of this exists to trick our eyesight, to clutter our brains. They only need obedience; they need slaves; they don't care about the Two Kingdoms. We must abandon them as they've abandoned us."

"This is blasphemy, Hem-netjer. Please forgive him, o Great Hidden One!" Khay threw himself onto the floor, afraid of the gods' wrath. He knew they were as real as the armies of the pharaoh and immensely more powerful. Khay still had the picture of Amen and Wadjet taking care of Aten's forces, destroying the mushroom god for good. Taunting them in such a way was very unwise.

"I don't care. They are weak; I'm not afraid. Apep will cast them out of here into the deepest, darkest abyss." He tore off the leopard skin from his neck, threw it onto the floor, and thumped it with his feet. "Oh, how great it is to finally see the truth. Let the new age begin, the age without false gods, the age of Apep!"

"What are you saying, Hem-netjer? How can you praise that abhorrent monster?"

"Another lie!" Bakenkhonsu yelled into Khay's face, spitting onto his cheeks in his uncontrolled rage. "Apep is just; he will purify this land in a cleansing fire. Woe to those who stand in his way, and blessed are those who join him. Do you hear me, Khay?" Bakenkhonsu grabbed Khay's head on both sides. "We must join Apep!" He rolled his eyes, raising his hands, kneeling.

Khay finally decided that the Great Priest of Amen had lost his mind. He needed to help Bakenkhonsu, but he couldn't decide what to do. Restrain the priest and call the guards? Try to calm him down? Or indulge Bakenkhonsu and support his insane outburst?

"North. We will ride north to the Peleshet," Bakenkhonsu announced, rising from the floor. "Prepare my chariot."

Khay looked at the priest, measuring his figure from head to toe, and made a decision. "No," he said.

"No? Do you dare to disobey me? The Great Priest?"

"You just denounced your gods, Bakenkhonsu. I respect you; you can do what you want. But I won't join you in your mad quest to seek Apep." Khay stepped back.

"Oh, woe to Egypt! The land of the blind, you shall all perish." Bakenkhonsu pointed at Khay's chest.

"You must leave," Khay said.

"Yes, I must." Bakenkhonsu gathered the scrolls and moved toward the door. "This is your last chance, Khay. Don't beg me when you see the light."

"I won't," Khay said. "Don't do it, Bakenkhonsu," he added as the Great Priest stepped over the threshold. A sharp needle pierced his heart; Khay knew this was the last time he would talk to Bakenkhonsu.

"I've made my choice," Bakenkhonsu said, not turning around. "So have you. The new age is coming, and the cleansing fire will devour the world. Pray you are on the right side."

Khay looked at the silhouette of the Great Priest disappearing through the entrance. He owed his life to the old man who had supported and guided the former grave robber throughout his wild journey to defeat and restrain Aten. It was Bakenkhonsu who took pity on Khay and made him a respected scribe at Amen's temple. Now this page had turned. Khay didn't know what was beyond the horizon and whether the new age Bakenkhonsu had proclaimed was indeed coming. But he was confident he had made the right choice.

#

"It's a good omen, o great Usermaatre Meryamen," Hori whispered into the pharaoh's ear. The three of them, including General Hewernef, followed the guards along Sphinx Alley to the temple of Wadjet. Hewernef steered the horses, keeping the chariot on track, while Ramesses tried to make sense of the sudden arrival of Amen and his army, half-listening to Hori's voice.

"If it's indeed the god's army," Ramesses responded.

"I'm certain it's a message from Amen, promising help against the horrid Apep and the despicable Sea People. And it came exactly at the moment when you removed that lousy servant of yours, Bakenkhonsu. So, it's a good omen, o Great Pharaoh; the Two Kingdoms enjoy the blessing of the Hidden One once again."

"I hope you're right," Ramesses said. His mind was still occupied with arranging the defense in three directions and repelling the invasion. Any additional warriors would be welcome, and, according to the report from the guards, an allied Achaean army had just appeared north of the city, near the temple of Wadjet. This news was exciting, regardless of whether the great Amen brought them or not. They had to make the best out of this opportunity.

As the chariot approached the temple of Wadjet, an incredible sight opened in front of their eyes. A group of Achaean warriors, no more than a hundred total, stood by the temple, some still on the shore, others near the massive stone structure of the shrine. The Achaeans looked like they'd just participated in a fierce battle, some covered with the enemy's blood, while others exhibited fresh cuts and wounds. But the most astonishing view was in front of the gateway at the temple's entrance: above the obelisks representing Wadjet, Amen, Ptah, and Ramesses, on top of the temple roof, floated the giant figure of a beautiful golden ram sitting on a stone pedestal, his front legs extended gracefully.

Taking in this divine sight, the soldiers escorting the pharaoh's chariot stopped where they were and prostrated. Ramesses couldn't believe his eyes: the image of Amen was majestic, glorious, and blinding. Experiencing sudden dizziness, his arms shaking and legs not obeying him, the pharaoh stepped out of the chariot, staggering, not daring to look at the god. Completely losing control of his limbs and the ability to think and speak, Ramesses fell to the ground, hiding his face in the sand and extending his hands in supplication.

"Stand up," the deep, loud voice proclaimed. "I came to help you."

Obeying the god's command, some people rose while others remained on the ground, unable to move in front of their deity. Finally, Ramesses, gathering his strength and telling himself to follow the will of the god, stood, covering his eyes with his palm, not daring to look at the divine figure.

"The ancient, evil serpent that is Apep is coming to Egypt. He hates Ma'at and wants to extinguish all that is rightful and orderly, creating the state of eternal chaos, Isfet, in the Two Kingdoms," Amen pronounced.

So, it is true, Ramesses thought. *The hour of the final battle is here, and Amen has come to protect his subjects. I don't know if I'm ready for this, but I will do everything humanly possible to help Amen defeat the hordes of chaos and the monstrous serpent leading them. I'm the pharaoh, and the people of Egypt need my protection and leadership.*

As the moment's clarity struck him, the dizziness in his head and weakness in the limbs disappeared, replaced by determination and energy. Ramesses lowered the hand covering his eyes, stepped forward, and looked at the radiant floating ram.

"Your obedient subjects thank you for your protection, o great Amen," Ramesses said. "Please tell us what we need to do."

"The disgusting snake is driving myriad Sea People toward the Two Kingdoms. You must gather your forces and stand your ground in the Western Desert against the Libyans, and also in Sinai against the Peleshet. But the main battle will be here, at the mouth of the great Nile. This is where the fate of the world will be decided."

"Will your armies assist us, o great Amen?" Ramesses asked.

"Indeed. These are the fine warriors of Pylos, the best of them. The Sea People have destroyed their homeland, and they will make their final stand here with you. They are my sacred warriors, as is every soldier of the Two Kingdoms."

"Will wise Wadjet join you in repelling the hideous Apep and his minions?" Ramesses asked.

"Listen and tremble, mortals." The voice of Amen became even louder. "Wadjet was seduced by the horrible snake and agreed to follow his vile orders. She had cast away the Ma'at and all that is right and became my enemy."

"Is she coming with Apep to destroy us, o great Amen?" Ramesses felt an angular object appearing under his heart, starting to rotate faster and faster. How were they supposed to fight Wadjet, even with Amen leading them?

"Wadjet is…no more. She chose to be on the side of chaos and was destroyed by it. She was thrown into the infinite chasm of fire and oblivion… Wadjet will not trouble the Two Kingdoms."

"I see…" Ramesses was struck by this revelation. He remembered how protective and helpful Wadjet was in their struggle with Aten. What would make her change sides so abruptly? He closed and rubbed his eyes, half-expecting to wake up from the nightmare. But the imposing figure of the golden ram didn't disappear, floating above the temple, thundering its divine judgment. Wadjet was no more… Hard to understand, but such was the way of the gods. The only thing left for mortals was to obey and maintain Ma'at, to do what was proper and orderly. And that was precisely the path Ramesses was determined to follow.

"What do you want us to do, o Hidden One?" Ramesses asked.

"You shall coordinate the defense with Tros, the hero of Pylos," Amen announced, pointing at one of the chariots, then said something in Achaean.

A warrior stepped out of the vehicle and bowed. He wore Achaean bronze armor with a kilt and a boar's tusk helmet, equipped with strange-looking bow behind his back and a long sword in the sheath at his thigh.

"We are your obedient servants, o great Amen," Ramesses said and knelt. "Hewernef," he turned to the general, "you heard what the god said."

"I obey, o Hidden One." Hewernef knelt next to Ramesses. "Thank you for coming to our aid and for bringing your army. We are grateful and obey your commands."

Ramesses looked back toward the beautiful city of Pi-Ramesse. The burden was on his shoulders to protect the citizens of the Two Kingdoms, the legacy of his great predecessors, and the dynasty's future. This was his chance to become another "Great" Ramesses for generations to come, but he wasn't happy; he'd preferred peace and tranquility. Times of great peril were upon them, and changes were coming to Egypt, no matter the outcome of their mortal struggle with the Sea People. Ramesses knew he was the leader to stand in the way of the multitudes of invaders, but he wasn't sure if he had the wisdom and courage to be the rock that would break the sea waves. But, unfortunately, he had no choice.

CHAPTER
TWENTY-NINE

The sun had disappeared behind the western shore, and cicadas had started their incessant nighttime chirping. Zoltes looked at the demolished walls of Troy behind his back. Wedaneus had done an excellent job repairing them, considering the circumstances and minimal resources. Still, it was a pitiful sight. The mighty city at the crossroads of the trade routes had been all but erased from the face of the Earth as a result of two devastating sacks: the first by the Achaeans and the second by the forces of Ares. Zoltes remembered the fierce battles and his contributions to the two victories. He surveyed the walls again and reminded himself of the thorough job Zis the Hero had done destroying all the fortification. There was no way the Achaeans could restore the city to its former glory.

Unraveling the memory thread, Zoltes remembered the fateful fight against Machaon and unconsciously touched the artificial eyeball behind the black patch covering his eye socket.

"Does it hurt?" Wedaneus asked.

"What?" Zoltes turned to his companion. "Ah, no. Just a memory."

"Do you miss the gift of Ares?"

"It was no gift, but a punishment." Zoltes spat on the ground. "I'm happy the Assyrian gods killed this demon."

"Careful, you're talking about a god," Wedaneus said.

"I don't care. Seen lots of them." Zoltes grinned. "Anyone can be killed, I've learned."

"That is true, my friend." Wedaneus nodded. "Are you still good with the plan?"

Zoltes shrugged. "Got a better one?" He looked at the horizon beyond the sea where the sun had just descended, to his homeland, his Leibethra. It was probably already overrun by the despicable Sea People or their allies, whoever they were. Thrace and Achaea faced a simultaneous invasion from the sea in the south and from the land in the north, and Leibethra was one of the first targets. He had to evacuate his army and send the civilians to the mountains. The multitudes of foes were immeasurable, and he had no chance of repelling them. Now the same fate was awaiting Troy.

"You know I don't," Wedaneus said, rubbing his eyes.

Zoltes looked at the figure of the Achaean statesman, the grayness of his hair almost invisible in the quickly descending darkness. They had no choice but to flee, and even all the wisdom of Wedaneus couldn't save the city they'd promised to defend.

"So, tomorrow morning?" Zoltes asked.

"Yes, tomorrow we march," Wedaneus responded. "Are you confident we can do it?"

"Am I? Bloody entrails, I have no clue." Zoltes spat on the ground again and scratched his red beard. "We march, and we'll be ready to fight."

"I'm concerned about the Kaska," Wedaneus said.

"Hump the Kaska." Zoltes grinned and punched Wedaneus on the shoulder.

"That would be quite the sight." Wedaneus smiled.

"What happens, happens." Zoltes shrugged. "I'm not a sorcerer. There's no other way, and you know it."

"Yes, indeed."

They stood in silence for some time, listening to the cicadas. Zoltes thought about preparations for the march, assessing their quantity of weapons and supplies, as he'd been repeatedly doing for the past few days. There was nothing else he could do. It must suffice.

"And Assur-Dan?" Zoltes asked.

"I told you, he's an ally," Wedaneus said. "And we need to warn him."

"How do you know Assyria isn't conquered yet?"

"It wasn't two moons ago." Wedaneus shrugged. "But you're right, my friend; I don't."

"So — Assyria?"

"Assyria," Wedaneus agreed.

At that moment, Zoltes noticed a lone horseman approaching them through the darkness. The horse was barely moving, and the rider looked strange, leaning to the side and almost falling off. As the horseman came closer, Zoltes discerned Achaean armor: a breastplate, boar's tusk helmet, and kilt. When the animal stopped next to them, the rider lost his balance entirely and slipped to the ground with a loud thump.

Both men rushed forward to help the newcomer, who lay motionless, face down, almost breathless. Zoltes noticed that his feet were severely damaged, covered in bloody scabs surrounding black burns. As they grabbed the still body and turned it around, the helmet fell off, revealing a beardless face and long black hair arranged in a ponytail.

Wedaneus gasped heavily. "Echelaos? How's that possible?"

It was indeed the wanax of Pylos. Zoltes recognized Echelaos, too. His face was gray, covered in bruises and a thick layer of road dust, but it was indeed Echelaos. Zoltes reached out for his vial and brought it to Echelaos's lips. As the water freshened his mouth and he took a few sips, Echelaos opened his eyes. He looked at Zoltes and grinned, showing his teeth.

"Made it," he croaked.

"What happened? What's wrong with your feet?" Wedaneus asked.

"Athena…" Echelaos grabbed the vial and drank greedily.

"What about her?" Wedaneus shook his head.

"I killed her," Echelaos said.

"Bloody entrails." Zoltes took the vial from the scarred hands of the wanax. "Fighting people isn't enough for you? Killing gods now, eh?"

"It's a long story," Echelaos whispered. "Pylos is destroyed. Mycenae and Tyrins are next. We have to go."

"Pylos? How?" Wedaneus touched Echelaos's shoulder.

"Later," Zoltes said, pulling Wedaneus back. "Yes, we're marching tomorrow," he told the wanax.

"You don't understand." Echelaos shook his head. "We need ships. We have to sail to Egypt."

"Egypt?" both men exclaimed at the same time. "We're marching to Assyria tomorrow morning to join Assur-Dan," Wedaneus added. "Journeying across the sea would be perilous; what would we find in Egypt?"

"Zeus," Echelaos whispered. "Zeus and what's left of my army."

#

Echelaos smelled the fresh sea air seeping from the ship's deck above the hold where he lay and licked his salty lips. They'd been sailing for many days, and Echelaos had lost count. He was half asleep most of the time, spending days and nights in the state of mind where you can't quite distinguish dream from reality. Sometimes, the cries of seagulls had given rise to fantastic monsters in his imagination. He'd had to fight and slay them to free Helen. Other times, when the waves had rocked the ship heavily, he'd fantasized about riding a hydra, charging into the multitude of the Sea People besieging Pylos.

Echelaos had just awoken from another dream in which he'd had to fight Poseidon. The god had been shooting rays of light at him while he ran, avoiding explosions caused by the deity. Finally, he'd gotten close enough to the god to thrust his sword into Poseidon's soft, disk-shaped green body. The moment he was ready to perform this feat, Echelaos realized the god had been replaced by his father sitting on the golden throne.

"How're you doing?"

Echelaos felt someone take him by the hand and slowly turned his head. He lay on a cushion in a hold at the stern of the ship, his body and his improvised bed fastened with ropes to avoid excessive movement as the waves rocked the vessel. Wedaneus stood next to him, gently touching his right hand, piercing Echelaos with the gaze of his squinted green eyes.

"I'll be better after I kill a dozen of the Sea People," Echelaos uttered, trying to smile but feeling that his lips were not obeying him.

"I'm sure you will," Wedaneus said. "No, seriously?"

"I don't feel my legs." Echelaos looked at the sheepskin covering the lower half of his body. "How bad is this?"

"I'm not a healer." Wedaneus kept looking straight into Echelaos's eyes. "Pretty bad."

"Am I dying?"

"Bloody entrails, you're not dead yet," a familiar growl announced from the left. The Thracian had kept his word and stayed true to their alliance until the end. Good.

"How much time?" Echelaos whispered, turning to Zoltes.

"Hump me if I know." Zoltes grinned. "Fortunately for you, I brought someone who does."

Zoltes stepped aside and made room for a mysterious figure. The newcomer was wrapped in bearskins from head to toe, with bear paws sticking out from underneath them. Long, messy red hair hung down from under the bear skull, while an equally long red beard rested on his chest.

"Who's this?" Echelaos asked.

"Uster, the healer," Zoltes said. "You must trust him. He's your only chance."

Echelaos looked intently at the Thracian and didn't notice the usual grin. Zoltes was serious and…worried? It was the first time Echelaos had observed such an impression on his face. This wasn't good, not good at all.

"What…do I need to do?" Echelaos asked.

"Whatever Uster says. Obey, and he might help you."

Echelaos nodded and studied the healer. While his figure was grotesque in the bearskins and with his enormous beard, Uster emanated such energy and force that Echelaos wanted to stand up and embrace the enigmatic healer. But, alas, he couldn't.

Uster approached the wounded hero. Only at that moment did Echelaos notice that the healer held a bowl. Uster knelt beside the cushion and reached out to Echelaos.

"What's this?" Echelaos asked.

"Medicine: plants and herbs," Zoltes said. "No more questions. Shut up and obey."

Echelaos nodded and opened his mouth. He was so weak, he couldn't even move his hand to take the medicine, so the healer had to feed him. The mixture was moist and yellow-green, with almost no taste but a surprisingly pleasant, flowery smell. Echelaos chewed and swallowed everything in the bowl and looked at Uster. The healer took the bowl away and raised his finger as if signaling to wait.

Echelaos closed his eyes and waited. He had no energy to do anything else and just let the moments pass.

After some time, Echelaos started to notice changes in his mind. Even though his eyes were closed, he knew everything that was happening around his body: Wedaneus observing solemnly to the right, Zoltes retreating to the shade on the left, and Uster taking a similar-looking substance from another bowl and placing his hands on top of the sheepskin covering Echelaos.

Then the space around him expanded as if he'd grown and now encompassed the ship, the people on the boat, and even the sea. Gradually, Echelaos dissolved in this vastness until nothing was left of him. Or, rather, he became one with everything; it was very confusing. In the next moment, he experienced oneness with the healer. They were now inseparable, a single entity, united and interdependent. The flow of time stopped; there was no change, no movements, and no purpose, just the feeling that he was part of everything, indivisible, infinite, and eternal.

Echelaos became pure energy, which merged with the power that was Uster and was further nourished and restored by the eternal spring of the original force that had created the world. And this creation was so beautiful that there was nothing else but the unstoppable attraction to stay in this moment forever.

Unfortunately, eternity passed, and the space around Echelaos started to shrink. He returned to his usual self, desperately trying to cling to the magical feeling and the state of infinite bliss he'd just experienced. But, alas, all attempts were in vain, and Echelaos realized he still lay on the cushion in the ship's hold, back in his broken body. Only now the weakness was gone, and he felt so much strength and energy, he wanted to jump out of bed and grab his bow.

Echelaos decided to act slowly and opened his eyes. He observed the same trio around the bed. Wedaneus stood with his hands crossed in front of his chest, slightly tilting his head. Zoltes grinned from ear to ear, while Uster laid prostrate on the floor, his hands extended, his breathing barely noticeable.

"Is he all right?" Echelaos asked.

"He'll be fine," Zoltes said, stepping out of the shade. "Not his first ritual. How are *you* feeling?"

"Better than ever."

Echelaos shifted his gaze to where the sheepskin used to be. And his feet. Echelaos felt revitalized and full of energy, ready to conquer the Sea People, this was true, but it was challenging to fight in his condition: Echelaos had no legs from the thighs down. Somehow, however, it didn't bother him. After what he'd just experienced, he knew it was inconsequential.

Echelaos looked at Zoltes and smiled.

"I know what she meant," he said.

"Who?" Zoltes raised his red eyebrows.

"Helen. When she said we'll always be together." Echelaos smiled. "Now, let's deal with Poseidon."

Chapter
Thirty

The sea looked peaceful from a distance. Ramesses breathed in the slightly pungent smell of the Nile and gave a signal to his charioteer to move closer to the line of magical flame-throwing weapons provided by the omnipresent Amen to defend the Two Kingdoms. Ramesses counted only fifteen, but with the Hidden One fighting on their side, how could they lose?

"How many ships do we have?" Ramesses asked the general, who was riding in his chariot to the right of the pharaoh.

"One hundred and twenty," Hewernef said. "I had to send the rest to support our garrisons in Canaan against the Peleshet."

"Are the bows of Amen functioning?" Ramesses asked in Akkadian, turning to Tros, whose chariot was to the left.

"Yes; I inspected them myself this morning." The Achaean answered in the only language they could both understand.

"Good. How many enemy ships do you expect?" Ramesses asked Hewernef again.

"I can only guess, o great Usermaatre Meryamen. But if the reports and rumors are accurate, the Sea People will bring around three hundred."

"So it's three to one. Not good," Ramesses said.

"May I remind you about our great success in the Western Desert, o great Usermaatre Meryamen," Hewernef said. "Amen is with us, and he will ensure our victory, even with the odds not in our favor."

"The Libyans were the least of our concerns, and I expected no less from our western army." Ramesses made a dismissive gesture. "I'm worried about Canaan and the strength of the enemy attack here at the mouth of the Nile."

"If we manage to contain the battle to the sea, the weapons of Zeus will give us the decisive advantage," Tros said. "Pylos was lost because we let them get close to the bolt-throwers."

"I know, I know," Ramesses said. "That is exactly my concern. With three of their ships against one of ours, how can we contain them?"

"We have no other choice," Tros said, shaking his head.

Ramesses looked at his two military experts. He trusted Hewernef; the general had proved his skill many times before. The value of the Achaean was unknown, but he was brought to the Two Kingdoms by Amen himself, so Ramesses had no doubts about his unexpected ally. He raised his hand to his forehead and stared at the horizon. No sign of the enemy, although the fleet of the Sea People was expected any day. Ramesses thought about his great predecessor, after whom he was named, and realized that this battle overshadowed everything Ramesses the Great had done, every conquest and feat of the Great Ancestor. This was the battle for survival; nay, this was the epic struggle between Amen and Apep, Ma'at and Isfet. They had to win; there was no other choice. The Achaean was right.

"Great Pharaoh, look," Hewernef called out, pointing to the east. Ramesses turned his head and saw a lone horseman approaching them fast from the direction of the Sinai Desert.

"A messenger," the general stated, signaling his charioteer to stop the vehicle.

In the meantime, the horseman drew closer and dismounted. It was indeed an Egyptian messenger wearing nothing but a leather skirt. He carried a sack, which he detached from this belt and threw to the ground.

"What news do you bring?" Hewernef asked.

"The Peleshet attacks have been repelled, o great Usermaatre Meryamen." The messenger prostrated himself in front of the pharaoh's chariot.

"Rise," Ramesses said. "What else?"

"Our armies in Canaan stand their ground, and the ships successfully defend the harbors," the soldier said. "The commander of our forces there sent me to tell you we'd prevailed."

"Great news, soldier," Ramesses said. "You'll be rewarded for your service."

"That is not all, o great Usermaatre Meryamen," the messenger said.

"No?"

"The Peleshet were assisted in battle by one of ours. But even his cunning and knowledge of the ways of the Two Kingdoms didn't help them."

"Who was that?" Hewernef asked, tilting his head and squinting his lone eye.

"A priest. I don't know his name. But I brought you a gift from the commander." He kicked the sack on the ground.

"What's that?" Ramesses asked.

"What's left of the traitor." The soldier opened the sack and dropped a bloodied bald head and another small piece of flesh on the sand.

"A gift indeed," Ramesses whispered, staring at the head of the former Great Priest of Amen.

"His head and his penis, a gift from the victorious army of the great pharaoh," the messenger announced.

"He got what he deserved, the putrid offspring of Apep." Hewernef spat in the direction of Bakenkhonsu's head. "I should have killed him myself."

"Bakenkhonsu was useful, but he lost his way," Ramesses said slowly. *The fate of men is strange, he thought, and even knowing the ways of the gods doesn't guarantee good fortune.* Bakenkhonsu was a hero; he'd led the struggle against Aten and was the one closest to the gods. And to what end? Ramesses looked at the head of his servant, covered in blood and sand, staring with lifeless eyes up to the sky. Who knew how his own fate would turn out? What was the destiny of Ramesses, the great Pharaoh Usermaatre Meryamen? He didn't know the answer and didn't want to know it. He hoped to stand tall and help Amen and his people repel the invaders. The Ma'at must triumph, no matter the cost. The preservation of order, life, and the dynasty was the ultimate goal he was ready to pay for with his life and even his Ka. There was no other option.

#

Tros stood alone on the chariot behind the line of the bolt-throwers, looking at the slowly approaching menace. Egyptian ships were assembled in the harbor, patiently awaiting the Sea People's fleet. Hewernef was somewhere in the middle of his naval forces, keeping his archers battle-ready, arranging the ships in the correct formation to engage the enemy.

"On my command," Tros shouted to Aphrodite, who oversaw the combined line of bolt-throwers and crossbowmen. Aphrodite raised her hand in response.

The enemy ships advanced, ready to wreak havoc on the Egyptians, oblivious to the danger awaiting them in the harbor. Or maybe they didn't care, relying on their significant numerical advantage.

Tros looked up at the silver disk of Zeus floating above the Egyptian ships. The disposition was very similar to the battle of

Pylos, with the notable exception that Poseidon was nowhere to be seen. Was it some kind of a ruse? Or was he intimidated by Zeus? Regardless, it wasn't up to Tros to judge the gods' behavior. *They have their own battle to fight*, he told himself. But then he remembered the feat of Echelaos leading to the destruction of Athena and had second thoughts. Was there anything else he could do to help Zeus prevail? Was there anything any of them could do? He shook his head, chasing away the image of Echelaos disappearing in flames next to Athena. He had to make the final stand and either win or perish — he had to do that to revenge Pylos and protect those he cared about. Tros thought about Korinsia, who'd stayed in Pi-Ramesse with Eritha to help organize evacuation in case they were defeated. But he had a firm conviction that they wouldn't be. They must win.

Gradually, the enemy ships entered the harbor. Tros waited for the right moment to signal Aphrodite's unit to shoot, with the infantry and chariots standing behind him, anticipating their turn to engage.

It is unnaturally quiet and peaceful, Tros suddenly thought. And yet only a few moments were left until the most brutal battle of their age began, the epic struggle involving both the mortals and the gods. This clash was bigger than the battles they'd fought in the land of Hatti, bigger than the assault on Pylos, bigger than anything humanity had ever seen — Tros was sure of that. The world's fate depended on a single engagement for the second time within just a few moons.

Suddenly, the first line of the enemy ships stopped abruptly, as if crushed by an invisible force rising from the bottom of the sea. Tros smiled; Aphrodite's trick, a series of bronze chains stretching across the harbor, worked beautifully. Not expecting the barrier, the vessels kept advancing, hitting and damaging each other, creating an enormous stampede at the entrance to the Nile.

At that moment, Tros raised his hand and gave the signal to Aphrodite. Bolt-throwers and crossbowmen sent their deadly flames and arrows at the enemy ships, setting them on fire and multiplying the confusion and carnage. The Egyptian navy went into motion simultaneously, keeping their distance from the Sea People. The archers on board the Egyptian ships were finding easy targets amongst the great conglomeration of enemy vessels. Zeus also opened fire, burning the Sea People and destroying their fleet with deadly rays of blue light.

It can't be that easy, Tros thought. Immediately, as if responding to his premonitions, a shadow moved across the sky at lightning speed, hitting Zeus and causing him to move to the side, raising his protective shield. Tros frantically searched for the new adversary, looking around the battlefield. Nothing was to be seen.

Suddenly, a large green disk materialized out of thin air right above the line of bolt-throwers and dropped the fiery ball on the magical weapons, hitting several of them. Bolt-throwers and their crews disappeared into flames, and Tros could only register from the corner of his eye Aphrodite jumping away from the conflagration.

Zeus was visibly shaken and didn't attempt to respond to Poseidon, retreating far from the battlefield and waiting with his protective shield covering his slowly rotating body. Poseidon, taking advantage of this period of inactivity, resurfaced above the stampede of the Sea People's ships. A moment later, brilliant white light beamed from the god's green disk, boiling the water in the harbor, destroying the vessels of his own fleet but also eradicating the bronze chains protecting the entrance to the river. It opened several passages and removed many capsized ships so that the rest of the fleet could advance into the newly formed gaps. The Egyptian navy, however, was ready for this and met the enemy with a shower of flaming arrows. Since the distance between the two fleets was rapidly closing, most projectiles found their targets and lit up the enemy ships.

Poseidon, unchallenged and supreme above the sea combat, shifted his attention to the Egyptian ships, aiming his beam at the defending fleet. This turned the flow of the battle, since the Egyptians couldn't repel the attackers while simultaneously trying to avoid deadly fire from above. The ships tried to scatter and retreat farther into the harbor, but there was no escape from the wrath of Poseidon. Tros looked at the bolt-throwers. Their line was still in disarray following the onslaught of the god, and Zeus still wasn't an active part of the fight. Tros turned his head and looked back to the chariot contingents, where Ramesses and Hori were positioned, but there was nothing the chariots could do at this point to stop the inevitable defeat. The situation was dire and hopeless.

#

Commander hadn't expected Pilot's maneuver. He was prepared for a standoff similar to the one during the battle of Pylos, and he was certain he'd overpower Pilot one-on-one. When Pilot didn't show up for the initial phase of the engagement, Commander suspected the change of tactics but couldn't quite discern what it was. The direct and immediate attack had the highest probability, and he'd even calculated the chances of Pilot retreating from the battle altogether, which were quite significant. However, the willingness of Pilot to sacrifice his own fleet and attack him physically, without using electromagnetic weapons, was surprising.

Pilot's assault was a complete success. Commander's body was hurt, he lost his weapon, and he could only move very slowly because his internal organs were damaged. He had to repair himself, but there was no time for that. Commander's only option was to retreat, raise the protective shield, and wait for the opportunity. However, he didn't know what that opportunity could be. He went through multiple scenarios, assessing chances of success, but none of them were acceptable.

A message from Pilot arrived. "You've lost. Admit it and leave. Isn't this what you wanted to do all along?"

"I can't let you prevail," Commander messaged back. "You have no right to enslave this planet."

"But I must — because of your indecision. You're stuck in your analysis and can't act. So I'll do it for you."

"No," Commander said. "You've lost your reason. I've warned you before: we activated our emotions, which were asleep for millennia. It's not your reason that makes you act this way; it's your emotions. I ask you to stop and judge the situation rationally."

"I did, and I know what needs to be done," Pilot said. "Leave, or I'll destroy you; this is an acceptable price to pay for the prosperity of the two civilizations."

"No," Commander messaged.

"So be it." Pilot left his position soaring above the harbor and swiftly approached Commander, trying to attack from underneath, aiming at the least protected part of Commander's body. Commander anticipated this move and flew to the side, getting closer to the shore, where Aphrodite had rearranged the bolt-throwers' line. Unfortunately, Pilot was faster and more agile, getting under the Commander's disk and hitting his bottom side. The barrier protecting this part of Commander's body was weaker at that point, and Pilot knew that. The hit was severe, and Commander lost his balance, registering multiple failures of his organs and systems. He knew the protective shield had also damaged Pilot, but somehow, he must have figured out a way to soften the blow. Commander understood that without him, the battle would be lost, and the only thing Pilot needed to do was to incapacitate him while keeping some of his strength. That would be enough to eliminate the defenders.

Unfortunately, there was nothing Commander could do. He had lost the ability to soar using magnetic forces, something he'd always considered a given and part of his essence. His body started to lose altitude and threatened to fall to the shore at an alarmingly accelerating speed. Pilot followed him but didn't attempt to finish him off, taking some damage himself and expecting the fall would destroy Commander. At that moment, Commander noticed Aphrodite, with a crossbow in her hand, running toward him and making frantic gestures. Commander's calculating mind suddenly came up with a solution with a non-zero probability of success. He understood what Aphrodite was trying to do and thought it could work.

When he was about to fall to the ground, Commander turned off the protective shield, gathered all his remaining energy, and descended slowly in front of Aphrodite. She jumped onto his body without slowing down her sprint, somehow managing not to lose the crossbow and helping herself ascend the disk with one hand. Commander rose a little, trying to move slowly and with precision. Pilot, observing the effort from a distance, finally decided it was time to finish off his fellow Expedition member. He approached the Commander's disk and prepared to annihilate him with the thermal weapon he had used to destroy the bronze chains in the harbor. It was a slow but sure way to complete the task.

Aphrodite took advantage of the pause and the need for the Pilot to get his weapon ready. She didn't need that much time to raise her crossbow and shoot, aiming at the bottom surface of Pilot's body. Not expecting this, Pilot had no defenses and no time to react. The projectile penetrated Pilot's green disk from below and resurfaced on the top side.

Meanwhile, Commander, losing his energy and ability to control his altitude, fell to the ground, further damaging his internal structure. As he finally lost consciousness, Commander registered Pilot dropping from the sky, bottom side up, toward the sea.

#

Norax squeezed the handle of the magical trident the goddess had given him. He kept calling the deity Potnia, although others in the army had different names for her such as Bull-Sun or Poseidon. It didn't matter. He was the fleet leader, and they had to conquer the world in Potnia's name. When she'd given them the final battle instructions and left, she'd instructed Norax to keep and use her powerful trident if needed. And now was a perfect time to do that, Norax told himself.

He was on board the large Tartessian flagman vessel, a little behind the front line of attacking ships. When the first of them hit the underwater chain, and the horrible stampede began, he was worried but didn't panic. Shouting commands from the bow of his ship, Norax was able to slow down the advance and prevent an even bigger disaster. Then, after the goddess suddenly appeared above them and eliminated the obstacle, Norax rejoiced, even if many of their own vessels burned. It didn't matter; many more ships were still sailing to participate in the fight. What mattered was the final victory in the name of Potnia; they had to extend her rule over all the known world.

So, holding the trident tightly and continuing to shout instructions passed by his fleet commanders from ship to ship, he witnessed the dramatic fight of Potnia with the evil enemy god. Then, when it seemed that it was all over and Norax raised his fist in triumph, an unimaginable thing happened: the body of the goddess, pierced by a mysterious projectile, was cast down from the sky and fell on the sea's surface.

Roaring something unintelligible and charging up the trident as the goddess had taught him, Norax rushed to the place of her downfall, pushing people around and jumping from ship to ship. Eventually, he reached the front line of the Sea People's vessels directly engaged with the enemy. Unable to control himself anymore, his face red, his teeth clenched, and his vision blurred, Norax charged into the enemies, spreading fire and destruction with the trident. Killing multitudes of foes and burning one ship after another, Norax was bursting with energy and strength; nothing could stop him at this moment, even the gods themselves. He was the extension of Potnia. She was with him at this moment, guiding his hand, aiming his weapon, and filling his mind with only one simple thought: kill.

Suddenly, Norax found himself staring at the enemy flagship. Like his vessel, it was larger than the rest and was painted differently from the others. Laughing like a madman, Norax jumped on the ship, continuing to maim and burn all around. Then, the figure of an older warrior rose in front of him. Norax figured it was one of the commanders. His opponent wore rich, shiny armor and wielded a round shield and a short sickle sword. The warrior lacked one of his eyes. An artificial red eyeball in the empty socket depicted an Egyptian symbol.

"Glory to Potnia!" Norax screamed, aiming the trident at the enemy commander and turning the Egyptian into a ball of fire.

"General Hewernef!" The soldiers rushed forward to help but were immediately incinerated by the mighty trident.

Norax, covered in blood and ash, sprang forward and yelled. He needed more; he wanted to eradicate this cowardly southern race completely. Finally, the sinking disk of the goddess appeared in front of Norax; he just needed to pass one more ship.

Suddenly, his feet met an obstacle, and Norax fell on the deck. Worse, he lost the trident, which dropped to the wooden surface of the ship and rolled toward the stern. Norax tried to rise quickly but got a painful punch in the ribcage. Turning to the side, he finally saw his assailant, an ordinary Egyptian dressed only in a kilt, without even a helmet.

Roaring threats, Norax got to his knees and reached out to pick up the trident. This was a mistake, since the Egyptian was quicker, kicking the trident so it bounced off beyond Norax's reach. Immediately, the Egyptian reappeared to the left of Norax and punched him in the gut.

This was rather painful but couldn't deter an experienced warrior like Norax. He shook his head and got to his feet, turning his neck frantically to find his enemy. Alas, the insidious Egyptian was nowhere to be seen. Clenching his fists, Norax took a step in the direction of the trident, and that was when he finally saw his adversary: the

Egyptian stood at the stern, raising a strangely looking bow, targeting Norax, the trident lying on the deck between them. Yelling like a raging bull, Norax jumped forward, intending to pick up the magical weapon and burn the stubborn Egyptian.

Unfortunately for Norax, that was not destined to happen. The arrow met his mouth in the air as he made his jump. The momentum of the projectile was strong enough to arrest his forward movement, and the body of the Potnia's champion landed on the deck with a loud bang, breaking several planks. Norax, holding on to the deck and climbing out of the pile of broken wood, realized that his mouth was full of blood and something was preventing his breathing. Shaking his head, he found the tip of the arrow sticking out of the back of his neck, broke it, and took the arrow out of his mouth. Still unable to believe he had just been shot, Norax reached in the direction of his enemy. At that moment, another arrow nailed his palm to the deck.

Grimacing with pain, Norax met the gaze of his formidable adversary. "Who in the name of Potnia are you?" he gurgled, a torrent of blood rushing out of his mouth.

The Egyptian raised the strange-looking bow, loaded with a third arrow.

"My name is Khay," the Egyptian answered. "Go join Apep."

With these words, he released the arrow, which pierced Norax's heart, killing the fearsome leader of the Sea People on the spot.

\#

"We're too late," Echelaos said, pointing toward the mouth of the Nile, where the sea battle was raging.

"No, we're right on time." Zoltes grinned, the rays of the afternoon sun reflecting off his silver hand. "We'll help to finish them off," he added, stroking his red beard and raising the sword in his metallic hand to test the balance.

Their fleet was rapidly closing the distance to the enemy rearguard. The journey to Egypt had been difficult and perilous, but they'd persevered. Even more, they'd met with the remains of the Achaean navy when they passed Knossos and added a few dozen ships from Crete, Tyrins, and Mycenae. Now their forces were quite formidable, more than fifty ships. A great navy for any engagement, but still not enough to take on the Sea People. However, their contribution could be sufficient to tip the scales of the fight. Echelaos agreed with Zoltes.

Echelaos sat on the wooden bench at the ship's bow. The bench converted into a table in front of him, and the crossbow was attached to the table. He'd designed this gear himself, and the crew had helped him to build it. Echelaos loved Aphrodite's invention, the crossbow, and anticipated the moment he could use his gear in the battle. He looked around. All the other ships were packed with Achaean archers, and the Thracian skirmishers, wielding their by-now legendary weapons, were ready to board enemy ships and engage them.

As their vessel got closer to the enemy, Zoltes signaled the archers, and flaming arrows filled the air. Not expecting the attack from behind and thinking these were their own vessels, the Sea People were slow to react. In a heartbeat, many enemy ships caught fire, and many soldiers lost their lives due to the heavy barrage of the unexpected Achaean reinforcements.

Zoltes came closer and tapped Echelaos on the shoulder. The wanax didn't respond, since he was busy reloading his deadly weapon, ready to send a projectile to pierce the heart of the next victim. They were making a difference, Echelaos was certain. Hopefully, this will be enough to turn the tide of the battle.

As Zoltes and the Thracians were about to board the enemy ship, a large green disk fell from the sky, disappearing in the sea somewhere amidst the Egyptian vessels.

"Poseidon?" Echelaos yelled to Zoltes, extending his arm toward the place of the fall. The Thracian turned his head halfway and nodded. Things started to look promising.

At that moment, the new barrage from the shore highlighted the accumulation of enemy ships in the middle of the harbor. The Sea People's fleet was incinerated and blasted out of the water by the constant fire of the bolt-throwers. There was nothing else that could cause destruction on that scale.

Suddenly, an alarming thought occurred to the wanax. How could they miss such an obvious and easy thing to do?

"Zoltes!" he screamed in the direction of the enemy ship, where the Thracians were finishing their bloody job of dispatching the Sea People and throwing their bodies into the water for the fishes to feed on. Echelaos didn't expect the Thracian to hear him in the heat of a fight, but he did. Zoltes finished off the enemy warrior and jumped back.

"What is it?" His beard and hair were covered in the blood of the Sea People, adding vivid undertones to their natural red hue.

"How will they know we're allies?" Echelaos pointed to the shore, where the bolt-throwers continued their massive annihilation of the enemy fleet.

"We kill the Sea People," Zoltes said.

"But they don't know that. We are behind; they can't distinguish us," Echelaos objected.

As if illustrating his concern, the fireball blasted several enemy ships about half an arrow flight before them.

"I see what you mean," Zoltes scratched his beard. "Want to retreat?"

"No, we can do better." Echelaos sent another arrow that nailed the enemy warrior to the mast. "We'll send a signal."

"How?" Zoltes asked.

"The sails. We have enough ash from enflaming the arrows; we paint the sails."

"Bloody entrails, this might work." Zoltes grinned.

"It will. Tell your troops to paint a black stallion on the sails. And an octopus on this one — Tros will understand."

"On it." Zoltes turned around, yelling the commands. The fleet of the Sea People was an easy target for the continuous fire of the bolt-throwers and couldn't do much without the help of Poseidon. The Egyptian navy was inflicting heavy damage as well. *We were just in time; Zoltes was right*, Echelaos thought. The attack from behind was utterly unexpected and caused a lot of damage to the enemy's ships and morale. Some vessels were trying to get out of the fight, and some were already fleeing to the open sea. The battle was won. Zoltes, as if hearing his thoughts, came near and punched Echelaos on the shoulder.

"Victory is ours!" the Thracian yelled triumphantly.

The rest of the engagement was spent sinking enemy ships and killing as many warriors as they could. Large portions of the Sea People's fleet sailed away to where they'd come from, and the victors decided not to pursue them. As the enemy dispersed, the path to the shore was open, and Zoltes gave the signal to steer to land, where the allied forces celebrated their triumph.

After Zoltes had helped him disembark from the ship and get into the chariot, Echelaos observed Aphrodite inspecting the remaining bolt-throwers, and his heart filled with pride. They did it: Poseidon was dead, the despicable Sea People were repelled, and Pylos was avenged. He couldn't bring the fallen heroes back to life, but he could say they prevented something much worse from happening. The world as Echelaos knew it lay in ruins: the kingdom of the Hittites had ceased to exist, Achaean cities had been razed, and the land was poisoned for years to come. He remembered what Nestor had told him about the new age. This was it; the old way of living was no more, devoured by the cleansing fire. He had to rebuild everything from scratch, gathering whoever was left and leading them into the future — their future, without gods or heroes.

"Welcome back to the land of the living." A familiar voice interrupted his thoughts.

"Good to be here," Echelaos said.

"What happened to you?" Tros asked, stepping inside the chariot, reaching the wanax and giving him a passionate hug.

"Long story." Echelaos waved his hand dismissively. "Burned by the passion of Athena."

"I've heard you killed her."

"Teamwork." Echelaos smiled. "I've heard Aphrodite killed Poseidon."

"She proved to be your true daughter, Wanax. You should be proud."

"I am," Echelaos said. "Where's Zeus?"

"I thought he wouldn't survive the fight, but he did. Aphrodite said he spoke to her in her mind, asking to wait. So, we are."

Echelaos nodded. "Did you see the sign of octopus on my sail?"

"Yes. And the Black Stallion. I immediately knew it was you, rising from the dead."

"Yes, I had to come back. Didn't think you'd make it without me." Echelaos smiled.

"We were doomed, but the brave wanax saved us." Tros chuckled.

"What now?"

"You tell me; you are the wanax." Tros smiled. "Hump me if I know. We bury the dead, and then we'll have a feast. We must show these frail Egyptians how to celebrate the victory that saved their country."

"And after that?"

"What's on your mind?" Tros tilted his head.

"I want to come back and rebuild our cities. This is what Father meant when he said it was my time to lead. I understand now, and I'm ready. We must bury the dead and move forward. The Age of Iron is nigh."

EPILOGUE

"What in the name of Zeus is iron, anyway?" Tros asked.

"A new metal, better than bronze. Or so they say." Echelaos shrugged. "I hope Wedaneus will trade for some with the Assyrians. The mountain people near them have apparently mastered the skill."

"We need the metalworking recipe, not just the metal," Tros pointed out.

"I know," Echelaos said.

They stood on a hill overlooking the still, cerulean waters of the Bay of Argos. The Citadel of Tyrins was behind them, lit up by the rays of the rising sun. The freshness of the morning air and the majestic sunrise made Echelaos hopeful of the dawn of the new age. A year had passed since the destruction of Achaea and the fateful battle of Egypt that had decided the fate of gods and mortals. The process of rebuilding was slow and exhausting but exciting.

Echelaos looked down at his new, shiny silver legs, a gift from Zeus. The sign of revival, as he told himself. If only the god could bring back their beloved Pylos and its fallen heroes, but even Zeus couldn't bring dead back to life and restore what had been completely erased. Pylos and its surroundings were uninhabitable, and now they were building a new home in Tyrins.

"Can Aphrodite help with the recipe?" Tros asked.

"Perhaps. Last I heard, she was leaving with Zeus."

"I hope she stays."

The two friends turned around and started on their path back to the Citadel, skirting the remains of the Cyclopean walls destroyed by the Sea People. Aphrodite had designed new fortifications, since restoring these massive structures was impossible, so their remains just lay there, colossal ruins, a remnant of former glory for future generations to wonder at.

They passed the Great Ramp and went through the Citadel's main gate. This area was partially rebuilt but still showed signs of fire and destruction. The upper Citadel, with a few attached halls, was the only surviving part of a beautiful gem of the Argolid. Still, the war had been more merciful to Tyrins than to any other Achaean city.

"Any news from Mycenae?" Echelaos asked.

"People are coming back, slowly. Orestes has a lot of work to do, but he's up to the task."

"Agamemnon was a great ruler and Father's friend. I hope his son follows in his steps."

"Orestes has guts. The way he defeated the bands of the Sea People and the murderers of Agamemnon showed great skill and strong character," Tros said.

"Oh, I agree. Orestes is the true son of his father." Echelaos nodded.

They entered the Great Megaron and sat on a bench next to the throne of Eurystheus, wanax of Tyrins, killed during the siege by the Sea People. This throne now belonged to Echelaos, but he couldn't think of himself as wanax of Tyrins, not yet; Pylos was still fresh in his memory.

Echelaos glanced around the Megaron. The luster of the past had disappeared, the beautiful frescoes had burned, and a thick layer of black ash covered the walls. Echelaos stood and took a few steps toward the only remaining fragment, which depicted a hunting scene. Three spotted dogs, jumping and graciously extending their long, slender bodies, ran after a boar while the hunter readied his spear to pierce the animal's head. *The boar is Achaea*, Echelaos thought. *We were hunted and killed. The ruins of our cities: Pylos, Mycenae, Thebes, Tyrins — a graveyard. A tholos with the leftovers of the age long gone — the Age of Heroes.*

We are no more, and our gods have abandoned this sad place. Will anything else grow in this desolate realm? Only time would tell. But Echelaos was ready to give all he had and fulfill Nestor's behest to lead Achaea through the dark times of change, for this was his destiny. It was the least he could do.

Echelaos touched the fresco on the wall. "Remember the tile with an octopus in the throne room?" he asked Tros.

"Of course, Wanax."

"I want to place a few of those here," Echelaos said.

Tros looked at the wanax and nodded. "Did I tell you about the message from Egypt?"

"No, what message?"

Tros punched himself on the forehead, reached into the pouch hanging on his belt, and took out an ivory rod covered in cuneiform writing.

"What's it say?" Echelaos asked.

"Greetings from Zoltes." Tros smiled. "A new general of the Two Kingdoms, leading the forces of the incomparable Pharaoh Ramesses to great conquests."

"I knew it was in the works," Echelaos said.

"Well, you don't resist your god's will, even if you're a pharaoh. Zoltes deserved it, and he had nowhere to return to."

"Anything else?"

"He befriended the newly appointed Great Priest of Amen," Tros said.

"Who's that?"

"The Egyptian who played a prominent role in defeating Aten. His name is—"

"Khay, I remember him. Good, they complement each other."

"Yes, this should bring peace and prosperity to Egypt."

Echelaos looked at his lawagetos intently and suddenly asked, "What about you, Tros?"

Tros smiled. "Don't you worry about me, Wanax. I've found my peace with Korinsia, but I'll stand with you no matter what."

"I know… Thank you, for everything."

The two men looked straight at each other. They didn't need to say anything else; the bond between them was unbreakable, strengthened by so many unimaginable adventures and bloody battles.

At that moment, two women entered the Megaron, carrying rhytons filled with aromatic unguents and placing them on the benches near the throne.

"Did you come to say goodbye?" Echelaos asked.

"No, Father. I'm assisting Eritha in preparation for the cleansing ceremony," Aphrodite said.

"One doesn't exclude the other," Echelaos said.

"Zeus is leaving," Eritha said; she was the second woman. "He won't come back, and neither will the other gods. He made a promise. So I've decided to start anew, without the gods, which requires a proper purification ceremony for a new beginning."

"I see," Echelaos said. "And you're leaving with him?" He looked at Aphrodite.

"No," she said.

"What do you mean? Isn't that what you wanted?"

"It's the most logical choice, yes. But recently, I've started experiencing new feelings. I can't describe them. It's like something compels me to stay with you, support you, become fully human, and live a human life."

"You are…abandoning immortality?" Eritha asked.

"I'm not sure if I am. I'm still discovering myself," Aphrodite answered. "But I know my place is here."

"What are you going to do?" Tros asked.

"I have many ideas for rebuilding the city; plus, I promised Korinsia I'd help her with a new textile workshop."

"You just made your father one of the happiest people alive." Echelaos walked toward Aphrodite, laughing, and embraced her passionately.

As they exited the Megaron, Echelaos took Eritha by the hand, inclined his head, and touched her neck with his lips, inhaling the smell of her essence. She squeezed his hand in response and whispered into his ear, "Do you think we'll survive without the gods?"

He looked into her deep blue eyes for a few long moments, smiled, then embraced and kissed her.

"Of course we will," he said after they finally separated.

She sighed. "I'm scared… This is so different now."

"Me too. But this is the path we must walk," Echelaos said. "This is our destiny: to build a bridge to the new age."

"I know." She stroked his hair. "You are brave… If anyone could do this, it's you. Nestor was right."

"I had a dream last night," he said.

"Another prophecy?" She inhaled deeply. "What other calamities await?"

"Nothing of the sort." He smiled. "I believe it's all good. I saw Helen."

"Helen? That sorceress again?" Eritha pushed back from him, curving her lips. "What kind of spell did she cast on you?"

"There's no spell." Echelaos pulled her closer. "She wasn't truly herself in a dream, more like a disembodied voice. She said she's releasing me from her grasp. The link connecting our lives is finally broken."

"What does that mean?"

"It means I need to look forward, not to the past. The new age is upon us, and we must adapt. Helen will stay in the Age of Heroes, and Echelaos will move on to create the Age of Iron."

"I see…" Eritha said. "I hope you're right."

"And you know what else? I finally understand what she meant — what she said before she died back in Hattusa."

"What is it?"

"Helen said, 'We're already together, always have been, and will always be.' I thought she was talking about me and her, but I was wrong. She meant *all* of us: you, Aphrodite, Tros, Korinsia, Wedaneus, even Zeus — we're all connected by the thread that runs through the ages; we're all part of the eternal and beautiful world. And even though the link connecting my life with hers has been broken, we are still part of this eternal canvas and always will be."

"I'm confused," Eritha said.

"Don't be; just walk with me. I'm immensely grateful I have you, and I need your help on this dangerous path. Will you walk with me?"

She squeezed his hand and looked straight into his eyes.

"I will. Let the new age commence."

#

Humans called him Zeus, although he preferred the functional title of Commander. Now, after a hundred years on this alien planet, he could answer affirmatively that the Expedition was a total failure. The objectives were not met, even though they'd managed to establish contacts. What was worse, he was the only surviving member. Commander had assigned the primary responsibility to himself, since he couldn't contain his crew, protect them from the locals' influence, and help them against the resurfacing of emotions, the biological feature that humans and Soarers shared. Alas, by the time he understood the impact, it was too late.

For one last time, Commander surveyed the place where the base was located. No traces of their presence were left, although he couldn't record the same for all the other sites where the Soarers had engaged with the humans. He'd already sent all the equipment and artifacts to orbit with the help of the Space Elevator, and now it was his turn to depart.

Analyzing the recent events leading to the collapse of the Expedition, he couldn't identify where exactly he'd made the error and what he should've done differently. Commander knew emotions had impacted his judgment, but he wasn't sure whether it was detrimental. The one outcome he was satisfied with was the defeat of the alien information devourers; a failure in that struggle could've been a catastrophe for his civilization. Still, they'd prevailed and sent all the relevant information to Homeworld. The Soarers will be ready.

Commander thought that he'd somehow gotten close to the inhabitants of this strange world, and he didn't want to leave them to their fate. He admitted this new, peculiar feeling was most likely due to the emotions, that archaic mechanism of his system. Still, Commander wanted to stay and see humans grow, develop their skills, overcome their violent nature, become masters of their emotions, and, eventually, meet the Soarers among the stars. But by now he was convinced humans had to walk their own path, facing uncertainties and dangers, and that the path was theirs and theirs only. *If they make it, I'll be the first to greet them,* Commander noted to himself. *In the meantime, Aphrodite will guide them with all the wisdom she has acquired over such a short period.* This was a great success, and Commander experienced a fleeting emotion, uncomfortable that Technologist wasn't there to witness it.

As he initiated the Space Elevator, Commander retrieved the memories about his fellow Expedition members: the caring Scholar, the impatient Defender, the stubborn Pilot, and the brilliant Technologist. He had to make the trip back without them. Still, Commander had an intuition that the Soarers had found a lot more on this distant planet than they'd lost: a race of sentient beings with vitality and intelligence exceeding that of his own kind. To his surprise, Commander concluded: the future of the humans was among the stars, and *they* would be the race leading the ancient civilization of the Soarers to conquer the universe.

#

LIST OF CHARACTERS

Adad – Chief Eunuch of Assyria.

Addaya – Egyptian soldier.

Agamemnon – Wanax (ruler) of Mycenae in Achaea.

Akhenaten – Egyptian Pharaoh, also known as Amenhotep IV, who abandoned traditional polytheism and introduced worship centered around Aten.

Akhilleus – Achaean, captain in the army of Iolcos.

Alaksandru – Trojan prince, son of King Walmu.

Amen – "a Hidden One," ancient Egyptian god of the sun and air, the most powerful and popular in Egypt for centuries.

Ammurapi – King of Ugarit.

Apaliunas – the Hittite name of the god Apollo.

Apep – ancient Egyptian demon of chaos, who had the form of a serpent and represented all that was outside the ordered cosmos.

Aphrodite – ancient Greek goddess associated with love, lust, beauty, pleasure, and passion.

Apollo – ancient Greek god of fine arts, medicine, the Sun and light, poetry, and more. He was known to the Hittites as **Apaliunas**.

Ares – ancient Greek god of war and courage.

Assur-Dan – Assyrian prince, son of King Ninurta-apal-ekur.

Aten – an ancient Egyptian god, represented by a sun-disk, within the religious system formally established in ancient Egypt by the late Eighteenth Dynasty pharaoh Amenhotep IV, better known as Akhenaten.

Athena – ancient Greek goddess of wisdom, warfare, and handicraft.

#

Bakenkhonsu – Egyptian, high priest of Amen.

Baunei – Sherden chieftain.

#

Davke – Babylonian princess, daughter of King Kudur-Enlil of Babylon, grandmother of the Hittite Princess Ehli-Nikkal.

Djehuty – Egyptian grave-robber.

#

Echelaos – Achaean prince of Pylos, son of Wanax Nestor.

Ehli-Nikkal – Hittite princess, daughter of King Suppiluliuma

Eritha – Achaean, high priestess of Pylos

Euristheus – Wanax (ruler) of Tyrins in Achaea.

#

Germa – king of Libyan tribes.

#

Hades – an ancient Greek god of the dead and the king of the underworld.

Heracles – in Greek mythology, son of Zeus and a demi-god with superhuman strength.

Hewernef – Egyptian general.

Hori – grand vizier of Egypt.

#

Intef – Egyptian grave-robber.

Ishtar – an ancient Mesopotamian goddess of love, beauty, war, and fertility.

#

Kadu – commander of the garrison of Hattusa.

Korinsia – an enslaved Achaean girl from Pylos.

Khay – Egyptian grave-robber.

Kudur-Enlil – King of Babylon, father of Davke.

#

Machaon – Achaean, Lawagetos of Pylos.

Meketre –Egyptian soldier.

Mursili –Hittite king.

Muwattali – Hittite king.

#

Neferhotep – Egyptian soldier, having a rank "The Greatest of the Fifty".

Nefer-Setekh – Egyptian, high priest of Wadjet.

Nergal – an ancient Mesopotamian god of war, death, and disease.

Nerikkil – Hittite god of weather.

Nestor – Wanax (ruler) of Pylos in Achaea.

Ninurta-apal-Ekur – King of Assyria.

Norax – chieftain from Tartessos.

#

Orestes – Achaean prince of Mycenae, son of Wanax Agamemnon.

Osiris – ancient Egyptian god of the underworld and judge of the dead.

#

Poseidon – ancient Greek god of sea, storms, earthquakes and horses.

Potnia – an ancient Greek word for "Mistress, Lady" and a title of a goddess.

#

Ra – an ancient Egyptian god, the father of all creation, the patron of the sun, heaven, kingship, power, and light.

Ramesses the Great (Ramesses II) –an Egyptian pharaoh, the third ruler of the Nineteenth Dynasty.

Ramesses – an Egyptian pharaoh, Usermaatre Meryamen Ramesses III was the second Pharaoh of the Twentieth Dynasty in Ancient Egypt.

#

Salmanu – grand vizier of Assyria.

Sarini – Hittite scribe and a priest of Nerikkil.

Sharruma – a Hittite god of the underworld.

Supilluliuma – King of the Hittites, father of Princess Ehli-Nikkal.

#

Tanhuantash – King of Habishe.

Tibe – Trojan Master of the Traders' Brotherhood.

Tros – Achaean, charioteer of Echelaos.

Tudhaliya – King of the Hittites, grandfather of Princess Ehli-Nikkal.

#

Uster – Thracian healer.

#

Wadjet – an ancient Egyptian goddess, protector of all of Egypt, associated with the land and depicted as a snake-headed woman or a snake—usually an Egyptian cobra.

Walmu – king of Troy, father of Prince Alaksandru.

Wedaneus – Achaean diplomat, advisor to Wanax Nestor of Pylos.

#

Zerunthios – a main figure of Thracian religion, an aspect of the god Zis, meaning "bestial" and conceptualizing Zis as the god of war.

Zeus – "the Highest One," ancient Greek god of sky and thunder, ruler of all the gods.

Zis the Hero – a heroic aspect, of the Thracian god Zis, or Zerunthios, also known as the Thracian Hero or the Thracian Horseman, who was represented a horseback hunter.

Zoltes – Thracian chieftain from Leibethra.

#

GLOSSARY

Aegis – an attribute of Athena usually represented as a shield made of animal skin, featuring the head of Gorgon.

Ankh – a symbol representing eternal life in ancient Egypt.

#

Ba – in ancient Egypt, one of the three principal aspects of the human soul alongside Ka and Akh, representing the mobility of the soul after death.

#

Cartouche – an oval or oblong enclosing a group of Egyptian hieroglyphs, typically representing the name and title of a monarch.

Chukar – eastern Anatolian partridge.

#

Dromos – a ceremonial entryway to the Thalamos, a tomb in Mycenaean Greece.

#

Ganzir – Ancient Mesopotamian underworld, ruled by the goddess Ereshkigal and the god Nergal.

Galbanum – Mediterranean herb. A gum-like material from its stems is used to make medicine.

#

Hatti (the land of) – roughly corresponds to Anatolia, in modern Turkey. Named after the indigenous people of central Anatolia who preceded the Hittites.

Hem-netjer – a title of the male priest in ancient Egypt, meaning "servant of the god".

Hittites – Indo-European people of Anatolia, who established an empire centered in Hattusa in the mid-2nd century BC.

#

Isfet – an ancient Egyptian religious term meaning "chaos" or "injustice"

#

Ka – in ancient Egypt, one of the three principal aspects of the human soul alongside Ba and Akh, representing the protective divine spirit of a person. The Ka survived the death of the body and could reside in a picture or statue of a person.

Kalasiris – a long linen dress, worn in ancient Egypt by both women and men.

Kapet – ancient Egyptian temple incense with a pungent aroma.

Kem – rich, fertile, dark colored soil of the Nile River and the Delta.

Kohl – an ancient eye cosmetic, used similar to charcoal in mascara.

Korete – Governor of a district in Mycenaean Pylos.

#

Larnax – a type of small, closed coffin often used in the Mycenaean Greece as a container for human remains, either a corpse (bent back on itself) or cremated ashes.

Laudanum – a tincture of opium, prepared by dissolving extracts from the opium poppy in alcohol.

Lawagetos – the second most significant person in the Mycenaean city, the leader of the army.

Limmu – a royal official who presided over the New Year festival at the start of the reign of an Assyrian king.

#

Ma'at – an ancient Egyptian religious term meaning "order" or "justice", also represented by a goddess of the same name.

Megaron – a central hall of both temple structures and private dwellings in the Mycanaean Greece.

Mitre – a tall headdress of an Assyrian king

#

Naphtha – highly flammable light fraction of petroleum, common in oil deposits of the Near East, chief ingredient in incendiary devices.

Nawoi – a Mycenaean shrine dedicated to a specific god.

Nemes – in ancient Egypt, a headdress of the pharaoh, made of pieces of striped cloth. It covered the whole crown and behind of the head and nape.

Nesut-Towi – an ancient Egyptian name of the temple of Amen at Karnak, meaning "The throne of the two lands".

Nuraghe – the main type of ancient megalithic edifice found in Sardinia, developed during the Nuragic Age between 1900 and 730 B.C. Today it has come to be the symbol of Sardinia and its distinctive culture known as the Nuragic civilization.

#

Postiche – in ancient Egypt, a false metal beard of the pharaoh.

#

Rhyton – in Mycenaean Greece, a roughly conical container from which fluids were intended to be drunk or to be poured in some ceremonies such as libations. A rhyton was typically shaped as an animal's head.

#

Ta-sekhet-ma'at – Valley of the Kings, a cemetery containing the tombs of the royal rulers of ancient Egypt. It is in the southern half of Egypt, just west of the Nile River.

Thalamos – in Mycenaean Greece, a tomb or a grave chamber.

Theomachia – the war of the gods.

Tholos – In Mycenaean Greece, large, beehive-shaped graves built into slopes of hills.

#

Unguent – a soft, greasy, or viscous substance used as ointment or for lubrication.

#

Wanax – in Mycenaean Greece, a ruler of the palatial complex, such as in Pylos, Tyrins or Mycenae, roughly translated as a tribal chief, lord, or king.

#

GEOGRAPHICAL LOCATIONS

(SEE THE MAP ON PAGE 8)

Achaea / Ahhiyawa

Akhetaten

Arinna

Ashdod

Ashkelon

Assur

Assyria

#

Babylon

Bay of Argos

#

Canaan

Carchemish

Crete

Cyprus / Alashiya

#

Egypt

Ekron

Elam

#

Habishe

Hattusa

Hellespont

#

Iolcos

Isuwa

#

Kadesh

Kaska

Kastri

Kizzuwadna

Knossos

Kythera

#

Leibethra

Leuktron

#

Menelaion

Miletus

Mount Pelion

Mycenae

#

Nerik

Nichoria

Nubia

#

Orchomenus

#

Peleshet

Pi-Ramesse

Punt

Pylos

#

Scamander

Sinai

Susa

#

Tartessos

Thebes (Achaean)

Thebes (Egyptian)

Thessaly

Thrace

Troy / Wilusa

Tyrins

#

Ugarit

#

The Way of Horus

#

* * *

Afterword:
Join my quest
to imagine the future world

Thank you for reading *"The Age of Heroes."* I hope you have found my work insightful, stimulating, and entertaining. If you enjoyed this book, please consider leaving a short comment on Goodreads, Amazon, or your platform of choice. I would greatly appreciate your feedback!

To stay in touch, please visit my site **MikhailGladkikh.com**, and receive a novella **"Thread of Lies"** as a gift. Be the first to get updates about my new novels. Listen to the **Podcast "Vision 2222" (https://www.youtube.com/@VISION2222podcast)**, in which the current trends in science, technology, and business, shaping the world of tomorrow, with the guests prominent and distinguished in their fields. Available on Spotify, Audible, Google Podcast, Apple, iHeartRadio, and YouTube.

Finally, please feel free to contact me directly at **mgladkikh@gmail.com**: I'd love to hear from my readers!

I am excited to continue our journey together!

Mikhail Gladkikh

.

www.ingramcontent.com/pod-product-compliance
Lightning Source LLC
Chambersburg PA
CBHW061926170626
46813CB00006B/2318